KNIGHT
OF
SWORD
&
SHADOW

AVA SPEIRS

KNIGHT
OF
SWORD
&
SHADOW

For my friend and long suffering partner in my insanity, Montana Ash. Her friendship and advice are two things that I can count on in this book world without question, and I am grateful for every ounce of support she gives me. I'm also grateful for the fact she lets me bounce all my ideas off her, she helps me with book titles and always reads (and tweaks) my blurbs.

Thank you for choosing to pick up a copy of **Knight of Sword & Shadow**. I feel like I've been waiting to write this fantasy series my whole life…and I am so excited for you to read it!

If you enjoyed this book, it would mean so much if you considered writing a short review. Reviews are helpful to other readers, but mean even more to authors, and I would appreciate it so much if you took a moment to share your love of this book!

Ava x

In a world of shadow, can one hero shine?

When scandal and disgrace fall upon the Order of the Conclave, Bastian and his Order are forced to hide who they are proud to be. Cast out, shunned and scorned by those who were once honoured to use their services, Bastian and his men are left with no choice but to become mercenaries. Moving across the Five Kingdoms, they restore peace for coin, shedding blood for others' gain.

Tasked with the job of escorting a noblewoman and her handmaiden across the Sand Seas, Bastian soon realises not all is as it should be. Something evil poisons the lands, as whispers of revolt and rebellion are once again murmured among the courts.

In the halls of his Order, Bastian is entrusted with a mission. He knows this shouldn't be his fight, but the duty to his Order, his comrades, and his mysterious travelling companions weighs heavily on him.

The mission is so dangerous and deadly only a fool would take it…and only a coward would refuse it.

**This is book one in a continuing series. This is an epic, high fantasy series that includes action, adventure, political intrigue, a reluctant hero and a horse with a serious attitude problem.*

GLOSSARY

The Five Kingdoms: Each kingdom has their own leaders and their own conflicts, just as each kingdom has their own allies and, indeed, enemies.

The kingdoms comprise the following nations: *Kestornia, Bordyre, Eloysth, Kalzynia* and *Tzenyth.*

Kestornia (ke-STOR-nee-ah): Considered by some to be the strongest kingdom, Kestornia is home to the city of Pavolyn (*PA-voh-line*), which is nicknamed the Golden City. The city is the centre for politics, trade, and religion.

Bordyre (bore-DIRE): Bordyre is the kingdom of warriors. The noble houses will send their sons and daughters to train in the Academy of Warrior Excellence within the Maroon City to be the finest soldiers of the Five Kingdoms. Bordyre shares a boundary with the Barrens.

Eloysth (EH-lo-isth): An island nation, its boatbuilders are sought by many. Eloysth is a nation of fisherman and boatbuilders and is known for its spiritualism. The kingdom may be small and isolated but has the strongest fleet of ships, therefore making it a strong kingdom, with its most populated area being termed the Blue City.

Kalzynia (kal-ZIH-nee-ah): An agricultural nation, most farms are to the south in the nation. Land is held by noble families and worked by commoners, who provide a tithe to the landlord. To the north, the land is hard and unforgiving, and Kalzynia has its own academy where warriors of the Gods are sent to train in the Grey City.

Tzenyth (ZEH-nith): The Prairie lands are wild and free, with no formal city, but instead, nomads occupy the land. Tzenythians follow the migration pattern of the wild *bulsyn*, never taking more from the land than what they need. The nomads call their whole nation the Green City in mockery of the other four kingdoms and their desire to be permanent.

The Order of the Conclave: Once seen as warriors of the Gods, the Conclave is made up of five Orders, all named after birds, as birds are seen not only as messengers but also as the unopposed rulers of the sky, where they fly closest to the heavens. The Orders are Cardinals, Hawks, Falcons, Starlings, and Ravens.

Great Unrest: A dark time in the recent history of the Five Kingdoms. The old Gods were cast aside when deceit and deception were discovered in the upper chambers of the Order of the Conclave. A plot was uncovered where some members of the Conclave conspired to overthrow the rulers of the kingdoms. Acts of treason against not only king but country were not forgiven lightly. Battles and wars ensued, tearing mankind further from the heights of heavenly glory to the discarded earth and dirt beneath them. When all seemed lost and hope gone, new Gods emerged from the ashes of chaos, promising redemption, and restoration.

Temple of the Maiden: Servants of the new Gods, the temples welcome only women within their walls, as the new Gods have only gifted their power of healing and miracles to women.

The Ages: Scholars say that there are different Ages. The Age of Remorse has long since passed. The Age of Redemption passes slowly, but the wind is shifting, change is coming, and a new Age is ready to be born.

INTRODUCTION

Thousands of years ago, the world was broken. What was once great fell under the need for power. In fragmented lands and continents changed forever by destruction and greed, mankind slowly picked its way out of the wreckage. And with a spirit born of the need to survive, mankind restored order.

New kingdoms rose from the ashes, but in the Age of Redemption, mankind has failed again.

The Order of the Conclave was once seen as warriors of the Gods, but since the Great Unrest, the old Gods are being cast aside. Cries of deceit, corruption, and hypocrisy still hang heavy over the Order, and what once shone as a beacon of hope is now cast in shadow.

Some knights have returned to their homelands, a chance to start a life they never thought they would have. For others, the sword is all they know, and their Order is still their home, no matter how broken. Forced to take any work, soldiers become mercenaries, and as time passes, the ethics and principles of the Order are dwindling…fading.

As whispers run wild of more rebellion and new Gods are worshiped, replacing the old, unrest is once again rife within the Five Kingdoms.

CHAPTER 1

IN THE GRIM SHADOW OF MORNING, A LIGHT DRIZZLE OF RAIN fell uninterrupted upon the weary warriors as they made their way quietly through the streets of the town. A town which they had spent the last two days defending against raiders. Behind closed, locked doors, their lungs fit to bursting as they held their breath, the citizens watched the silent combatants as they departed in a slow single file procession, making their way to the main gate.

Peering through the grey light of dawn, the soldiers remained silent as they approached the barricade that had already been swung open to hasten their departure. As they passed through in single file, not one word was uttered until the banging thump of the wooden bar lock dropping into place echoed in the empty streets of the town they left behind.

"Ungrateful scum," one of the men muttered, gratified to hear some mumbles of agreement among the line.

"Quiet," another mumbled. "They got what they paid for, and we got paid what they owed," he reminded them. More muttering rippled through them as they headed south. The feeling of the townsfolk no longer wanting them there now that their job was done, was a sour reminder that they weren't welcome. Bitter but familiar, a feeling they knew only too well in the last few years of change.

"Ax, Xan," the one who led in front spoke. "Go get the horses. Meet us at the destination," he instructed, and two of the men moved out the line and slipped out of sight.

"Men, we travel for a time on foot. We'll clear the outlying villages, and then we'll rest before we ride."

"Are we still on course to head back to the Golden City?" his nearest companion queried as the order to march filtered back through the ranks.

Bastian turned his head to look at his comrades as they pulled hoods low and hitched their packs higher up their backs, settling themselves for the walk ahead. "We are," he answered.

"You still feel out of sorts?"

Bastian glanced at his closest companion. "I do," he confirmed to Khaldan.

"Not like you to move on a *feeling*," Khaldan commented softly, a glance back to make sure they weren't overheard.

It was true, it wasn't like him to act on a feeling. He had fought in wars and battles and trusted his gut instinct on where to strike next in a hand-to-hand combat, but to move his men on a…*niggling* sensation that something was wrong? That wasn't the kind of leader he was.

"Might be the weather," he said instead and was gratified when his friend's grunt told him exactly what he thought of that, but nevertheless, it stopped the line of questioning.

Bastian's thoughts focused inwards as they walked the uneven terrain, the hardened trade tracks softening to trail tracks as they left the village of Skersa behind. They had taken the job to defend the town and rid it of its bandit problem. A group of outlaws had been moving south through the kingdom, raiding and pillaging as they travelled, and had hit Skersa twice now. It was a small town, population around five hundred or so, and they made their living through trade and agriculture. Their farms had livestock taken by the bandits, and some of the wealthier merchants had suffered from their wagons being cut off and their goods stolen.

Bastian and his men had been travelling along the same trade route, fresh from a completed job further north. When they heard of the town's need, Bastian had sent two of his men to the town to negotiate terms.

The routine was a practiced one. The only difference these days was that they demanded payment for their services. Actual payment. Not the promise of one or the acceptance that a payment may be called for at a later time. Those days were gone and had been that way for eight years now. The transition to this new way of life was a difficult one for both Bastian and his men *and* the people who now paid for their services.

Once, the sight of Bastian and his men would have brought relief and calm. Now, they were viewed with the same cynicism as the Order was, the Order they once openly represented and now served from the shadows. The Age of Redemption was supposed to be exactly that, redemption from the Age before it. An Age where men crawled in the dirt, civilisations a distant memory in the years that had followed since the world fell apart and only the strongest survived. Bastian snorted in the cold morning light. Strongest? He wasn't too sure it didn't mean stupidest.

Over a thousand years ago in a world that looked nothing like it did today, men and so-called *leaders* of countries, hungry for power, tore it all down. The history books called it explosions from bombs, but from what historians understood, these bombs had a terrible impact, and the world as it was, was destroyed. It was the chemicals in the bombs, they said, that made the earth die. Soils lay dead, vegetation withered and fell to rot, and animals became scarce. Oceans and seas dried up, and water, when it could be found, was poisonous. With nothing to sustain them, the world of man fell.

Small pockets of humanity remained, but the damage was so severe these small pockets became isolated. Alone and vulnerable, they no longer fought each other, but focused on the fight to survive.

The destruction was so violent on the world that the earth's plates jarred against one another as parts of land broke off and, over hundreds of years, moved and formed new land masses.

A scholar of Bastian's once described the Re-Shaping as if it were a jigsaw puzzle. Only, once you shook all the parts up of what there once was, there were so many missing pieces that you made good with what you had left.

And through sheer stubbornness, Bastian was sure, the willpower of men persevered. Slowly, the poisoned rain stopped falling. The water cleansed from below the earth's crust and was purified in natural springs. Green returned to the charred blackened earth. Habitats of once isolated pockets spread further.

Man began to rebuild.

The Age of Remorse was one of regrowth, rebuilding and new beginnings. Faith was reborn. Man once more turned his sights skyward, and the Gods answered.

It took centuries of painstaking progress, but cities and towns were reconstructed. Relics of past architecture were restored or replicated. Technology may have been lost and forgotten, but creativity remained.

The old world had science, but the new world had *magic*.

Bastian was sceptical about the origins of magic. The old texts said that it was nature's reward to the humanity that survived. It was said that, even before the land broke, their ancestors would have had the same capacity for magic, they just couldn't access it. But the result of the radiation poisoning in the bloodstream of the survivors changed that. It was not only the world that was shaken on its axis from the force of the destruction, but people were as well. However, there were others that said the gift of magic was from the Gods themselves, to prove to man that they had not abandoned them.

Whichever theory you wished to follow, there were rumours of the gift of magic failing. Fewer and fewer were known to wield the power, and as magic faded, so did the faith in the old Gods.

Bastian knew that, in the old world before the Before, there had been separate faiths, each claiming their God was the one true God. Bastian was still not convinced this wasn't the root of the problems that caused the bombs to fall. It seemed that no matter the Age, faith was ever constant and ever changing.

Around fifteen years ago, the old shrines of the old faith were torn down, new shrines built, their spires higher, their towers wider, their doors open and more welcoming. Their collection plates were just as heavy, Bastian had noticed.

It was the older Gods that Bastian and his men's Order served, even though none of them were particularly religious, but the Order of the Conclave served the Gods first in a world of men. And from man's perspective, whether regarding the served or the servants, where one failed, it was only a matter of time before the other would follow.

The Order of the Conclave was the knights of sanctuaries and shrines. Holy men who served a higher purpose. Warriors who fought for right and the good of man. Or most of them believed that to be true. But where there is man, there is corruption and deceit.

During the Great Unrest, as faith in the Gods wavered, scandal and treachery were discovered in the higher echelons of the Order of the Conclave. What was once seen as holy and devout was now exposed as false and twisted. Personal gain and wealth had long since replaced the virtue of the devoted servant.

Knights of honour and duty were now thought of no more highly than the beggars in the streets.

Monarchs and leaders, who had previously relied on the Order for peace and order, were quick to act. By turning the common people's attention away from themselves and their own failings, they painted the Order of the Conclave as the culprit and face of treachery.

When the final order came down from the Grand Master, that the knights could return home, their calling served, there was little left of those whose core purpose was what it had always been.

Only one kingdom of the Five Kingdoms remained openly amicable to the Order of the Conclave, and that was in Kestornia, in the city of Pavolyn. In the heart of the country's Capitol, the headquarters of the Order still stood proud. The doors may be a little beaten, the gates more rusted than before, the shine of the stone dulled with negligence, but the structure was still sound, and what the Order once stood for was no less diminished within its seemingly tarnished halls.

When the call came through for the disbandment of the Orders in the other kingdoms, where some men were pleased to return to their families, there were other knights who had nothing to return to. Their calling to serve in the Order had been exactly that, a calling. A lifestyle choice. A purpose served. All they knew how to do was train and fight. The kingdoms may have turned their backs on the very men who had served the old Gods loyally, but the need for peace-keepers or mediators was still there. Those knights made their way to Pavolyn and made the Order of the Conclave their home.

Bastian frowned at the path in front of him. Distrust of his Order was high, and quickly he and his men learned that to survive, they needed to be clever. What was once offered as a service from the Gods was now offered for a price.

Mercenaries. Sellswords. Brawlers.

"You lost in there, old friend?" Khaldan asked him quietly.

"I think I may be," Bastian admitted as he pulled his hood lower.

"We'll find a boarding house on the way, wash off this shit and blood. A hot meal and a warm bath, that's what you need," Khaldan assured him.

"You think everything is better after a bath," Bastian teased him gruffly as he gave his companion the side-eye. Khaldan did not give the impression that warm baths were in his list of favourite things. Standing at around six feet four, his shoulders seemed as broad as he was tall. His heavy beard needed trimming, Bastian noted, and the scar above his left eye was more prominent in the morning light. Khaldan's brown hair was kept short, unlike Bastian's longer, darker hair.

"Clean body, clean mind," Khaldan replied with a grin.

"Of course," Bastian grunted in amusement.

"And of course, there is the pressing problem that I'm too much of a gentleman to point out to my learned friend," Khaldan said as he looked over Bastian with a grin.

"And what's that?" Bastian asked him dryly.

"You stink."

Bastian barked out a laugh despite his current heavy thoughts. "Is that right?" he asked in amusement.

"You think the men are grumbling because they're walking?" Khaldan said conversationally as he straightened his pack. "It's because they're downwind of you."

"I can always count on you to keep me grounded," he grumbled as he smiled ruefully at his companion's banter.

Khaldan reached over and patted his shoulder. "I'm the gift that keeps on giving."

"Sure," Bastian snorted. "If you say so." They walked through the morning and into the early afternoon. The rain never became more than a persistent drizzle, and the sun remained shy as it hid behind clouds, causing the whole landscape to look grey and uninviting.

After several hours, Bastian heard the faint whinny of a horse further up the hill they had been steadily climbing. When it was followed by another, he heard Khaldan beside him grumble something that sounded a lot like "about time." As they crested the rise, Ax and Xan were sitting on a rock as the horses grazed lazily beside them.

"You took your time," Ax greeted as he and Xan rose to their feet. "It's a filthy day to be sitting on a rock waiting for you lot," he added with a growl. "Especially when he's with me." Ax jerked a thumb at Xan and rolled his eyes.

"Yeah?" Khaldan asked as he shared a look with Xan. "What did Xan stop you from doing?"

"Nothing!" Ax protested wildly as the others moved around them to get to their horses.

"Check the tightness of your girth!" Xan called to his companions. "I gave up trying to check them all; he was just undoing them again."

As Bastian headed towards Ghost, the black stallion gave a short snort of recognition. Ghost stood sixteen hands tall, and with his powerfully muscled build, thick mane and flat nose, he was truly a magnificent looking horse. Magnificent he may be, but it was soon discovered by any who approached him that Ghost was a mean son of a shrew, and even Bastian had been on the receiving end of Ghost's hooves a few times himself. He was a trained warhorse, and Bastian, having broken the stallion in himself, wouldn't trust any other mount to take him into battle.

"Mount up," Khaldan ordered. "We reach Hylones before morning"

Strapping his pack to Ghost's saddle, Bastian didn't bother checking the girth. Both Xan and Ax knew not to linger too near to *this* horse. Mounting the steed, Bastian ignored the horse's disgruntled huff as he settled in the saddle.

"You ready?" Khaldan asked as he manoeuvred his own mount closer while he kept a watchful eye on Ghost. "That demon horse is looking more pissed than normal."

"Ghost hates the rain." Bastian patted Ghost's neck twice in commiseration. "Let's try to reach Hylones before dawn, or it won't be just the horses that are hacked off."

"Ten men on horses travelling at speed—we won't be missed," Khaldan said quietly as he looked over at Bastian, taking in the firm, straight back of his companion. His hood hid his expression, but Khaldan didn't need to see Bastian to know his lips would be twisted in a smirk, his pale blue eyes mocking.

"I don't intend to be missed." Bastian's tone was firm. "We have our orders."

"Okay, so our intentions are what?"

"Right now? To be dry before sunrise." Bastian nudged his heel into Ghost's side and began a brisk pace south.

Khaldan shook his head as he followed suit. "Dry *and* noticed. Everyone will see us coming. Wonderful. *Exactly* what we need."

CHAPTER 2

As Bastian had intended, they arrived in Hylones before dawn, and although the rain had let up, they were still damp from the day previously. They had been in the town many times before, and Bastian led the men to the inn that they usually stayed at. Although run down and the white paint had turned grey a long time ago, the building was still sturdy. The bonus for those who knew and had been inside before was that the innkeeper's wife was considered "obsessive" in her cleaning, which meant although outside gave the impression of ill kept, the inn inside was clean and well maintained.

As Bastian dismounted from Ghost, he heard Ax rouse the stable hand, talking to him quietly, alerting him to the fact there were ten warhorses ready to be wiped down, fed and watered.

"He's by himself," Ax said as he approached Bastian, who was unhooking his pack from Ghost's saddle. "I'll leave one of the men with him?"

"Are you telling me or asking?" Bastian continued to see to Ghost's saddle, loosening the girth and leaving the saddle loose. The stallion whinnied gently, and Bastian gave him a reassuring pat on his withers. "Is he new or one who we've seen before?" He looked over to the stable hand, who had come out of the huts, still rubbing the sleep from his eyes, which were rapidly opening as he looked around at the different horses.

"Your mean mount bit him last time," Ax said as he

eyed Ghost warily. Bastian's horse had been known to snap at Ax one time too many as well.

"Then he'll know to avoid his teeth." Bastian hefted his pack onto his shoulder as he handed Ax Ghost's reins. "He likes his straw dry." Ax's faint protest was ignored by Bastian as he winked at Khaldan, who had been listening to the exchange with a barely concealed grin.

As the two of them approached the inn, the door was opened by the innkeeper's wife, who glared at them with disapproval. "I just washed the floors," she said as she eyed their muddy boots with clear distaste.

"We can take our boots off," Khaldan told her amicably as he sniffed the air. "I smell oats and…" He paused for another dramatic effect. "Bacon?"

Bastian and Khaldan had both frequented this inn before, and for whatever reason, the mean-eyed, sharp-nosed, tight-lipped wife of the innkeeper seemed to like Khaldan. If Bastian hadn't witnessed it himself, he would think his friend was exaggerating. Every time she looked at Bastian, it was as if she swallowed something sour that left a bad taste in her mouth and a look in her eye that gave the clear message that she wished she hadn't taken a taste. But when she looked at Khaldan, she almost, *almost* smiled.

"There's bacon, milord," she simpered as Khaldan beamed down at her.

"Bastian, your boots." Khaldan nudged Bastian as he kicked his own boots off, careful of the mud and prompting Bastian into action. With a suppressed sigh, Bastian stopped and unlaced the boots before awkwardly hopping onto the front stoop, one stocking-soled foot at a time until his boots were in his hand, and he was inside the warm hearth of the inn.

"S'pose you'll be wanting them cleaned?" she asked with a sniff of disapproval as she eyed the boots with the same look she usually reserved for Bastian.

"If you could add it to the tab," Bastian answered gracefully. His polite manner was lost on her as she snatched the boots off him and turned on her heel to head to the back of the inn. "Tell the others—no boots off, no entry."

"Does no entry mean no bacon?" Xan called after her. He had walked up behind Khaldan and Bastian during the exchange.

"No boots, no nothing!"

"I swear to the Gods she gets meaner every time we see her," Xan muttered as he kicked his boots off and left them by the doorway.

"I think she's delightful," Khaldan announced loudly, losing his smile when he caught Bastian's flat look. "Anyway, let's get rooms."

Bastian passed the innkeeper as he hurried down the stairs past him. "Oh milord, the room is clean."

"Very good."

"I'll have hot water sent up, milord. How many rooms?" the innkeeper enquired as he pushed his shirt into his trousers, obviously woken by their early morning arrival and not yet ready to start the day.

"Six, if you have. Five if you don't." Bastian pushed open the door to the room he had been in every time he was here. It was beside the back exit, had a clear view of the stables, and if he stood just at the right angle, he could see the main gate into the town.

"I have five?" The innkeeper had followed him back up the stairs and now stood hesitantly in the doorway.

Bastian looked around the familiar room, the two single beds housed a cot under one of them. He knew the other rooms were the same. "Five is plenty," he told him with a sharp nod. Khaldan would haggle the price and the meals, but for now, all Bastian was interested in was getting out of his clothes. Unbuckling the clasps of his heavy cloak, he caught it before it fell, and tossed it on a chair. Next, he worked at the buckles on his cuirass. The rigid leather was fastened tightly across his chest, and he was struggling with one of his buckles when Khaldan entered the room.

"Let me help," Khaldan offered as he crossed the room, hissing quietly when he saw the dark blood staining the white shirt beneath. "You told me the bleeding stopped."

"It did."

Khaldan began to berate him but instead stopped himself; it would fall on deaf ears. "Five rooms, for three nights, two meals each, and food and water for the horses. Although, I had to give an extra silver coin for Ghost and his oats."

Bastian tugged his shirt off over his head, which hid his grin from his companion. "He'll appreciate the extra care."

"Your horse is hated by everyone," Khaldan grumbled as he started working on the buckles of his own cloak.

"I like him," Bastian countered as he took the leather tie from his hair. In the corner of the room stood a tin bath, and going over to it, he began to move it closer to the fire.

"Eager for a bath now, aren't you?" Khaldan's knowing look earned a laugh from his companion.

"I fear I may be deprived of bacon if I turn up at breakfast with days' old blood on me."

"True."

Both men busied themselves with their packs, pulling out clothes that were still presentable. They had been on the road for many days, and there was little that was still clean. A knock on the door pulled their attention from their laundry problems.

The innkeeper and two young boys stood in the hall, buckets of warm water in each of their hands. As they filled the tub, Bastian watched the boys try to hide their curious stares.

"Clothes washing," he said, suddenly causing the youngest one to jump. "How many coins for some garments to be cleaned?"

"Well, I'd have to ask the wife," the innkeeper said as he avoided looking at Bastian.

"I can wash clothes," the youngest boy spoke up. "It's me that does it anyways," he added with a little bit of defiance as he saw that the innkeeper was glaring at him, but he wasn't correcting him.

"Is that so?" Bastian looked him over and then to the innkeeper for confirmation. He received a shrug in return. "And how many coins would you take?" he asked the boy.

The boy's eyes were darting between Bastian and his employer, his tongue repeatedly swiping out and licking his bottom lip, showing his uncertainty. "Five," he blurted. "Copper."

"Five copper?" Bastian's eyebrows rose in surprise as he glanced quickly at Khaldan, who had his hand pressed against his mouth. "Five copper is a high charge for some shirts. No?"

"No." The boy shook his head, his back straightening as he took a step forward. "How many shirts have you?" He looked at the bed with the pile of laundry. "I see at least three. Trousers too, and there will be socks." His nose wrinkled in disgust. "And I counted ten of you, so if everyone has that, that's..." His eyes screwed shut as he thought about it. "That's five and ten, then ten, and ten." When he started using his fingers, Khaldan's shoulders started to shake as he repressed his laughter. "It's a lot," he finished boldly.

"I didn't realise five was for all of us," Bastian countered. "But still, that's half a copper per man. You think that's fair for..." He pretended to consider the pile of clothing.

"At least thirty pieces of clothing," the innkeeper announced grandly. "I think he's giving you a bargain," he said with a disgruntled look to the boy.

"And how much will you take from his five coins?" Bastian asked the innkeeper, his amusement with the boy waning as he eyed the greedy innkeeper.

"One."

"One?" Bastian asked, his head tilting slightly to the side. "Just one copper?"

"Yes." The innkeeper didn't meet his eye, and Bastian knew he was lying.

But it was the boy who uncovered the lie. "One? Really, I can have four coins?"

The innkeeper looked as if he wanted to leave the room in a hurry rather than commit to an answer, but Khaldan was arranging his laundry and was by chance blocking the door.

"We can talk about it," the innkeeper tried to assuage the youth.

"Confirm your cut now," Bastian spoke over what the young boy had been about to agree to, his steely gaze fixed on the innkeeper.

"Two copper," he said with a sigh. "Two for me, for using my soap, my water, my tubs, you understand. Still, it's three for the boy."

Bastian noted with disappointment that the boy was still thrilled at the idea of three coins for a full day of heavy laundry. "Two to him. Is that fair to you, boy?"

The boy's dark hair fell into his eyes, but it didn't hide the glee. "Yes, milord, oh yes, indeed." He looked to the other boy, who was also nodding enthusiastically.

"You can go," Bastian directed towards the innkeeper. "I'll add your two coppers to the bill."

The innkeeper nodded quickly and rushed out of the room. Khaldan stepped out into the hall and watched his retreat and gave Bastian a quick look of confirmation that he was no longer in range to overhear.

Bastian crouched in front of the boy, who stood no higher than his hip. "You'll wash three shirts, two trousers and *all* the socks…" His lips tipped at the corners as the boys shuddered. "For me and each of my men. Yes?"

"Milord." The young boy nodded.

Bastian looked between the two boys. "Both of you?"

"Yes, milord, it will be done quicker," the other boy spoke, and Bastian realised he seemed older but was definitely led by the younger one.

"Very good." Bastian rose and reached into his pack. From his coin bag, he took out a handful of coins and counted out three copper coins, which he dropped into the boy's hand. He then added a silver coin to the pile and met the wide-eyed gaze of the youth.

"Milord? That's…that's too many," the young boy said almost with regret at his own honesty.

Bastian didn't acknowledge him and counted out the same again. He held the four coins out to the other boy. "Keep it between us. I expect cleaner than clean, understand?"

When they realised that they were both getting to keep the coins, *each*, the coins disappeared into pockets at alarming speed with a rushed "yes, milord" as they hurried to the beds to take the clothing.

When they had gone, laden down with washing and closing the door behind them, Khaldan dipped his hand in the bath water, testing it was still warm. "Generous of you."

"My clothes are stained from our last two skirmishes; they'll need harder cleaning than some of the others," Bastian stated as he started to loosen his trousers. "I won't be long," he added as he looked between the door and the tub.

"I'm going." With a shake of his head, Khaldan pulled the door open. "I'll tell the others about *laundry day*."

When the room was clear and the door closed firmly, Bastian pushed his trousers down and stepped into the tub. The water was lukewarm, and the tub was only half full, but still, he felt his muscles begin to relax as he leaned back. On a small wooden board that hooked over the side of the tub sat a rough bar of soap and a washcloth. Ignoring both of them for the moment, Bastian tipped his head back and stared at the ceiling. The beams were cracked and split, but as Bastian stared at them, he realised they were decorative only. An odd choice when it seemed that the original beams had been cut out.

The pitch of the ceiling was a mix of timber and mud blocks. Bordyre was a land that had two commodities, the salt and the coal mines, and for everyone else whose calling was not to work underground, it was the training academies for the warriors. Neither was a very promising future. The mines were dangerous. Tunnels collapsed on a regular basis, or strange explosions caused fatalities. For the mothers and fathers who sent their sons and daughters to the warrior schools, they knew that there was the strong possibility that their child was not returning to them. Odds of living to an old age in Bordyre were slim.

Within the Five Kingdoms, it was very rare that the lands or their lords weren't battling over one thing or another. Neither *thing* Bastian had ever found to be worth dying for, but still it was his duty to serve.

Hearing laughter in the hall and the soft murmuring of some of the men as they passed, no doubt being tempted below by the smells of bread and bacon, Bastian felt his own stomach grumble at the thought of warm food. Forcing himself to sit up, he washed the days of dirt and blood off himself. Using the soap, he washed quickly, taking care of the wound to his side. It was a graze more than a wound, and he was pleased to see the broken skin was red but not angry. Cleaning it thoroughly, he then washed his hair. His hair was the fashionable length that sat on his shoulders, but he kept it mostly tied back when travelling. Many a time, he had wanted to cut it, but propriety demanded he wear the style of his peers. With a light lather on his hair, he reached for the leather roll that housed his razor, and after soaping his face and using quick practiced strokes, he gave himself a rough shave.

Finally, as the water turned murky with his cleansing, he stood and picked up the one remaining bucket of water and poured it over himself, washing away soap and dirt that clung to him from the bathwater.

Dressing in casual, comfortable clothing, with his coin purse secure in his belt, he emptied the tub using the buckets. Outside the window, there was a drainpipe that was halved to allow waste and water disposal. Bastian made a few trips to the pipe at the side of the window, and when there was only a small amount of water left in the tub, Bastian left the room for the innkeeper and the boys to remove the excess water, clean it and refill it for Khaldan.

The hall of the upper level of the inn was narrow as were the stairs, and Bastian had to stoop on the way down to avoid hitting his head on the ceiling. The rough, uneven walls had been painted white and showed wear and tear from current use. There was white everywhere, Bastian noted as he entered the common room and made his way to the large table the men were at. Again, a strange colour of choice in an inn that catered to the soldier more than the nobleman. Taking a seat, he reached for a warm bread roll as Ax poured him a mug of coffee.

"It's good," Ax told him conversationally.

Bastian looked him over quizzically. "Why are you in your undergarments?"

"Some dark-haired imp stole my clothes," Ax told him

around a mouthful of food. "I believe we have you to thank for that?"

Bastian looked to his other men. All of them were either in their travel clothes or in more comfortable attire, like he was. "You gave them everything?" he asked sceptically.

Ax swallowed loudly as he shook his head. His roll was full of bacon, Bastian noticed as Ax pointed it at him. "Let's be clear. I was in this"—he pointed at his long johns—"and this little hobgoblin ran into the room and nabbed all my clothes."

"And Xan's clothes?" Bastian asked as he looked over to his other companion, who was eating his breakfast and looked to be content to do so without a word spoken. "He's dressed appropriately for breakfast."

Ax tore another chunk from his bread roll. "You see, he wasn't there."

Bastian saw Xan's top lip curl, and as he looked towards Bastian, there was a glint of glee in his light brown eyes. With a sigh, Bastian reached for his coffee. He knew exactly what had happened. Khaldan would have told the men that the boys were doing laundry, and Xan had seized the opportunity to mess with Ax, which would have been payback for Ax messing with the horses.

"If the innkeeper's wife screeches when she sees you, you owe us all ale." Bastian began to butter his roll, and Xan passed him the platter of bacon. Sure enough, when his roll was filled with juicy, delicious bacon, his hand jerked to a halt, stopping the approach of food to his mouth, when the ear-shattering scream of the innkeeper's wife pierced the air. With one hand flung up to cover her eyes at the scandalous sight of Ax in his underclothes, she fled the common room, and as his men erupted in laughter, Bastian took a hearty bite of his breakfast roll. The taste of the smoky-flavoured bacon burst on his tongue, causing him to close his eyes in appreciation.

"I think she was bringing sausage," Ax announced remorsefully.

"I'll go," one of the others said as he stood, clipping the back of Ax's head as he passed.

"And get more coffee!" Ax called after him as he rubbed his head while he reached for more bacon.

"Well, if you wanted to be noticed and *keep* being noticed," Khaldan said to Bastian quietly as he leaned into him so he could be heard over the morning chatter, "you got it."

"That's what we want."

CHAPTER 3

ON THE SECOND DAY OF THE STAY AT THE INN, BASTIAN WAS
sitting by the hearth in the common room, enjoying a coffee
and carefully mending his travel cloak. The young boys,
whose names he learned as Wilhelm and Gurt, were doing a
good job of making sure his cup was never empty. Wilhelm,
the younger one, was a constant shadow, but Bastian was
enjoying his company and, even more so, the comical facial
expressions the young lad pulled whenever the innkeeper
hollered for him.

"You sew like a woman," Khaldan told him as he took a
seat beside him, careful to move the chair, allowing both
men a clear view of the entrance.

"Thank you," Bastian murmured as he finished with his
repair, tying a knot in the thread.

"It's not a compliment."

Shaking out the cloak, Bastian eyed his handiwork. "I
think it is. Look." He pointed proudly to the hemline.
"Flawless."

Khaldan snorted as he reached for his friend's coffee.
"Where's your shadow gone?" he asked, referring to
Wilhelm as he took a drink.

"Ax has found more laundry for him."

"Of course he has," Khaldan snorted. "Found more, or
muddied what he had already cleaned?"

"Safe bet to assume the latter," Bastian answered as the
innkeeper's wife walked into the common room.

When Khaldan had asked for more coffee, he waited

until they were alone again before he spoke to his companion. "How long are we waiting?"

"One more night," Bastian confirmed quietly.

"It's not good for us to be in one place too long."

"It's been one night. We stay one more and the third night if we have to." Bastian stretched his legs out in front of him. "We're hardly taking up residence."

"You let five of the men out last night."

"I did."

"They went to the brothels and the other inns. They're not as well"—Khaldan hesitated—"maintained as here."

"I can imagine." Bastian waited for his friend to get to the point. He knew it was coming, but he was a patient man. Khaldan and he had known each other for a long time. Both were natives of the kingdom of Kalzynia, both born with warrior blood. They had trained in the academy together and come up through the ranks at the same time. As Bastian waited for his friend to spit out what was worrying him, he lounged in the seat, appearing at ease. Lazy even.

Khaldan's left eye twitched. It was slightly hooded due to the scar he had over it. It made his brown eye seem lighter than the other, which Khaldan used to his advantage when he was younger and trying to impress the ladies. "How much attention do you want, Bastian? We make ourselves any more known here, and we may as well paint a flag and hang it out the window."

Bastian sniffed slightly. "Hardly seems subtle," he commented dryly.

"Exactly!" Khaldan scoffed as he saw the innkeeper's wife return with new coffee and a plate of sticky buns.

"Thank you, Halver," he told her warmly as she placed the plate as close to him as possible.

"Milord." She left him with a small smile and hurried back to her duties but cast one look over her shoulder to ensure that Khaldan was taking a bun.

"I got half a pot of coffee," Bastian observed gruffly as he reached for a bun. "You get a feast."

"I told you, she's a good woman."

"She's a harridan that likes your bearded face too much for a married woman."

Khaldan grinned as he took a big bite of the bun. As he chewed, he gave Bastian a wink, causing the other to laugh. Quietly they enjoyed the buns and the coffee before Khaldan began to get restless again.

"One more night," Bastian cut off anything he was going to say. "Send out five again tonight, and make sure Xan is with them."

"And Ax?"

"Stays with us."

Khaldan shook his head slowly. "Sending Xan out without him is going to be a problem. You know he'll only sulk and pout."

"Pfft." Bastian tossed the last of his bun to one of the inn's hounds that lay a few feet from him. The speed with which the hound moved to eat the scraps caused Bastian to raise an eyebrow. "Wasn't sure that thing was still alive. I haven't seen it move since I sat down."

Khaldan turned to look at the dog, which had resumed its former position and closed its eyes again. The dog was shaggy haired, with long legs and a long snout. Its tail was short, and its ears were pinched. "What breed is it?"

"All of them?" Bastian suggested as they studied it. "Little bit relieved it moved. Wilhelm talks to it."

"You need to stop adopting strays," Khaldan warned him as he got to his feet.

"Nothing wrong with a stray," Bastian said as he studied the dog before standing also. "Speaking of, I better check Ghost."

"And then?"

"A walk through the town, I think. I have an inkling to get more cotton. My socks need darning."

Khaldan gave him a flat look before he shook his head and started towards the stairs, mumbling about it being better off hanging a flag. Bastian grinned at his friend's retreating back and left the inn to check on his horse.

Ghost was in a corner of the stables, his back to the wall, his side protected. Bastian couldn't help but smile as he assessed the horse's defensive position. Ghost whinnied in greeting and then promptly ignored him. Unperturbed, Bastian reached down to look at the feeding buckets, checking the horse had enough oats, picking out and tossing the straw aside.

When he was finished, he gave the stallion's coat a quick brush and checked his hooves. Xan had already told him that Ghost refused to give his hoof to the stable hand, and Bastian made quick work of checking.

"You're good," he told the horse as he dropped the leg back down, and Ghost snorted again as if to acknowledge the comment. "Stop being difficult," he added as he walked away, and the horse's snap of his teeth was definitely for his benefit that time.

Slowly he made his way through the town, heading to

the area where he knew the market was. Hylones was a town much like other towns where the first settlement had grown and morphed into a township as more and more people stopped moving around and settled in one place. The days of roaming were past for most, settlements took shape, and towns and cities were born. The town of Hylones had a fair trade that ran through it this close to the border of Kalzynia, and Bastian knew that merchants always needed their wagons guarded as they made their way west to the Golden City.

Bastian didn't try to hide who he was; he kept his face uncovered, and his travelling cloak was pushed back over his shoulders showing his leather cuirass beneath. He ignored the sly looks or the barely concealed stares. He was here to be noticed, and so far, it was working. He and the men had been working small menial jobs for weeks, things that never lasted more than a few days, and although this meant that payment was frequent, it meant there was no longevity.

Merchants were notoriously greedy, but those who had valuable goods to protect were willing to pay for the privilege, especially if they recognised the cut of the men who were protecting the supply.

The market was like any other. Numerous stalls, some set up and ready to be dismantled with ease, others more permanent under a wooden canopy that kept their goods and sellers dry when the weather turned. Bright maroon-coloured pennants of Hylones's colours flew in the wind, declaring the town's loyalty to the kingdom of Bordyre. Some merchants chose to fly their own colours, but even with the small show of nationalism, the predominant colour in the market was maroon. The market was roughly square in shape, large in size and was bordered with homes and businesses on either side. The buildings didn't open onto the market, which made a very imposing stone and brick frontage leering over the square. It was quietly suffocating, Bastian thought as he looked around, and also limited options of escape should one need it.

In the market, Bastian spotted the exact merchant he needed. The silk trade was always lucrative, and the cloth was always in demand in the higher houses' clothing armoires. Making a few stops along the way, picking up his cotton and some sweetmeats, Bastian stood and haggled the price of a small bag of the jellied treat that he had taken a liking to a few years ago. The sweet was cut into small cubes, a smooth firm jelly, sometimes flavoured with rose water and then rolled in powdered sugar. It was hard to come by, something to do with the curing process and the temperatures needed to be cool to let the jelly set, and as the markets got closer to the border, the weather fared warmer.

"Two silver is ridiculous," Bastian told the stall keeper with a laugh. "Two copper is too much, but because I see you have the blackcurrant rose, I'll give you three coppers."

"One silver." The merchant was round and bald, a bit like the sweet he sold, smooth and juicy looking. Bastian eyed the small pouches behind him and then around at the other market stalls.

"It's mid-morning," Bastian said casually. "I imagine that you've sold little of your treats today."

"Afternoons are better," the merchant grumbled.

"In this heat?" Bastian said as he looked to the sky. The sun was nearing its peak. "Strange that it would be better fare in the warmer weather when you just told me the lengths you need to take, and the cost, for keeping the sweets good." When the sweet dealer frowned, Bastian grinned at him. "Three copper." He held his hand out for the bag. "And I'll be on my way."

The merchant seemed to think about it and then with a grumble, tossed the small bag to Bastian and snatched the three offered coins out of the man's hands. Bastian indulged in one of the sweets before he tucked the rest in beside his coin purse. He made his way through the market and lingered at a silk merchant's stall. As his fingers traced over the delicate silk material, he kept his hand resting on the pommel of his sword.

"Seems a heavy wagon," he spoke conversationally to the merchant at the wagon, not the one on the stall. The man at the wagon was in heavy woollen and thick socks, with thick wrappings around his boots, whereas the man to the side wore a gaudy smock over tight woollen breeches. It was obvious which one was in charge.

"Aye, does it?" the wagoner spoke with a quick perusal of Bastian. "Order?"

"Silk merchant?"

"Trader." The man spoke as he got off the step of the wagon and made his way towards Bastian. "Hawk?"

"Too lofty for the likes of me." Bastian smiled slightly as he moved his hand off his pommel, and the carving of the Raven was revealed.

"Ah," the merchant said with a dip. "How many have you got?"

"How many do you need?" Bastian asked as he looked towards the corner of the market where there was a soldier in a deep maroon cloak watching him. It seemed that the soldier's nose had been broken and never set straight, his eyes were flat and beady, and his hair cut short. Far too short for a native of Bordyre.

"Could do it with six, would prefer eight, but I'd sleep comfortably at night knowing it was ten." The merchant smiled sadly. "Not many of you left in groups of ten."

"Pay?" Bastian asked as he gave the merchant his attention, while watching the maroon-cloaked soldier straighten when a comrade joined him. He knew their heads were dipping together, and he knew he had a few moments before they made their way over to the merchant and the stall.

While trade was encouraged in the market, trading for protection was not. The lord of the town took a percentage of the profit for the stalls, but there was no profit he could take from a mercenary offering protection outwith his town.

"How many?"

Bastian looked at the merchant and winked. "Your bed will offer the gateway to a dreamless sleep."

"I can't spare the wagon or the horse."

"How many bolts?" Bastian asked quietly as he saw the soldiers finally make the decision to move.

"Ten and twenty."

"We can take them; we have our own steeds." Bastian eyed the wagon. "It will be a heavy load though."

"I'll add on five," the merchant allowed.

"Gold?"

"Silver."

"Three gold and two silver, per man," Bastian conceded as he pulled out his coin purse. "I'll have the small silken purse," he told the one at the stall who had remained silent throughout. "For my sister."

"It is a fine choice," the man said graciously as the soldiers arrived.

"No soliciting in the market," the one who had just arrived barked at Bastian, as Crooked Nose stayed quiet. Watching.

"Surely that contradicts the nature here." Bastian looked around slowly. "And if the purpose is not to sell, then you walked by all these others peddling their wares to get to me."

"The merchants are allowed to sell; you are not."

"What am I selling?" Bastian extended his arms in supplication. "I have no goods."

"You're selling your sword." Crooked Nose glared at the weapon as if it personally offended him.

"I am?" Bastian looked down at the long sword at his side. His hand brushed over the top of it familiarly. "I can assure you that I mean to keep this. My father gifted this to me when I was but a lad."

Crooked Nose looked at him and then the sword and appeared momentarily confused. "No!" he exclaimed as he took a step forward. "You're a sellsword."

"I am?" Bastian asked dubiously. "I merely buy a purse." He held up the delicate silk purse. "For my sister, well, my nephew actually," Bastian offered a fond smile. "He had cut his first tooth and soon he will lose it," he added conspiratorially.

"The purse is for a babe?" The first soldier who had spoken and appeared more reasonable spoke again.

"Yes, but he is too young to appreciate the fine delicate work. My sister will, and she will know it is a worthy purse."

"For your nephew?" the soldier asked dubiously.

Bastian glanced at the purse. "Well, not him, just his teeth. Or tooth."

"It is a fine purse for such a thing," the merchant in the gaudy smock spoke up. "Or perhaps a lock of a lover's hair," he said to the soldiers as he held up another, like any merchant always ready to make an additional sale. "For your sweet love."

The more belligerent of the two lowered his head to inspect the purse and was rudely elbowed in the side by his companion.

"You need to come with us," the Crooked Nose said with determination to Bastian.

"Why?"

"You're soliciting."

"Said who?" Bastian queried quietly.

"Me." The soldier took an authoritative step forward.

Bastian frowned and looked down at himself before looking back up at the two soldiers. "You? Well, *you*, I have a task for you. Prove it." Whether it was the change in his stance, the fact his hand now gripped his sword rather than rested on it, or the mere challenge in Bastian's eyes, the soldiers hesitated. "I have a purchase in my hand, as you can see." Bastian indicated to the purse. "I've yet to pay for it, I admit that, but that's because you fine fellows interrupted our barter."

The quieter of the soldiers looked to his companion and the stall owner with the gaudy smock. "Is this true?"

"I gave my price, but he thinks that the finest silk from the basin of the Mumbling Mountains is worth only one piece of silver." The merchant gave a nonchalant shrug. "I thought that's why you came over because you saw the worth of the product yourself."

Bastian fought the smile as the soldiers looked between themselves, suddenly unsure.

"What's your price?" Crooked Nose asked the merchant.

"One and a half silver."

"For that?" the other soldier blurted out.

"Exactly what I said," Bastian spoke up quietly. "Surely just the silver coin will do," he appealed to the soldiers.

"Well, it's not for us to say," the one who had voiced his disbelief mumbled. "It's for your niece you said."

"Nephew," Bastian corrected him easily. "Just cut his first tooth. The whimsical design will appeal to my dear sister."

"And your sword?" Crooked Nose asked.

Bastian regarded him casually. "A faithful companion since I left the academy."

"Which one?" he asked as he studied the long blade with the intricate handle.

"Both of them," Bastian said with a quick grin, and he took small delight in the way they both involuntarily stepped back.

"You were Order?" Crooked Nose asked.

"I *am* Order," Bastian corrected. He reached for his coin purse and stifled his snort as the two half drew their own swords. "One silver." He tossed it to the merchant. "Your silk may be good quality, my man, but of the Mumbling Mountain, it is not."

The merchant went to protest and instead bit the coin to

test the quality of the silver, and with a grunt, the coin disappeared in his pocket. "It's still good," he muttered.

"It is." Bastian glanced quickly at the other merchant still at the wagon, and the older man nodded subtly. "Gentlemen," Bastian addressed them as he dipped his head and left the market.

Khaldan waited at the corner, and as Bastian approached, Khaldan pulled his hood up. "Are we ready to leave?"

"We may be, my friend," Bastian told him as he pulled a sweet from the pouch and popped it in his mouth.

"Your teeth will rot on them," Khaldan chided him with a frown, choosing to ignore Bastian's smug grin when he was offered his own treat and took it. "Goods or people?"

"Goods," Bastian told him in a low voice. "Three bolts of quality silk each if I'm right."

"Pay?"

"To be finalised but should be a good price."

Khaldan cursed under his breath. "Pay first, then terms," he reminded him.

"Is that how it works?" Bastian asked him in wonder. "Why did no one ever mention it?"

"You're a son of a goat," Khaldan grumbled as they headed back to the inn to gather the rest of the men. They had a job to do, and now that they had drawn enough attention, they would wait one more night to see whether their time here was over.

Chapter 4

Bastian waited patiently in his room as the night darkened, his attention on the main gate as the background noise of the inn lowered to a steady mumble as guests retired to their rooms after their meals were over. The gates to Hylones were large and wooden and were not substantial enough to withstand a pointed attack, a fact that Bastian wanted to share with the ruling authority of the town but kept his counsel to himself. These days he never knew if he was going to be part of the attacked or the attackers. In case of the latter, he was keeping his options open.

Around midnight, he saw the side door of the main gate open, and a low-lit flame of a torch bobbed conspicuously in the night. Counting the beats before the door was closed again, Bastian guessed three, maybe four people had been admitted into the town after curfew. The torch was quickly dimmed, and with a rapid knock on the adjoining wall, he summoned Ax through from the other room.

Moments later, the door to his room was opened and Ax slipped in. "Am I allowed out yet?" he asked sullenly as he stroked his blond beard.

"Town gates just let in three, maybe four stragglers. Torch was heading north of here," Bastian told him.

"You want me to try to find three people in this town in the middle of the night?" Ax asked him incredulously.

"No, they let three in, but they let two *out*." Bastian turned back to the window and pointed towards the distance. Two very dim lights could be seen. "I want to know who was let out in the dead of night, after curfew."

Ax came and stood beside him, his eyes on the two faint lights before he turned to Bastian. "Your plan worked then?" Ax asked with a slight smile. "Flushed them out?" When Bastian gave a slight shrug, Ax turned back to the window. "Next stop is where?"

"Base of the Teeth."

"I'll meet you there." Ax clasped Bastian's shoulder as he passed on his way out of the room. A short while later, Bastian watched the door in the gate open again, and then when there was enough distance between the gate and the land, a flare of light blazed briefly in the night, and he watched as it bobbed in the darkness for a few more moments before the light was extinguished. Ax had let him know he was out and on the trail.

Even so, all night Bastian watched the gate. When Khaldan came back from being with the men in the alehouses, he told Bastian before taking to his bed, that the merchant would have the silk ready for the morning. Through the night, Bastian remained vigilant on watch. Before dawn broke the night's rest, Bastian and his men were in the market, the bolts of cloth rolled tight and ready to be transported.

"I gave your man the details last night," the merchant told Bastian as he loaded Ghost with three bolts of cloth.

"Aye, he shared it." Bastian tightened the girth, ignoring Ghost's huff of displeasure. "You paid all of it?"

"Order may have some problems," the merchant said gruffly, "but the Order is *still* Order."

"Yes, we are," Bastian agreed solemnly.

The nine of them rode out of Hylones as the dawn broke, and on the way out of the gate, Bastian caught Khaldan's eye and, with a jerk of his head, waited for Khaldan to give the order.

"Xan, he has six hours on you. Can you catch him?" Khaldan asked as he looked over his shoulder at his comrade.

"Catch him? I'll be in front of him," Xan boasted as he pulled on his horse's reins.

"Five silver says Ax is at the meet before you," one of the others called from the back.

Bastian smirked as the wagers started, amused at Xan's growing outrage as the consensus was reached that he wouldn't catch up to Ax. Calling for one of the others, soon both men were breaking away from the column and following the trail of Ax.

"And then we were seven," Khaldan murmured as he pulled up alongside Bastian. He looked over at the dark-haired leader, not at all surprised to see that Bastian was unconcerned. "If we're followed?"

"We'll deal with it," Bastian told him easily. "Did you get all that we need?"

"I did."

"Good."

They rode at a gentle pace through the morning. The barren countryside began to be speckled with greenery the further south they ventured. In the distance, the Dragon's Teeth reared ahead of them, the harsh black rock rising imperiously into the sky, piercing the peaceful blue sky with sharp, ragged points that contrasted harshly with the surrounding area.

"I hate the climb," Khaldan offered conversationally.

"Think how the horses feel," Bastian quipped as he pulled his hood low over his forehead.

"Rain?" Khaldan looked to the cloudless sky.

"Maybe I just want privacy," Bastian countered.

"Aye, sure you do." Khaldan scoffed as he pulled his own hood low and tugged his travelling cloak tight around him.

The men rode in silence through the morning. The unit had served in the Order in one form or another for a long time. They were used to each other, used to their command, and used to the way that Bastian ran things. Although the Order had fallen out of favour due to politics, greed, and accusations of corruption—the majority of which were still unfounded—the men in Bastian's company still held true to their training. Some days it was a looser hold than there had been before, but a hold it still was.

When darkness began to fall, Khaldan rode ahead to find a spot to stop for the night. With practiced moves, the men spoke little as they set up a small camp, the weather still mild at this time of year as they headed south, and with fresh food from the inn, they forwent any fire.

After a light supper of bread, cheese and some beef, Bastian unfurled his bedroll, positioning his pack under the material to provide a pillow of sorts. Ghost stood apart from the other horses, his head cocked to the north where the faint howls carried on the night air.

"Could be timberwolves," Khaldan commented as he looked northwards. "Surprised we've not seen them yet."

"Could be," Bastian agreed as the cries pierced the air

again. "They're not near, but if they've not come nearer, and our scent will carry on the wind the same as their cry, then they may be more than the grey wolf."

"I'm not in the mood for *zyvarg*," Khaldan grumbled as he rolled out his own bedroll, referring to the larger, more vicious wolf-like creature. When the world crumbled and fell, and radiation soaked the soils and spoiled the water, it also bred mutations. New variants of animals that had survived the fall of the world were born. From the majestic, almost regal, large grey wolf, the zyvarg were created. Larger in size, with fangs that dripped venom and sharp talons that could slice through flesh and bone, sharper than any blade, the zyvarg were an unwanted companion in the open.

"Blanyon, Fylip, first watch," Bastian ordered as he stood by Ghost. "They move closer, we move out."

"Understood," Blanyon said as he moved through their small camp. "I'll take the higher ground," he called softly over his shoulder to his companion.

"Rest, boy," Bastian spoke to Ghost. "It's a long day tomorrow." Back at his bedroll, he pulled his cloak firmly around him and lay down to sleep.

Shadows of night covered the damp ground. A light rain had fallen earlier, and Khaldan had glared at Bastian as the men travelled, as if he were personally responsible for the drizzle that seemed to soak their clothing. With the sounds of his companions settling down for a few hours' sleep, Bastian too closed his eyes. His thoughts took longer to quieten, but as he listened to his surroundings and the familiar sound of night, he was lulled into sleep.

"Bastian," Khaldan whispered fiercely. "They're here."

Springing to his feet, Bastian reached for his sword with one hand while rubbing sleep from his eyes with the other. "Close?"

"Almost on top of us," Khaldan growled as he cast a glare to Fylip. "The sergeant took his eye off the horizon," he added with scorn.

Cricking his neck, Bastian took the flask of water his companion handed him. "Easy to do in the dark," Bastian conceded diplomatically, pointedly ignoring Khaldan's huff of displeasure. Swallowing half the contents of the flask, Bastian handed it back over. "Okay, I'm awake. Where are they?"

"You think the zyvarg were waiting until your thirst was quenched?" Khaldan asked in amusement.

"It's the polite thing to do." Bastian secured his belt, turning slowly in a circle, intent on sensing their enemy.

"They're circling," Khaldan muttered. "Sensing the weakest points, no doubt."

"Clever scurs that they are," Bastian acknowledged. "So," he said, coming to a stop and facing to the west. "They're sticking to the darkest areas." He looked around one more time. "Makes sense." Turning quickly, he searched the area and saw the dark coat of Ghost in the dim light. "Speaking of sense," he said as he gestured to his horse, "that one would have made a better watch on a night like this."

"Aye," came the grim reply.

"And here they come," Bastian warned as the zyvarg slowly approached. Midnight black coats of fur blended with the lingering darkness, while eyes of dull orangey-red like that of the slow burning embers of a dying fire came into focus as the zyvarg advanced.

"Smooth and silent," Bastian cautioned his men. "It's going to be bloody."

The zyvarg attacked as one. Their arrow-headed formation leapt into the camp, and soon men and beast fought in a tangle of claws and swords. The men were no stranger to fighting the zyvarg, and with practiced strokes and known weaknesses, they gained the upper hand fairly quickly. The creatures knew when to cut their losses, their cunning intelligence the reason they were a formidable opponent. As they retreated into the grey of the approaching morning, Bastian wiped his sword with a handful of torn grass.

"That was easy," he said to no one in particular.

"Agreed," Blanyon said as he walked over to join him. "Assessing us or too young?"

Bastian frowned. "They weren't as grown as I've seen, but they were no pups."

"Trained?" Blanyon suggested.

"Rumours have been coming out of the north of Bordyre for a while now about warriors *riding* zyvarg," Khaldan muttered as he kicked the carcass of one of the fallen creatures. "I can see the appeal," he said as he crouched down warily, ensuring the animal was dead, and then turned it over. "They aren't as delicate or as vulnerable as horses."

"Those that live near the Barrens are crazy enough to think they can tame them." Blanyon joined Khaldan as he examined the zyvarg.

"They should know better; you can't tame something

truly wild," Khaldan disagreed. "It will always turn back to its true nature."

Bastian said nothing as he checked on Ghost and the other horses, and the men got rid of the dead zyvarg and prepared to move on. Death, of any kind, drew too much attention in this part of the land.

The group moved on fairly soon thereafter, alert and ready for the zyvarg to return. For two days, they rode and in that time, although they could hear the monsters, they weren't approached by them again.

On the third day, they were at the base of the Dragon's Teeth, where Ax, Xan and Medan were already waiting.

"And?" Bastian asked as he dismounted.

"Three travellers, well protected, I think; they knew to be careful. Lost them in Byx. They obviously had something arranged. They arrived at night, and which house they went in I do not know," Ax told him as he frowned. "We watched the town all night. They didn't leave."

"They'll come this way," Bastian mused.

"No other way to go now," Xan grunted. "If they're heading south still."

Bastian nodded his agreement. It would make no sense to travel from Hylones to Byx to then turn north again. The Teeth were the only thing blocking them.

"They could be heading west," Khaldan said. "Skirt the base of the Teeth, take the long way."

"No, they'll come this way." Bastian considered the mountain range. "It's the only way that makes sense."

The Teeth were a range of treacherous mountains with a narrow trail that ascended at a sheerness that made it hazardous to climb in the dry months and impossible to pass in the winter. With nothing more to add, the men spoke little as they brushed down their horses and made a small makeshift camp for the night. After a meal of dried beef and stale bread, they braced themselves for the drop in temperature that the night would bring, and when the land was silent around them, they attempted to sleep.

The pale light of the morning crested over the peak of the mountain. The cold air that swirled around Bastian was made no less biting by the golden sunlight lighting the sky above him. The bedrolls were huddled close together in the attempt to be a windbreaker from the strong wind as it raced down the side of the mountain, roaring free in the hollow at the base. The close placement of the bedrolls may have proved to be some way to ease the cold, but it had proved no shelter from the wind that tugged relentlessly all night on loose corners of cloaks or blankets, eager to chill the bones of the men as they lay at the foot of the Teeth. Lighting a fire was not possible here, as the men were exposed, open, and vulnerable. Fire here would only illuminate their presence against the black rock, signalling to all across the valley of a presence there.

Instead, the men had fought off the cold by relying on extra blankets from their packs. Wrapped tight in their outer clothing and blankets, they had wished for warmth as they chased sleep across the miserable night.

Like his men, Bastian had been awake for most of the night and ended up relieving Khaldan of his watch long before he was due. Hearing movement, Bastian turned his attention to the dip of the mountain basin and watched as Ax arrived from a night of scouting, his heavy woollen cloak draped over his shoulders. Seeing that it was Bastian on watch, Ax frowned at him before searching for Khaldan. On silent feet, Ax approached Bastian and took the waterskin from him.

"Why are you awake?"

Bastian reclaimed his waterskin, his attention on the mountain. "I was contemplating the wonders of the universe alone in silence."

Ax glanced at his companion. "Uh-huh." He spat to the side, and as he wiped his mouth, his scowl was now also on the mountain. "And what message of *wonder* did the shrew have for you?"

"She said *come back later, she's busy*."

Ax laughed lowly. "Yeah, they're all too *busy* for the Ravens." He pulled his cloak up and over his head, pulling it low, keeping out the cold as much as possible. "You should have slept," he admonished as he tilted his head to the black rock face behind us. "It's going to be a heck of a climb. No sleep means you're weak, and heck knows you're already clumsy."

"I have faith you'll catch me if I fall, brother."

"You do?" Ax's grin was wicked. "I lost faith in mumbo jumbo a long time ago, brother." He walked over to the bedrolls, and Bastian watched as Ax started to nudge his companions, rousing them. "Wake up, soldiers. Today we *fly* up a mountain."

Turning his attention back to the climb, Bastian shook his head wistfully. Their Order was Raven, and it was a pity they couldn't actually fly, as it would mean they would be out of the shadow of the mountain a heck of a lot quicker. Bastian scowled back along the open landscape because he could feel a deep unease in his bones.

Striding over to his own bedroll, he began to tidy the camp as the men got ready to start the day. They worked with efficiency and practiced ease, and Bastian knew that they all felt it, that they needed to get out of here and get out soon.

Something was stirring in the land.

CHAPTER 5

THE CLIMB OVER THE TEETH TOOK THREE DAYS. GOING UP was hard. Going down, especially with horses, was harder. Ghost had managed with a lot of biting, kicking and flat stares that conveyed his displeasure throughout to his rider. Bastian had taken the horse's punishment silently, knowing how difficult it was for the animals. The others fared the same. Khaldan's horse had slipped and fallen, and luck was with them that despite the scrapes and cuts, the mount was mostly uninjured.

As Ghost strutted off his displeasure at the base of the mountain, Bastian sipped from his waterskin. Ax was last down, and once he had checked his horse over, he handed the reins to one of the other men who was walking the horses to let them lose their fear and anxiety with the others.

"Any sign?" Bastian asked him softly.

"Heard a scream before I reached the peak," Ax told him as he pulled his cloak from his pack. "Didn't hear a crunch, so I doubt they fell."

"Probably a rattler," Bastian suggested. "Or a disagreement," he added dryly.

"Whichever it was, it slowed them down."

"Still climbing?"

"Yeah, they lit a fire." Ax's look to Bastian conveyed his thoughts on that particular decision.

"Reckless," Bastian mused. "Or stupid?"

"Both?" Ax suggested. "The zyvarg started the climb."

Bastian cursed under his breath, for that was not good news. "Well, the beasts may solve the problem for us," he told Ax grimly.

"Aye, a full belly does tend to slow one down."

"Stops us from knowing who it is too," Bastian said as he looked back up the mountain face.

"You sure our presence in Hylones made them move?" Ax asked him as he watched his companions shake off the fatigue from the days in the Teeth.

"It's what we do, flush out the guilty or the ones with something to hide from us." Bastian tipped his head back as he took another drink.

"True, we're Order. You let it be known in the town that we were. Even your negotiations with the merchant weren't subtle." Ax cast him a sideways look. "We were Order when it meant something." He grunted as he kicked at the ground before pulling his cloak around himself. "Now… Well, now they look at us as if we're just another bunch of cynical mercenaries looking for their next pay day."

Bastian looked at the man beside him, his eyebrow raising in question. "Is that all you are, sir knight? A man with a sword to sell?"

Ax dipped his head at his leader's softly spoken words. "Of course not," he muttered as he took a deep breath, rubbing his hands over his eyes. "I'm sorry, it just—"

"Gets under your skin, and you rage at the unfairness of it all?" Bastian said knowingly. "I know, soldier, by the Gods do I know."

Ax smiled at his companion with respect. "We served them so long and so freely for what? To be cast as the villain when it all went to shit?"

Bastian grunted in agreement. "Who are we to disagree with the rulers of our kingdom," he said with bitterness.

"The men who fight for it?" Ax pointed at Fylip, who was tentatively approaching Ghost. "Your horse hates him. He's going to bite him. Why can't you make your horse be normal?" he asked, changing the subject onto matters that were within their control.

"He is normal."

"He's an animal."

"Indeed he is." Bastian grinned as he watched his horse snap at Fylip.

"I mean he's a rabid animal," Ax stressed as he flinched in sympathy when the sergeant leaped back as Ghost successfully bit him.

"I like him," Bastian told him amiably as he headed over to his horse as Fylip scurried away from him.

"You would!" Ax called after him. "You're just as bad!"

Bastian stood in front of his mount and raised his eyebrows. "You missed out on the last of the apples," he told him. Ghost nickered and tossed his glossy black mane. "Fylip was being nice," Bastian continued to admonish the horse. Ghost gave him a flat stare. "This is why none of the men will share with you." Ghost pawed the ground with his hoof. "I know, you don't care, fine." Bastian met the fiery tempered horse's look. He fought the smile that tugged at his lips as he reached into his pouch and brought out an apple. "Behave until we get to the Golden City, boy."

Ghost ignored him as he happily munched his treat. When Bastian turned away, Khaldan was behind him, arms crossed and wearing a disapproving look.

"What?" Bastian asked, wincing internally at the slightly defensive tone of his voice.

"You give him treats when he doesn't deserve them." Khaldan looked over Bastian's shoulder. "You treat him like he's human."

"I like him better than I like most humans," Bastian told his friend.

"He bites you more than anyone," Khaldan reminded Bastian.

"Aye, but he doesn't bite me to hurt me." Bastian looked over his shoulder at his horse, who was pointedly ignoring everyone. "He's fine."

Khaldan snorted and then gestured to the men behind him. "You want to wait for the ones up there, or are you keen to keep moving? This silk needs to be delivered. After all, we took the payment."

"I know." Bastian rocked his head from side to side as he loosened the tension between his shoulders. "We'll do the job we were given."

"And the strangers?"

Bastian looked at the horses laden with the silk and then back at the mountain. He had made their presence known in Hylones simply for reasons like this. With the Order in disgrace or not, the guilty still fled when soldiers of the Order were in town. He and his men may have lived as mercenaries now, but those who knew him as a soldier of the Order of the Ravens knew that, although the majority of the rulers of the Five Kingdoms had turned their back on the Order of the Conclave, there were some within those Orders who hadn't turned their back on their kingdom.

Bastian and his men were such men.

"Xan," Bastian called. The tall man straightened from his pack, and seeing Khaldan and Bastian together, he reached into his coin purse and tossed a coin Ax's way, glowering at his companion's victorious laugh. Making his way over to Bastian and Khaldan, he was still tightening his purse strings when he stopped beside them.

"Silver?" Khaldan asked him conversationally.

"Aye," Xan said as he turned his back on Ax, who was still laughing with his companions. "So, you want me to go back up the Teeth, find out who they are, and then catch up with you?"

"It's like you can read my mind," Bastian mocked, not altogether happy about that.

"We knew we were either waiting for them to get eaten or killed, whether you're here when it happens or not, was the bet." Xan shrugged as he pushed his daggers into their holsters better. "Take my horse?" he asked Khaldan. "I'll be quicker on foot."

"Ax can do it; consider it payback," Khaldan told the man beside him.

Xan pushed his hair out of his eyes as he turned to look at Ax, the grin already forming. "Always knew I liked you for a reason," he joked. Pulling his hood up over his dark hair, he looked up at the Teeth. "Who knows, maybe they died already."

"Charming," Bastian murmured.

Xan turned to his leader and rolled his eyes in exasperation. "I ain't here to charm," he reminded them. "I'll catch up. Make sure he waters my horse first."

Xan strode away from them, Ax called out a farewell, and the single finger salute over his shoulder was Xan's reply, which caused a few to chuckle as they got ready to leave.

"Fall out," Khaldan called when he was mounted on his horse. "We have a long way to go yet."

They rode through the night and well into the next morning before they stopped for a few hours' rest. They saw little by way of any other travellers. The Dragon's Teeth bordered Kalzynia and the kingdom of Tzenyth. Tzenyth was the land of the Plains people, and Bastian and his men travelled with comfort through the high grasslands, always vigilant for others.

As the days turned, Ax began to fall back further as they waited for Xan to catch up. On the fourth day, he was gone completely, and Khaldan and Bastian merely exchanged a look before they set off on their day's travelling.

Bastian was leading the company, enjoying the warmth of the sun on his back when Khaldan drew alongside him.

"We stop?" Khaldan asked him casually.

"No."

"And if they're hurt?" Khaldan tried to keep the frown from his face, but Bastian knew his friend too well.

"They heal. This isn't new to them."

"And if they're dead?" Khaldan asked more harshly.

"Then we mourn them," Bastian replied simply. Turning his head, he looked at his companion. "You growing soft on me?"

"They're our responsibility."

"They are." Bastian nodded. "And?"

"The old you would have stopped and checked, or at least waited."

"The old me is exactly that, old and in the past." Bastian

turned in his saddle as he looked back at the men riding behind him. "You turned into a worrier, my friend. Xan will be fine."

Khaldan kept his opinion to himself, but when they stopped for rest that night and they had caught some rabbit for dinner, he sent two more men back to scout for their companions once they had eaten their meal. Bastian observed him quietly but said nothing as he ate his portion of rabbit. Khaldan didn't address the challenging look in his companion's eyes and made a point of looking after the horses.

In the morning, Bastian had made a decision that he knew would not be popular with his men. As he broke his fast on a meal of cold rabbit and water, he heard Khaldan groan. Looking up, he found his friend shaking his head.

"I knew you would do this," Khaldan told him as he reached for a piece of meat. "Where are we offloading the horses and silk?"

"Three can take them to the nearest port," Bastian replied as he leaned back comfortably.

"Three? For ten horses?" Khaldan shook his head in disagreement.

"Three is fine," Bastian stated firmly.

"You really want to send five of us into it?"

"Seven," Bastian corrected him, pointing to the horizon. "Your strays have returned."

Turning swiftly, Khaldan saw Ax and Xan riding towards them, both sharing the one horse. The other two men behind them. They were unharmed and greeted their companions when they were at camp. Fylip took the horse to the others, and Xan made his way to Bastian, Ax lingering behind, his interest already on the food from the night before.

"Trouble?" Bastian asked Xan as the other man squatted down to be at his eye level.

"It's strange."

"Strange?" Khaldan asked sharply. "How?"

"There were three of them. I didn't get too close to tell you if they were male. One definitely was."

Bastian and Khaldan exchanged a look. "Why did you keep your distance?" Bastian asked.

"I couldn't get nearer," Xan told them. "I tried everything I know, and when I thought I was closer, I was suddenly back where I had been."

"Magic?" Khaldan whispered in disbelief.

"It had to be. They didn't try to get closer to me either, just maintained a distance, and I couldn't see them."

"They were shielded," Bastian growled as he stood. "They are behind us still?"

"Yes, I figured there was something odd, so at the base, I hid in the trees and waited for them to come out of the Teeth."

"Did they?" Khaldan asked quietly.

"I don't know," Xan admitted. "I saw nothing. I waited a whole day and nothing."

"We do not need them following us," Bastian said grimly as he looked at Khaldan. "Well, I'm already decided."

Khaldan reluctantly nodded in agreement, and Xan rose to his feet, looking between the two of them. "No, really?"

Bastian clasped him on the shoulder as he looked west. "Think of the adventure."

Ax walked up to them, chewing his breakfast. "Sand Seas?" he guessed.

"Only you would be excited at the thought of burning in that blasted desert," Xan grumbled as he walked over to the small food area to get his own breakfast.

Ax looked at Bastian, giving him a small shrug. "Where's his sense of adventure?" he asked innocently, frowning when Khaldan groaned, and Bastian started laughing. "What? What did I say?" he asked, but his companions just walked away from him. "What did I say?" Ax asked the remains of his breakfast. Receiving no answer, he tossed the bones into the long grass and prepared to set off again.

In the end, it wasn't quite as Bastian predicted. They ended up using four men to take the horses. Ghost needed a handler of his own, and only Blanyon was brave—or stupid—enough to take the black stallion on.

"It's said that, in the Before, they used horses to make something they called glue," Bastian told no one in particular as Blanyon yelped as Ghost nipped him.

"Glue?" Khaldan repeated. "How?" he asked curiously. "Nothing of them is sticky."

"Doesn't glue come from trees?" Xan asked a moment later. "Gum trees, or did I get that wrong?"

"Glue is still made from the carcasses of animals," Bastian told them as he tightened his pack. "It comes from skin, tissue and bones," he added, completely ignorant of his companions' horrified faces. "I believe they heat it to separate the substance…" Looking up, he stopped, his face showing his surprise at their expressions.

"How do you know this?" Khaldan asked him with a

shake of his head. "The thoughts in your head are truly dark."

"It's a process of extraction," Bastian defended himself. "If you asked anyone, other than you three, someone would be able to tell you."

It was obvious his companions didn't believe him, and each went to check their own packs. Bastian made his way to Ghost, who immediately turned his head from his owner and snorted his discontent.

"Try not to bite too many," Bastian warned him as he ran his hand over his mount's withers. "And be good to Blanyon; he was the only one brave enough to offer." Ghost turned his head to look at his rider, and Bastian hid his smile at the unimpressed stare. "Be good, lead the others, don't drown at sea."

Dancing backward, he avoided his horse's teeth, and laughing, he stood back as his horse huffed in displeasure.

"It's as if he can understand you," Xan commented with a wry grin from where he watched the exchange. A safe distance from the stallion's wandering teeth, Bastian noticed.

"I am under no illusion he doesn't understand me perfectly," Bastian said as he popped a sugar cube in his mouth and laughed when Ghost stomped his hoof. "You see, had you not been a beast, I would have told you that I was adding them to your pack," Bastian taunted his horse.

Ghost reared and Blanyon cried out in alarm, thinking the horse was escaping. Grumbling at the absurdity of it all, Xan snatched the pouch of sugar cubes off of Bastian and approached the unruly horse, holding the pouch out as a peace offering. When Ghost had eaten two cubes, he and the rest of the horses and their handlers left the camp, leaving six behind.

"Promise we get one night in Blazyth before we enter," Ax asked.

"One night, no more," Bastian conceded. "And if you drink too much, I'm leaving you to dehydrate where you drop," he warned him.

"Drink too much?" Ax laughed. "Is there such a thing?"

The men began their march to the town of Blazyth and the Sand Seas beyond. As they left their small camp, Bastian looked over his shoulder to the horizon. The feeling that he was being watched had been sitting in his gut for the better part of the day. Grimly he faced forward. He was hopeful he would find them in the town of Blazyth, and if he didn't, well, there was no shelter in the Sand Seas. If they were being watched, it wouldn't be long before they knew by who.

In fact, he was counting on it.

CHAPTER 6

Blazyth was a small town, once a trading post that had become more established than its original intention. Sitting perched between the Teeth and the Sand Seas, it was a town that didn't have a lot going for it. You were either running from something or running *to* something, and a stop in the town on an otherwise perilous journey through the Teeth or a suicide mission across the Sand Seas was the perfect spot to either hide or take a moment to choose your options. And sometimes that choice became that you didn't want to do either, and if going back wasn't an option and going forward wasn't either, then you stayed where you were. As more and more people chose the option to stay where they were, the trading post transformed from semi-permanent structures to buildings, whether homes or houses, and the town grew.

The town was technically in Kalzynia, but as it almost touched into the kingdom of Tzenyth, the kingdom of Kalzynia turned a blind eye to the ongoings of the town. The people of the Prairies had no desire to climb the heights of the mountains or cross the dry plains of the Sand Seas, which meant that Blazyth was made use of to keep in touch with the rest of the kingdoms. The small town offered snippets of information for those who avoided the only permanent structure on the plains, the Fort. The Fort provided the delegates and ambassadors of the other king-doms a place to gather and to make demands of the nomadic tribes who cared little for the movements and squabbles of their fellow men. Men who were tied to structures and obligations, men like those who had caused the world to fall once before and no doubt would again.

Tzenythians followed the pattern of the *bulsyn*, the wild bovine animal that migrated over the plains with the changing of the seasons. Tzenythians cared for what they had and what they gave back to the land, land that worked and provided for them as hard as they worked for it.

As Bastian stood in the darkness of an alley, leaning against the wall of a small shop, the night was heavy and muggy around him, despite the light drizzle that had been falling steadily for the last hour. Bastian could hear the roars of laughter from the tavern. With his cloak pulled low over his eyes as he kept watch, he blended well into the shadows of the darkness. The tavern that Ax had led the others to was smaller than the ones he could have chosen, and in a small tavern, knights were more susceptible to discovery.

In Hylones, Bastian wanted attention, but in Blazyth, he wanted the men to blend. They had each shed their cuirass before they ventured out looking like simple men in simple clothing—black trousers with shirts of grey or black, which showed signs of previous mending. Their boots were in varying stages of being thick with mud, a sight that made Bastian itch to find the polishing cloth. Their cloaks were thick and heavy woollen of dark grey or brown, a sign of few options on which to spend your hard-earned coin. When money was tight, you went for practicality and picked the cloak that would serve you all year round, not just a light travelling cloak for the summer months. The men wore the clothes of poorer men, which were as far from their normal dress choice as they could be.

But no matter how they dressed, they were still soldiers. Knights and sergeants of the Order of the Ravens, and there were some disciplines and idiosyncrasies that, no matter what their clothing, were hard to disguise. Ax was able to blend into any surrounding, anywhere. He'd taken cover in a brothel once, and twice Bastian himself had walked past him thinking he was one of the girls for pleasure —a mean feat considering Ax had a thick blond beard. Khaldan was also apt at blending, but Khaldan attracted too much attention sometimes from certain women, the rarity of finding a travelling man who was married, and happily at that, proved too tempting a challenge to some. Xan was almost as good at disguising his appearance and nature as Ax, which they should be, because the two of them tested each other at every opportunity. But there were two more men with them: a sergeant and a newly joined knight who they had collected from Bordyre on their most recent commission from the Conclave. Men who didn't know how to blend with the ease of the others.

It was because of them that Bastian stood outside in the rain, watchful of the shadows, knowing that there was the possibility that within the deepest shadows, he was being watched back.

The crossing of the Sand Seas would be hard. He had done it three times before, and each time, he had been sure that the infernal punishing heat would be the end of him. As he stood in the rain, Bastian reached his hand out, taking the moment to savour the feel of the wetness on his skin. The Sand Seas sucked every drop of moisture out of you, or close to it. Xan had started the conversation earlier about a wagon in order to take their packs across for them. The added weight was not a kindness in the Sand Seas. Travel light and swift if you could, that was the trick to crossing. Which is why the horses were taking the long way around. Bastian didn't have time for the long way. He knew there was a need to return to the Golden City, he just didn't know why, but the nagging feeling in his gut was telling him to make haste.

And haste meant crossing the Sand Seas. But a wagon meant a horse, and a horse was just another body that needed water in the heat of the desert.

Hours later, Khaldan, ever the responsible one, led the others from the tavern. With more swagger in their walk to make onlookers believe they were deep in their cups, Bastian knew their act would fool anyone else watching. They split up as they staggered their way to their beds, ensuring that if they were being followed, they made the job harder by making their tails follow one or two rather than six.

With care, Bastian tracked them, making sure that they all got back to the lodgings for the night, and when they were inside, he circled the inn and the walkways once more to be sure they hadn't been followed. Finally, after a long damp night, Bastian sought the comfort of his bed, leaving the first watch of the night to Xan.

Morning came too soon, and with reluctance, Bastian agreed to the purchase of one wagon and a horse that had outlived its former employment. Ax assured his companion that he had received a good price for it, to which Bastian said nothing. Had he been told Ax paid more than he should to ensure the horse's survival, he wouldn't have been surprised. Ax was always a soft touch when it came to animals.

They left the town of Blazyth with as little fanfare as they entered. Khaldan and Xan loaded the wagon with water and food, and as they loaded, Bastian covered their supplies with old tarp that Ax had handed him and he hadn't asked where he got it from, knowing better than to question. Bastian and Khaldan took the wagon out first, and over the course of the morning, the others joined them.

Now, standing in the shadow of the Teeth, Bastian regarded the start of the Sand Seas. Little of the *sea* was sand anymore. As he stood facing forward, Bastian looked over his shoulder to the trail they had left. The grass had started to cut back long before they arrived at the edge of the Sand Seas. Rocky terrain had replaced undergrowth, and Bastian knew that further in, the land was dry and cracked in places, more so in the centre, with the heat of the unforgiving sun that beat down upon it relentlessly. There was little reprieve from the harsh rays in the summer months. Barren land that few things could survive amongst stretched before him as far as the eye could see. The knights knew what they faced travelling this way: the heat, the lack of shade, the lack of water and the lack of life.

The wagon creaked as Khaldan and the others shrugged off their packs. It would be difficult in the coming days to look after themselves in the unforgiving plains, but to have to care for an animal too made the burden heavier. *Better the horse carries the weight than us*, Xan had argued. In the end, Bastian had allowed it, but his gut and his former experience of crossing the Sand Seas told him that he had been soft. The horse would become a burden, and no matter what Ax promised, it was unlikely to survive the crossing.

"We wait 'til the sun sets?" Khaldan asked Bastian as he

stared over the land before them, assessing the land with a grim stare.

"No, we make a start now; no point waiting for it to be easier," Bastian told him as he looked over his shoulder to where they had come from, once more. "We left *easy* the moment we chose this route."

"So, pain, suffering and misery from the outset?" Khaldan stated wryly, his tone as dry as the land in front of them.

"Why change old habits now?" Bastian asked with a grin as he set forth knowing that his men would be at his back, as always.

* * *

THE DAYS CROSSING THE DESERT WERE LONG AND torturous. Living hell was the most accurate description for it. The air burned all around them. Breathing was painful, every hot inhale seared the mouth and dried their throat. Hacking coughs were the steady beat to march to with aching, tired feet. Lungs that had little chance to be full left the men with ragged and gasping breaths. The night brought no relief, with temperatures dropping so dramatically that they lay shivering under stars that gave light to the shadows but offered no warmth as the chill entered their bones and threatened to never leave.

The men did not complain. They had known it would be hard. Some, like Bastian, had crossed before, but that passing previously didn't make it easier. Bastian watched as the water rations for the day were filled into flasks, the amount so small that it would not quench their thirst. A full flask was unlikely to be held again until they had fully crossed and fresh water was nearby once more.

"Dust cloud!" Bastian heard the call and turned to watch the desert dust rise and swirl around the approach of newcomers. The dust concealed their numbers, and Bastian felt that now familiar nagging return to his belly.

"Weapons at the ready," he bit out.

"They could be friendly?" Xan suggested as he half turned back to look at his companion.

"They could be," Bastian replied, when he saw Khaldan nodding in agreement with Xan. "We're not." He ignored Ax's snort of laughter as Ax drew his sword. "Xan?" Bastian called out softly.

"I see them," Xan said from his vantage point. He had climbed into the wagon, using the extra height to give him a better view. "Three, I think," he told the others. "One is slight…"

Bastian looked back out over the land. The sun was reaching its highest point, and soon the sun would be the only enemy they had to fight. "A woman?" he asked him with surprise.

Xan shrugged in answer as he dropped down from the wagon. "Or a child? They have at least one male with them though."

"No one in their right mind brings a child into the Sand Seas," Khaldan rumbled as he walked forward.

"Easy, soldier," Bastian cautioned him. "You were the one who just agreed with Xan when he told me that they could be friendly."

"That was before," Khaldan grunted.

Ax kept his attention on the newcomers, but Bez was

looking skywards. "We need to move," he said gruffly. "They may pass right by us."

"We're six men exposed in the middle of the blasted desert, with a wagon," Xan replied sharply. "Only a fool is passing us by without seeing what's under that tarp."

Bastian walked forward and stood beside Ax, causing Ax to look at him with suspicion.

"Bastian?"

"I'm still wearing my cuirass and my knives," he told Ax. "You're practically defenceless," he pointed out, referring to the fact that Ax, like the others, had shed most of their protective clothing in the heat of the sun.

Ax lifted his sword. "And this is what? A toothpick?"

"It's useless if any of them have a bow." Bastian gripped the pommel of his sword. "Fall back. It's my turn to do the meet and greet anyway."

Ax shook his head but said nothing. Had he moisture in his mouth, he would have reminded Bastian he was not the most sociable person, but a dry throat and a drier mouth were not the time to argue semantics with his fellow knight.

As the riders neared, they slowed in their approach, a fact that only irritated Bastian more. Several feet from where the men were gathered, the riders stopped. Even from where he stood, Bastian could see little lather on the horses' coats, signs they had been pushed and pushed hard in the uncompromising heat.

A male with bronze skin, black hair tied in a topknot, and the sides of his head shaved in the style of the nomads, he was clean shaven, broad and tall. He dismounted from his horse and pulled his sword from the saddle. With a glance at his two companions, he walked towards Bastian.

"I hope you have water," Bastian started. "Your horses are about to die without it."

The man looked back at his horses and turned back to Bastian. "I know horses," he told him harshly.

"Well then, you'll know they're not sweating, there is no lather, I can see ribs, and their eyes, especially on that one" —Bastian pointed to the horse the smallest person sat on— "are sticky."

"They need watered," Khaldan agreed as he stepped up beside Bastian. "And we have none to spare."

"I know horses," the stranger reiterated. "And I have water."

"You do?" Bastian looked at the three horses and the other riders. He could see no obvious sign that they were carrying water. "Then why have you stopped?"

As the stranger went to reply, a cry from behind him made him spin around, and with impressive speed he raced to the sound as the person making it slumped in their saddle.

"Not just the horse that needs watered," Khaldan observed quietly to Bastian.

"Don't even think about it," Bastian warned his friend.

"Seems like the right thing to do," Khaldan murmured with an easy half shrug.

"No."

"She's failing," Xan said from behind them. "The other woman isn't much better."

Bastian scowled at the trio as he realised his companions had noticed what he hadn't. The other two strangers were both women, and the male was either a guard or a husband.

They watched as the man reached up for the woman, her hood falling back, revealing her delicate features and thick lustrous black hair as he lifted her from the saddle.

"That skin will burn like a cinder in a roaring fire if she's out in the sun too long." Xan leaned into Khaldan. "The tarp would cover her."

"It would," Khaldan agreed.

"They aren't our problem," Bastian reminded his friends.

"We know, they weren't," Khaldan said as he gave him a quick smile. "They are now." Striding forward, he and Xan both offered to help the newcomers, leaving Bastian behind them.

The male looked past them to Bastian and raised an eyebrow in question. Feeling the silent agreement from his men behind him, and the fact Xan was already helping the other woman off of her horse and pointing to the wagon, Bastian knew he couldn't say no.

Which is exactly what his friends were counting on.

CHAPTER 7

Bastian watched as Ax offered to take the girl off the male and was ignored as the man lowered her to the ground. The man pulled her hood back over her head, protecting her from the rays of the sun. Xan had already helped the other woman off her horse and was offering her his arm as she swayed in the heat. Her light travelling cloak was a good choice; the heavily embroidered dress was not.

"You have water?" Bastian asked as he moved closer, watchful of the male as he helped the girl to her feet.

"Yes," the male answered tersely. "Are you okay?" he asked the girl gently.

"I'm fine, Kase, I didn't mean to faint." Her voice was soft and husky, and as she turned to look at Bastian, he was surprised to see she was older than he thought. Slight in frame and small in stature, she would easily be mistaken for a child, but as he met her curious stare, he realised she had to have seen at least twenty winters. "Thank you for stopping to offer aid," she spoke to Khaldan, but her green eyes stayed trained on Bastian.

"We didn't stop to offer aid. Your thanks are misplaced," Bastian corrected her. "The speed you were travelling at, we were unsure if you were friendly." His tone made it known he still was unsure.

The woman held his stare for a moment more before she turned to the other woman leaning on Khaldan's arm. "Milady," she murmured as she crossed the short distance to her. "Let me help you." She held her arm out, and Bastian noticed the brief hesitation from the other woman before she moved to the support of the younger woman.

He watched the three of them interact as Ax and Khaldan gave them space, his head cocking to the side as he observed them. With a glance to the sky, he turned his attention to Khaldan and raised an eyebrow.

"Are you running from someone? Something?" Khaldan asked the three of them.

"No," the man, Kase, answered.

"You were crossing at some speed," Khaldan carried on. "Almost urgently."

"It's hot," Kase answered as he crossed his bare arms across his chest.

"Not like a plainsman to cross the Sand Seas," Ax spoke up as he moved his hand up and down in front of him in reference to the man's attire: brown leather trousers, sleeveless leather tunic, soft leather boots, and his arms held strappings for knives. Around his waist hung a thick belt with his long sword secure against his hip.

"I've not been on the Plains of Tzenyth for a long time," Kase grunted as he looked over his shoulder.

"Expecting someone?" Khaldan asked him.

"We're not being followed," the younger woman spoke up. "We were told the crossing would be treacherous; we thought that speed would help."

"Interesting," Bastian spoke quietly as he watched her.

"Is it?" Her stare was bold and challenging, but he could see the sweat on her forehead, the sway of her body as she fought to stay upright.

"Put the women in the wagon," Bastian instructed Ax. "Cover them but leave the sides loose."

"The wagon?" the other woman spoke for the first time. Her uneasy look was not unnoticed by Bastian and his men.

"It's not comfortable," Xan told her, "but it keeps you out of the direct heat of the sun." He looked over the two women and then back to Bastian. "They'll fare better with less on."

Bastian ignored the outraged gasps of surprise as he assessed them both. "Lay your cloaks on the bed of the wagon, dresses off, stockings too if you're wearing them. Lie in your shifts. It's not cooler under the tarp, but it's not quite as hellish as being on horseback in this heat."

Neither woman moved and Bastian looked to Kase. "They go under the tarp, or they die in the saddle. Talk to your women. We've wasted enough time."

The man regarded Bastian, and Bastian did not back down. With a nod, Kase turned to the two women, whispering quickly as he kept looking back at the men.

"Brilliant idea," Bastian commented dryly to Khaldan.

"Would you rather they die out here?" Xan asked from his other side as they watched the three exchange words. The lady seemed to have the biggest objections, but Bastian kept his attention on the raven-haired woman, who was watching him back.

"I don't care if they live or if they die," Bastian told them both coldly. "I care that they're wasting daylight and, as we rot in this heat, we aren't moving any further forward."

"Bastian," Khaldan's tone held a warning.

"This is pointless," Bastian said gruffly as he shook his

head. Turning from the newcomers, he walked back to the front of the wagon. Tipping a small amount of his water from his flask into his hand, he let the horse wet its tongue and mouth. "Move forward," Bastian told Bez.

As they moved out, he knew that the women had stripped as he had instructed. He heard the horse's huff of discomfort as they scrambled into the wagon, the wagon groaning as it was jostled from side to side as they settled into place.

Without looking back, he knew Khaldan and Ax had fallen into formation, and about an hour later, he looked to his left to see the tall Tzenythian had walked up beside him.

"Long way from the Plains," Khaldan spoke up, breaking the silence.

"Long way from anywhere, in here," the man replied.

"Feels like that," Ax agreed. "Name's Ax."

"Kase," he offered in reply.

"Khaldan."

"Greetings." Kase acknowledged the pleasantries. They walked further, the sweat running down their necks, soaking their shirts, burning their skin relentlessly. "You have a name?" Kase finally asked.

"There's a lot of power in a name," Bastian answered him finally.

"Are you powerful?" Kase asked, his tone slightly mocking.

"No," Bastian looked skyward again, cursing under his breath. "Let's stop here," he called out to the others. "Night will fall hard tonight."

Kase looked around, disbelief evident on his face. "Here?"

"You know of somewhere better?" Bastian challenged him as he pulled the leather tie from his hair, shaking it loose before pulling it back from his face and retying the tie once more.

"You don't want to try and seek shelter?" Kase asked them as the men around him seemed to be settling where they stood.

"There is no shelter in the Sand Seas," Ax spoke jovially. "Barren and burned, you stop before *you* drop, or the temperature does."

"You've crossed before?" Kase asked Bastian. The other man looked at him as he loosened the ties to his cuirass.

"I have never seen shelter on those occasions either."

"Occasions?" Her voice was quiet in the noise of the men as they settled for the night. Bastian watched her as she came around the side of the horse, her cloak over her white shift, her hood pulled back, black hair spilling over her shoulders. "My lady queries why we've stopped."

"Does she?" Bastian asked her ruefully. "Well, tell your lady that night comes suddenly in the Sand Seas, and it's better to have stopped before the cold stops you."

"Cold?" She looked around and saw the men were pulling on cloaks of their own. "The shift is so sudden?" she asked sceptically.

"As unpredictable as a woman's temper." Bastian took his own cloak from Xan, who hid his smile.

She said nothing, but he saw the flash of irritation at his words. With a pointed look to Kase, she turned on her heel and retreated to the end of the wagon.

"Your companions are?" Xan asked as he watched her retreat.

"The Lady Tyria and her handmaiden, Beth." Kase looked skyward once more. "We were travelling so long yesterday I thought I imagined the speed of sunset," he told them. Xan was quick to answer, and soon they were discussing the perils of the crossing.

Bastian watched and listened as he checked the horse and then went back to check the other three horses. He chose to say nothing in regards to the not-so-subtle change of subject from the bodyguard. Bodyguard or protector? He wasn't quite sure.

Eyeing the third horse, he let out a low sigh. The horse would be dead by morning. As he stroked its nose, he considered walking it from the makeshift camp.

"I'll go," Ax spoke from behind him.

"Makes sense to ration the water between the other three rather than waste it on this one," Bastian admitted as he reached up to scratch the poor beast's ear.

"The vultures will be glad of the meat," Ax told him as he took the reins.

Bastian's hands tightened on them, making it hard for Ax to leave. "Don't stay with it. Let it die alone or kill it yourself. I don't want you out there alone for too long. They have secrets, your new friends."

"I'll be quick," Ax confirmed as he tugged the reins from his friend's grip.

"Here." Bastian handed him his flask.

"For me?" Ax asked as he took it. "Or the horse?" he added with a sad smile, knowing his friend *too* well and that Bastian was giving the horse water despite his earlier words.

"Cruelty has already happened to this beast," Bastian

told him, confirming Ax's thoughts. "We don't need to inflict more before its end."

Bastian returned to the camp, the men now silent and fitted close together. It was Xan's and Bez's turn to take camp under the wagon, but he noted with disgruntlement that neither had taken the spots.

Bez refused to meet his stare, but Xan had no issue. "What?"

"Are you being serious?" Bastian asked him.

"It's not right." Xan looked away as he spoke.

Bastian waited and then with a huff of displeasure, he dropped low and took up the space under the wagon. If the idiots weren't going to use it, he would, happily. It didn't provide warmth or shelter but simply gave the illusion of doing so, and an illusion was sometimes all you needed to feel safe enough to sleep.

"How many are following you?" he heard Khaldan ask Kase.

"I...I don't know what you mean," the man stumbled his reply.

"Been on the road a long time, friend," Khaldan told him gruffly, and Bastian heard the tell-tale sound of Xan's whetstone sharpening his blade. "No one rides that fast unless someone's chasing them."

"I, we—"

"No one picks the Sand Seas either, unless they're desperate," Xan added. "Especially a man from the Prairies of Tzenyth."

Silence fell on the camp, and with a satisfied smile, Bastian closed his eyes. Yes, he was a suspicious bastard, but so were his men. Which is why they were *his* men.

"Five," Kase admitted. "They took our possessions and valuables," he said with disgust. "They even took the food."

"If they took it all, why are they still following?" Khaldan asked shrewdly.

"I killed one of them," Kase explained. "I believe he was a brother of the leader."

"Ah," Xan grunted. "Never mess with brothers. They hold grudges."

"Do we need to leave?" Kase asked quietly. "We caught sight of you and thought safety in numbers."

"You took two women into the camp of six men who you know nothing about," Khaldan snorted. "You're either very trusting or very stupid."

Bastian smiled wider in the darkness at his friend's tone.

"I think I may be both," Kase answered truthfully. "This is not where we're supposed to be."

"Where are you heading?" Xan asked.

"The Golden City."

Silence descended and Bastian knew they were waiting. When he remained silent, he heard someone move closer to him. Opening his eyes, he saw a shadow fall across the wagon.

"We'll escort you to the city," Khaldan told Kase as he crouched low. "Three gold for the trouble."

"Mercenaries?" Kase asked them in surprise. "I thought you were…"

"Different?" Ax spoke up as he joined them. "Nothing is what you expect," he said as he dropped his sword gently to the ground. "How many?"

"Five," Xan answered.

"Won't be hard to spot," Ax said as he stretched. "I'll

take the first watch," he told the others. "Kase? That your name?"

"Yes."

"You're on third watch," Ax instructed. "Get some sleep. We move at dawn."

Bastian lay awake for a while longer, listening to the shivering of his men as the night stole the heat from them and the land around them. As he felt the pull of sleep tug at his awareness, he startled slightly when the wagon moved above him. He hadn't forgotten the women were above him, but he hadn't expected the sounds of the wagon to be so loud.

Faintly he heard the quiet murmurs, and then the wagon was once again still. Closing his eyes again, he drifted off to sleep.

The wind whipped around him, his hair blowing across his face as he turned to hear the crashing of the waves behind him.

Waves.

Bastian reached for his sword and realised his scabbard was empty. His black tunic was tight fitting over his thick black woollen trousers. Pushing his hair from his face, he slowly turned around. He was on a beach with the sand blackened, and the cliffs above him were dark rock. He was in no place that he knew. In the distance, he saw the hooded figure running from the beach to a small trail that led away from the water. With a curse, Bastian ran after them, yelling for them to stop.

The figure halted and looked back, raising their hand sharply, and then they were running again.

Bastian heard a loud crash and turned, ready to defend himself. Instead, a giant wave engulfed him, and with a start he jerked awake.

Sitting upright and forgetting he was under the wagon,

his head cracked off the undercarriage. "Gods," Bastian groaned as he rubbed his forehead.

"Which one?" Khaldan grumbled as he turned onto his side. "Is it my watch?"

"No, brother," Bastian assured him as he slipped from under the wagon. "Sleep."

Quietly Bastian walked to where Xan was standing, looking over the deserted land. He had been asleep longer than he thought. "All good?"

Xan glanced at him and then back over the land. "All quiet. You're early."

"Or just in time," Bastian muttered as he pointed to the horizon and the shapes moving over the darkened land, shapes that were too low to the ground to be men. "Is that what I think it is?"

Xan peered into the darkness, looking up at the blanket of stars above them, wishing for more light. "Zyvarg? Here?"

"What in the Gods' names are they tracking?" Bastian asked the night.

Xan groaned as he looked towards the horses. "The dead horse?"

Bastian shook his head. "Ax knows better than to spill blood here." A long cry sounded in the night. "I think the vultures have found it anyway."

"Not going to lie," Xan told Bastian quietly. "I don't have the energy needed for this fight."

"None of us do," Bastian told him tightly. "Wake everyone, we need to move."

"The wagon?" Xan asked as he moved away to do as he was bid.

Bastian made the decision. "Put as many of us in it as it'll hold. Give the horses more water, hydrate them. Let's hope our new travelling companions share their horses and that they have enough speed in them to put distance between us and the zyvarg."

CHAPTER 8

THE HORSES DID THEIR BEST IN THE FRIGID TEMPERATURES. With the women in the wagon along with most of the others, Khaldan and Bastian took the horses, and Xan ran alongside the horse pulling the wagon. Xan was originally from Pavolyn, and with his slighter frame than the others, he was also their best runner. The wagon was loaded down with the extra weight of its passengers, and although it lent them speed, it still wasn't as fast as it could be. The zyvarg could easily catch up to them.

Bastian and Khaldan stayed behind the wagon, watchful of their pursuers, Bastian's anger mounting more and more as they tried to rush across the hardened land. When Khaldan's horse faltered, Khaldan immediately dismounted, urging the horse on with the promise of water as he jogged alongside it.

The zyvarg kept a constant pursuit, gaining no ground but a constant presence behind them. Their behaviour puzzled Bastian, but he was more intent on keeping the distance between them than stopping and dealing with it.

"Stop!" Ax called from up front. "You need to see this," he told them as he slowed the horse that was leading the wagon. The sun was cresting the horizon, and they knew they didn't have long before the heat washed over them.

Bastian nudged his horse to the front and dismounted as he stared ahead at the sight before them. "Everyone off the wagon," he ordered.

"What is it?" Xan asked as he walked up to stand beside them. "By the Gods, it's gotten worse."

In front of them was a broken land. The sun had long since burned and scorched the earth, removing all the moisture, which had led it to be cracked and split, but now, as the men looked across their way forward, the land was literally crumbling to dust beyond them.

"We split up?" Khaldan asked Bastian as they tracked possible routes across.

"And if one of us falls?" Ax asked as he took the offered flask from Khaldan. "That looks a lot like holes to me," he added, pointing across the ground to the holes that had been uncovered as the crust crumbled.

"I've never seen land like this," Kase said as he joined them. "If we walk single file, will it hold?"

"There are nine of us," Xan reasoned. "Three threes?"

"No." Bastian shook his head in denial. "I'll lead, follow in pairs." As he studied a potential route across, he heard the howl behind them. "The heat will slow them down; let's not let it slow us." Bastian looked over his shoulder and met the gaze of the handmaiden, Beth. "You'll be safe," he told her, his eyes shifting past her to the land that lay behind them. "If we play this right, we may lose our trackers too."

"Pity it's sunrise and not sunset," Khaldan grunted in agreement. "Xan, you're with me. We'll take the back."

Bastian nodded and when Kase paired with the handmaiden and not Lady Tyria, he kept his silence. Beth seemed to notice the slight to their ladyship moments after Bastian, but she also seemed to realise it was too late to go unnoticed. However, she still moved forward and stood beside Ax, who smiled down at her, and within moments,

Bastian saw her blush prettily at whatever his friend had commented to her. He made a mental note to remind the younger knight not to flirt with the handmaiden. They had enough problems for this journey to deal with.

"And the horses?" Kase asked as he saw Xan and Khaldan unhook the wagon from the horse.

"Will walk with us," Bastian told him. "But they're not our priority."

Kase licked his lips, ready to argue, but his attention flicked to Beth, and with lips pressed tight, he looked away in defeat.

"You any good with that sword?" Xan asked him as he straightened from freeing up the mount.

"As good as any sellsword," Kase bit out tersely.

Xan smirked at the arrogance but ignored the taunt. "Fine, you can keep the horses with you. We'll switch." He walked up to join Lady Tyria, and when he was beside them, he looked Kase over once, a challenge in his stare. "You're holding us up," he mocked him as he jerked his thumb over his shoulder. "Move."

Gripping his sword's handle, Kase made his way to the rear and, still grumbling, accepted the reins off a grinning Khaldan.

"Let's make this as quick as we can," Bastian told them as he faced forward, and with determined steps, he began the walk across the pockmarked land.

Each step that he took, he could feel the difference in the land. The ground that was firmer had a slightly more substantial feeling to it. Had the land not burned to the touch from the merciless sun, Bastian may have contemplated walking barefoot. His bare skin would be more receptive to the slight fluctuations of the density of the land, but he did not have that luxury.

Bastian didn't look back at his companions. They were paired, and the newcomers were with one of his men, men who knew how to follow in formation. Still, the zyvarg following them niggled at the back of his mind. Zyvarg were large and predatory. They had more than enough options to hunt for prey in the Plains or Kalzynia. Why would they enter into the Teeth? For him? His men? He doubted it. They weren't that important. Yes, they were Order, but they were good at disguising it. And as far as Bastian knew, zyvarg didn't care what the colour of his cloak was, man was man. A beast didn't care who they were making their meal.

Unless they did?

Bastian paused and he heard Xan mutter a curse behind him as he pulled up short before walking into his companion's back. "Sorry, milady," Xan quickly apologised to the lady who he was paired with. "More warning, friend," Xan grumbled.

"What is it?" Khaldan called from the back, causing Bastian to turn around and look behind him. They were in their pairs, close enough to catch one another, but not too close that they walked into each other. Well, unless you were Xan.

"Why are you so close?" Bastian snapped at Xan. "If I fall, you fall right behind me."

"You stopped because I'm too close?" Xan asked him in disbelief. "If you hadn't stopped, I wouldn't *be* too close."

"Why did you travel through the Dragon's Teeth?" Bastian asked the lady beside Xan. She was slightly taller than her handmaiden. Her hood was pulled over her hair to protect her head from the sun, but she hadn't pulled it low, so her red curls were still on display. She had pale skin with a smattering of freckles, a curse of most redheads. Her eyes were a deep brown, and they were staring blankly at Bastian as her mouth opened and closed…struggling for something to say?

"We didn't," Beth spoke up for her mistress, and Bastian flicked his eyes to her, seeing Ax reach out and catch her arm as she made to move forward.

"I asked *you*, Lady Tyria, why do you travel to the Golden City through the Teeth?" Bastian's look was hard and cold, the only thing that was cool in this desolate land. His head cocked to the side. "Those zyvarg, are they yours?"

"Why would they be ours?" Kase exclaimed as he strode angrily forward. He stepped past the handmaiden, who reached out to grab him, to halt him, and he didn't notice when Xan stepped out of his way to let him approach Bastian. "I don't like your tone, or your questions, sellsword."

Bastian regarded the man in front of him casually, a small smile playing around his lips. "I don't really care what you like," Bastian told him. "And I wasn't asking you, Tzenythian." Bastian met the startled brown eyes of the lady one more time. "I was asking Lady Tyria. Tell me, lady, where's your lord?"

"Dead," Kase growled as he stepped closer to Bastian, his hand on his sword. "Tell *me*, mercenary, what's your name? Whose lord do you answer to?"

"I answer to no one," Bastian said with a wide smile. "That irks you, I can see." His gaze swept over the former plainsman, and he nodded thoughtfully. "Banished more than left by choice, I reckon." He turned to Lady Tyria. "Running to something rather than from something, I think, but not a husband. No…" Finally, they landed on Beth, who met his stare with no fear in her eyes. "You, you're more than you seem," he spoke quietly.

"I'm merely a servant, standing in the boiling sun, with a pack of zyvarg following this group, and a temperamental son of a heathen in front of me, playing dice with my life."

Bastian grinned at her tone. "I can assure you my father is a devout man," he said with a small tip of his head. "May the Gods watch his soul."

"Why have we stopped?" Beth asked him. "Really?"

"You passed through the Teeth." Bastian watched as her tongue flicked out to wet her bottom lip, but she never denied it. "These zyvarg, they're not following me *or* my men. They're following *you*. Why?"

Beth glanced behind her, frowning. When she turned back, she spoke to Kase. "Is he right?"

"It's possible."

"Why are they following us?" Lady Tyria asked the plainsman.

"That's what I asked," Bastian murmured and winked when Beth turned her glare to him.

"I don't know why they follow us," Kase bit out. "So we took the Teeth. We'd just been robbed; we reckoned that the bandits wouldn't follow us into the Teeth."

"Why would they still follow?" Ax spoke up. "They took all you had, you said."

Kase spoke to Bastian when he answered. "I'm one man

with two women; there was still something that I had that they wanted."

Bastian clenched his jaw as he recognised that the man's words could be true. With a curt nod, he turned back to the way ahead and resumed walking.

"That's it?" Kase asked in surprise. "We just resume walking like he hasn't just stopped us all for no reason?"

"You want to hold us up any longer?" Xan asked him as he began to follow at a further distance behind.

Grumbling a range of curses that made Beth clear her throat in disapproval, Kase took his position back at the rear.

As they walked further and the sun rose higher above them, their steps became slower, but with Khaldan at the rear and Bastian calling orders from the front, they encouraged their group to remain behind without too much space growing between them.

"Bez!" Khaldan barked. "Stay steady, man, you're swaying like a dancer in one of the dancing tents of Henka."

"It's so hot," the sergeant complained. "I never wanted to see more of Ax than I am, but right now, I can see three of him."

Bastian held his fist up for them to stop. "Everyone take your rations."

The men took a small sip from their flasks while monitoring the newcomers. When Lady Tyria raised her flask again, Xan reached out to stop her. "No, milady, that's enough."

"I'm so thirsty," she whispered hoarsely, clutching the flask to her chest. "One more sip?"

"No," Xan said with an easy smile. "You'll need it, we're not even halfway."

Bastian watched as she struggled with Xan's order, and then with a nod, she hooked her flask to her belt.

"All good?" Bastian asked, his eyes lingering on Lady Tyria. When she realised that he was waiting, she gave a small nod. "Let's move."

Time passed slowly and the men were miserable and fighting to stay upright, but the howl of the zyvarg was so sudden and so loud that the horse Khaldan was walking beside reared in fright, causing him to jump out of the way. When the horse's hooves thundered back onto the fragile land beneath it, the ground gave way, and the horse's front legs buckled from the loss of solid ground. The horse screamed in terror, and the other horse jumped back in fright, pulling Kase with it.

"Get back!" Bastian cried to Khaldan and Kase, who scrambled out of the way of the panicking horse. "No one else move!" Bastian yelled as he saw the others had broken apart. "Bez!" Bastian called the sergeant. "Do *not* move."

His words were drowned out as the horse screamed again, its attempts to regain its footing causing more and more of the sinkhole to grow under it.

"Khaldan!" Bastian cried as his friend tried to get to the horse. "Leave it!"

Khaldan looked up and towards Bastian. He struggled with the command and then stepped backwards as the horse fell forward and into the sinkhole, its death waiting in the maw of the open hole. Kase was still trying to calm the other horse, as the land gave way around them and the zyvarg howled louder.

"They're coming," Ax shouted, loud enough to be heard over the horses.

"Move!" Bastian bellowed. "Plainsman, leave it!"

Kase looked like he would ignore him, but the zyvarg howled again, much closer, and with a cry of disgust, Kase tossed the reins from him as he picked his way over the disintegrating land. The horse, taking the moment of freedom to rear on its hind legs and then turning, ran across the way they had come, right into the path of the zyvarg.

Khaldan grabbed Kase's arm when he stumbled, and Bastian waited one more moment to ensure they were okay before he started a steady jog over the deadly terrain. "Keep up!" he called over his shoulder. "The horse will only slow them down for a short time."

As they ran, the land crumbled in some places but not as badly as the sinkhole they left behind.

"Bez!" Fylip yelled, and Bastian spun on his heel. He saw the young sergeant try to righten his footing as the sudden chasm opened under him, and Bastian raced to catch him, throwing his pack to the ground as he ran.

"Bastian!" Khaldan screamed in warning.

Bastian jumped as the ground gave way, and twisting in the air, he reached out and caught Bez's arm as the other man fell into the chasm.

"Bastian!" Khaldan cried again, and Bastian could hear his men running.

"Don't let me go," Bez pleaded as he looked up at him.

"I won't." Bastian pulled but he had landed at an odd angle, more on his side than flat, his right arm trapped under him. To move would loosen his hold on Bez, but Bastian could hear it, the rapidly crumbling earth underneath him. A cry of alarm behind him, and he knew his men were struggling to catch up. More of the ground fell, and Bastian had no choice but to flatten onto his stomach, his grip loosening on Bez allowing the man to slip some more.

"Bastian!"

"I have you," Bastian said through gritted teeth. "Pull yourself up." He tried to brace himself, but there was nothing to grip against.

Bez's legs flailed under him; with nothing to push against, he hung uselessly. "Help me!" he screamed as dry desert land rained down around him.

Bastian felt hands suddenly grab his ankles and tug. "I'm here," Khaldan grunted as he pulled.

Bastian suddenly lurched forward as the land crumbled from under his chest, causing him to fall forward into the sinkhole. Bez jerked in his hold, and his grip loosened once more.

"Bastian," Bez pleaded with him as he stared up in desperation. "Please."

The dissolving earth had allowed Bastian to free his other hand, and he reached forward to grab Bez, but more land gave way.

"Stop bloody moving!" Ax called out. "You're making it worse!"

"I can't catch him," Bastian yelled back as he stretched forward. More land gave way, and he jerked forward more. The hole was rapidly getting wider and bigger, and Bastian's eyes widened as he saw how deep it was underneath them. There was no end.

"Bastian, stop!" Khaldan yelled again.

Bez slipped further, and Bastian was pulled further into the hole. He felt the grip on his feet loosen, and then a mad grab jerked him to a stop.

"Khaldan?" Bastian called.

"I can't hold you," Khaldan told him urgently. "I can't hold you both."

"Khaldan!" Bez screamed as Bastian's eyes closed at the severity of the words. "Bastian, don't you leave me! Don't let me go!"

Bastian tried to tighten his grip, and his right arm stretched one more time as Bez swung fruitlessly below him.

"Try to catch my hand," Bastian encouraged him. Again, the other man's hand tried to make contact, but his endless movement, sweat-slicked palms, and terror were overriding his chances. "Bez…" Bastian forced his voice to be calm.

The ground groaned and the chasm widened. Bastian registered the yell behind him, and he felt his body jerk backwards. The jerk swung Bez, and the man's hand loosened.

"Bez, no!"

"I'm going to lose you both!" Khaldan warned them.

Bastian saw the decision in Bez's eyes the moment he made it. "Bez!" He scrambled forward, kicking free of the hands that held him, straining to secure the man below him as Bastian lurched dangerously forward himself.

"Fly high, my friend." Bez let go.

CHAPTER 9

BASTIAN TOOK THE CUP OF WATER WITHOUT A WORD AS AX bound the cut to his upper arm. The men were sombre as night began to fall across the desert plains. He grunted involuntarily as Ax tightened the bandage, but said nothing as his companion rose to his feet, clasping him on the shoulder as he walked away to give him some space.

Khaldan and Xan had pulled Bastian back when Bez let go, the task made easier with the extra weight gone. Slowly they had dragged him back until he was on firmer ground. Strong familiar hands had helped him rise, his leg buckling slightly with the injury he had sustained when he fell trying to help his comrade.

Bastian's arms were cut and scratched, a particularly bad cut to his right arm where he had landed on it in his initial fall. Ax had told him he would clean and bind the wound. Bastian heard him but his stare was fixed on Khaldan, who returned the weight of his accusatory stare with no expression.

Bastian had looked around the terrain at the damage of the sinkholes and couldn't believe that they were still standing. Well, some of them were. The ground looked like the hard cheese with the holes in it that his sister had preferred when they were younger.

"Sit down," Xan had told him gruffly. "Before you fall down."

Bastian had done as he was instructed, and then he had steadfastly refused to talk to Khaldan or any of the others.

He heard Fylip telling Xan that the zyvarg had fallen behind, the last horse had ran in fright when they were trying to save Bez, no doubt the zyvarg would make a meal of it too, and then there was silence again. Bastian took a mouthful of water and swirled it in his mouth before he spat it to the side, the water discoloured with dirt and blood.

"Bastian?"

Her voice was still soft and husky, and Bastian automatically looked up into the deep green eyes of the handmaiden.

"Do you want to talk about it?" she asked as she hovered above him.

"No." Bastian took another sip of water, knowing it was an indulgence.

"He was your friend," she began.

"He was a soldier," Bastian told her gruffly as he got to his feet. "Soldiers fall."

Beth didn't hide her surprise at his callousness. "I—"

"We need to find a better place to rest," Bastian spoke to the others. "Mousetraps in the night won't stop them from their hunt. They'll sense our weakness." Striding forward, Bastian grunted as he bent over to pick up his pack. "Let's move." Pulling his pack on, he turned and began to walk. When he heard no one else move, Bastian turned and looked back at them all. "Did I mumble?"

Khaldan hesitated once more, but then with a shake of his head and a string of unpleasantries, he picked up his own pack, Ax and Xan following his actions.

"And this one?" Beth challenged as she watched the mercenaries pick up their things and carry on as if they hadn't just lost a companion, their friend.

Bastian faltered before he turned and met her angry glare, her finger pointing in accusation to the solitary pack left behind.

"Leave it," he told her as he turned his back to them all and began to walk.

Beth wanted to rage at him, she wanted to scream, shout, throw something at the infuriating man who walked ahead of his companions but was so clearly alone. She felt the need to reach out to him and shake him.

It was obvious he was grieving, just as it was obvious that they were hardened warriors, but his closed-off attitude was beginning to grate on her nerves. He had been sullen and suspicious long before the loss of their friend this afternoon.

"We need to follow them," Kase spoke quietly in her ear.

Looking up at the much taller warrior, Beth rolled her eyes. "Do we?"

Kase's lips twitched as he looked towards the men's retreating backs. "He may be a hard son of a goat, and a distasteful one at that, but he knows these Seas better than I do."

"How much longer?" Tyria asked them. "I'm ready to burst into tears at any moment," she confided quietly.

"I don't think I have moisture left in my body to cry," Kase told her with a small smile. "They're grieving," he told Beth. "It's hard to lose someone, especially like that." He rubbed his hand over his hair, slicked back into its normal topknot. "We need them, for now."

Beth gritted her teeth as she looked to the figure in front of the men, leading them away from where they stood. "Fine, but the moment that we don't, we leave them."

"As soon as I see green, we're gone," Kase assured her.

"Are they not taking us to the Golden City?" Tyria whispered to them.

"We'll see," Kase answered softly. "We don't owe them anything, especially gold."

Partly assuaged that Kase agreed, Beth hooked Tyria's hand through her arm and tugged. "You're doing well, just a little bit longer."

Tyria dipped her head in acknowledgement, and with nothing left to say, the three stragglers followed behind the mercenaries.

The day turned into another, then another, sinkholes opened up randomly but nothing like the ones that they had encountered that fateful day. Soon the day turned to a week, and on the turn of the eighth day, Beth heard the howl of the zyvarg. Immediately her attention was drawn to Bastian as he rose from his spot on the edge of their small camp.

He'd kept himself on the fringes of the group as they travelled, speaking little, and his cloak at night was wrapped tight around him, a barrier warding off not only the cold but any who approached him.

"Khaldan?" Bastian queried. "Have they rested enough?"

Beth watched as Khaldan swept his gaze over them all, and then with a terse nod to Bastian, he began to pick up his pack. "Let's move, there's no sleep to be had tonight."

"I don't think I can," Tyria said in a low voice. Beth hurried to her as she dropped her face into her hands, her shoulders drooping.

"You can, milady," Beth urged her as she sank on the ground beside her, her small hands prying Tyria's fingers loose from where they were weaved together. "Lady Tyria, please," Beth implored her.

Tyria raised her head and looked at the handmaiden, her brown eyes swimming with tears. "I'm so tired," she whispered hoarsely.

"Be tired or dead," Xan spoke above them both. "We've lost enough. I'm not losing any more men. Get up."

Beth scrambled to her feet. "That's not fair!" she cried, poking Xan in his chest. The man didn't budge and merely looked down at her with a tiredness of his own.

"If she can cry, she's more hydrated than we are," he told Beth with a gruffness she didn't expect from him. "You follow, or you die here."

He turned and joined his companions. Beth stared after his back, and in the dim light, she could feel the heavy stare of Bastian as he watched her before he turned his back, and the men began to walk.

"She isn't a pack in the dirt!" Beth screamed after them. "You can pick her up! You can't leave her in the dirt like his pack!"

She watched the others turn to look at her, varying looks of disbelief and horror at her outburst on their faces, as she referenced the discarded pack of Bez's. Beth didn't care about their reactions; her attention was on one man only, the leader, the cold distant one.

He didn't turn.

He didn't speak.

He did…nothing, and then he resumed walking, as if it didn't matter if Tyria was with them or not.

Beth went to shout again, anger, frustration, tiredness, hunger and thirst ready to pour out of her in her anger, but a cool hand on hers made her stop. Tyria was standing, her free hand wiping her face, and she gave a watery smile.

"Hush now." Tyria swallowed back her tears. "We should make haste."

"I…"

"Beth," Kase spoke quietly. "Come."

Closing her eyes against the unfairness of it all, Beth took a deep breath, and then holding tight onto Tyria, she started to follow the band of mercenaries, who as far as she could tell, had no mercy at all.

<hr>

THE DAY THAT BASTIAN REALISED THEY HAD CLEARED THE Sand Seas, he barely realised the accomplishment. He walked many steps before he registered the difference of the ground underneath him. Frowning, he looked down and green shoots of grass looked back.

Struggling to swallow, his tongue felt thick and heavy. The water had run out days ago, but finally he croaked out Khaldan's name, and as if in a fog, he heard the others stop.

"Thank you, Gods," he whispered as he sank to his knees to run his hand over the green. Quickly, he was on his feet again, his gaze searching the surroundings. The vegetation was thicker to the west of them, and with renewed energy, Bastian made his way there. He heard someone behind him, and as he sank to his knees once more, his hands dipped into the clear pool of water.

"Oh Gods," Xan mumbled beside him as he splashed

his face. Greedily his hands scooped water to his mouth as Bastian did the same.

After a few grateful gulps, Bastian pushed to his feet and looked back at his companions. Beth had fallen two, maybe three, days ago, and the men had taken it in turns to carry her. Ax currently held her still, and Bastian hastened over, taking the lady from him and returning her to the pool. Gently he wet her lips with water and waited until she was alert enough to drink from the pool herself. By that time, the others had made their way to the pool and were savouring the taste of water again.

"It's fresh?" Kase asked as he drank again. "I don't see a stream."

"It's behind the shrubbery," Beth told him, her voice raspy and drier than normal. Wearily she got to her feet. "Tyria, come, follow me."

As Bastian wet his face, he watched her lead the other woman to the greenery. Tyria stumbled and the slighter woman caught her, holding her up easily. Too easily, he thought as he watched them, for a woman who had been carried for days.

"If there's a stream," Khaldan spoke, breaking the sounds of splashing, "it means we can wash."

Ax was watching the edge of the Sand Seas and turned back to look at them. "They're not far behind us, and I feel better for the water, will feel even better to be wet all over, but I need to sleep. I need sleep before I can fight them, Bastian."

Bastian rose to his feet, nodding already in agreement. "We need to fill the flasks and the spares and keep moving. Xan, where are we, roughly?"

"Could be Selkta," Xan said as he looked at the way they had come. "Teeth are that way. I can see the Tooth of the Dragon over there," he said as he pointed. "Puts us south-west, more south than west," he amended. "Selkta should be three to four miles that way." He pointed beyond them.

"What's in Selkta?" Kase asked as he hovered between the pool where the men were and the vegetation where his mistress and her handmaiden had dipped behind.

"Water, beer, food and beds," Ax told him as he filled flasks. "And if there are no beds, haylofts." He squinted up at the tall Tzenythian as he continued his task. "You object to a hayloft?"

Kase's forehead rose as he shook his head. "Not at all, I'm ready to sleep here," he admitted tiredly. Turning to look back at the Sand Seas, he spat on the ground. "You've done that more than once?" he asked them as he looked around at the gathered men. "You're crazy. I will never go through that again."

Khaldan rose from the banks of the pool. "Never say never, plainsman. Desperation makes you do desperate things."

Bastian grunted in agreement as he took one final drink of water before securing his flask. "Get your companions. We're not free of danger yet."

The men had started to walk at a slow pace, their feet still dragging with tiredness, their bones still heavy with lethargy, and their hearts still weighed down with loss. A few gulps of water at the side of a pool were not enough to quench the thirst of their souls.

Bastian turned to see Beth and her lady emerge from the

bushes. Tyria looked much better, and his eyebrows rose when he saw that Beth was dripping wet, but when she met his look, she turned away, making a pretence of wringing the water from her hair.

"She jumped in?" Ax asked softly with some surprise.

"Looks like it," Bastian murmured as he faced forward again.

"Well, good for her," Ax mumbled as he looked over his shoulder towards them again. "She looks better for it."

Bastian said nothing, but as he checked his companions again, he noticed that Tyria and Kase *both* looked better, far better than two people who had merely been refreshed with a few handfuls of water. Again, his attention snagged on the handmaiden. She had colour in her cheeks, and her eyes were bright. She looked refreshed, she looked more than refreshed. Beth caught him watching her again, and he saw her back straighten as she returned his stare, her own one bold.

Distant howls reminded him of the more important problems they had, and with one more look to the woman who drew his attention more than most, he focused on the path ahead.

Night had fallen by the time they reached the outskirts of the small farming town of Selkta. Bastian could almost feel his men's relief as they skirted the town, and he would be a liar if he didn't feel it himself. The zyvarg had reached the pool about an hour, maybe two, after they had left. The yips and yelps as the creatures found water as they had, had rumbled in the air, a reminder that where he and his companions were refreshed, so were the beasts following them. With water in their bellies, the speed of their pursuit would quicken.

"Where to?" Kase asked Bastian as they hesitated at the edge of the township. "Is there an inn for my lady?"

"One, far corner of the town," Bastian answered him. "It's where we're heading."

"Why at the edge?" Kase asked suspiciously.

"They have a large stable," Khaldan told him. "Good soft hay too," he said as an afterthought.

"My lady is not sleeping in hay," Kase told them firmly.

"Your lady can sleep when she finds a place to lie down," Xan grunted. "As will we all." Pushing past the plainsman, Xan headed towards the inn, the rest of the men following. Bastian turned back to the sound of a lone cry, and as he waited for the answering call, Beth joined him.

"Bastian, I, um, I didn't get the chance to…"

"To what?" Bastian looked down at her. She really was slight in stature with her head barely reaching his shoulder. "Thank us? You can hold your thanks; you're not in the Golden City yet." Moving forward, he wasn't sure which of them was more surprised when Beth's hand grabbed at his wrist, halting him.

"I wasn't thanking you," she told him, releasing her hold hastily.

"Of course not, why would you?" Bastian scoffed as he turned from her again.

"I meant to apologise!"

"Meaning to and doing it are not the same thing," he called over his shoulder.

"Ugh!" She felt like screaming. "You know what I mean!"

"Nope, can't say that I do." Bastian saw the others were already at the inn, and he was eager to be too.

"Bastian!" Beth called. He ignored her as he kept on walking. "Bastian!" She almost stomped her foot in irritation as he continued to walk away from her, but she knew she couldn't let him affect her like that. Kase hurried back to her and looked between her and the object of her frustration.

"It's okay, we'll be in the Golden City soon," he assured her. "You'll never have to look at any of them again." Kase rubbed her shoulder in a comforting way. "After tonight, we can leave them. Remember what you said in the Sand Seas, we can go whenever we wish? And honestly, I think we need to; we don't want to be with the likes of them."

"What do you mean? You think they're dangerous?"

"I do."

Beth frowned as she looked towards the shadows that were the retreating soldiers. "But wouldn't they have…done something by now?"

"Let's talk more in the morning." He tugged her hand. "Come on, tonight you sleep in a bed," he said with an eager grin, and allowing herself to be distracted with the idea of a bed, Beth nodded enthusiastically, and together they hurried to the inn.

CHAPTER 10

The innkeeper wasn't overly content to let the men in at the time of night that they arrived, but when Ax "accidentally" dropped Lady Tyria's name, the fact that there was a lady on his doorstep prompted the innkeeper to be more forthcoming.

He had three bedrooms still available, and the ladies took one, and Kase was ready to sleep outside their room until Beth, Bastian noticed, assured him they would be fine. The innkeeper, on hearing Beth's gentle arguments to the tall Tzenythian, took it upon himself to march the inn's own guards out to demonstrate the security of his inn and more importantly, his guests.

The other two bedrooms had twin beds in both, and Ax was already making his way to the stables when the innkeeper called him back and told him he could provide cots for each room.

"A cot?" Kase asked dubiously. "For a babe?"

"They're roll away beds," Xan explained as Khaldan confirmed the cots would indeed be welcome. "They're akin to a mattress only thinner, to allow them to roll for storage. Think of it like sleeping on the ground only comfier."

Kase looked around the men to see if he was being mocked but instead only saw tiredness and weariness weighing the men down. "How long are they?"

"Fylip will take one," Xan said matter-of-factly. "Then it's the next shortest one."

Bastian didn't bother looking around. He knew neither Khaldan, Kase or himself were sleeping on the floor.

"So, you then?" Kase asked, and it was obvious by his tone he was waiting to be told it was him.

Xan looked around and huffed out a small laugh. "I guess so. I really need to up my game in the training room," he jested with an easy smile.

"Doesn't matter how wide you are, brother," Ax said with a clap on his shoulder. "It's height and you know it."

"How long will you be here?" the innkeeper asked them tersely, not in the slightest bit amused by their easy banter.

All eyes turned to Bastian, and the innkeeper, realising he was in charge, gave him his full attention. "My…lord?" The hesitation was brief, but Bastian recognised the slight for what it was. He knew how they looked, but he would challenge anyone to walk through the Sand Seas and come out looking fresh.

"It depends on the lady," Bastian countered with a nod to Lady Tyria. "We are at her command."

"*Me*?" she squeaked. "You are?" When Beth nudged her slightly, she regained her composure. "Two nights at least."

Bastian hid his smile when he saw Kase look away, fighting to keep his face straight and his frustration in check.

"Very good, my lady," the innkeeper bowed. "If you'll follow me." He paused and looked them over. "Your carriage?"

"Misplaced," Xan answered gruffly.

The innkeeper's eyebrows rose as he looked over Tyria again. "Horses?"

"With the carriage," Ax told him with a wide grin as he

thumbed the pommel of his sword. The innkeeper wisely chose to ask no more questions and instead led them to the narrow stairs, which led to the floor above.

The inn was laid out well. The main door led into the common room, and in a small corner of the room was an alcove in which the innkeeper kept his books and greeted new guests. In addition to the main common room, there was a separate dining area for the more discerning or noble guest, and to the rear of both rooms was the kitchen.

All of the rooms were above, and there was also a small annexe to the rear that housed the innkeeper and his family. He led them to the far end of the hall. All doors were closed, and Bastian could hear some of the occupants of the inn moving around. In some rooms, they could hear the loud snores, and in one room nearer the end, the cries from within he noticed brought a blush to the handmaiden's cheeks.

"Here." The innkeeper pointed to two rooms beside each other and one room across the hall. "This one is larger for your ladyship." He opened the door to the room by itself.

"They'll go here," Bastian told him as he pushed the door open to the corner room. With a quick glance, he knew it was smaller than what the innkeeper was offering the women, but Bastian knew for anyone to get to this room, they had to pass the other two first.

"I want the bigger room," Tyria blurted, surprising most of them as she had been meek and mild for most of their journey so far.

"I want a room to myself, a hot meal and a solid bed beneath my bones," Xan told her. "Wanting doesn't mean getting." He pushed the room door open beside the one Bastian had picked for the women. "This will do us," he told Ax and walked inside. "Tzenythian, you're with us," he called over his shoulder.

"I'll stay with these two," Kase said as he looked at his lady and her handmaiden, but he jerked his thumb at Khaldan and Bastian.

"How can we possibly refuse?" Khaldan murmured to Bastian as he walked into the room opposite them.

"Easily," Bastian countered. "Xan takes a cot. You're either in here with us and on the floor, giving Fylip your bed, or you take a bed in there."

Kase stared at the two rooms, and then he looked over Fylip, who was smaller in height to the Tzenythian by a good few inches. With an angry grunt, Kase followed Ax and Xan into the room, slamming the door behind him.

"Do you need anything?" Bastian asked the two women as the innkeeper wisely stayed quiet during the negotiations.

"A bigger room and a tub of hot water," Tyria mumbled, but with a waning smile, she spoke to the innkeeper. "A washbasin?"

"Inside, my lady. I'll rouse one of the boys to get hot water brought up to you." Giving her a quick bow, he made to walk away, but Bastian stopped his departure with his hand on his arm.

"Hot water for three rooms," he told him as he produced a silver coin. "For your boy's trouble at this late hour."

The innkeeper took the coin and hurried to the stairs, leaving Bastian and the women in the hall.

"You going in?" he eventually asked them, and Tyria,

realising that they were simply standing in the hall, turned quickly and entered the room. Beth remained outside, returning Bastian's cool appraisal. "What now?" he asked her with a sigh.

Beth went to speak, but a loud cry from one of the rooms had her cheeks flaming. "Are you going to stand outside all night?"

"Nope, got a bed to go to."

"Then why are you not in it?" she challenged him.

Bastian looked down at the younger woman as she stood with her arms across her chest, her posture stiff. "I will see you both settled for the night," he told her easily. "It's only right."

Beth found that she actually had no argument to that, and with a nod, she entered the room. Bastian leaned against the doorpost as he waited for the water to be brought. Khaldan stuck his head out the door once to ensure he was okay, and Bastian noticed with chagrin that his friend had already removed his cuirass and weapons.

Eventually the innkeeper's son arrived with two large pitchers of steaming water, the innkeeper behind him with the third. Taking one off the boy, Bastian took it into the room where Tyria and Beth were both removing their boots. They seemed to have been waiting until the door was closed, but fatigue got the better of their patience.

"Sleep well," he told them, and he heard Beth murmur her thanks as Tyria began to fill the small washbasin, and he closed the door behind him.

Waiting for the innkeeper to come out of his own room, Bastian stood with his hand held out.

"Sir?"

"Key for their room."

"It's in the door," the innkeeper quickly replied, his face paling when he saw Bastian had it in his hand.

"No, it's not. Now the other one." When the innkeeper went to protest, Bastian smiled. It was not friendly. "I've stayed in my share of inns, my good man, I know there is always another key."

With a huff and a grumble, the innkeeper reached into his pouch and handed over the extra key.

"All three rooms." Bastian's voice was low, and with another mumbled protest, the innkeeper did as he was bade. As the innkeeper walked away with his son in tow, Bastian waited until they were both descending the stairs, and then he turned and swiftly locked the door that the women were in.

"Hello?" Beth was at the door, and ignoring her, he opened the door to where Xan and Ax were.

"Here," he said to Xan, noticing that Ax was already asleep and Kase was shirtless at the washbasin. Xan caught the key, dropping his cuirass on top of his cot. "Sleep well," Bastian told him as he glanced at Kase, who had straightened and was now looking at him over his shoulder.

Closing the door firmly, he heard Xan lock the door. Beth was rattling her door handle, but she was in the corner room, and Bastian had noticed when he saw the three rooms that the smaller room had the thicker, more soundproof door. She would not be happy, and with a contented smirk, Bastian went into his room, ready to shrug out of his clothes and wash the dirt and grime from his face.

Sleep was calling to him, and he was ready to greet it.

"You don't understand." Beth was careful to keep her voice low. "He locked us *in*."

Kase looked around the common room as he listened to Beth's grievances. In truth, he wished he'd thought of locking the room door himself to keep the women safe, but judging by the fury in Beth's eyes, he was keeping that observation to himself.

"Well?" Beth demanded as she stabbed her spoon into her bowl of porridge.

Kase blinked rapidly as he considered his words. "I'll ask for the key this evening."

It was the wrong thing to say.

"Aren't you going to ask him why he did it?" Beth asked in outrage.

"I—"

"I did it so you would be safe," Bastian spoke from behind them, and Beth whirled in her seat to see he had come through the front door. "You're welcome," he added as he took a seat beside Kase.

"Where have you been? And safe from who? You?"

Bastian ignored her questions as he reached for a warm bread roll sitting in a basket in the centre of the table. Breaking the bread, he took a hearty bite. "You feel like you'll never be full again," he said conversationally as he chewed, "after coming out of the Sand Seas, but then anything you eat makes you feel nauseous, so you can never eat too much."

"How long does it last?" Kase asked as he looked down at his own half-eaten food in his bowl.

"Few days." Bastian finished his roll before he looked fully at Beth. "You saw an inn of people retired for the evening, but never believe the shadows don't have eyes. Someone is always watching. We were tired last night, exhausted. Some of us were asleep before our heads were on the pillow." Bastian had also lowered his voice so as not to be overheard, but his words were firm. "We are not known for sleeping heavy, but it's a hard journey over the Sand Seas, and a sleep that hard makes it difficult to hear noises in the dark. It was safer to lock the door."

Beth held his stare, ice blue eyes cool and frigid as they held hers. Firm. Resolute. She was fairly sure this man would have locked her door should they all have been well rested. He just seemed to ooze control issues.

"It was a good thought," Kase said much to her dismay, and she knew he was avoiding her as he kept his attention locked on his bowl. "One I should have thought of myself," he admitted without raising his head.

"It's been a long crossing," Bastian told him as he rose to his feet. "That's why you rely on those around you, as they do you." Bastian spared Beth a glance, and she hurriedly looked away so he wouldn't see her distrust. "Bread will help soak the porridge, stopping the queasiness."

He crossed the room and headed up the stairs, and when he was out of sight, Beth turned her attention to Kase. "You agreed?"

"He makes sense," Kase said as he rubbed his hand over his topknot. "By the time I washed the dirt off my face and hands, I don't even remember lying down. I didn't hear a thing until morning when Ax came *into* the room, not out of it."

Beth chewed the inside of her cheek as she thought about it. She and Tyria had both cleaned their faces and hands, and then the two of them had fallen into a deep slumber. She didn't want to think of how long Kase had been knocking at the door before she woke up. Of course, by that time, his High-Handedness had already unlocked the door. Obviously because his men were already on their feet and moving about the inn.

Once she had carried out her morning ablutions, she had gone looking for the arrogant mercenary, but he was nowhere to be found.

Pompous ass.

Loud laughter caused her to startle, and she saw that the blond-haired Ax, the more approachable of the men they travelled with, was dripping wet. Xan and the quieter man, Fylip, were both laughing loudly at their comrade.

"What do you think happened?" Beth asked Kase, smiling as Ax shook his long hair like a dog.

"I think he was causing mischief," Kase said with a reluctant smile. Ax saw them and raised his hand in greeting but didn't come over. They heard Xan tell him to go to the room and fix himself, and then Xan and Fylip both left the inn.

"Where are they going?" Beth asked Kase as, through the window, she watched the two men head into town.

"Will I follow?" Kase asked as he turned in his seat to watch them.

"Yes."

"You sure?" Turning back to face her, he looked at her in surprise. "You will both be alone if I go."

Beth thought about it for a moment, but heavy footsteps

on the stairs as Khaldan joined the common room made her decision easier. "Go and be quick before he notices you."

Kase nodded and stood abruptly, ready to follow the men. "Stay to the room. Don't come out until I'm back," he ordered her, and just as he was about to leave, he hesitated and grabbed a roll, heeding Bastian's words. "Don't leave the room," he said again, and then he was out the door, hurrying to follow the other men.

Beth watched him go and then turned in her seat to see Khaldan talking to the innkeeper, but his attention was on her. "Don't leave?" she muttered as she shoved her spoon into her now cold porridge, turning slightly in her seat to avoid looking at him. "Difficult when they're always watching."

Hurriedly she finished her food. Taking two rolls, she stood to go back to her room, stopping short when she realised Khaldan was behind her.

"Sir?"

"You eat enough?" he asked her pleasantly.

"Yes, you?"

"I did." Khaldan looked around the room, and she braced herself for him to ask Kase's whereabouts. "Your lady?"

"Sleeping when I left her," Beth told him and showed him the rolls. "I'm taking these up to her to see if she wishes to break her fast."

"Tell the innkeeper to prepare a tray. She'll need more than that." Khaldan moved past her, heading to the door. "Tell your lady not to eat too much. It takes time to adjust to the food."

"You're leaving too?" Beth blurted.

He paused and turned. "There is enough here to protect you." His voice was gentle, and Beth realised he meant to reassure her she was safe. "You'd be better out of the common room though," Khaldan continued. "If your lady wishes to eat at a table, there is a dining room for her to use. Not here."

"Of course." Beth nodded in agreement, not wanting to tell him that if she used the dining room, she wouldn't see their comings and goings. "I'll make sure she uses it."

She knew he heard the insincerity in her voice. His eyes crinkled at the corners, but he didn't call her out on it. Instead, he gave a brief dip of his head and left the inn.

Cursing herself for a poor liar, she hurried up the stairs to the room. Maybe Kase was right, the room was the safest place for her, away from their ever-watchful eyes.

CHAPTER 11

"WHY ARE YOU SMILING?" KHALDAN ASKED BASTIAN AS HE walked into the room. "And should I be concerned Fylip isn't downstairs?" he added as he looked around the room. Bastian was lying on his bed, in only his trousers, his arms folded behind his head as he stared up at the ceiling.

"Are you saying I shouldn't smile?" Bastian asked as he turned his head to look at his companion. "And Fylip is with Xan; they're scouting for the zyvarg."

Khaldan raised his eyebrows as he heard the update and sat on the corner of his bed. "This bed feels like a rock," he said with surprise.

"Not the best," Bastian admitted. "Never noticed it last night. Will probably notice it tonight."

Khaldan nodded and let out a sigh, his shoulders drooping with fatigue. "Might not notice," he admitted ruefully. "I could sleep for a week."

"I could eat for a week," Bastian told him as he rubbed his belly. His body was one of a warrior, thick with defined and corded muscles and scattered with scars.

"It was a hard crossing," Khaldan spoke quietly. "You should not blame yourself, brother." Bastian said nothing, his attention returning to the ceiling. "Bastian," Khaldan growled at him. "We are no longer ten years old, and your silent treatment was never amusing even when we were."

Bastian felt his lips twitch as he concentrated on the wooden beams above. "There are cities still from the old time," he said quietly. "There are those where castles sit on the precipice, and still, they hold their ground. The earth beneath them is crumbling and hollow, but still they hold."

"You are not a castle sitting on the edge of a rock, held fast to the ground with a deep foundation, my friend. You are naught but a man, with tired arms, yes, but your grip was ever strong."

"I should have held on," Bastian spoke quietly.

"He let go, Bastian." Khaldan stood wearily and crossed the small room to the washbasin. "You can only do so much, and that's not much if the one you're holding on to lets go."

"He saved me."

"He did." Khaldan looked down at the plain smooth wooden bowl with the clear water inside. His reflection looked back at him. Thick brown hair hung shaggy. His beard needed trimming, his hair too, he mused. Brown eyes stared back at him in his reflection, and his attention stayed caught on the scar above his left eye, neatly cleaving his eyebrow in two. "You can't save everyone," Khaldan said gruffly before dipping his hands into the water and splashing his face. As he patted his face dry with the linen provided, he turned back to Bastian, who was watching him quietly. "What?"

"Nothing."

"It's never nothing, it's always something." Khaldan sat back down on his bed. "We both know you'll tell me eventually, so let's stop the charade and tell me now."

"You need more sleep." Bastian returned to his study of the ceiling.

"I..." Khaldan cut himself off. Twisting his head from

side to side to loosen the knot at the base of his skull, he tried not to rise to Bastian's small idiosyncrasies, but sometimes it was hard. "I *do* need more sleep," he said, instead of what he wanted to say, which was to demand the other man stop being so infuriating. Looking over, he saw Bastian smiling again. "You're a son of a goat. You know that, don't you?"

"I think my father would object." Bastian was grinning widely now. "He's very un-goatlike."

Khaldan groaned as he lay back on his bed, imitating his friend's position. "Do I need to wait?" Silence was his answer. Gritting his teeth, he tried a new tactic. "Why were you smiling when I came in?"

Bastian huffed out a laugh as he sat up, swinging his legs over the side of the bed. "Do you notice she's the worst handmaiden?"

"Worse than what?" Khaldan closed his eyes, getting comfortable.

"Half the time she forgets to wait on her lady, the other half she's making moon eyes at the plainsman, and him? How many times has he looked at her instead of his lady?"

"I don't think I've been paying as much attention as you have," Khaldan told him dryly.

"They're hiding something."

"Of course they are."

"We need to find out what before we escort them to the Golden City," Bastian said as he stood and reached for his shirt.

"Sounds good." Khaldan moved slightly, his body moulding to the firm bed beneath him after all.

"I—" Bastian halted as he realised Khaldan was almost asleep. "Never mind." Grabbing his sword and cuirass, he left the room.

When the door was closed firmly, Khaldan opened his eyes to slits to ensure he was alone. It was his turn to grin as he settled further into position and closed his eyes again. Bastian was always suspicious, but Khaldan had also noticed how often Kase looked to the handmaiden for direction and not his lady. If they were lying, time would tell—it always did—and they were still a long way from the Golden City.

Bastian finished lacing his cuirass as he entered the common room. Ax was at a table to the back of the room, a tankard in front of him. Making his way over to him, Bastian noted the other guests, mentally assessing them and filing them as foes or friendly.

"Must you scowl at everyone?" Ax asked him as he sat beside him.

"I scowl?"

"You glower and you know it," Ax told him as he took a long drink of his ale. "What did you do to Khaldan?"

"Left him to sleep," Bastian answered as he raised his hand to the innkeeper, getting his attention and pointing to Ax's tankard. "And why do people keep asking me what I've done with my men?" Bastian grumbled as he got comfortable. "First Khaldan asks what I've done to Fylip, and now you're asking what I did to Khaldan."

"Bez's death has made you paranoid. It's a turn of phrase; no one expects you to have *done* anything," Ax told him easily as he took another drink. "We are soldiers, brother. We fall."

Bastian scowled at Ax but said nothing. There was no

point, not with Ax. He had an outlook on life that was not shared by Bastian, and he learned a long time ago not to argue with him over it.

"The lady and her handmaiden?" Bastian decided to change the subject.

"In their room all day. The lady broke her fast there, and they got lunch sent up to them an hour ago, along with enough pitchers to suggest bathing," he added enviously.

Bastian nodded his thanks to the innkeeper as he placed the tankard in front of him. "Still a long way to travel," Bastian said as he took a long drink, his face registering his surprise at how pleasant the ale was.

"For a small town, it's decent," Ax commented as he drank his own.

"It is," Bastian conceded. "Your thoughts on our companions?" Bastian asked him casually.

"The lady is no lady," Ax said with a grin. "The Tzenythian, bodyguard or protector, I think, not a soldier," he added. "But with a little training, he could be," he added as an afterthought.

"And the handmaiden?" Bastian asked softly.

"Not sure. She's difficult to read. Too outspoken to be a servant, too opinionated to be nobility of standing. He watches her constantly."

"He does," Bastian agreed.

"Lovers eloping?" Ax suggested.

"Three of them?" Bastian was sceptical.

"It's been known to happen."

"When?" Bastian shook his head at Ax's wild assumptions, and he took another drink. "Her accent is hidden."

"Not hidden, Eloysth."

Bastian considered it. "Would fit."

"*Does* fit," Ax corrected.

"She's a long way from home," Bastian mused.

Ax raised his hand to the innkeeper, indicating two refills. "Aren't we all, my brother. Aren't we all."

They stayed at the inn one more night, but when Xan and Fylip reported signs of zyvarg having ventured closer to the town, Bastian and his men gathered their weapons and sent Fylip to find a wagon.

"Why do you need a wagon?" Lady Tyria asked them as she watched them check their holsters or tighten their cuirasses.

"It's for you, lady," Khaldan, ever the diplomat, told her with a smile.

Lady Tyria chewed her bottom lip, her gaze continuously darting to Kase. "For me? I don't understand."

"You and the handmaiden need to be in the wagon and sent ahead of us," Xan supplied as he stretched his arm over his head.

"As bait?" Kase growled, his hand tightening on his sword.

"Don't be foolish," Khaldan scoffed. "The women will be in the wagon, with you driving it, and we'll take care of our followers once and for all."

They were all more or less in Bastian and Khaldan's room, as it was bigger, and the men were moving between the two rooms.

"Followers?" Beth asked, her attention, as always it seemed, fixed on Bastian.

"We are careful with our words when there are other ears listening," Bastian told her as he buckled his sword belt. Beth frowned but said nothing.

"So, you are sending the three of us first?" Kase asked carefully, his gaze flicking to Beth's once, and Bastian noticed she made a great effort not to look Kase's way.

"Four," Xan answered. "Ax goes with you."

"Why?" Lady Tyria asked as she regarded the blond male.

"Our packs will be with you," Ax piped up. "I'll keep you honest," he told her with a wink.

"My lady *is* honest," Kase bit out savagely.

"You then," Ax joked back with an easy shrug. "Either way, I'm going with the wagon, and the wagon is going with me on it, as are our packs."

"And we can go with it, or not?" Beth guessed.

"Sounds about right." Bastian met her cold look with one of his own. "Is there a problem? Handmaiden?"

Beth tilted her head slightly at the inflection of his tone but chose to ignore it. "No problem here, sir."

"Wonderful."

A while later, when Xan had settled their bill at the inn and none of the men commented on the fact that Kase nor his Lady Tyria were anywhere to be found to pay their share, the men unloaded their packs onto the wagon. Beth and Lady Tyria sat on the bed, the packs more or less securing them in.

Kase sat up front with Ax right beside him, completely at ease with the hostility emanating from Kase beside him.

As they walked out of the village, their voices were a low murmur. Bastian walked behind as he sometimes did, and he pointedly ignored the steely green stare of one of the wagon's passengers.

"She glares at you much more, people are going to start wondering if you compromised her honour," Khaldan muttered under his breath, causing Bastian to chuckle as they walked side by side. "Should we swap with Xan and Fylip?" Khaldan asked him.

"Xan knows the way," Bastian told him amicably.

Khaldan pushed his cloak over his shoulders, ensuring the clasp was still secure. "Well, there's one thing for sure, she won't forget us."

At the fork in the path, they heard Xan speak to Ax, who looked over his shoulder at Bastian and Khaldan. With a quick wave of his hand, he cracked the reins and let the horse pick its pace.

"And then there were four," Fylip said when they joined them. "He'll be okay?"

"Ax?" Xan asked with a look over his shoulder at the wagon as it moved quickly beyond them. "He'll be fine. I worry for them more than him."

Facing east, the four of them began to walk back to the Sand Seas. "And you definitely think they are still here?" Khaldan asked Fylip.

"Would you go back across that dead land if you had the choice?" Fylip asked. "They may be animals, but they aren't stupid. They're here. Waiting."

"Waiting?" Bastian asked sharply. "For what?"

Fylip shrugged under his leader's glare. "The towns-people to become complacent?"

"The town doesn't know it has a pack of zyvarg on its fringe." Khaldan turned to look at the small dust cloud the wagon was producing.

"But the zyvarg do know their prey was in it." Bastian gripped his sword. Just then, the low howl echoed in the rocks further west of them.

"They've been *waiting*?" Khaldan asked in astonishment.

"What in the name of Hoxka did they do to that pack?" Xan asked no one in particular as they watched the creatures emerge from the stones where they had settled to wait, the zyvarg's attention on the wagon.

"When you followed the strangers and the zyvarg in the Teeth," Bastian said suddenly, "you said they never got closer to the three strangers, that *you* never got closer?"

"You think *they* were the three in the Teeth?" Xan asked, his eyes widening in realisation.

"I think our travelling companions are liars," Bastian snarled. "It's *us* that needs that wagon, not them. Let's move. If we're right, we'll catch the zyvarg only because they won't get closer, and we can thank the Gods that Ax is protected by default."

The four soldiers set an easy, steady running pace, knowing they would need their speed the closer they got to the wagon.

"If you say I told you so," Khaldan panted as they ran, "I will skewer you where you stand."

Bastian grinned as he ran. "If *you* say you told me so, I get the first kill." He quickened his pace. "Or maybe I'll just outrun you!" he called as he pounded across the ground, knowing his companions were behind him.

Despite the fact it should have been impossible for them to catch up to the pack of zyvarg, they did in fact find themselves closing in.

"There's a lot," Fylip panted as he forced himself to maintain the pace of his peers.

"Aye," Bastian grunted as he loosened his sword and then barked out the command to Xan. "Get their attention."

Xan slowed slightly, and with two fingers in his mouth, he let out an ear-piercing whistle.

The zyvarg stopped chasing the wagon and turned as one pack to face the four men running after them.

"Definitely more than we thought," Khaldan said as they slowed, bracing themselves for the fact a very large monster pack was running straight for them.

"The whistle may have been a bad idea," Bastian admitted as he freed his sword.

Khaldan glared at him before getting into position to defend himself and his brothers. "Gee, ya think?"

Had the zyvarg been intelligent enough to comprehend it, they may have wondered why the prey they were racing towards were laughing as they grabbed their sharp sticks and stood firm at their advance. But the zyvarg were merely godless creatures, created from a toxic land after a catastrophic change to the world that once was.

When spurred to hunger and desperation, they attacked on sight. They had followed this prey across lifeless lands, and many of their kind lay dead behind them. They did not like this land. They did not like this prey. They wanted to return to the lands they knew. It was too warm and too dry here. The prey here was small and did not fill the ache in their bellies.

This prey was not small. Eager to feed, the first of the zyvarg reached Bastian and his men and with a loud snarl, leaped forward, its fangs bared, ready to feast on fresh meat that would finally ease the gnawing hunger inside.

CHAPTER 12

Bastian's sword cleaved into the side of the zyvarg as it leapt, his short dagger sinking into its neck as it fell. Kicking the dead beast off of his sword, he was swinging for the next one before the first one landed at his feet.

Khaldan ducked as one of the monstrous beasts launched itself at him, and with swords in both hands, he attacked the pack as it in turn attacked them. He heard Fylip yell, but with two of the beasts in front of him, Khaldan was unable to tell if it was a cry of battle or one for help.

Xan cursed as he spun and fought. The beasts were showing no sign of fear, and after the dogged persistence they had shown by following them across the Sand Seas, Xan was ready to tear them limb from limb.

In the warrior training academies, he had been taught to defend against all foes, but it was hard to train against a pack of creatures who didn't understand formation or strategy. Fighting the pack was like fighting madness; there was no rhyme or reason to the attack, as beasts fought amongst themselves to attack the men.

"Fylip?" Bastian called out as he fought. He had heard his companion's yell but was loath to take his eyes off the enemy.

"I'm fine," Fylip grunted. "Bit my leg."

"Xan!" Bastian commanded.

"Covering," Xan replied with a heavy grunt as he smashed his dagger into one of the beasts' eyes.

The number of beasts around them was diminishing, so movement was hindered as they manoeuvred around the fallen. Fylip stumbled and as he fell, the zyvarg sensing his weakness pounced only to be met with a gleaming sword that bit savagely into its side, its scream of pain echoing around them.

Bastian quickly removed his sword and plunged it into the creature again, as Fylip regained his footing.

"I'm up," Fylip shouted as he turned to fight off another zyvarg.

"Almost there," Xan growled as he removed the head of a smaller beast. Hearing a rabid growl behind him, he turned to see the biggest beast he had ever seen. "Ah sh—"

The beast struck him, and he went down. Wildly he fended the snarling jaws off of him as the beast snapped and bit at his arms, which were protecting his face.

The snarling stopped as a gleaming blade plunged downward, through the back of the neck of his assailant. Pushing the beast off of himself, he looked up as Ax grinned down at him.

"You could have struck me!" Xan growled as he took his friend's outstretched arm and was pulled to his feet.

"I know." Ax grinned widely as he turned and fought another zyvarg, but having his friend there, Xan realised that the majority of the pack were dead, with only a few remaining and the others fleeing back the way they had come.

Bastian looked up from the dead zyvarg he was cleaning his sword on, seeing Khaldan inspecting the cut to his bicep. "Deep?" Bastian asked him, noticing for the first time that Kase was there too, pulling Fylip to his feet.

"A scratch. It will need to be bled though." Khaldan grunted as he squeezed the wound. Zyvarg saliva had a toxin within it that caused hallucinations, and if it took hold within the bloodstream, it was slowly poisonous.

"Don't prod it," Ax scolded as he slapped Khaldan's hand away from the wound. "Fylip, are you bleeding?"

"Aye," Fylip groaned as he used Kase for support. "Brute bit deep," he said as he examined his leg.

"Into the wagon with you," Ax barked out orders. "Khaldan, you too."

"I don't need the wagon," Khaldan protested, but Ax fixed him with a look and turned to Bastian for support, but Bastian was staring at the wagon, one eyebrow raised in query. Khaldan turned to look and saw that Beth sat up front, the reins in her hands. Her cloak had blown back, her black hair loose in the slight breeze, her cheeks were rosy, and she was holding Bastian's stare with her own.

"I'm not touching that," Xan said beside Khaldan softly.

"Huh?"

"Them two," Xan confirmed. "I've seen friendlier war councils."

Khaldan huffed out a laugh, his face straightening when Bastian turned his attention to them.

"Let's clean this up," Bastian instructed. "Fylip, Khaldan, you heard Ax, move it."

Khaldan opened his mouth to argue, but Xan nudged him, and with a grunt, he headed to the wagon, where Ax was already digging through his pack.

"You need help?" Kase asked Bastian.

Bastian looked the plainsman over. His bare arms had

marks on them, but no blood was drawn. "You came back? Why?"

Kase blinked in surprise. "My lady saw the pack follow and then saw you behind the pack, chasing them."

"Your *lady*?" Bastian glanced at the wagon and then fixed a hard stare on the plainsman. "Or the handmaiden?"

Kase pursed his lips as if forcibly restraining himself from answering. "The beasts?" he asked instead as he pointed at the creatures around them.

"Pile them up," Bastian ordered as he sheathed his sword and bent to the task.

Khaldan was leaning against the wagon as Ax pulled out his medical pouch and wordlessly handed him his flask when the blond warrior looked around for his own.

"You know the art of healing, sir?" Beth asked as she moved closer to the bed of the wagon.

Ax gave her a quick grin as he started pulling jars and a stone mortar and pestle from his pouch. "I can do a little," he admitted. "Nothing like the true healers, of course." Ax considered the younger woman. "You?"

"A little, sir," Beth told him as she moved closer. "I can help if you require?" She looked at Fylip's leg. "It'll take hold soon."

"It will. Your aid would be appreciated," Ax told her as he pulled himself into the wagon and turned. He held his hand out. "Hope you're not squeamish," he said as he pointed at Khaldan. "If I mix the salve, then you could apply it to Khaldan?"

"Of course," Beth told him as she pulled her cloak off and pushed the sleeves of her gown up slightly.

Ax noticed the black ink on her wrist, his eyes flicking to

Bastian. "You may want to wrap linen around your wrists," he said conversationally. "Not everyone is partial to the signs of the new Gods."

Beth yanked her sleeves over her wrists and looked for Kase, seeing him working alongside Bastian and Xan. She startled when Ax laid a hand on hers. "It's fine, lady, just be careful," he cautioned.

Khaldan had been watching the others build a zyvarg pile, but seeing they were managing fine without him, he turned his attention to the wounded, wondering what Ax could have possibly done to the handmaiden to make her look so edgy.

Lady Tyria had been at the front with the horse, calming it and making sure it had water. Finished with her task, she returned to the wagon. "The horse will be fine," she told them. "We need to move it if they intend to burn the beasts."

"A wise suggestion," Khaldan agreed. "Tell me, lady, which family are you from?"

"We've been travelling together for weeks, and you ask this now?" Beth asked as she finished wrapping the linen cloth that Ax had provided her with around her wrists.

"It's hardly been a leisurely stroll," Khaldan retorted with a show of teeth that was anything but a friendly smile. "Those zyvarg were intent on pursuing you."

"And you think it's because I am nobility that they wanted to kill us?" Lady Tyria scoffed. She looked down at her dress and took in the wear and tear of her travelling habit. "I admit I look…less, but I am a lady of a high house, although I have never heard of the zyvarg to be so discerning of their prey," she mocked.

"Of course you are noble." Khaldan paused as Beth pushed his sleeve up with more force than he thought necessary. "Which noble house would that be?"

"You know every house in every kingdom?" Lady Tyria challenged him.

"Know of? I'd say so—fought most of them, or for them." Khaldan grunted as Beth rubbed his arm, kneading the flesh, forcing the blood to spill. "Did I offend you, hand-maiden?" Khaldan asked her as she cleaned his wound.

"It needs to be thorough," Beth grumbled as she worked.

Khaldan turned his attention back to Lady Tyria. "Lady Tyria, you're from Bordyre, if I'm not mistaken. Your house?"

"Barsgaard," Lady Tyria told him coldly. "And I do not appreciate being questioned."

Khaldan dipped his head slightly in acknowledgement. "Of course," he conceded. "Are you quite done?" he asked Beth as he looked at his arm. She was spreading the salve over his wound with vigour, and at his tone, she seemed to realise that she was being too rough.

"You're covered," she said as she dropped her hands from his arm.

"Thank you," Khaldan told her politely. "Ax, how goes it?"

Clearing his throat, Ax concentrated on his task at hand. "Got most of it," he said. "Running low on Jezberry, but it should be enough." Ax was gently cutting around Fylip's leg as he cleaned the wound and pressed his salve into it.

"He feels no pain?" Beth asked, fascinated.

"The zyvarg poison numbs the flesh; he feels nothing," Ax explained, and Fylip grinned at her.

"Thought I was impressing you with my threshold for pain," Fylip said, laughing as he watched Ax work on his leg.

"You are also numb?" Beth asked Khaldan, her voice tinged slightly with accusation.

"Khaldan's scrape is merely that, a scrape," Ax spoke instead. "See, here." He pointed to Fylip's leg. "The flesh is red and angry, but when pressed, it turns white." He demonstrated. "Khaldan's arm stayed red, yes?"

Beth frowned as she thought about it. "Yes, I think."

"It was," Ax confirmed reassuringly. "I was watching." He smiled as Beth flushed. "If it stays red, then the skin is actually tender, and the wound feels prickly and painful."

"Oh." Beth looked at Khaldan. "Maybe I was a little bit rough."

"Apology accepted."

"I wasn't actually saying sorry," Beth bit back angrily.

"I know, I was being polite."

She snapped her mouth closed when she saw Bastian and the others coming to join them.

"We good?" Bastian asked as he peered at Fylip's leg. "Feeling no pain?"

"I could dance on it," Fylip told him with a grin.

"Let grace favour us so that *that* doesn't happen," Xan rumbled beside them.

"How much longer?" Bastian asked Ax.

"I can work as we move," Ax said as he carefully kept up his work on Fylip's bite.

Bastian looked around, taking in the fact Kase had

moved to stand beside Lady Tyria. "Then let's mount up and move on."

It was a short time later that the packs had been moved to make room for them, allowing Beth, the lady, Ax, Fylip and Xan all to be in the back of the wagon, albeit a tight fit.

Khaldan sat beside Kase up front, and Bastian took the opportunity to walk alongside the horse, enjoying the animal's silent company. They travelled into the night before he spotted a suitable shelter for them. Ruins of cities and towns were still scattered across the kingdoms, and Bastian, after checking the structure of this ruin, told them to stop for food and sleep.

"An old place of worship," Ax said as he stared up at the stone arch, the only remaining wall still standing high. The others were in various degrees of disrepair, and tumbled broken bricks littered the land.

Xan looked up at the arch. "Pity it lost its roof; rain's coming."

"Three will fit under the wagon," Bastian told them as he dropped his pack. "A small fire, I think," he told Khaldan, who was already gathering debris for one.

"Just enough to heat water," Khaldan confirmed. "I'll take my first watch." The others volunteered their watch, and Bastian said nothing as his men purposefully left him the last watch.

"If you're going to be asleep the longest," Xan said casually as he arranged his pack as a seat, "you should take rest under the wagon."

Khaldan was suddenly concentrating very hard on starting his fire, Ax was inspecting Fylip's leg, and Xan was trying his best to look innocent.

"Subtle," Bastian snorted as he picked up a broken stone from the fallen structure. "As subtle as this across the back of the head," he mocked. "Fylip goes under," Bastian instructed. "Lady Tyria and the handmaiden."

"Why is it always *the* handmaiden and not her handmaiden?" Beth snapped at him.

"No reason," Bastian answered easily as he climbed up onto the wagon. "If you're all so determined for me to sleep," he told his men, "then I'm going to sleep." Wrapping himself in his cloak, he closed his eyes and shut out the lowered talking from his men, letting sleep take him.

Ax woke him for his watch. The night was still holding on, but the land knew the dawn was coming, and stirrings of life could be heard. Bastian moved quietly from the wagon, careful not to disturb the three people keeping dry under it.

"Black night," Bastian said as he took a mouthful of water from his flask, observing the overcast sky.

"It was." Ax touched his arm, getting his attention, and with a jerk of his head, he led Bastian out from the ruin.

"What is it?" Bastian asked quietly. "Fylip?"

Ax shook his head. "The Lady Tyria claims to be from a noble house of Bordyre."

Bastian grunted as he drank more. "Explains the colouring and the accent she's trying to hide. Which house?"

"Barsgaard," Ax told him dryly.

Bastian snorted as he swallowed and quickly covered his mouth to stop from spitting out the mouthful of water. "Reckless," he said when he recovered. "To pick one of the most well-known houses in the kingdom."

"Yes," Ax agreed.

Bastian eyed his friend in the dim light. "What else?"

"The handmaiden has black ink on her left wrist."

Bastian's eyes narrowed as he turned to look at the wagon. "Get some rest," he told Ax.

"Aye."

Bastian watched Ax take his place on the wagon and then turned his attention to the land in front of him, his mind racing with questions. Questions he couldn't ask the newcomers, not yet, but when they reached the Golden City…well, that would be a different story.

CHAPTER 13

The next few days, the group travelled with few issues. Fylip's leg proved to be more challenging than Ax had predicted, and it slowed them down slightly as he attended to it. The wound required a more thorough cleaning, and since the toxin had been successfully cleared, the numbness had worn off and Fylip was in a great deal of pain. Each time Ax needed to treat him, he insisted the wagon stop, and with the unexpected interruptions, Bastian was grudging the lost time.

Beth gave Ax assistance each time, and Bastian wasn't the only one to notice that Fylip became more comfortable and in less pain when she was near. Having known the man for a long time, Bastian knew his character, and he wasn't the type of man to play up for female attention.

Bastian also paid more attention to the handmaiden, for the reasons of the black ink, or that was what he kept telling himself anyway. The black ink was a delicate art, a painful one at that. Small hollow needles holding black ink pierced the skin, marking it permanently. Bastian was no stranger to the art of marking, and he had fought alongside many men who displayed the markings on their skin. The people of the Plains were more akin to using it on themselves, although he had observed none on Kase. Was that why she had it? Because she was closer to the Tzenythian than they were alluding to?

Or was it for a more holy matter? The shift to the worship of the new Gods was still too *new* for some, but it didn't detract from the fact that the new Gods and their faithful flock marked their skin in holy reverence. Bastian still hadn't understood the why or the how of it or how it mattered to their faith, because many of the new sects were very secretive of their devoutness.

With the Age of Redemption almost over, people were looking for new Gods to worship, ones who hadn't, in their eyes, failed them. With the old Gods, there was wonder, faith and magic. Magic had created a lot of the reconstruction of the buildings from the time before, but it wasn't infallible. Nothing was. More and more, the magic that was called from the old Gods failed, the power dwindled, and from the south, there came whisperings of new Gods gifting miracles, healing…the sceptical would even say…magic?

But their believers were quick to cast aside the claims of magic, or witchcraft as they called it. The powers of the new Gods weren't a parlour trick, they were *gifts* from the new Gods, and the power was only available to the devout. The believers. The faithful.

Bastian had witnessed the more zealous disciples of the new Gods, and they left a bad taste in his mouth. Eyeing the handmaiden as she spoke quietly to Kase in the wagon, he wondered at her. She didn't seem overly passionate, well, not about religion anyway. She was very…excitable about some other matters.

Watching her accept some of Kase's food, Bastian considered the fact that she ate meat. Rumour had it that the newer devout worshipers shunned meat completely. Bastian recalled the efficiency with which Beth had cleaned the flesh from the rabbit leg she had for supper last night. She was definitely not shunning meat, which was underlined by the fact she was happily chewing on the dried beef her companion had just handed her.

"You stare at her much longer, my friend, and she will be thinking you want a courtship," Khaldan said to Bastian with his head turned away, as if they were discussing the route to take.

"I'm not—" Bastian caught Khaldan's smirk and stopped from defending himself. He *had* been staring, and he'd been caught. Thankfully not by her, because that would have been hard to explain. Bastian turned his body slightly, not deliberately blocking Beth from view, but enough so she wasn't in his direct line of sight. "I keep waiting for them to slip up, make an error," he told Khaldan quietly.

"I keep waiting for them to slit our throats in our sleep," Khaldan grumbled as he scanned the horizon. Bastian let out a low chuckle at his friend's negativity. "But they haven't, and we're what, five days from Pavolyn?"

Bastian turned fully to look at the landscape in front of them. The town of Werzka was only a day's walk in front of them, and then once they entered and manoeuvred through the small town, they would hit the next bigger town and then the next, and within days they'd be at the gates of the Golden City.

"They'll leave before we reach the gates of the Golden City," Bastian mused.

Khaldan looked at him in surprise. "What makes you think that?"

Scratching his jaw, Bastian thought about it. "It's what I would do." Glancing at Khaldan, he gave a half shrug. "It's what you would do too."

Khaldan went to protest and then thought about it.

"Aye, probably." They both looked westward for a few more moments in silence. "We let them go?" he asked questioningly.

"We earned that coin," Bastian said bitterly, but still he hesitated. "He's pulled his weight when it counted."

"They're also the reason his weight needed to be pulled," Khaldan reminded him.

Which was true, and Bastian didn't appreciate the reminder. "Still, he has helped."

Khaldan snorted. "Just *him*?"

"Aye, just him," Bastian growled as he turned and headed back to the wagon. It made no sense. Khaldan was right—they were *owed* their pay from adding the three of them to their party. They had caused more trouble than they were due, zyvarg packs, extra rooms at inns, irritating *questions*…losing Bez. Bastian glared at the wagon as he passed, his eyes inevitably being drawn to *her.* As usual, she was watching him. With a reprimand to himself, he jerked the reins of the horse, encouraging it to walk. "Move out," he barked at his men.

Ignoring his men's mutters and feeling her stare heavy on his back, Bastian forced himself to think of the bigger picture. Five more days, less if he guessed correctly about their intent, and then they would be free of this charge. He really hoped he guessed correctly, because he was eager for them to be gone.

Werzka was moderate in size, in truth an overspill from the next town over, Wrazyth, and it had been said that the town of Werzka arose from the displacement of a jilted lover, who was shunned from their village and cast out, but not cast far.

Werzka was on slightly flatter land. The nearby woods meant carting supplies was easier with timber on hand to make wagons, and it also, strategically, slowed anyone down who had survived the journey through the Sand Seas, which Bastian suspected was the main reason the town had sprung up. Only the desperate went through the Sand Seas, and the first populated place, so close to the capital, was the best place to check what made those people desperate.

"Will we be stopping in the town?" Kase asked as he joined him up front.

Looking over at the tall plainsman, Bastian considered him. Slightly shorter than Bastian, Kase had a heavier bulk to his shoulders and biceps, which Bastian had noticed restricted his sword arm slightly. Bulky men and the art of mastering the sword did not always go hand in hand.

"You choose the sword," Bastian commented to Kase as he looked at his weapons belt. "Two daggers on your belt, one in your boot."

Kase looked at Bastian's own array of weapons he was carrying. "Your point?"

"I've met and fought with a fair number of the Prairie men before, and the axe is usually a preference over sword."

Kase's snort was not complimentary. "Stereotyping? You?"

Bastian thought about it and noted with some surprise that Kase was right. "You're right, that's like me saying every man from Kalzynia is a hard-faced brute with no sense of humour."

Kase gave Bastian a sideways glance as they walked. "Aren't you Kalzynian?"

"Yep."

Despite himself, Kase grinned widely, and the two walked in companionable silence, the voices of the others in their party low murmurs in the background.

"So, do we?" Kase asked eventually.

"Hmm?" Bastian was pulled out of his thoughts. "No, we carry through to the next town. More inns and a better choice of comfort for your lady."

"Agreed."

Bastian met his look with one of his own. "I wasn't aware it was up for discussion."

"Your sense of awareness is not my problem," Kase told him and then turned on his heel to inform his lady of the planned stop, leaving Bastian standing with a small spark of appreciation for the wit of the Tzenythian.

Wrazyth left little to be desired in Bastian's opinion. It was a large enough town to have a clear hierarchy of those who were wealthy and those who were not. The town had a large wooden fence around it, which was more symbolic than effective. There were two gates into the town, and as he always did, Bastian took the one further from the more established houses and merchants, and selected to enter the poorer part of the town.

His men were all out of the wagon, bar Fylip. Kase was walking beside the horse, with the women both seated up front.

The people of the town barely glanced at them as they looked like any travelling party. The men had their travelling cloaks around them, covering their weapons. Bastian and some others had their hoods up. Nothing suspicious, as a light rain had fallen earlier. As they made their way through the town, Bastian gave the signal to Xan. Xan, who had been waiting for it, slowed down, lingering at a food stall, and then slipped away without the others breaking stride. He was so efficient at blending into the crowd Kase never noticed he was gone.

Before the next turn onto a busier street, Khaldan also broke off, melting into the bustle of the townsfolk. Bastian noticed Kase drop back from the horse to address his lady. Catching Ax's eye, Bastian gave a slight nod. Smoothly Ax dropped back, and with ease he reached up and swung himself into the wagon beside Fylip.

Bastian slowed his steps, allowing the wagon to reach him, and Kase took the opportunity to join him. "What's going on?" Kase asked, keeping his voice low.

"Scouting." Bastian kept his attention in front of him.

"For?"

"Fun."

Kase glared at the man beside him. "Is this the time for jest?"

"When is it not?" Bastian countered.

"I don't like it."

"You don't like fun?" Bastian pretended to think about it. "I'm not surprised."

Kase went to speak, but a small cough from the wagon stopped him. Turning, he saw Beth looking back at him, a warning in her look. Biting his tongue, Kase turned away.

Bastian watched the exchange and saw Ax hadn't missed it either. Sitting low in the wagon, Ax pulled his hood slightly lower as they travelled through the town. Bastian took them to an inn he had frequented before. It was clean, reasonably priced, and offered decent fare.

A stable hand lounged against a post that led to the stable area, and as the wagon approached, he straightened, his hand already rising to catch the harness to slow the horse's progression.

"Need unhitching?" he asked Bastian as the boy patted the horse's withers.

"Yes, a good check on him too," Bastian instructed.

"Aye, milord."

Kase had helped both women from the seat, and they clustered together as Ax slipped off the wagon. "Need a hand here," Ax called to him as he pointed at Fylip. The plainsman hesitated as he looked to Bastian, who was steadfastly ignoring him as he walked to the entrance of the inn.

As Bastian walked into the inn, he knew the two women were at his back, and turning to them, he addressed them quietly. "Let's keep this low-key, no titles here," he instructed them quickly. "Your coin doesn't stretch that far."

Beth's eyes narrowed at the dig, but she wisely stayed quiet.

"How many rooms?" the young man asked as he kept his attention on the book he was reading. "One?"

"Four if you have," Bastian's voice was as curt as the man's was disinterested.

With a sigh, the man looked up and then put his book to the side and looked at the ledger beside him. "Can give you two with two beds, one with one."

"Or you can give me three with two, and I'll take two folk for the hayloft."

The attendant looked down at the ledger at the mention

of the hayloft, and Bastian pulled his hood back slightly. "Oh, I didn't realise it was you," the man said with a little more friendliness when he looked at them again before he looked back at his ledger and turned it for Bastian to look. "I have what we have," he added apologetically.

"What's on?" Bastian asked as he looked to the common room, which was empty, and back to the man.

"Some festival about the moon and"—he paused, thinking—"lilies?"

"Jasmine," Beth spoke up quietly behind them. "It's a festival for the flowers that bloom at night."

Bastian turned to look at her in question, and Beth lowered her eyes to the ground, avoiding Bastian's stare.

"You're almost full for a new Gods festival for flowers?" he asked, turning back to the man in front of him.

"It took us by surprise as well," the man laughed. "The rooms we have left are neat," he confided. "You'll sleep five. How many travel with you?"

"There are eight of us," Bastian told him as he chewed his inner cheek, thinking. "Give me what you have. The hayloft should hold three unless it's full as well?"

The man shook his head, confirming it wasn't, and soon he was leading the three of them to the back of the inn. "One down here, the other two above," he told them as he opened the door to a small, compact room with two narrow beds situated close together.

"Tell me the two rooms are together?" Bastian asked as he stepped back.

"Of course." Leading them up a wooden stairs, he showed them the other two rooms. The double room was slightly larger, but the single was no more than a large cupboard.

"It'll do," Beth said, walking into the room past both of the men. "Tyria and I will be comfortable, and Kase will be just next door." She looked to Bastian as she finished talking, the challenge in her eyes clear, waiting for him to correct her and tell her that Kase would sleep elsewhere.

"Excellent," Bastian said with a smile, pleased when she lost her smug look at thinking she had outsmarted him. Leaving the room, he made his way down the stairs, and seeing Ax and Kase with Fylip between them, he directed Ax to the smaller twin room. As soon as Kase was free of Fylip, he left them, searching for his charges.

"You look pleased with yourself," Ax commented dryly.

"Do I?" Bastian helped lower Fylip onto the bed.

"She didn't realise she's trapped above us yet?" Ax realised as he looked upwards.

"Don't believe so," Bastian said evenly, keeping his face straight. "Thinks she's clever," he added as he straightened.

The rooms above were accessed only from the stairs that were right beside the door to the room Fylip and Ax would be in. The door to the back of the inn was next to their room and led straight into the stables, with the hayloft above them. There would be no slipping out in the night for Beth or her companions, not without Bastian or his men knowing.

When they heard the thump above them, which sounded suspiciously like a foot stamping in temper, followed by a slamming door, Bastian started to laugh.

CHAPTER 14

DINNER THAT NIGHT IN THE INN WAS TENSE. BETH'S attention was fixated on her plate, Kase was scowling, and Tyria was so nervous she had an irritating twitch in her eye. Bastian on the other hand was outwardly relaxed, which only seemed to irritate Kase more.

Ax was speaking to the occupants of the neighbouring table. They had travelled to Wrazyth solely for the Festival of Moon and Blooms. Bastian was half listening to the conversation as he ate his meal, Khaldan beside him. The other man had joined them a short while after Beth realised her folly, or more accurately, once Kase had explained her folly to her. He had also received an accusatory glare as she joined them for their evening meal, but Khaldan had merely greeted her pleasantly as he always did.

"I don't even know which other flower, apart from jasmine, that flowers at night," Ax said conversationally.

"Nightflower," the older man at the table beside them told him.

"I thought that was jasmine," Ax said as he scratched his beard thoughtfully.

"No, nightflower is rare," he told Ax easily, but Kase's snort drew the man's attention. "You got something to add to the conversation?" he challenged.

Kase looked down at his half-eaten meal of beef and vegetables and back to the man across from him. "I'm merely eating my meal."

The man's glare lasted a moment longer before he resumed talking to Ax.

"Careful, plainsman," Bastian cautioned. "We do not need unnecessary attention."

"Why?" Beth asked as she pushed her potatoes around her plate. "You think you go unnoticed? Trust me, you don't." Raising her head, she looked between the three of them. "Where's Xan?"

"Not here," Bastian answered amicably. Reaching over, he picked up the pitcher of ale in the middle of the table and topped up both his and Khaldan's cup. "More?" he asked Kase, who nodded and held his cup out for a refill. Both the women were on water, but Bastian had noticed that Tyria followed the pitcher with perhaps slightly more attention than she realised. "Would you like some, Tyria? Perhaps some wine?" Bastian's voice was pleasant, and he wasn't surprised to hear another huff of displeasure from the man across from him.

"She doesn't want wine," Kase answered for his lady. Bastian was going to argue the point because it was clear that Tyria would gladly accept some wine, but he wisely kept his mouth shut and his opinion to himself.

As the table reverted to silence once more, there was no other choice but to listen to Ax asking about the festival. The more the stranger spoke about it, the more irritated Beth seemed to get.

"Your thoughts are very loud," Khaldan told her as he swept up the last of the gravy on his plate with a hunk of bread.

"Excuse me?" Beth asked him in surprise.

"You don't need to agree with our neighbour," Khaldan

told her easily. "But if you could keep your disagreement from your face, we'd appreciate it."

Turning her head, she looked to Kase for support, but Kase simply shrugged. "I'm not allowed an opinion?" Beth challenged Khaldan.

"Course you are," Bastian scoffed. "I'd just rather your opinion wasn't aimed at an officer of the Town Watch."

Bastian watched as the handmaiden and the plainsman both looked at the stranger again. She didn't see it, but Bastian watched as Kase registered what he and Khaldan already knew. The shorter cut hair, the short sword and dagger on his hip, the plain clothes, the boots that were good quality but worn, and the telltale baton at his side, which he had tried to conceal with his tunic, which was beside him.

"They do this sometimes when there are too many travellers within their walls," Khaldan explained. "They take off their outer tunics, and they sit in taverns and inns and converse with the new faces, see why they're here."

"And right now, *we* look suspicious," Bastian broke in. "So perhaps we could pretend to look less like enemies and more like a group of friends enjoying our supper?" He wasn't expecting much, but he was slightly frustrated at Kase's grunt and Beth's shrug.

"So, Tyria," Bastian started. "How was your meal?"

The red-haired woman looked at him in alarm, and he wasn't sure what had garnered that reaction from her. "Um, good. Slightly salty."

"I agree." Khaldan wiped his mouth with the linen cloth that had been by his plate. "More seasoning was needed," he said. "What would you have added?" he asked. "I think more herbs. Thyme, maybe?"

Tyria was nodding. "Basil," she answered, and when he nodded, she smiled and seemed to relax more. "And perhaps some rosemary—brings the flavour of the beef out more." Tyria dipped her finger in the remaining gravy on her plate, tasting the gravy again. She wrinkled her nose as she thought about it. "A dash of red wine would have helped."

Khaldan was nodding as he drank his ale. "Yes," he told her as he placed his cup down. "Adds a richness."

"It does." Tyria beamed at him, and Bastian realised that was the most he had ever heard her speak, at least when he was present.

Ax turned back to the table as the man he was talking to said goodnight and left the inn.

"Are we good?" Bastian asked behind his cup as he watched the watchman leave.

"Might need to split up," Ax said with an easy smile as he reached for the pitcher of ale, his words in contrast to his outward appearance. "He was already suspicious. The seating arrangements could have been better," Ax admonished them. "May as well have drawn a line down the table."

Bastian grunted in agreement. "True, we should have mixed it up."

"I don't understand," Beth said as she looked over her shoulder to the door where the man had exited.

"Attention on us," Khaldan reprimanded her, making her head whip around in guilt. "We're sitting as a group, but with you both together and us over here, it's clear you are not our women."

"*Your* women?" Beth's tone was incredulous.

"You travel with six men. There are two of you," Bastian told her bluntly. "He probably thinks you are whores." At his declaration, Tyria spat her water out in shock at his terminology, and Ax grunted in surprise as he got a face full of water. Ignoring them, Bastian continued. "We should have made it clear that at least one of you was married," Bastian muttered as he looked between the three of them.

"I can't marry my lady!" Kase looked outraged at the very idea.

"We weren't sending you to the friars," Khaldan snipped. "Pretending to be married is better than the alternative, or would you rather she was thought a whore?" Khaldan asked lightly, causing the other man to scowl at him.

"Well," Beth spoke up, her hand resting lightly on Kase's arm, no doubt to stop him from snapping at Khaldan. "What's done is done."

"Indeed," Bastian murmured.

Kase looked down at her hand on his arm and then up at her before he nodded. "Maybe an early night for you both, away from the prying eyes, would be best."

Bastian was sure she would argue, but she gave a small nod instead. Standing, he clapped Khaldan on the shoulder. "You be okay here?"

"Where are you going?" Kase demanded as he watched him prepare to leave.

"For a walk," Bastian replied as he picked up his travelling cloak. "You're in with Fylip?" he asked Ax.

"Of course." Ax saluted him with his cup as he ate the last of his meal.

"Where are you walking to?" Beth asked him.

"I heard there was a festival," Bastian said mildly as he fastened his cloak. "I like festivals," he added blandly.

"I'll come." Beth was on her feet before Kase had registered her words and could protest.

"I don't think that's a good idea, do you?" Bastian asked, somewhat surprised at her boldness.

"If that man's watching, what better way to throw suspicion off of us?" Beth was ready for an argument, and Bastian knew it. "You said it yourself, we're either men with their wives or we're…" She licked her lips in discomfort. "You know. And I don't think it's *walking* that men do with those women."

Bastian was going to argue it was too late to pretend anything else, but the fury in Kase's glare was enough to have him agreeing to the proposal. "Fair enough," Bastian conceded, "but it *is* perhaps too late," he warned her.

Beth rolled her eyes as she smoothed her blue travelling dress over her hips and turned to collect her cloak. "Well, it won't hurt to try." When she had her cloak on, she looked to him in expectation. "Well? Are we going or not?"

Khaldan tried to cover his snort of laughter with a cough, but he earned a glare from Bastian anyway as he and the handmaiden walked away from them.

"Have fun," Ax called jovially, completely ignoring Kase's murderous glare. "Don't be out too late."

It was Bastian's turn to shoot him a look as he and the handmaiden left the inn. The two of them walked at a steady pace, and having been to Wrazyth before, Bastian was very familiar with the layout of the town and knew his way to the town centre. With Wrazyth being a town in the kingdom of Kestornia, gold was a predominant colour of the town. Bastian heard the sound of revelry as they approached the centre of the town, and conscious of the number of people gathering, he pulled his hood up, placing it over half of his head.

Beth already had hers up, like his, sitting comfortably enough away from her face so she could still look around.

"I think you need to take my arm," she said to him in a low voice. "If we are to be convincing, I believe the menfolk give their lady wives their arm."

Bastian was about to ask her what she knew about menfolk, but instead, he offered her his right arm, and she slipped hers through his, her hand resting on his forearm. Bastian looked at her hand on his arm, noting the long slender fingers, the thinness of her wrist covered by the linen she was using to hide her markings.

"My hand irks you, husband?" Beth asked him casually as they moved amongst the townsfolk.

"No," Bastian answered gruffly as he looked over the town centre. Beth made a noncommittal noise, but it was clear she didn't believe him, and Bastian opted to remain silent.

The market stalls that usually housed vegetables, meat, cloth and the like had been replaced with stalls of flowers and baskets of bulbs, while garlands of greenery hung all around a large wooden frame. The market square was dimly lit, and in the centre of the market square was a large square. Inside it were hundreds of baskets filled with plants.

Beth slowed to a stop as she gazed at it. Lifting her

head, she saw the steps and the ladders that had been positioned around the square, with small wooden platforms above them. Glancing at the sky, she let go of Bastian's arm and clasped his hand instead. Pulling him forward, she hurried to a ladder. Seeming to change her mind halfway through, she looked between the square and the sky once more. Changing direction, she tugged Bastian forward, stopping at a ladder leading to one of the smaller platforms.

"We go up," she told him as she started to climb. "These are viewing platforms," she told him over her shoulder as she made her way up.

With no choice but to follow her, Bastian climbed behind her. As she went to pull herself onto the platform, Bastian's hands on her waist stilled her. "Easy there," he told her as she looked back at him. "You should have let me go first," he chided. "I would have helped you up."

Beth rolled her eyes at him as she moved a step higher. "I've climbed far more dangerous a thing than this," she told him as she grasped the long posts on either side, effectively pulling herself up the short distance and onto the wooden platform. Bastian was swiftly behind her, and the two of them shared a look of alarm when the wood beneath them creaked loudly.

"Mayhap someone didn't need that second helping of bread with supper," Beth said as she averted her face from Bastian, pretending to smooth her cloak. She heard his huff of laughter, and pleased she had finally gotten the stoic warrior to laugh, Beth pulled her fallen hood over her hair again.

Bastian looked upward to the edge of the cloud that

covered the silver of the moon, and then down to the area of the market mapped out.

"You've been to a Festival of Moon and Blooms before?" Beth asked him, and when he nodded, she looked him over quickly. "You don't seem the type," she confessed, "to look at flowers," she explained when she saw his jaw clench.

"I move around a lot," Bastian told her as he watched the people below. More were taking to the ladders and the platforms. "You picked a good one," he complimented her.

"Praise?" Beth placed her hand on her chest and dropped her mouth open. "I may be speechless," she teased.

"But yet, you can still speak," Bastian joked back. "Our viewing area only holds two," he clarified.

Beth's peal of laughter caused several below them to look up. "The platforms are roughly the same in size and shape, it's just that you are so…big." Her smile faded as she considered the hard mercenary in front of her, struggling to find the word to adequately describe him.

"Big?" Bastian looked her way with amusement. "Isn't everyone big to you?" He gestured to the fact she hardly reached his shoulder.

"Funny," she answered, her tone dry. "No, *big* isn't right…imposing," Beth corrected as she turned to face him, thinking of her word choice. "And big," she reiterated with a smirk.

Bastian was going to ask her why she chose *imposing* when she looked upwards, her eyes on the moon. Then, turning to look down, she breathed a small gasp as the flowers burst into bloom, the sound drowned out by the noise of the crowd.

Having seen the sight many times before, Bastian needed his focus to be more on the woman in front of him and the mystery that she presented, rather than the flowers that bloomed at night, but as he glanced down, his attention was snagged on the design the baskets had been laid out in.

The larger blooms were laid out creating a curved design. Bastian moved forward. Within the design, there were three clear lines with no baskets in it. He heard the murmurs getting louder from the platforms around them.

"Beth," he said as he turned to look at her, to tell her they needed to leave, but the words stuck in his throat as he looked at the young woman beside him.

Beth felt like she was frozen as she took in the splendour of the design. Large blooms of jasmine fragranced the night air, with the small purple nightflower spread amongst it, and in between it all was the blackthorn lily, a rare poisonous flower that was rumoured to be only found at the edge of the Barrens. But it wasn't the flowers that held Beth's rapt attention. It was the design.

"Handmaiden," Bastian spoke quietly beside her. "We need to leave," he told her.

"It's a teardrop," Beth told him as she took it in.

"I know what it is." His voice was grim. "And it's much more than a teardrop."

Beth looked away from the bold display and met steely blue eyes. "Yes," she breathed. "It is. It's a *sign*."

Bastian considered her, as she looked at him, green eyes wide with excitement and a flush to her cheeks. "It's a sign we need to move," Bastian told her gruffly. "Not everyone is as enraptured as you with what that represents."

At his tone, his closed expression, Beth pulled her attention away from him and looked around. Some of the towns-people looked delighted, but most of them looked shocked, and more, she noticed, looked angry.

"Blasphemy!" someone shouted, and Beth whirled around to see a torch fall into the design.

"No!" she protested, but her voice was drowned out as the crowd reacted. Bastian grabbed her arm and almost dragged her to the ladder. The flowers burned rapidly, and dimly she heard him tell her to move.

"Beth!" Bastian barked. "*Move!*" When she hesitated, she heard him curse, and then he was bending slightly, and she was over his shoulder as he took them both down the ladder.

"Bastian!" Beth suddenly found her voice as she hit his shoulder in protest, but he didn't hold her for long, and she was soon on her feet.

"Walk," he ordered briskly. "We need out of this before the riot starts or the air poisons us."

"If you were worried about my safety, I think a platform out of the crowd was perhaps the best choice," Beth sassed at him as she was practically dragged through swells of people.

"Because the safest place to be in an enclosed fire is a wooden platform." Bastian gave her a scathing look, and Beth bit her tongue. As if to emphasise his point, when Beth turned back to look because she heard screaming, the fire was eating at the ladders to the platforms above.

Soon they were back at the inn, and Beth was not surprised to see his men waiting for him. Kase was standing slightly apart with Tyria cowered close to him.

"We leaving?" Ax asked. He almost sounded casual, and

Beth marvelled at his ease at the sky lit up with the flames from the fire.

"The town is burning," she snapped at him.

"Good point," he said with an easy grin. "Definitely time to leave."

CHAPTER 15

Beth gaped at Ax and was only brought out of her stunned speechless inaction when she realised that no one else was disagreeing with him. "We need to help," she said as she looked at the men in front of her.

"*We* need to leave," Ax told her with his normal quick easy smile, like they were discussing the weather.

"The town is *burning*," she told them again as she watched Xan shoulder his pack and head to the stables. "We cannot leave," she hissed at Bastian, capturing his arm as he took his pack from Khaldan.

Bastian looked down at her hand and then up at the handmaiden, his look questioning. "What's the problem?" he asked as he shook his hand free.

"The problem is that the town is on fire, and you and your men seem to be leaving it to burn!"

"We're not responsible for the town burning," Khaldan told her as he fixed his travelling cloak, pulling his hood up to cover his dark hair.

Beth watched them, feeling like she was missing something, something important, but all she could focus on was the horror that these capable men would leave. "We could *help*," she told them as her attention landed on Bastian.

"The town has a Watch that is taking action as we speak," Bastian told her tersely. Looking over his shoulder, he could see people running to the town centre as just as many ran from it.

"Who would willingly walk away from people who

needed help?" Beth asked them in wonder, seeing Xan leading the horse from the stables, the wagon already hitched. "What kind of men are you?" she asked, her voice barely a whisper.

"Mercenaries," Bastian answered sharply. "We good?" he asked the others, and Beth turned to Kase for support.

However, her trusted companion merely shook his head, telling her not to push it. Taking her arm gently, he led her to the wagon, and with a heavy sigh, Beth got into it, taking the far corner, wrapping herself in her cloak. Avoiding looking at anyone else, she closed her eyes. The familiar presence of Tyria settling beside her gave her comfort. The wagon rocked gently as more got in, and she didn't try to hide her snort at the fact that they were all riding out of the town, a town she could help.

But he had told her, they were naught but mercenaries. Sellswords. Men for hire.

Her eyes snapped open. She felt slightly guilty at seeing everyone around the wagon and not in it like she had suspected, because they had made sure Fylip was laid out, as he was still recovering from his wounds.

"If you were to be paid, would you stay?" she demanded.

"Let it go, handmaiden." Xan was walking nearest to her side of the wagon. Twisting around from where she sat, she looked to see who was driving the wagon, seeing Khaldan with Kase beside him. Ax and Xan were on either side, and leaning over the side, she knew who would be in front. Sure enough, the tall dark figure who walked beside the horse was him. Bastian.

"Why won't you help?" she asked Xan, settling back to her seat. "Can't you hear the screaming?"

"I can," Xan told her, his voice tight.

"Is it truly all about being paid? I could—"

Tyria elbowed her sharply in the ribs, cutting her off.

"You could what?" Xan asked her. "Pay?"

Knowing what she was revealing, Beth ignored the warning voice in her head and the slight ache in her side from Tyria's sharp elbow. "If I could pay, would you change course?" she asked the man who walked beside her.

"You haven't paid us yet for the first hire," Khaldan said from the front, and she realised that Kase had turned towards her, the warning in his eyes clear. "Keep your coin, handmaiden, for the debts that you *already* owe."

Tyria jabbed her side again when she went to argue, and with Kase's angry stare boring holes in the side of her head, Beth gave up. Pulling her hood up, she slouched lower in the wagon. Hearing rustling, she knew Kase had turned to face forward.

"Where's your man?" Kase asked Khaldan, suspicion lacing his tone. Beth sat up straighter, leaning back to see the front of the wagon. Xan's huff of amusement had her settling back in embarrassment.

"Ahead," Khaldan answered, his tone light and unconcerned.

"I can't see him." Kase peered ahead.

"Okay." Khaldan shook the reins slightly to encourage the horse to go faster.

"Why are we going faster?" Kase demanded, his hand already slipping to his sword.

"Because blackthorn lily is poisonous," Ax told him dryly. "And it's currently burning in the town centre, which means it is in the air, and if we don't get away from it, we're going to have more problems than where Bastian is and what speed we're travelling at."

The blond warrior met Beth's stare as she realised why they were refusing to help. It wasn't because they were mercenaries or men with no hearts, it was because to stay meant harmful consequences, maybe even death. She dipped her head in acknowledgment of his reprimand, and Ax gave her a wink and a smile, which made her feel better, but she knew had it been anyone other than Ax, she wouldn't have received such a light rebuke.

"We should go faster," Kase urged Khaldan as he looked to the night sky worriedly.

"Should we?" Khaldan rolled his eyes at the fickleness of the warrior beside him.

"We're still getting to know one another." Kase surprised him with the admission. "It takes time to build trust."

Looking to the Tzenythian beside him, Khaldan studied the man, whose face was averted to avoid eye contact as he accepted his error in judgement. "We are," Khaldan agreed. "And trust is *earned*; time has nothing to do with it."

Kase went to argue, but there was no point because he actually agreed with him. He had known men his whole life and trusted none of them, and he had known these men a handful of weeks and trusted them more than he was willing to admit.

As they drove the wagon through the town, the streets became busier as people either raced to the centre to help or, like the men knew, ran to avoid the poisonous air. As more and more people joined them on the streets, the wagon slowed and Ax and Xan dropped back to the rear of the wagon, guarding them from unwanted passengers.

"How long do they have before it fades from the air?" Tyria asked Beth as she huddled close, covering her mouth and nose.

"They need a good rain," Fylip said from where he lay. "It'll still hang around, but it will stop it from spreading." The injured man grunted as he pulled himself into a sitting position. "Contain it."

"Rain?" Beth asked him sharply, looking upwards to the cloudless sky.

"It would help with the spread of the fire too," Fylip added. "Water always beats fire." Looking to the sky himself, Fylip didn't see the small smile that the handmaiden gave to her companion.

With an increasing urgency, Khaldan knew he needed to move this wagon faster through the throngs of people. "Ax! Xan!" he called loudly. The wagon lurched behind him, and he knew his companions had jumped on. "Everyone hold on," Khaldan warned and then cracked the reins. The horse leapt forward and kept his steady pace, irrespective of the people in front, and when it started to slow, Kase surprised them all by jumping onto the horse's back, and bending low, he whispered in its ear.

Khaldan dropped his hold on the reins as the plainsman sat back and took them for himself, their departure now in his hands. With confidence and skill, Kase manoeuvred the horse and wagon out of the town of Wrazyth.

As they reached the town's gate, a shadow detached from the darkness, and Bastian ran up to the wagon and jumped. Khaldan grabbed his arm and pulled him onto the wagon without it slowing, steadying him as he took the empty seat.

"Left it a little late," Khaldan grouched as they both settled.

"Nonsense, I timed it perfectly," Bastian told him as he settled his cloak around him, his attention on Kase, who was looking at them both. "Eyes to the front, plainsman; we're not in open Prairie now."

Kase's eyes narrowed as he glared at the gruff leader of the men, but he was right, he was still needed to steer the horse. "Which way?" Kase asked as he faced forward.

"Southwest," Bastian told him, feeling the stare from his friend beside him. "Problem?" he asked Khaldan quietly.

Khaldan shook his head as he looked forward. "Nope, no problem, not from me."

Bastian said nothing and let it rest. He knew his companion would say plenty later when the men were alone.

Kase led them away from the burning town of Wrazyth as the others looked back on the town, the night sky illuminated in orange as the flames licked higher.

"Would you look at that." Fylip broke the silence as they travelled deeper into the night.

"What is it?" Bastian turned in his seat to look behind him.

"Rain," Fylip answered.

Bastian grunted and turned back in his seat,

dismounting from the wagon to stretch his legs. "You've seen rain before." He would have said more, but Kase was turned around in his seat, his face twisted in an angry scowl, which to be fair, it wasn't unusual for him, Bastian mused. But Kase wasn't looking back at the town, he was looking at the handmaiden and the lady. Both of them had their heads down and looked to be almost avoiding the eye of the plainsman.

What was going on there? Bastian wondered, not for the first time. Too many secrets. He hated secrets.

On Bastian's instructions, they travelled past the next town, keeping to the outskirts, far enough away to avoid suspicion.

"Why do we travel so far from the towns?" Beth finally asked on the third day. "Instead of this blasted wagon, we could be in an inn with a bed and food."

"With coffee," Tyria grumbled beside her.

"Ah, I forgot you had a hidden purse full of coins," Bastian replied as he walked alongside the wagon, his cloak hiding his features from her.

Beth glared at Xan, who merely grinned back at her from his spot beside Fylip. Kase had resumed his seat in front, and Khaldan had jumped down a few miles back, as he and Ax had gone to hunt for supper.

"It's not that full," Beth protested.

"And it will be less full when you hand over payment for our services," Bastian countered.

"We're not in the Golden City yet," Kase growled from his seat.

"And nor will we be any time soon if we keep taking the long way around," Beth added in exasperation.

"They say patience is a virtue," Bastian commented as he walked beside them, his eyes watching the horizon. Xan and Fylip both chuckled, and Bastian fought his own smile, knowing why his men would laugh at his hypocrisy.

"*You* lecture me on patience?" Beth asked incredulously. "You are the least patient man I have ever met."

"Really?" Bastian pushed his hood back slightly to look at her. "That can't be right."

She knew better than to ask, she did; her inner voice was screaming at her to say nothing. "Why not?"

"You travel with Kase," Bastian told her honestly. Ignoring her building frustration and the grunt of displeasure from the front of the wagon, he added, "And I can't be the only man who's lost his sense of serenity in your company."

"You!" Beth snapped at him, and a small cough from Tyria made her bite back her temper. "You're…*not* a nice man," Beth added sullenly.

"Never claimed to be," Bastian told her as he pulled his hood back over his head, settling it low, covering his eyes as he turned from her with a small smirk.

As they had skirted the towns, which were becoming closer and closer, Bastian had kept a watchful eye on the landscape.

"The monastery is close," Xan commented, breaking the silence that had covered them for a while.

"Aye," Bastian grunted, turning to look south.

"A roof may be welcome," Fylip added as he pointed upward. "That doesn't look friendly."

Glancing up, Bastian took in the deep grey clouds and considered his options.

"What's the monastery?" Kase asked as he looked up at the sky too.

"Clue's in the title," Bastian quipped.

"Are there still friars?" Tyria asked smoothly, cutting off any retort from the men. She was tired of the peacocking and just wanted to be warm and in a bed with a roof over her head.

"It's abandoned," Fylip informed her. "The friars and the devout got an upgrade," he told her.

"An upgrade?" Beth asked curiously. "I don't understand."

"Well, the ones who protested too loudly at the new Gods got sent along to meet their old Gods." Bastian felt the familiar anger in the pit of his stomach at the brutality of what had happened within the sacred walls by the so-called *devout*.

"They killed them?" Kase asked. "Where is this place?"

Bastian pointed to the hill to the west. "Behind there. It's set in a small valley."

"Is it safe?" Kase asked.

"Is anywhere?" Xan turned to look at Bastian. "Night's coming, they're not back yet, and the valley keeps our fire unseen."

"How will Khaldan and Ax know how to find us," Tyria asked them, "if we move off this path?"

"They'll find us," Bastian told her as he looked at the sky again. "It's only water," he spoke to Fylip. The large crack of thunder that sounded caused Tyria to jump in surprise, and even Xan winced. "Fine, we'll seek shelter."

"The roof may have fallen," Xan spoke to no one in particular. "It may not be a solution."

"The whole place should have been toppled," Fylip grumbled.

Bastian hated the place, but he disagreed. The massacre that happened within the walls should never have been forgotten. "That it still stands strengthens their memories even more."

"You knew them?" Kase asked as he directed the horse towards their new destination.

"No, I just protest the slaughter of innocents."

Kase said nothing further, and as they crested the hill, the first fat drops of rain started to fall.

Below them were the ruins of the monastery. A spire, which had once stood true and had risen from the small tower to pierce the skies above, now lay toppled in a heap. Part of the roof still held, but two of the walls had fallen further into disrepair, leaving huge gaps in the structure.

"So, it's not completely watertight," Fylip joked as Kase hurried the horse forward.

Once inside, Kase unhooked the horse from the wagon and began to rub the weary mount down. Xan and Bastian moved the wagon between them to the side of the entrance. It wouldn't stay completely dry, but it proved a barrier against anything that may try to seek shelter too.

The wind was picking up, and as Beth and Tyria helped Fylip walk to the back of the building, they sought areas where the roof still held.

"Do you think it will hold?" Tyria asked Beth quietly over Fylip's head as Fylip lowered himself to the ground with their aid.

"I know nothing about structures," Beth said to her as

she looked upwards to the wooden rafters. "They look sturdy enough."

The men joined them, and once Xan had broken up some discarded wood and furniture, they set about lighting a fire.

"Is it safe?" Kase asked as he looked between them.

"Should be," Xan said as he struggled with his flint.

"*Should* isn't reassuring," Kase muttered.

"It's the best I have," Xan said as he looked up at the tall plainsman.

A cry on the wind caused Bastian to turn his head, looking towards the entrance.

"What is it?" Beth asked him as she stepped closer.

"Khaldan," Bastian told her, his hand gripping the pommel of his sword.

"Why do you reach for your sword?" Her voice was anxious, her worried gaze also on the entrance.

"Because he is not alone." Bastian began to move forward. "Xan, with me."

"What? Wait!" Beth moved forward to follow.

"No," Kase said, catching her arm. "You stay here." Looking down at her, he jerked his head towards Tyria. "Stay, I'll go."

Hurrying after the other two, Kase loosened his sword, catching Xan looking over at him.

"You wish to fight beside us?" Xan asked curiously.

"Better fighting beside you than lying dead from an ambush."

"What a choice," Bastian commented dryly as he drew his sword. "Stay close," he instructed. "Both of you."

"Aye," Xan said grimly. "Let's see what trouble Ax is in now."

Bastian gave a firm nod at Xan's words. "Let's," he agreed.

Moving past the wagon, which was supposed to keep others out and them in, Bastian, Xan and Kase stepped out into the night to face the unknown danger.

CHAPTER 16

"You should sit," Fylip told Beth as she paced in front of him.

"Sit?" She stopped her pacing as she turned to him. "I have been sitting. I've been sitting and waiting for an age."

"And you have not been alone," Fylip reminded her gently. "Nor have you actually sat."

"My lady," Tyria began, but Beth's stern glare cut her off. "Oh!" Tyria looked at Fylip, her eyes wide in panic.

The sergeant grinned at her. "It's just me here," he said with a low laugh.

"You don't seem surprised." Beth smoothed the skirts of her blue travelling dress under her as she sat beside Tyria.

"That you're not her handmaiden?" Fylip asked with amusement. "No."

He watched as Beth and Tyria exchanged a worried look. "Does anyone else…suspect?" Beth asked him.

"Suspect?" Fylip shook his head. "No." The two women breathed a sigh of relief. "We all knew early on," he continued.

Beth flinched at his honesty. "Oh." She stared at her hands. "I thought…" Beth gave a shrug of her shoulders.

"We've seen a lot," Fylip told her gently. "We can read people."

Beth nodded but she still felt slightly foolish. "How long have you known?"

"Me?" Fylip asked her as he looked between the two of

them. Beth nodded again and his face twisted in a grimace as he thought about it. "The second day?"

"Wow." Tilting her head back, she stared up at the empty rafters. "And the others?"

Fylip looked away as he avoided Tyria's stare. "Can't speak for the others," he told them gruffly.

"He knew immediately?" Beth said flatly as she looked over at Fylip, her lips pressed together, forming a thin line. When Fylip didn't answer, she dropped her head into her hands letting out a low groan.

"It wouldn't have been immediately." Fylip tried to console her.

"But soon after," Tyria said as she rubbed her forehead. "Well…that's…" Huffing, she wrapped her arms around herself. "That's disheartening."

"Why has no one said anything?" Beth asked as she stood and resumed her pacing.

Fylip raised his hands as he shrugged. "Guess you must have been lying for a reason."

"That's…" Beth thought about the right word. "Preposterous."

Fylip laughed, long and loud. "I've walked this world a long time. Trust me, you have no idea what's preposterous."

"Have you always been a mercenary?" Tyria asked him, trying to change the subject. She could practically *feel* her lady thinking beside her.

Fylip sniffed and flicked the end of his nose, clearing his throat. "I have," he told them.

"Why?" Tyria asked, genuinely curious. "You seem like a good man."

Fylip looked at her with a puzzled frown. "I am a good

man, well…as good as any," he told her. "My job doesn't take that away from me."

"But fighting for money." Tyria shivered. "It's so…"

"Mercenary?" Fylip finished for her with a grin. "You think soldiers in the service of lords and ladies don't get paid?"

Tyria flushed at his words. "Of course they do, but that's different."

"How?" Fylip challenged.

"Well, they're…" She trailed off as she saw his cynical smile.

"Loyal?" he scoffed. "I've seen more underhanded back-stabbing from a *loyal* soldier than I ever did from a man who sells his swords to fight for right."

"For right?" Beth asked him, pausing in her to and fro across the small area. "Does a man who sells his sword care about such things?"

"We took you with us," Fylip reminded her. "You saying you're the wrong kind of person we should help?" he challenged.

"No." Beth paused. "I, uh, I mean, we're different."

Fylip nodded as he looked to the entrance. "Course you are," he said as he struggled to stand. "You tell yourself that."

"Where are you going?" Tyria asked in alarm, half rising from her seat.

"Entrance. Stay here," he told them as he reached out to grab a discarded piece of furniture. "Wind's picked up, and I can't hear naught else."

"Would they call for us?" Beth asked as she stopped walking and looked at the wagon.

"No," Fylip told her firmly. "Which is why I'm going to look." He looked between the two women. "Stay here."

Tyria and Beth watched him hobble off to the front of their dilapidated shelter.

"I didn't mean to make that mistake, my lady," Tyria spoke quietly to Beth.

"It's fine." Beth shrugged it off. "It's probably for the best. Fylip is right, I don't think we were fooling any of them," she admitted ruefully.

Tyria sat and looked into the flames of the small fire that they had kept burning in the hope of some food. "Do you think they're okay?"

Beth nodded as she rubbed her hands together. "They are skilled warriors."

"I hope so," Tyria sighed softly. "Do you think we'll be in the Golden City soon?"

"We will," Beth assured her. "I think Kase was right."

"Right about what?" Tyria asked curiously as she watched her mistress get to her feet and resume her pacing.

"We need to leave, before we get to the Golden City," she told her with a glance to the entrance. "When Kase comes back, we'll tell him it's time."

"Are you sure?" Tyria asked worriedly. "What if they are watching?"

"We'll give them their gold," Beth told her as she thought over all their options. "Let's prepare to leave," she said as she thought through how they would slip out.

Recognising the look on her mistress's face, Tyria twisted her hands together. "Do we need to slip out if we pay them for their protection?"

Beth inhaled deeply as she thought about it. "Let's be

ready to go," she said instead.

"We've been ready since we met them," Tyria scoffed.

Beth was nodding fervently. "Good," she said as she began to bite her thumbnail. "That's good, Ty, we need to get to the Golden City."

"We will," Tyria assured her as she rose to her feet. "You need to stop overthinking; they mean us no harm." Tyria reached out, her hands resting lightly on the upper arms of her mistress, bringing her pacing to a halt.

"And would they think that if they knew the truth? The reason?"

Tyria's hands dropped. "I would like to think so."

"Thinking and knowing aren't the same." Beth shook her head. "No, we need to go."

Tyria recognised the look on her lady's face and bit back her protests. The men they had travelled with had been nothing but respectful. Yes, the one in charge, Bastian, was harsh sometimes, and he absolutely did not tolerate any of her lady's more…vocal protestations. But apart from that, the men had protected them. Tyria truly hoped they didn't take offence from the way she and her companions were planning on leaving.

***

BASTIAN, KASE AND XAN MOVED THROUGH THE NIGHT making as little noise as possible. The rain was impeding their vision, but for this, it suited their purpose. They didn't need to be running in blind; slow and steady won the race after all.

"Can you see anything?" Kase asked them, wiping his

eyes of the rain that fell heavily around them.

"I see rain," Xan grunted.

"You definitely heard a cry for help?" Kase asked Bastian as they moved forward.

"No."

Kase faltered and almost stumbled. "What? What do you mean *no?*"

"I heard Khaldan," Bastian spoke, his voice barely above a whisper. "That was enough."

Kase saw that Xan was nodding in agreement. "He's in trouble?" Kase asked.

"Something's not right," Xan spoke this time. "Bastian?"

"Go."

Kase looked over his shoulder, and the other man was gone. "Where did he go?"

"Scouting," Bastian answered. "Now, no more talking." He looked around in the downpour. "Who knows who is out here."

Kase kept his sharp reply, that they knew Khaldan was out there, to himself. Silently, he followed the mercenary, the scowl on his face openly displaying his disapproval.

"This way," Bastian murmured as he tracked the mud that surrounded them.

"If you can track in this," Kase grumbled, "you're a better tracker than anyone I've met."

Bastian looked at him over his shoulder and winked. Kase wasn't completely sure what to make of that. Was he telling him that he was a better tracker? Or was he telling him he wasn't? Kase gripped his sword tighter. These men were full of contradictions. They acted like paid swords for hire, but they were loyal. *Too* loyal. And their interactions with each other? Kase hadn't seen a brotherhood like it. Not even on the Prairies.

"Head with me," Bastian ordered quietly. "Now is not the time to have a lapse in concentration."

Kase blanched at being caught with his thoughts wandering, especially by this man. "I'm here."

"Good, stay with me," Bastian told him curtly. "And keep your ears open," he added.

"What am I listening for?"

"A raven's call."

"The bird?" Kase asked in confusion.

"You know any other raven?" Bastian asked him tersely. "Listen for a shrill call. You'll know it."

Kase doubted it but nodded to show he had heard his instruction, even though he understood nothing at all. What he did know was that he and his lady needed to leave these men. They were a day's ride from the Golden City, and the urgency to get there was nipping at their heels.

Already the man beside him had caused him delays with his "approach" to how they progressed to the Golden City. Kase was only beside him now because he didn't trust him, or his men, and he wanted to ensure they weren't bringing any more trouble to his lady.

And now they were creeping about in the night in a rainstorm, looking for his men who he had chosen to leave. How was Kase supposed to hear any sound over this downpour, never mind identify it as a raven? Shaking his head, he glared at the back of the man in front of him. When Bastian stopped suddenly, it took all of Kase's agility not to knock him over as he hastily sidestepped, avoiding a collision. Bastian's body whipped around to the left, and he was completely still. Straining to hear, Kase heard nothing other than the sound of rain hitting dirt.

Dirt that he was standing in, in the middle of a storm.

Bastian moved quickly forward, and Kase saw that he was now armed with a short sword in his left hand. Whatever the man heard, he was prepared to meet it with weapons. Bastian moved forward with such purpose that Kase wasn't sure he remembered he was behind him.

When Xan slipped noiselessly in between them, Kase almost shouted out in alarm, not immediately recognising the man in front of him or, more importantly, expecting him to appear as if from nowhere.

Xan's hand landed on Bastian's shoulder, and he leaned forward, speaking directly into his ear, and Kase couldn't hear what he said. Whatever it was, Bastian took off running. Kase was prepared to run too, but Xan spun to face him. His brown hair was wet, rain ran down his face, his hood lay around his shoulders.

"Go back," Xan instructed Kase.

It took a moment for Kase to process the words, but when he did, he looked at Xan in astonishment, and then over his shoulder to see a dark shape disappear into the tree-line. "No!" Kase argued. He wasn't sure why—he would rather be with his lady and out of the rain—but being told to go back infuriated him.

"Go, it's not safe," Xan told him, leaning closer. "We'll be okay!" He patted Kase's shoulder, and turning, he ran the way Bastian had.

Kase hesitated. He was being given an out. Yet he was running after Xan, despite his own desire to head back, because he was more determined to find out what they were running *to* and why they didn't think he could go with them.

The weeks he had been travelling with these men, Kase was amazed at how fast Xan could run. Bastian was already out of sight and Xan close to disappearing into the treeline. Kase knew he couldn't shout out, in case whatever they were running towards heard them. Throwing caution to the wind, he crashed into the wooded area not long after Xan, yet he couldn't see the other man at all.

The tree canopy stopped some of the rain, but it also provided a screen against the night sky, and within the trees, the wood was black. Kase had never been this far southwest, and the terrain was unknown to him, but a wood was still a wood…wasn't it? He was soon to find out, he thought to himself as he moved around the trees, his sword in hand and a throwing dagger in the other. Of the other two men, there was no sign, and silently he raged that the reason they were out here was because they had split up to start with.

Hearing a shout, Kase froze, straining to hear it again. When it sounded, he turned and headed west, running through the woods with no idea what he was running towards. His foot caught and he stumbled, losing his dagger as he flailed to catch purchase on the nearest tree trunk, and bit back his cry of alarm when the tree caught him.

"Easy," Xan whispered. "You make more noise than a baby troll taking its first steps," he grumbled.

"I thought you were a tree," Kase grumbled sullenly as he straightened. Looking around, he searched the woodland floor. "Dropped my dagger."

"Leave it," Xan urged. "Move," he commanded. "Quietly," he hissed when Kase stepped forward.

Kase couldn't see the other man clearly, but he could feel the glare of reproach. Biting his tongue, he slowly moved forward, and together they moved through the wood. He wanted to ask where Bastian was, and then he heard it again.

The shout of alarm.

A soft chuckle beside him made him look at Xan in question. The other man never looked at him but continued to move amongst the trees like a wraith. Peering into the darkness, Kase realised he could see better. Light flickered through the trees, and as it got brighter, Xan slowed down.

"Fire? In rain?" Kase whispered to Xan.

"Have you ever fought an atchen?"

Kase stared at Xan in the dim light. "Are you serious?"

"Deadly." Xan looked at Kase's sword. "You may wish you had one of your countrymen's axes." Xan jerked his head to the side. "You okay for this?"

Kase wasn't sure. Atchen were myths. High tales of fancy that his mother used to scare him with when he wouldn't do his chores. Humanoid in appearance, with long claws instead of fingers, and fangs where teeth once were. The stories said they were once men, cursed by an angry spirit and driven to an insatiable hunger. When they had gorged themselves on the food the land provided them and when the bulsyn lay dead on the Prairies, they turned on each other and feasted on the flesh of men.

Xan seemed to read Kase's uncertainty and took pity on him. "Aim for the heart, *only* the heart. Avoid the claws and teeth. They hold a poison in their gums." Xan waited. "Plainsman?"

"Yeah, yes." Kase shook his head as if he was clearing it.

"Heart. Got it."

"Take their head if you must, but make sure you go back to the body and drive your sword right through the heart until it shatters."

The ground felt unsteady under his feet, but Kase nodded. "Head, heart, shatter. Got it."

Xan assessed him once more, and then he rushed away from him, his sword out as he leapt forward, and Kase ran after him.

The clearing was illuminated in yellow light, but not from a fire, and Kase couldn't identify it as he almost came to a complete halt. There were several atchen in the clearing, and Bastian was fighting two at a time. They were tall, taller than Kase had expected. Their arms ended in long black talons, and he quickly realised that they used them as if they were swords. Faces twisted in rage, the atchen attacked. Xan was already engaged in his own fight, and Kase started towards the fray, but he heard someone calling his name.

Khaldan and Ax were tied back-to-back in a shallow alcove that seemed to be carved into the ground, creating a hollow shelter. A single torch shone above them, just barely out of the rain fall. Kase looked towards the two men fighting and made the split decision to free their companions.

"Good to see you," Ax greeted him as they both held out their hands to him. Kase heard the roar behind him, and he turned to look, only to see an atchen come lurching towards him. Grabbing a knife from his belt, he dropped it into Ax's outstretched hand and prepared to meet his foe.

It was his childhood nightmare that greeted him. About

twelve feet tall, hairless, with yellow glowing eyes, the atchen staggered towards him, its claws already slashing the air in front of it. When four razor sharp claws arced downwards, intent on slicing his flesh open, Kase parried the attack and engaged in a fight with a myth.

Shouts and cries surrounded them. He was dimly aware that Khaldan and Ax were free, but it was taking everything to keep this horror in front of him from skewering him on its talons.

"Stop dancing with it," Bastian barked from somewhere to the side. "Aim for the heart!"

Kase would never admit to them that he forgot about the heart. Head or heart. Fighting the atchen was one of the most surreal things he had ever faced, and he was holding his own, but piercing its heart was proving to be hard.

A dagger threw through the night, embedding itself into the chest of the atchen. Whirling on his feet, Kase's outraged stare met Bastian's cold one.

"Kill them, don't play with them," the man bit at him. "Xan, make sure all of them are dead." Kase watched as Bastian turned to Khaldan and Ax. "What happened?"

"Killed a boar," Khaldan told him tiredly. "Guess it was its dinner." He pointed to one of the atchen that lay dead.

"It saw us, decided pork was off the menu," Ax added. "Never saw the two that were with it until it was too late."

Khaldan snorted in contempt. "Can't believe they were out in the open like that. The Golden City is half a day's ride."

"Children's nightmares shouldn't have caught you unaware," Bastian reprimanded them. "We've seen them before," he added.

"In the Barrens, Bastian, not twenty miles from the capital," Xan said as he straightened from piercing a fallen monster's chest. "This?" He gestured to the ground and the fallen. "This is enough to catch you off guard."

"I've never seen them," Kase spoke up. "Wouldn't have believed you if you came back and told me," he spoke truthfully. "I still can't believe it and I'm right here."

"Well, if it helps," Ax told him as he rubbed his hands across his eyes, "you'll never forget the smell of them burning."

All of them grimaced, Kase noted, and a short time later, as he watched the fallen creatures burn, with his hand over his nose and mouth, he knew Ax was right. He would smell the putrid burning flesh for years to come, he feared.

"Where's the boar?" Bastian asked as he slid his sword into its scabbard.

"Who cares?" Khaldan grouched as he rubbed his wrists.

"I do," Bastian snarked back. "I'm hungry." He started to walk away from them, and muttering insults, Khaldan followed.

"These?" Kase asked Xan when he saw Ax leaving too.

"They burn quickly," Xan assured him. "Come, we need to find food. Your lady will be hungry."

Kase walked away from the pyre when he saw that the flesh was already crumbling to dust. His lady would be incredulous, he realised, but with a final glance over his shoulder, he met the dead glare of an atchen, and with a shudder as he turned away, he would prefer if he never had to tell her. She had enough to worry about without him adding to it.

CHAPTER 17

FYLIP RECOGNISED THE CALL OVER THE HEAVY RAIN AS THE shadows in the dark began to detach from the night and form the shape of his companions.

"You took guard?" Bastian asked as he approached, checking behind Fylip to ensure the women were still safe.

"The handmaiden was restless," Fylip told him. "Feared you were taking too long."

Bastian grunted as he walked past him and heard Ax start to admonish the sergeant about being on his leg and not resting. As Bastian walked to the rear of the ruined monastery, he saw her standing, her arms wrapped around herself as she waited impatiently for their return.

"You found them?" she asked immediately, looking over his shoulder for the others.

"We did," Bastian answered as he nodded in greeting to Tyria.

"Are they well?" Beth asked, but Bastian didn't need to answer when Kase came hurrying after him. "Kase." Beth sounded relieved. "Are you hurt?"

Kase looked at his clothing. Even soaked through with the rain, he still had bloodstains on his tunic. "It is not mine," he assured her gently.

"What did you fight?" Tyria asked Bastian as he peeled his sodden cloak off his shoulders and she saw the dirt and blood on his clothing, which the rain had not managed to wash away.

"Things that should not be here," Bastian grunted as he pulled off his boots. "Ax?" he called.

The blond warrior walked over to him and noticed the poor fire. "I'll build this up. We need heat," he told Bastian, dropping three rabbits at his feet and pulling flint and stone from his pocket. "You left this with Xan, I bet."

"The fire was fine," Xan grumbled as he sat beside Bastian and started to pull his own boots off. "My feet feel like they are swimming," he grouched.

"I can't feel mine yet," Ax complained.

"Are we safe?" Tyria asked them all as she looked between the group of bedraggled warriors all in a state of undress, within appropriate measure of course. Fylip was sitting down back where he had been, Khaldan ensuring he was well. Ax had made a bigger fire, and Bastian was on his feet again, tying rope around a low beam, securing the other side and then hanging his cloak near the fire to dry.

"We could put the cloaks up," he said to the others. "Serve as a barrier if it holds."

Xan was squinting up at the makeshift clothesline and nodding. "Used worse." He got to his feet and pointed to the opposite wall. "Needs support."

Bastian followed Xan's finger and saw the beam crumbling on the opposite end. Looking around, he spotted a long thick piece of fallen beam, and in his socks, he picked his path across the old stone floor, picking the fallen beam up as he crossed. He measured it against the wall, and then using a fallen brick, he made a temporary fix to the beam.

Turning back, he already saw that Khaldan and Xan had their cloaks over the line, and Ax was shaking his own cloak out away from the women.

"We won't see the entrance," Beth protested weakly, averting her eyes from the men stripping down out of their wet cloaks and loosening their cuirasses so they were in their shirts.

"You won't," Khaldan agreed. "We will."

"Kase?" Beth asked her companion for clarification.

"They want to rid themselves of their sodden clothes," he told her easily. "Their cloaks hanging from this means that they will be screened from you and the lady."

Beth flushed in understanding, realising that Xan was already pulling his shirt free of his trousers. Bastian was unbuckling his heavy cuirass, and Ax and Fylip were making light work of skinning the rabbits.

"Are we safe?" Tyria asked again. She had been watching them act like they weren't all covered in blood and the Gods knew what else.

Xan caught her eye and nodded. "Aye, they're dead."

"What were *they*?" Beth asked, taking her seat beside Tyria.

"Atchen," Ax told her as he spat into the fire. "May they freeze in the depths of hell."

"Atchen?" Beth's peal of laughter was loud in the monastery. "Kase, what was it really?"

"I do not lie." Ax's angry words cut off anything that Kase had been about to say. "Monsters of evil walked those woods, and they were far too close to the Golden City for my liking."

Bastian huffed in agreement. His cuirass was off, and he, like Xan, had pulled his shirt tails free of his trousers. "Far too close." Untying his hair and shaking it free of the leather tie, he accepted a linen cloth from Khaldan and began to rub it over his hair, letting the cloth soak up the moisture.

"Do you plan to undress fully?" Kase asked the mercenaries as more items of clothing were pulled free or loosened.

Bastian looked at him, taking in his still sodden clothing. "Yes," he answered, pointing at the rope with the cloaks over it. "That's why we have this," he added. "Ladies," he said as he dipped his head to the two women, and then he stepped behind the cloaks.

Xan was grinning at Kase and was already pulling his shirt up as he walked around the barrier, baring his back, pulling it over his head. Khaldan was behind him, and Ax followed, leaving Fylip to cook the rabbit.

Beth heard them talking in low voices as more articles of clothing were slung over the clothing rope. Exchanging a look with Tyria, who merely shrugged, Beth turned to Kase. "You can join them. You're soaked through."

Kase grunted in displeasure. "Water doesn't bother me," he told her with a frown aimed at the curtain between them. "You better hope that holds. My lady sees any of your skin, and there'll be trouble," he called to them.

"Atchen?" Tyria prompted. "Truly?"

Kase shook his head in disbelief. "I saw them with my own eyes, and I still don't believe it," he admitted tiredly as he sat down, ignoring the discomfort of his clothing.

"Tell us everything," Beth demanded, and as Fylip skinned and skewered the rabbit, Kase did, stopping only to remove the skin and innards of their supper away from the women.

Bastian sat with his back to the wall, ignoring the chill seeping into his bones from the cold stone behind him. Ax had started a smaller fire for them, and all four of them had their feet pointed towards it. He listened to the plainsman telling the women and Fylip of their skirmish with the beasts, and he was impressed with the simple efficiency with which he told the tale. There was no embellishment, no added drama, just a clean concise retelling.

It suited the Tzenythian perfectly. Similar to how he fought. No flourish and no flair. Simple, quick, and clean cuts.

After a thin supper, which consisted of a third share of a skinny rabbit and a weak cup of tea, Bastian tossed the bone into the fire. Closing his eyes, he tilted his head back, resting it against the wall. He knew Khaldan could see the entrance from where he sat, and while Bastian and the others rested, one of them would keep watch. He fell asleep immediately. He had always been able to sleep anywhere, anytime. The training of a good soldier meant you knew how to get sleep when the opportunity presented it.

Dark clouds raced too fast across the night sky. Dark gave way to grey, which gave way to light, then to dusk and then night again. Standing on black sand, Bastian watched the sky turn through its cycle of sleep. All around him, he heard a steady drumming. Looking down at the sand, he noticed with surprise his feet were bare. The black sand moved over his feet like a living thing, as if it were a million black ants.

Crashing waves on the shore made him turn to look at a sea that was almost black with fury. The pull towards it was strong, but Bastian had never been a fan of the sea, and his nature kept him on the sand. The scream that pierced the air had him whipping around to find its source. The dark figure was on their knees, hunched over, their head almost on the sand. Or maybe it already was—Bastian couldn't see for their hood that shielded their face. Another scream sounded and he realised with startling clarity that the scream wasn't coming from the low figure.

The figure rose to their feet, swaying slightly, unsteady in their movements. Another scream and the figure flinched as if struck. With a hesitant step, they moved towards the sea, and Bastian ducked down as a loud bang reverberated through the air. He covered his head as sound pressed down on him.

When he thought it was safe to look up, the figure was once again on the sand, laid low with the voice on the wind.

Cautiously Bastian started to make his way to them. He needed to know who this was. Who was screaming? Why was he here? Where was here? Questions with no immediate answers pressed into his mind.

Another cry, another unseen blow delivered to the hooded figure. Bastian picked up his pace. They were obviously hurting.

"Hey!" he called as he advanced, and the figure spun towards him. Like before, a hand was held up in warning as they began to back away from him. "No! Don't go!" Bastian yelled, but they turned and ran from him. Panic coursed through him, and he ran after them. He knew he couldn't lose them.

As he ran, the sand got deeper, wetter, heavier, and soon he was up to his knees in it. Wildly he looked around, not understanding why he was sinking into quicksand on a beach. The more he struggled, the more he sank.

As the sand swallowed him slowly, he coughed out as hot black granules of sand filled his mouth. A shadow appeared above him, and looking up, he saw that the hooded figure was back.

"Help me," he choked. He couldn't see their face, but he saw their *boot as it came up and rested on his head, and then…they pressed down.*

Bastian woke with a start. Disorientated, he took in his surroundings, his hands brushing away the grains of sand he could still feel spilling over his head.

"What is it?" he asked as he realised Xan was watching him.

"They're gone," he told him, his voice low.

"What?" Bastian asked, still pulling himself from his nightmare.

"The three of *them*, they're gone," Xan clarified.

Bastian got to his feet and walked around the barrier to see it empty, and walking forward to the entrance, he found Fylip lying unconscious. "He was harmed?"

"No," Xan told him from behind him. "Just knocked out."

"Horse is gone," Bastian grunted as he inspected the wagon.

"Yep."

Bastian picked up the three gold coins sitting on the seat of the wagon. "They paid their debt." Turning, he looked at Xan and held out the coins.

Xan glared at the coins, shifting his attention to the landscape beyond. "Did they?"

Bastian sighed, scrubbing his eyes tiredly, fighting the yawn. "Come, let's wake the others. We need to check him out," he told Xan, gesturing to Fylip.

"We follow?" Xan asked, following Bastian back to the others.

"No," Bastian answered, shaking Khaldan awake. "With

atchen in the woods, we need to get back to the Order, report our findings."

"What is it?" Khaldan asked groggily, sitting up, already wishing he could go back to sleep.

"Our charges did us a favour and left," Bastian told him. "Knocked Fylip out though," he directed to Ax, who was also awake.

"Well, that was rude," Ax muttered as he stood up. "I'll go check on him." Picking his cloak off the line and snatching up his boots, Ax stalked to the entrance.

"This hid their escape," Khaldan mused as he too took his cloak from the line, Xan mimicking him, opening the area up once again.

"Takes more than some hanging cloaks to make us all sleep through three people walking past us." Bastian looked at each of his companions. "Did you all sleep deeply?"

"I think so." Khaldan rubbed the back of his neck. "I think if you give me a few moments, I could sleep again."

"Agreed," Xan said with a mighty yawn and a huge stretch.

"So, they drugged the tea," Bastian concluded. "Ax was right," he told them, pulling his boots on. "That's just rude."

<hr>

THE SMALL COMPANY OF MEN ENTERED THE GOLDEN CITY IN a similar manner to the way that they left it, quietly and at night. Quickly they made their way through the streets, keeping close, a sense of wanting home urging them forward.

However, Bastian was careful in all things, and as eager as he was to be within the walls of the Conclave, he was also keen to make sure they weren't bringing too much attention to themselves. There was always someone in the shadows watching.

When the Order of the Conclave's white walls rose out from amongst the buildings around it, Bastian couldn't contain his smile at the welcome sight. The heavy wooden doors were closed, and he knew they would be barred. Making their way around the outer wall, Bastian led them to the side entrance, which was always manned, despite the hour.

Rapping his knuckles in the familiar knock against the wooden gate, he and his men grinned at each other at the sound of the wooden bar lifting. Slipping in through the narrow opening, the five were finally back within the familiar walls.

"My lord," the sentry greeted. "We were expecting you days ago."

Pushing his hood back, Bastian reached out and clasped the man's shoulder. "Blanyon," Bastian said. "It's good to see you made it back."

"We did, but the general's not happy," Blanyon whispered. "He's been watching that gate."

"He *is* watching," the stern voice spoke from the shadows. Moving into the light, the men stood straighter as the older man came into view. Vyka deVanya was not a man to be trifled with in his day on the field of battle, nor in his later days as general of the Order of the Ravens. Around his middle may be softer now, but his eye was as sharp as it had been on the battlefield, and his expectation of his men equally so.

"Bastian," he greeted, taking in the state of fatigue of his men. "Where in the hell have you men been?"

"It's a story," Khaldan said gruffly. "A story that can wait, I hope. I need a bath and a bed."

"And a healer for Fylip," Ax added.

Vyka looked each of his men in the eye. "Where's Bez?"

"Fell," Bastian answered gruffly. "He flies high." He dipped his head when he couldn't meet his commander's eye.

"Accident or foe?" Vyka asked, watching them all.

"I let go." Bastian looked up.

"*Bez* let go," Khaldan corrected, emphasising Bez's name. "We'd have lost them both if he hadn't."

Vyka placed his hands behind his back as he regarded his men. "You have a lot to tell." He seemed to think about it. "But not tonight. Go to your quarters, get some rest."

Gratefully, the men walked past him, but Bastian remained, his attention on Vyka, who had half turned to watch the men depart. Turning around, he looked Bastian up and down.

"You look like shit."

"Feel like it."

"They look like shit too." Vyka's tone held the reprimand. "You drive them too hard."

"They can handle it," Bastian countered.

"He's been waiting for your return," Vyka spoke quietly in the darkened garden of the Order's home.

"Shall I debrief you first?" Bastian asked his commander

despite the fact that weariness rode heavy upon his shoulders.

"No." Vyka shook his head. "Rest. Report first thing in the morning," he added. "To me first," he added in a quiet whisper.

Bastian hid his surprise well at being given permission to sleep. He must look really bad to be granted rest before reporting. "Aye, sir."

They began to walk to the living quarters, both men silent. When Bastian reached the stairs that led to his room above, Vyka's hand on his arm stopped him. "He let go?"

Bastian closed his eyes briefly, once again seeing the resolution in Bez's eyes just before he died. "I couldn't hold him."

Vyka heard the pain and the truth in his knight's words. "Sleep, Bastian, tomorrow is already waiting."

"Sir." Slowly Bastian climbed the stairs to his chambers. Inside his room, he didn't call for a squire to help him, he merely dropped his armour and his clothing behind him as he took them off, making his way to the washbasin.

The Golden City was reconstructed from a city of the world before, and magic had helped rebuild it to its former glory. Or what the creators believed was similar to the former buildings that stood there before the world that it had then been ended. Magic and the creators couldn't restore everything, but in the Golden City, plumbing still worked. It had taken many years to puzzle it out, but the restorers and the creators had fashioned indoor plumbing, and it was with a grateful sigh of relief Bastian splashed his face with warm water.

Dipping his head under the brass tap, he quickly

scrubbed his face and hands. With only his heavy black trousers still on, he scrubbed his upper body. Tiredly he pulled the rest of his clothing off, and with a grimace at the fresh white linen bedding and knowing he was still far from clean, he climbed into bed.

He had so much to tell his superiors, but first, he could sleep.

CHAPTER 18

The sounds of the familiar woke Bastian from a solid dreamless sleep. Daylight was doing its best to creep through the bedroom drapes, as a light breeze blew the heavy material gently. Bastian lay in his bed for a moment longer, relishing the feel of the sturdy bed beneath him, the soft blankets over him, the crisp white painted ceiling and the sound of the Order moving about and carrying out their morning duties.

The large four-poster mahogany bed took up most of his room in the Order, but it was a damn fine bed. One of the squires had placed white gauzy curtains around it at one point, arguing in the summer months it kept the bugs and flies from his bed, but Bastian had taken them down once the squire had left the room. He would have gotten away with burning the things in the hearth, but Khaldan had taken that moment to come into his room and, of course, felt it was his duty to inform the others at breakfast that Bastian had a taste for soft furnishings. Bez had offered to fetch fresh flowers for the room after breakfast and had earned an extra duty in the stables cleaning the stalls. Bastian smiled at the memory, but it was quickly replaced with the memory of the look of acceptance in the sergeant's eyes before he let go of Bastian's grip, choosing to fall to his death.

Pushing it from his head, he knew he had to move on. Stretching leisurely, Bastian lay for one more moment, and knowing hot water waited for him, he got out of bed.

Usually he made his bed, but knowing the sheets were soiled with the grime of his travels, he instead stripped the linens ready for the wash.

The palace of the Golden City had rooms with single washrooms adjacent to the bedrooms, but in the Order of the Conclave's building, washrooms were communal. In a cupboard near the door, Bastian collected a towel and a small compact pouch that housed his washcloth and soap.

Pulling on a pair of simple trousers that he usually trained in, Bastian headed to the washroom, eager to be clean. Despite his sleep, he knew it was still early when he saw he was the only one in the washroom. The large square room had a tiled floor and simple bare walls that were unremarkable; however, the decoration in the room wasn't on the walls, but more on the eight single bathtubs that were laid out in two simple rows of four. Eight tubs of enamel with iron clawed feet stood proudly in the room. The magic users had long ago infused them with magic to continually warm the water poured into them. Stripping off his clothes, Bastian sank gratefully into a steaming tub of water.

This may be better than being in bed, he thought to himself as he enjoyed the water enclosing him with its warmth. His eyes closed in appreciation as the warmth seeped into his bones, easing his aches and pains.

Soft muffled footsteps didn't disturb him; he knew the squires were merely checking the rooms, ensuring the water remained clean for the knights yet to rise. Bastian felt the presence beside him, and then the sweet aroma of coffee made him open his eyes.

Clem smiled as he stepped back. "They told me you came home in the night," he said quietly. "I knew you would need this." He gestured to the wooden tray that now lay across the bath, where two cups, both filled with coffee, sat waiting.

"Clem, you are a gift from the Gods," Bastian said with appreciation, reaching for a cup and taking a long drink.

"When you are ready, if you move to the next tub, my lord, you will feel better for it."

Bastian nodded as he finished the first cup and picked up the other. Clem took the empty cup and left the washroom.

"Morning," Khaldan greeted as he entered the washroom, heading for the tub in front of Bastian. He undressed and turned his back to Bastian as he got in with an appreciative sigh. "Oh, I need this," he said with quiet appreciation.

"Sleep well?" Bastian asked him as he drained his second cup. "I needed *that,*" he said as he placed the cup back on the tray.

"I did sleep well," Khaldan told him. "It's a good bed."

"But not home," Bastian mouthed along with Khaldan as Khaldan spoke the words out loud. "You'll be home soon," Bastian told him.

"Aye," Khaldan acknowledged him before sinking completely under the water, wetting his brown hair. When Khaldan rose again, Bastian was getting into the tub beside the one he had just been in. "You not soaking?" Khaldan asked him.

"Not today." Bastian picked up his soap and started to lather. "I need to meet with the general, give my debrief." Glancing at his friend, who looked pained at his words,

Bastian gave a low laugh. "You can soak, my friend. It only takes one of us to attend."

Khaldan looked at Bastian over his shoulder, hope in his eyes. "Really?"

"Really. Stay. Enjoy the tubs and then meet me for breakfast." Bastian hesitated as he looked around the room. "Or lunch?" As he began to wash, he wondered what time it was. "What time is it?"

"Still morning," Khaldan answered carelessly, leaning back in his tub. "I'm not getting out until the water's cold."

Bastian smiled at Khaldan's eccentric comment as he scrubbed his skin clean and washed the lather from his hair. He moved to the third tub, rinsing his body one final time. Wrapped in a towel and feeling better than he had in weeks, Bastian said goodbye to Khaldan and headed back to his room.

His bed had been remade in fresh linens, his clothes were laid out on the bed, and a fresh cuirass and scabbard had been polished and left by the bed.

Clem knocked on the door and asked if he needed assistance, but Bastian declined after thanking him for the clothes.

Bastian preferred the heavy black trousers they wore when travelling, but in the walls of the Order of the Conclave, he needed to dress the part, and with a resigned sigh, he picked up the black leather trousers that had been laid out for him. Thankfully, it was Clem who had placed his clothing out this morning, and the leather was soft and comfortable. His shirt was white with simple leather laces to tie at the neck. Bastian's boots had been replaced with another pair, no doubt from his closet, and with clean socks and boots that weren't worn at the sole, his feet felt good, almost comfortable.

The cuirass that had been left was heavy leather with a raven on a rock etched into the leather. Bastian stared at it for a long moment. His travelling cuirass was simple and undecorated, but this was a decorative piece of armour as well as a functional piece. Strapping himself into the thick leather chest plate, he looked over at the large rectangle of polished glass in the corner of the room. He looked like himself again, he mused as he buckled on his sword belt and slid his sword into the scabbard, adding several throwing knives into his belt and clothing.

Finally, he picked up a leather tie that lay on the dresser, and pulling his long shoulder-length hair back, he tied it low at the nape of his neck. Scratching his jaw, he realised he should probably have asked Clem to shave him, but he knew he was already late. If the squires knew he was back, so did the Lord Commander. Checking his appearance one more time, Bastian left the sanctuary of his room to go meet with the general.

The Order of the Ravens' wing of the Conclave was to the west of the main hall, and Bastian knew that Vyka wouldn't want him to go through the main hall. Bastian therefore walked the back corridors and halls, keeping away from the front of the wraparound inner balcony that looked down and into the main hall. Instead, he took the path that overlooked the walled garden and training square. Bastian could hear the sergeants bark orders at the recruits and trainees. Eager to see how many there were in the training, Bastian paused to watch.

He counted only twenty in the training yard. Twenty

was good, but the large empty space behind them told the story that once there were five times as many. Those days were gone. With the fall of the Orders, not many came to enter the ranks of a seemingly disgraced service anymore.

Eventually he reached his general's office, and rapping his knuckles against the solid door, he heard the command to enter. Pushing the door open, Bastian took in the small office Vyka insisted on keeping even though there were many larger rooms throughout the complex.

"My lord," Bastian greeted.

"Sit," Vyka said as he poured over papers on his desk. "Did you break your fast yet?" he asked without looking up.

"Not yet. I had coffee though," Bastian told him as he took a seat in a chair that he was sure was older than himself. "Why won't you move out of this room?" Bastian asked as the chair groaned in protest.

"Why won't you serve at the palace?" Vyka asked him, looking up from a parchment.

"You know why," Bastian grouched sourly.

"Then why ask me a question when you already know the answer?"

Bastian bit his tongue to stop from replying. Vyka returned his attention to the parchment. "Will I start?" Bastian asked him in amusement. He knew his general well —once he was puzzled over something, he would lose himself in it.

"Oh, yes," Vyka told him absently. "From the beginning."

"We went from here to the north of Kalzynia, spent some time in Kalzenyth."

"The fishing port?" Vyka asked in surprise. "You have a craving for snowtrout?"

"No." Bastian picked at a ragged piece of skin beside his nail. "We were following a rumour."

"Do I need to draw the details out of you?" Vyka's attention was back on the parchment.

Bastian barked out a laugh at his commander's taunting. "No, my lord, where was I?" he mocked, and when he saw Vyka's lips twitch, he sat back in his chair. "We left Pavolyn and headed north, as you directed. We took a few jobs for pay as you directed, mercenaries once again. I first heard the rumour of unrest at the Bordyre border."

"What unrest?"

"The people seem to be more divided than we thought in regards to the old and the new," Bastian told him. "The new Gods are sweeping across the southern kingdom and are reaching into the northern kingdoms as well. In Bordyre and even Kalzynia, places of worship where the old Gods were loved have been either burned down or destroyed." Bastian sat up slightly straighter. "In a town in the southern farms of Kalzynia, we heard that there was a prophet of the new Gods who could perform miracles."

"Miracles? You mean magic?"

"No, I *mean* miracles. Heal the sick, cure the lame, feed the hungry." Bastian shook his head. "Magic, as I understand it, is something that is taken in order for it to be given, but apparently the miracles need no such relationship. The prophet merely speaks, and the act is done."

Vyka frowned. "Did you find him?"

"No. The closest we came to him, her, them, whoever,"

Bastian said with frustration, "was in Kalzenyth, which is why we stayed longer than we should."

"They vanished?"

"Or they never existed," Bastian countered. "But in the town, we heard a rumour of something else. Heard it more than once as we travelled, and the people saying it, aren't just the ones in the towns and villages. They're talking about war."

"War?" Vyka frowned. "Whose war?"

"The *Gods' war*, that's what they're calling it," Bastian told him. "The old and the new, fighting for dominance. The Gods are at war in the heavens, and they will wreck ruin upon us mere mortals as they fight for dominance."

Vyka looked bewildered and sceptical at the same time. "The comings and goings of Gods are not for man to involve himself in," he said in consternation.

"Agreed." Bastian nodded. "However, man seems to want to pick a side. We travelled and we listened. There's a divide between the people, and it's growing."

"This is insanity," Vyka said, leaning back in his seat. "I mean, I heard the same reports, but you have seen this?"

"We have," Bastian confirmed. "I don't understand it. The new Gods are no longer *new*. Half of my life, I've known of them; it's not an overnight thing. But it gets worse." Bastian hesitated. "There are those who are claiming that they have seen them. In person."

"Blasphemy."

"I thought so too." Bastian nodded. "But I have spoken to these people, and they believe."

"Your thoughts?"

Bastian threw his hands up in the air. "They were

tricked, they saw what they saw, they saw nothing. Pick a day; my answer changes daily." He sighed heavily. "But as we left Bordyre, we heard a rumour of the Mystic, saying that the Mystic is preaching the end of days, the end of not only this age, but all ages." Bastian had his commander's full attention now. "I turned from our destination to track them. I made sure those who would recognise us for Order recognised us, in the hope that it would flush them out."

"Did you find him?"

"No. But"—Bastian inhaled deeply—"there is some merit to the claims. We fought atchen in the woods to the southwest of the Golden City. We were tracked and hunted through the Sand Seas by zyvarg."

"The monsters are far from the Barrens," Vyka said with a frown.

"Monsters roaming the lower kingdoms sounds like end of days stuff, no?" He raised an eyebrow at his commander, and Vyka leaned back in his chair with a sigh. "And the Sand Seas are crumbling, literally," Bastian added quietly. "Great chasms opening with no warning. It's almost as if they have been affected by the Barrens."

"Tell me how he fell."

As he filled his commander in on how they lost Bez, Bastian controlled the pain at the loss of his comrade. When he was finished, Vyka sat silent for a moment. "He was a good sergeant." Bastian remained quiet but his commander was not one for silence. "And these three companions you picked up for safe passage, their purpose in the Golden City?"

"The handmaiden has ink on her wrists," he said. "She had wanted to witness the Festival of Moon and

Blooms." Bastian recalled Beth's reaction to the symbol. "I would assume they are here for the new Gods." Bastian hesitated but duty commanded he share everything. "I attended the festival with her. The flowers were laid out in a pattern; I was on a raised platform, and I saw it plainly." Bastian met his commander's curiosity with a steady gaze. "There was a pattern in the display, a symbol. It enticed the festivalgoers to violence. The pattern of the flowers was destroyed, but I can recreate it. I am no artist, but you will recognise it. After all, you have seen it before, in battle."

Quickly he drew the teardrop and the symbol within it.

"No. He's dead, I killed him myself," Vyka swore as he dropped the paper Bastian had drawn on.

"Well, either the new Gods have resurrected him or there are men out there with similar beliefs."

"This will start riots," Vyka spat as he glared at the symbol.

"It already has. And if it entices…excitement…amongst the people, you can see why with this, the rumour of a Mystic and a fallen Conclave in every city but the capital, well…"

"War is an easy conclusion to make," Vyka agreed with disgust. "You should have interrogated the handmaiden."

Bastian almost choked in surprise. "I'd rather cross the Sand Seas again."

"Difficult?"

"Impossible," Bastian corrected him.

"And her lady?"

"Claims to be of the House of Barsgaard," Bastian deadpanned.

Vyka grunted in surprise. "Well, there's folly and there's just plain stupidity."

Bastian silently agreed.

"The Lord Commander needs to know all of this," Vyka told him tiredly. "He'll want you out there again, gathering information."

"I know," Bastian told him. "Can I request Khaldan stay behind?"

"Denied."

Bastian clenched his fists in frustration. "Can I request that we get at least a week at home? They need to see their families."

"Five days."

"Your generosity knows no bounds," Bastian mocked his superior.

Vyka stood, ignoring the knight's sarcasm. "Come, you need to report."

"My lord." Bastian followed his superior from the room, prepared to tell the whole story to his Lord Commander. Before they got to the rooms the Lord Commander occupied, Vyka turned to Bastian in the hall.

"Do not mention the symbol," he whispered hurriedly.

"To the men?"

"To *anyone*," he ordered, his eyes flicking to the closed door of the Lord Commander's quarters. "Not all of what you told me is news, but the symbol *is*. Keep it to yourself for now. I need to think how we approach this."

Bastian stared at his commander for a long moment before he nodded. "I was the only one of the men who saw it," he confirmed. "Myself and the handmaiden."

"Good," Vyka nodded. "Let's keep it that way."

CHAPTER 19

"Five days?" Khaldan's tone did not hide his displeasure.

"I tried for a week." Bastian avoided eye contact. "If you think about it, it's almost seven days."

"You know what's almost seven days?" Khaldan snapped. "Seven days."

"Um, well…" Ax cleared his throat. "Seven is not *almost* seven, it *is* seven. *Almost* seven would be six."

Bastian bit the inside of his cheek as he turned his head away so his friend did not see him laughing. "Or eight," Bastian murmured.

"You're both a pile of dung," Khaldan told them as he stood abruptly. "You want to come with me? See if you can tell Rhexynia that *five* days is almost the same as seven?"

"No, I'm…" It was Bastian's turn to clear *his* throat. "I'm good, here, I…eh, have…stuff. Vyka, you know, huge pile of stuff he needs from me."

Khaldan's snort was not complimentary. "You?" he asked Ax. "Do you also have *stuff*?"

"I do." Ax nodded quickly. "Really important stuff."

Fixing his sword, Khaldan looked them both up and down, and with a scoff of disgust, he turned and left them both standing in the entrance to the training yard.

"She's going to skin him alive," Ax leaned in and whispered to Bastian as they watched their friend depart.

"Aye," Bastian agreed as he scratched his stubble. "I have no intention of crossing her threshold until he's had at least three days to calm her down. Maybe four." He thought about it some more. "Perhaps not even then."

"A good and wise plan," Ax agreed sagely. "Never met a woman who can curse like Khaldan's lady wife," he confided in Bastian.

Bastian grinned widely as he thought about the blonde-haired gentle-looking woman who Khaldan had married. She appeared as frail and fragile as a delicate flower until she spoke. Or lost her temper. In fairness, Rhexynia was very easy to anger. There had been hopes from some that perhaps her children would bring out the gentler side of her, but she had borne four children now, and Rhexynia was still as quick to temper as she had ever been.

Bastian was quietly confident he was to blame for some of that. Until he stopped serving within the Order, Khaldan would also remain in service, and service meant that they were rarely at home.

"I am needed in the nave," Ax told Bastian. "Do you have a need of me here?"

Bastian shook his head as he looked his comrade over. Ax's hair had been trimmed since his return, the blond hair resting loose on his shoulder. His beard had also been trimmed, and his clothes were plain and simple. He was not wearing a cuirass, choosing a simple white tunic, with dark cotton trousers. "No, go," Bastian told him. "I'll see you at supper?"

Ax had been turning to go, but at his friend's question, he hesitated. "You'll need to show up at some time," he chided Bastian. "You cannot hide in the Order for five days."

"I'm not hiding," Bastian said with wide eyes. "Now go.

If you're late, Vyka will just ask me to find you." Bastian made a shooing motion with his hand. "Go."

"Supper!" Ax called over his shoulder, making his way to the inner sanctuary of the Conclave.

Alone and unsure with what to spend his time, Bastian scratched his jaw again. With a frown, he tugged at his beard, and with a plan in place, he went looking for one of his squires. After Clem had trimmed Bastian's hair and shaved him, Bastian had lingered in the tubs again, this time allowing himself to enjoy the soak. Once more dressed and enjoying the solitude, he decided to take a walk around the halls and enjoy the peace that he felt when he was within the Order's walls.

The Order of the Conclave consisted of five separate Orders. Their purpose was to be the soldiers and servants of the Gods and those who ruled in their name. It was said in the days of the Before that great giant machines flew across the skies, taking people to different lands. But now, the only thing that flew the high heights of the sky unchallenged were birds. Birds soared so close to the heavens; how could anything other than a bird represent the agents of the Gods?

Bastian stood in the great hall looking at the intricate tapestry of the Order of the Conclave, which depicted the five Orders. In the top right corner was the Hawk representing the Order of the Hawks. Strong and powerful, the Order of the Hawks were swift and agile, their talents lying in their strength and their ferocity in battle.

The bottom corner were four Starlings flying in tight formation, their short, pointed wings making the bird appear small and, in flight, like a four-pointed star. The

Order of the Starlings were also like the bird they represented, the smallest of the Orders, but their soldiers were quick footed and made for excellent infantry soldiers. They attacked as one and rarely were sent on solitary missions. Where the Hawks were sometimes used for information gathering, the Order of the Starlings were very capable of spreading the information, communicating the word of the Conclave to the masses.

Bastian turned his attention to the top left of the tapestry, the Falcon. Shown in the tapestry as a bird of prey in flight, the Order of the Falcons were fierce warriors and hunters as the bird they were named for. The Order of the Falcons fought with grace and ferocity. Favoured by the warrior kingdoms, the Order of the Falcons fought for glory and victory.

In the bottom left corner, the solitary black-feathered Raven sat perched on a rock, its head at an angle as if weighing the other birds within the tapestry. Bastian had always appreciated how the Raven sat and considered its options in the tapestry, whereas the other birds were in flight, already rushing in. Ravens were very much like the men who served in their Order, a double-edged sword. They were either seen as strong and wise or a bad omen associated mostly with death and ill tidings. A complex bird indeed, Bastian mused.

And in the centre of the tapestry, depicted in deep red, was the Cardinal. The brightly coloured parent bird that looked after its young. Confident and caring, passing on its wisdom to those it taught and also to those it advised. A group of Cardinals was known as a conclave, and even though the other branches of the Order under its wing were not all the same, the Cardinal governed the conclave with a tight fist.

Bastian studied the tapestry in front of him, digesting the strong message the tapestry told. The Orders were messengers of the Gods. They served the Gods and their emissaries in life. As soldiers of the heavens for over a century, the Orders had served. As fighters for freedom, they had bled, and as servants to the crowns, they earned their living. Until the very crowns they fought for no longer wished to pay for the upkeep of the retainers who had served them so well and so faithfully.

When the rumours of outlandish demands from the Order of the Conclave first reached his ears, Bastian had just left the smoking pyre of one of his brethren. The smoke of death had still hung heavy in the air when Bastian and his men had been escorted from the streets of the city they had just freed from oppression.

More and more, the rumours spoke of battles not in the name of the Gods but in the name of greed. Rulers who wished to gain more territory. Soldiers of the Orders were no longer treated with the respect they had known and perhaps in some cases—Bastian's eyes flicked to the Hawk in the tapestry—demanded.

Slowly the leaders of the kingdoms turned from the loyal servants they had heavily relied on previously and instead focused more on their own armies. Armies that had been trained by the very men they now rejected.

Kestornia had not cast the Order out. In the Golden City of Pavolyn, the king and his queen still relied on the counsel of the Lord Commander and the strength of the men at his command.

"You stare at that tapestry any longer, I will begin to think you see something that no other does," Xan spoke behind Bastian.

"Where have you been?" Bastian asked him, turning to see the dark-haired soldier. It was clear Xan had not visited the bathing chamber yet or slept from the look of the dark rings under his eyes.

"You think I would let them get away?" Xan asked him as he leaned against the wall.

"Find them?" Bastian asked as he looked around them.

"I found *him*. The women I have not."

"He left them?" Bastian asked in surprise. "Are you sure?"

"No, which is why I followed him."

"Xan, I care not for the storytelling dramatics," Bastian reminded him. "Get to the point."

"He is in the inn of the White Horse. I assume the women are too," Xan said with a grin. "But they'll be gone by the morning."

"Why?"

"The inn is fully booked from tomorrow, so they need to find alternative lodgings."

Bastian frowned. "Why? What's happening tomorrow?"

Xan grinned widely. "It's the king's birthday celebrations."

Bastian glared at the man beside him. "Tell me you're kidding and we already missed it."

"Nope." Xan looked positively buoyant. "The *actual* birthday is in three days, but the celebrations begin tomorrow."

"We have five days of rest before I leave again." Bastian

stopped walking, his hands on his hips. "I could take time to fast while I'm here."

Xan laughed loudly. "Vyka will skewer you himself for that dung heap of an excuse. Pomp and circumstance are already calling you."

"You are a sick and twisted man," Bastian grumbled.

"Do I leave in five days?" Xan asked with an arched eyebrow.

Bastian cast him a sideways glance. "I don't know. I have not yet received my orders."

Xan nodded as they walked. "I'll catch some sleep. I want to be on them again before they move."

"No indication of why they're here?" He thought about it. "I thought for sure that they would head to the nearest Temple."

Xan shook his head. "So far, they seem to be avoiding the Temples, old or new. I don't know why, but I plan to." He bid farewell to Bastian and headed to his rooms.

Bastian resumed his tour of the building and almost wished he had opted to fast when he met one of his least favourite people in the halls.

"They told me you were here," Kedda greeted him. Kedda was a big brute from Bordyre, and Bastian was sure the Order of the Hawks knight had nothing but air between his ears.

Bastian spread his hands out in front of him as he forced an indifference. "This is my home. Where else would I be?"

"Scavenging for coin like the carrion eater you are." Kedda's smile was nasty. Missing a few front teeth didn't help his looks.

"It's always a pleasure to see you." Bastian went to move

past the taller man, but a beefy hand gripped Bastian's upper arm.

"You broke my nose last time," Kedda growled down at him.

"Broke your jaw too," Bastian told him conversationally. "I can break it again if you wish?"

Kedda pulled Bastian closer to him, his lips twisted in an ugly snarl. "I await the day I get told I can skewer you like the pig you are."

"You should hold your breath until then." Bastian's voice was light, conversational, as he looked into the dark, angry eyes of the other man, unafraid.

"Let him go." The sharp command came from the side, and Kedda quickly stepped back in recognition of his superior's voice.

"My lord, I did not see you there."

Bastian did not step back from Kedda, forcing the other man to take another step away from him in his commander's presence.

"Crux," Bastian greeted the older man. A good soldier in his day, Crux had fallen foul of the soldier's curse, where instead of the glory of death on the battlefield, he would die of old age. "It has been a while," Bastian said, extending his arm, and the commander of the Order of the Hawks grasped it with a warm clasp.

"Bastian, it has been too long. Come walk with me, tell me how you've been," Crux directed, stepping in beside him. The two of them began to walk the direction Bastian had been heading when a throat being cleared behind them made Crux stop and turn. "Yes?"

"My lord, I..." Kedda looked flushed and hesitated under the commander's eye.

"You're?" Crux asked. "An imbecile? Incompetent? Dim witted?"

Bastian failed to hide his laugh as the smaller man looked at the huge burly soldier, earning him a glare of hatred from Kedda.

"I was talking to Bastian," Kedda finished lamely.

"You were?" Crux looked at Bastian. "Were you finished?"

"I hadn't even started," Bastian told him, seeing the mischievous sparkle in the commander's eye.

"Splendid." Crux held his arm out. "Help an old man, my boy," he instructed. Bastian offered the commander his arm, and they resumed walking. "Stop gawking, Kedda, you look like a snowtrout out of water," Crux called back over his shoulder.

Bastian and Crux walked in silence for a few steps, and as they turned down the hall to the Order of the Falcons' section of the Order of the Conclave, Crux leaned into Bastian. "Has the idiot gone?"

"No, still staring after us," Bastian told him. "He looks quite lonely."

"Insufferable," Crux grumped. "I take it he is still mad about the teeth?"

"Nose, I think." Bastian shrugged. "Maybe the teeth?" he added as an afterthought.

"You should have been allowed to joust with him," Crux spoke in a low voice. "Would have solved a lot of problems."

"You could just excommunicate him," Bastian suggested idly.

"I would, but you know my daughter, she'd take it personally if I kicked her husband out of the Order of the Conclave." Crux rolled his eyes at Bastian, who chuckled at the other man's humour.

"The Order of the Falcons may take him?" Bastian suggested. "Drykol loves a challenge."

"There is a challenge, and then there is Kedda," Crux said wisely. "I wish no one else that misery." Crux patted the back of Bastian's hand. "However, you spoil my time with you. Tell me your adventures." Easily Bastian recited the story that he had told Vyka, leaving out the parts as commanded by his superior. Crux may have been old, but his brain was still sharp. "And when do you tell me the parts you have left out?"

Bastian was not prone to deception, so instead he spoke the truth. "When my general permits it."

Crux huffed out a laugh. "Very wise, you should have been a Hawk."

Bastian laughed in the halls. "But you just told me I was wise; doesn't that rule me out automatically?"

"Funny as always," Crux said dryly. "My time draws nearer," Crux confessed as they walked. "I need someone strong and wise to lead my Order."

"Well, that definitely rules me out," Bastian joked. "Your Order has many good men," he reassured Crux. "Most of them see through Kedda's crude ambition. Have faith in your flock."

Crux stopped walking and looked up at the younger man. "If this is your idea of advice, I was wrong that you were wise." Crux tugged Bastian's arm. "Come, take me to the nave. I would see my nephew."

Bastian walked the commander to the hall of worship and left him in the company of Ax, who was delighted to see his uncle. As Bastian returned to his room, he knew he had accomplished one thing today and that was a reminder that he was best out on the field; politics was not his game.

CHAPTER 20

THE SUMMONS CAME A DAY LATER, AND ALTHOUGH BASTIAN was expecting it, he still felt a strong surge of resentment towards the thick parchment that was handed to him. Striding down to the nave, he sought out Ax, who was deep in prayer in front of the altar, and Bastian hesitated at the side, unwilling to disturb him.

"I can feel you hovering," Ax told him with a wry smile, his head still bowed in prayer. "One more moment and I shall be with you."

Bastian said nothing as he looked up at the plain stone altar with the seven Gods depicted in marble above it. Emblems of their divinity rather than faces of the Gods, because who could be so bold as to put a likeness of a face to the holiest of beings?

Hoxka, the powerful mighty one, whose hammer rang out amongst the heavens when his temper was tested, his sigil was carved in the marble as the shape of a hammer. Kob, a starburst of radiance, which depicted his beauty and fairness. Mankla, the crest of a wave for the God who ruled the seas. Zynia, a beauty so fair that none could rival it, her sigil was a rose. Beside her was the sigil of a mother and babe, for Pexdra, the Goddess of motherhood and fertility. In the centre of them all, the sigil for Xedan, the father of the Gods and the God of war. His sigil was three inter-locking symbols. The symbols were similar in shape to trian-gles, but their pattern was more of an intricate knot that had no start and no finish.

As Bastian stared at the marble carvings, he felt a presence beside him and was surprised to realise Ax had finished his prayer and was now standing beside him.

"Lost in thought?" Ax asked him with a soft smile.

"I guess I was," Bastian confessed. "More Gods than Orders. Sometimes I like to think which Order is favoured by which God."

"The Raven was favoured by Xedan. There are scriptures where they state he sat with one on each shoulder."

"Xedan is also the God of war," Bastian said to Ax. "Maybe that's why we feel like there is an affiliation with him," he mused.

"And they also say that a raven carries the soul to the underworld," Ax told him cheerfully as they both walked to the doors leading them out of the nave.

Bastian looked to the far side where a lone carving of marble was high on the wall. The skull was expertly carved into the stone, showing only half the head in profile as the other was said to wear the flesh as she would have in life. The skull's eye socket was hollowed out, but it still had the uncanny ability to make one feel as if it were watching and following a person around the room. Although the skull took up most of the stone, there was the smaller etching of two coins to the bottom corner, letting all who looked be reminded that payment was required for the passage to the underworld.

"Why is she never with the others?" Bastian asked Ax thoughtfully. "Tyxra is always alone, away from them."

"The Goddess shuns herself," Ax answered easily. "The Gods live in the heavens; Tyxra is confined to the underworld, her task to punish the dishonourable dead."

"You would think that death was punishment enough," Bastian muttered as they exited the nave and stood in the enclosed courtyard in the mid-morning sun.

"It is not for the way of the Gods that you have sought me out this morning though," Ax said with a knowing smile. Bastian handed over the parchment and ignored Ax's cackle as he read it. "And what? There is only me here to ask to accompany you?"

"You're the first person I've asked. I plan on finding Xan next," he admitted.

"It's a party," Ax told him as he waved the invitation in front of Bastian's face. "It's an invitation to celebrate a happy occasion."

"It's a summons, and you know it as well as I do." Bastian glared at the offending parchment. "Are you coming with me?"

"Of course. I wouldn't miss it."

Bastian's lips twisted into a grimace as he regarded Ax. "I should be offended that you look so eager to enjoy my discomfort," he grumbled.

"Now, my brother, would I do such a thing?"

With a shake of his head, Bastian started to walk away from his companion. "Aye!" he called over his shoulder. "Now come help me find Xan."

Ax's laughter followed him into the halls of the Order and merely got louder when they found Xan later and the two of them took great delight in Bastian's misery. But he knew he shouldn't complain too much—at least they were willing to accompany him to the charade.

The carriage arrived at the doors of the Order of the Conclave promptly at the seventh evening hour. The three of them were in their formal attire, and Bastian was glaring at his high-polished black leather boots with suspicion when Clem alerted them to the fact that the carriage was outside.

"I'm sure these aren't even mine," he spoke aloud as he studied the boots.

"They're nice boots," Xan complimented him as he placed his own boot beside Bastian's, comparing them with his own. "I like them."

Bastian rolled his head from side to side in the hope to stretch his neck in the bid to try and loosen up the tension he could feel settling at the base of his skull. "Well, let's get this dung pile over and done with," he told them grimly as he left the sanctuary of the Conclave.

The Golden City was named such because of all the ruined cities that had been repaired and rebuilt after the Before. Pavolyn had many buildings that favoured glass, and as the sun rose in the morning, the golden sun was reflected in many of the buildings. In truth, the actual buildings were stone and tile, reclaimed from fallen structures and ruins found throughout the kingdom. As the sun fell, the sheen was lost and there was nothing "golden" about Pavolyn.

They rode in silence through the streets, the curtains of the carriage drawn closed so nosey passers-by did not see the occupants within. Pavolyn royalty accepted the Orders still, but not all the residents of the city felt the same, and Bastian was in too eager a mood to knock a few teeth loose tonight, without adding stone-throwing citizens into the mix.

The palace was lit with torches and had ropes and ropes of small lanterns that were strewn along the walls like banners. Golden pennants flew high in the towers and the arches, music spilled onto the street from the enclosed walled garden, and the sound of merriment rang out, reaching the three soldiers when they exited the carriage.

They adjusted their cloaks over their formal attire, and with a shared look—two of amusement and one of determination—the three knights of the Order entered the palace compound.

***

BETH CLUNG TO THE SHADOWED CORNER OF THE GARDENS, even though Kase was an imposing deterrent to any who dared approach, and Tyria's fierce scowl was a further warning to any who perhaps thought to chance past Kase.

"How long do we have to wait?" Kase asked again under his breath as he tracked the approach of a rather rotund balding man who was in a garish tunic of orange and purple, heading straight for them.

"They said we would be seen," Beth reminded him. "Patience is a virtue."

Kase glanced at her but chose not to comment on the fact that she was quoting the irksome mercenary. Instead, he focused his full attention on the man in the hideous clothing.

"Lord Barka deVekyan," he announced himself. Kase said nothing, which seemed to confuse the lord in front of him, who clearly was expecting another reaction. "It's been so long since one of the Prairie graced a function. May I ask which Clan you belong to?"

Kase had not anticipated the lord asking about him; he was sure they were all trying to get to his lady. She was in her robes after all, but to want to talk to him…he was off balance. "What?"

The lord blinked in confusion at the harsh tone. "Your Clan?"

"My Clan is none of your concern." He glared at the lord until his message that he wasn't talking was received, and the man hurried away. Turning his head slightly, he saw Tyria laughing behind her hand, and Beth, too, had her lips pressed in a thin line, her eyes crinkling in amusement.

"These people are annoying," Kase snapped at them both. "It's not funny."

"It's a little bit funny," Tyria countered. "He barely reached your belt. It took great courage for him to approach you."

Kase folded his large arms across his chest, his glare all the hotter on the occupants of the gardens. "Courage? These spineless imbeciles don't know the word."

When Tyria went to scold him, Beth placed her hand on her arm, stopping her from antagonising their companion. "Perhaps some wine would be a good idea?" Tyria said instead. "I'll go find some." Slipping past Kase, she melted into the crowd.

"We have been here for some time," Beth spoke quietly. "I do not think it will be much longer."

Kase said nothing, just kept his eyes on the crowd, who all seemed to be keeping their eyes on them. He was eager for this evening to be over. After they had finished their second cup of wine, a steward wearing a uniform of white, heavily embroidered in gold, walked up to them. "Follow me," he instructed with a short bow.

Together they took a number of passages and halls until

they were before large ornate doors that, when pushed open, revealed a sitting room furnished in white and gold. Thick woollen rugs, stained gold, were strewn about the floor, while heavy golden velvet drapes hung from the ceiling at windows that were the height of the wall. Gauzy white netting blew gently over the open windows that led to balconies, which overlooked the gardens below.

Several couches and chairs adorned the room, and on the tallest backed chair sat the golden-haired queen of Kestornia.

Queen Aeryn smiled in greeting at the three of them as they entered her sitting room. The tall Tzenythian was imposing with his head shaved on the sides and his long black hair scraped back in a topknot. His leather tunic didn't hide his broad chest and only accentuated the bulge of his forearms. His fierce gaze full of distrust reminded her of another imposing male, and Aeryn found herself smiling widely at the plainsman, earning her a sharper scowl.

"Welcome," she greeted them, her attention shifting to the woman in the middle of the three strangers. Dark raven hair hung long down her back and over her shoulders. The blue silk dress, embroidered in silver at the bodice and the hem, with its plain round neck spoke of wealth rather than fashion. The heavy blue velvet cloak that sat back over her shoulders, with a simple silver clasp at the neck, spoke the loudest in the room. "Handmaiden," Aeryn spoke clearly, never one to shy away from controversy. "You are far from your home."

Beth smiled in greeting. "I am, your majesty. I have travelled far to meet you."

Aeryn gestured to the couch and chairs. "Please sit, refreshments are being brought."

Kase took the chair nearest the door, and Aeryn watched the red-haired woman sit tentatively on the couch, smoothing her plain green dress over her knees as her eyes darted around the room. The dark-haired woman sat with a grace that rivalled Aeryn's own, and she waited until they were settled.

"It is kind of you to grant us an audience," Beth began. "Especially tonight, when the festivities are in place."

Aeryn gave a dismissive wave of her hand. "The festivities will last for several days. You take me away from nothing." She paused as the house staff brought in trays of goblets of wine and platters of small delicacies. "Please help yourself," she encouraged as a plate was made for her.

Kase eyed the small pastries and delicate foods with wariness, but Tyria had no qualms leaning forward and making herself a plate as well as one for her lady. When they each had food and wine, Aeryn smiled at the handmaiden, encouraging her to start.

Beth's food lay untouched, and her goblet rested on a small table beside her. Wetting her lips, she met the dark blue eyes of the queen. "I had a vision," she began.

The queen dabbed delicately at the corner of her mouth with a napkin. "Please, tell me that you did not use the boon from your Temple to tell me that you had a vision?"

"If you would grant me some patience, your grace?" Beth said quietly. "I will tell you why I am here."

Aeryn looked her over once more, and with a sigh, she reached for her goblet of wine. "Very well, handmaiden, tell me your tale."

"A dream, my mother called it, only it recurred every night for two years, before she took me to the Temple. Every night, the detail never changed, the images never wavered in focus. Every night, the five figures emerge from the sea, they stand, not one of them wet, their clothes crisp and clean, their hair unbound and loose. Together they walk as one towards me. Their faces are never in focus, but I know they are a mix of male and female. They reach forward together, and all of them but none of them take my hands." Beth swallowed as she watched the queen, who was expressionless as she listened. "They pull me to the sea, and I resist, but inside, inside I know I want to go. I want to step into the waves and see where they lead me." Beth broke eye contact briefly with the queen. "I do not fear what lies beneath the waves. But they stop me before the water's edge. They hold me in place and a wave, a wave so big, rushes to the shore." Beth glanced at Kase, who was watching her. He had heard the story several times before, but still he listened with attentiveness. "I fear the wave—I do not fear the water—but the wave that will crash over me, *that* I fear. For I know it's not a wave."

"What is it?" the queen asked.

"Death." Beth took a sip of her wine. "I know the wave will harm me. I know the wave is not of the sea. I know the wave seeks to drown me."

"The wave is part of the sea, is it not?" Aeryn asked.

"No, it is different. The sea is clear and calm and tranquil, the wave is angry, dark in colour, froth of white churning at its crest. It is as different to the water beneath it as the sun is to the moon."

"And what do you think this means?"

"The five beings that came out of the tranquillity are the Gods." Beth sat straighter. "The wave is Mankla, the sea God, eager to wash away those that believe in the new."

"And the meaning?" Aeryn bit into a fluffy light pastry, appreciating its flakiness and buttery texture, as she listened to the woman across from her.

"The Gods are kind and gentle; they do not wish us harm. The old Gods are fearful of their replacement and will strike out at any who look to the new for guidance, comfort or shelter."

"You got all this from a wave?" Aeryn asked sceptically.

"No." Beth smiled indulgently. "One night, the vision changed. The figures emerged from the fire, the kind of warm and gentle glow that fills you with warmth, but from the depths of the fire, a spark ignites into a heavy wild flame that licks the air around it as it covers the room in thick smoke. It makes me choke. I cough and choke on the smoke, but it's too thick, too heavy. I have no choice but to inhale it into my lungs."

"And die," Aeryn surmised, and Beth nodded. "Are there more?"

"Yes, there is the earth that opens to swallow me, the flowers that turn to thorns to poison me, the tower that crumbles beneath me as I fall to my death."

"And in all, the safety is given in the arms of the new Gods?"

"Yes."

Aeryn looked between the three of them and reached for her wine. "You did not come all this way to convince me that you believe in the new Gods, handmaiden. What is it that you seek?"

Chapter 21

Beth met the unwavering gaze of the monarch without flinching. "My visions have changed. I am sure of my belief. I am a follower of the new Gods," she said as she uncovered her wrists and showed them both to the queen. "I did not ask for these. I did not sit and patiently endure the pain to ink them onto my skin. They appeared on their own, and they began the first year the vision changed."

Aeryn leaned forward and inspected the delicate black pattern around the young woman's wrists. "And this tells you…what?"

"These?" Beth shrugged as she covered them again. "They tell me that I do not necessarily have to be sleeping to receive a sign from the Gods."

"Are these the reasons your dreams changed?"

"No. I'm on the sand, the sea is angry and violent, and a voice is chanting beside me. A voice I know but do not know. I feel them, the Gods. They are within me, *I* am *their* voice, and if I strain, I can hear them, hear the words they are urging me to say as they speak beneath the sea. And then there is the other on the sand. He speaks his own words. They flow around me, but they are not the words from the Gods."

Aeryn frowned. "I do not know what you want from me? From my kingdom?"

"Can't you hear the words my lady tells you?" Kase spoke for the first time. "There's someone on the sand with her, someone who is not a God, but someone who is as *powerful* as one." Kase leaned forward in his earnestness to appeal to the queen. "There is a false prophet. He is dangerous. He is not the truth," Kase spoke instead of Beth. "As we travelled here, we heard rumours of him travelling through towns, whispers of his passing. He is real. He is walking amongst us."

"And who may he be? This false God," the queen asked Kase, taking in the ferocity of his glare, the tension in his shoulders. He was quite formidable looking, but Aeryn was a queen, and she was used to dealing with imposing-looking men. Even so, the man's next words caused a chill down her spine.

"He calls himself the Mystic."

Aeryn drew back in her chair, her expression closed off. "The Mystic is dead."

"Well, either someone lied or he's been born again," Kase growled.

"You know not of what you speak," Aeryn snapped at the surly man. "He is dead." She turned to Beth, her look no longer friendly. "Other than this, why are you here?"

Beth hesitated before she spoke again. "The time for the old Gods is over, and they know it, your grace, but they will not go quietly. They fight still. They rally the people to war using this man who calls himself the name which gives you fear. I know it, I have seen it. Evil walks amongst us. The creatures that dwell in the Barrens have come forth. They are moving south. It all points to this. To *him*. We need to stop them. We need to end this war before it even begins."

Aeryn looked at the small, graceful woman in front of her and laughed scornfully. "We? Or you?" Shrewd blue eyes watched Beth, calculating. "You are what, one and twenty if you are a day? How can *you* stop this? Even if it were true, which I have my doubts, what are your plans to scale the heights of heaven and wage war on Gods?"

Beth was not to be perturbed with the queen's mocking tone. "I have my faith, I have my gift, and I have a request of you, Queen Aeryn. That is why I am here. I need soldiers. I have a task to complete, and I need men who can fight, men who have seen war and are not scared to see it again."

"The Orders?" Aeryn's lips were pressed tight in anger. "The Orders who fought for and serve the very Gods that you say you are fighting against?"

Beth smiled. "I understand the scepticism and the seeming hypocrisy in my request, but my vision is clear. I need the men of the Order to help me find an artefact."

Aeryn's eyes narrowed further still. "An artefact? Which one?"

"I do not know."

Aeryn waited for more information, but the woman didn't offer any. "Say I believe any of this. Which Order? They are very different men within their ranks."

"I do not know," Beth confessed. "I see wings on leather but not which bird wings it is."

"It's a tall tale you bring to me," Aeryn told her with a heavy sigh. "Have you shared this with your Temple Maiden?"

"No."

Aeryn nodded. "I did not think so." Smoothly she rose to her feet. "You have given me much to consider, and I shall. It's a lot to process, handmaiden. For now, go, enjoy the evening. I shall call on you when I have thought more on this."

"But I don't have time," Beth protested. "I need to begin my journey. I've wasted so much time already; I don't have much left."

"Then I suggest you make some." With that, the queen swept out of the room, her manservants hastening after her, leaving Beth staring helplessly at the door as it closed behind her.

"Well, that was as to be expected," Kase said as he stood and stretched. "Are you okay?"

"No, I thought…"

"That the queen of Kestornia would hear your story and immediately fall over her feet to order men from the Conclave to march to war against an unseen enemy, in an unknown location, for a war that rids them of their Gods?" Kase reached down and finally plucked a pastry off of the platter. It was so small in his hand it seemed it was hardly worth eating.

Beth turned to look at him and couldn't conceal the twitch of her lips as she rolled her eyes. "Well, when you put it like that…"

"It's a lot to take in," Tyria agreed. She was sitting deeply back against the velvet couch, her feet skimming along the floor as she sipped from her goblet. She looked entirely comfortable in the queen's audience room. "When you first told me, I thought you were stark raving mad."

Beth turned to look at her, her eyes wide. "Truly?"

"Yes." Tyria nodded. "Why do you think I kept asking you to repeat it?"

"I told you when I was nine years old." Beth shook her head in amazement.

"I know, that's why I believed you." Tyria leaned forward and plucked a grape from the bowl. "The retelling never changed; not one word was altered. It had to be true."

"You believed me not because of what I see in my visions but because the details are the same?" Beth was incredulous.

"Of course I did." Finishing her wine, Tyria stood too. "I was eleven. What in the kingdom's name was I going to know about visions of Gods?"

Kase snorted out a laugh as he picked a few more items off the tray, chewing as he looked between them. "So, what do we do now? Wait?"

Beth sighed as she wrung her hands together, and then not knowing of any alternative, she nodded. "We wait. I was hoping to avoid the Temple," she confessed as they walked to the heavy doors and Kase pulled open the door for them. "No one will understand, and there will be so many questions—"

The three men in front of her were not what she expected to see. Bastian, Xan and Ax stood looking as shocked at their appearance as she was sure she was of theirs. She wasn't sure which stunned her more, the fact they were in front of her or what they wore.

"You're Order?" Kase scoffed as he looked them over. "I *knew* it."

Beth couldn't speak, her eyes glued to the long red cloaks the men in front of her wore. Bastian watched her as her gaze darted between the three, taking in the armoured breastplates, the long tunics under it, even down to their black polished boots, but it was their blood red cloaks that she kept looking back at. The mark of the Order was not only the bird sigil etched into their armour or on their leather cuirass, but it was also in the heavy bold cloak that each man wore, telling all who looked upon them that they served in the Order of the Conclave.

"You look surprised?" Bastian's voice was dry as he looked the three of them over. "And surprisingly…wealthy."

"What?" Kase laughed derisively. "You think you should have been paid more than three gold coins?"

"Not at all," Bastian said with a bland smile. "I didn't expect payment from you at all, given your want to sneak about in the night." His attention rested on Beth. "Fylip sends his regards. We all *thank* you for the tea."

Flushing at the blatant rudeness of the man, Beth looked up at Kase. "We were leaving, it's…" She had almost said it was good to see them, but it wasn't. It was awkward and tense. "Late." She ignored the mocking smirk that Xan wore or the amused laughter shining in Ax's eyes. "Yes, it's quite late." Gathering her skirts, she made to move past them.

The dagger to her throat stopped her passage as Bastian fixed her with an unwavering glare. "The Temple?" he asked, ignoring Kase's cry as he reached for his sword, Xan's sword already drawn and the tip resting on the plains-man's chest.

"What of it?" Beth asked quietly, seemingly unfazed by the dagger in front of her.

"You wear their sigil at your neck." He cocked his head

as he considered her. "You failed to mention you were an *actual* handmaiden."

"As you forgot to mention your red cloak, Sir Knight?" Beth mimicked his tone. "You may step aside."

"I may," he spoke quietly as he looked over her shoulder, "but I don't see the queen within her chamber, and I know how freely you share your tea."

"You think we harmed the queen?" Kase asked incredulously. "We had an audience with her."

"I bet you did," Xan said as he pushed his sword against Kase's chest. "Move backwards, slowly, so we can see for ourselves."

"I am a handmaiden of the Temple," Beth said in exasperation. "We had an audience with her majesty. I'm hardly going to spike the tea!"

"And besides," Tyria spoke up for the first time. "We had wine."

"Move," Xan commanded, and Kase had no choice but to walk backwards as Xan walked forwards, his sword steady.

As they advanced into the room, a house servant came into the suite through the opposite door. Seeing the situation, he stopped on the spot, completely still.

"Where's the queen?" Bastian asked him.

"I'll get her."

As the servant ran from the room, Bastian fought the urge to call him back and tell him that wasn't what he had asked him.

"Ooh," Ax said with glee as he picked up a small pastry with a cured beef filling. "The palace always makes the best finger food."

"Is the sword still necessary?" Kase asked Xan, glancing down at his chest to emphasise the point. "The queen is clearly unharmed."

"I'll be the judge of that," Bastian told him, but he did drop his own arm that held the dagger he had been pointing at Beth.

"How did you even get in?" Xan asked as he regarded them. "Sure, you look the part, but an audience with Aeryn is difficult to achieve."

Bastian watched as Beth's cheeks bloomed in colour. "A boon?" he guessed.

Beth was thankfully saved from answering when the doors to the other side of the room opened and the queen entered with a handful of guards and another man, who also wore the red cloak, but out of the corner of her eye, Beth saw Bastian stiffen.

Hastily Beth curtsied, as the Order men bowed, some more shallowly than others, she noted.

"What in the name of the Goddess is going on?" Aeryn demanded as she joined them. "And why are you still here?" she directed at Beth and the others. "Didn't I tell you to enjoy the evening? If I was not clear," the blonde queen snapped, "I did not mean in my audience chambers." Glancing at the knights, she rolled her eyes. "Really, Ax? Do they starve you in the Conclave now?"

Ax, who had happily resumed eating the canapés, laughed. "It is good to see you in such fine spirits, your grace."

Aeryn said nothing but turned to the older man beside her. "Lord Commander, these are the three I was telling you about."

The Lord Commander was older, but not too old that he no longer served in battle. Average height and build, he nevertheless commanded a strong presence. Greying hair, pulled back at the nape of his neck, a round face with a straight nose that sat over thin lips, moulded that way surely from the years he had pressed them together to keep himself quiet, he was a plain looking man.

"Lord Commander Draxon," Bastian greeted. "I did not know you received an invitation."

Draxon swept his gaze over the three men of the Order. "And why would I not be here?" he harrumphed. "So, you're the handmaiden?" He turned to Beth. "The Temple Maiden know you are here and of what you speak?"

"Handmaiden?" Xan asked sceptically. "Truly?"

"You seem so shocked," Beth mocked.

"Surprised," Ax interjected to cut off Xan's words. "Perhaps we should have enjoyed more tea over the course of the journey."

"We had no choice," Kase grumbled. "There were atchen in the woods. *Atchen.*"

"You know each other?" the queen demanded as she watched them all. "How?"

As voices vied to be heard over others, Bastian's hard tone cut through them all. "I don't think we knew each other at all."

Beth met his look and glanced away. "No, it would seem not."

"I'm going to need more wine," Aeryn declared, gesturing to the servants on hand. "Wine, a lot of it, more food too, oh, and some chairs."

"We can lift chairs, Aeryn," Bastian grumbled as he

walked across the room and demonstrated he could indeed lift the chairs that he brought to the small circle of people. "They're literally in the same room as you."

Aeryn ignored him, and Beth exchanged a wide-eyed look with Kase that no one reprimanded Bastian for calling the queen by her given name.

"You can tell your tale as we wait," Draxon spoke to Beth. "Who are you and what is your purpose?"

Beth stood slightly straighter as she felt herself being weighed and judged by everyone in the room. "I am a servant of the Gods," she said simply. "The new Gods," she added hastily.

"Your robes and ink tell me that, girl. What I want to know is who you are and why a girl from Eloysth is demanding knights from the Conclave."

"You demanded *what?*" Bastian asked her in disbelief.

Beth ignored Bastian as she gave the Lord Commander her full attention. "I am happy to discuss it with you in private."

"You discuss it now," Draxon barked. "Now, one more time, who are you?"

CHAPTER 22

BETH HELD HER HAND UP TO STOP KASE FROM SPEAKING. She knew him well, and without looking, she knew he would be away to snap in reply to the man who ordered her to explain herself.

"Lord Commander," Beth spoke with calmness and confidence. "It is a pleasure to meet you," she told him politely. "Please allow me to introduce my companions, for everyone's benefit." Turning to her left, she looked at Kase. "Kase Larsyd is my protector and bodyguard. He has been in my service for six years."

"Seven," Kase corrected her gruffly.

"You're Tzenythian," Draxon pointed out. "It's unlike one of your people to serve in the Temple."

"Unlikely but not impossible," Kase answered.

"Your Clan?" Draxon asked.

"None of your concern."

"I asked a question." Draxon's voice was cold and stern.

"And I answered it. In case you're deaf, I'll say it again, it's no business of yours. I am in the service of the Temple, and I do *not* answer to you."

Hoping to avoid either man's anger spilling over, Beth turned to Tyria. "This is Tyria deYarg. She has been with me since I was a girl and first entered the Temple."

Draxon looked the red-haired woman over and dismissed her. "I did not ask for introductions to your party, I asked who *you* were."

"My parents gave me the name Beth."

Draxon grunted and raised an eyebrow as he waited. "And the name the Temple gave you?"

Beth couldn't help but look at the three men she had recently travelled with. All three watched her, and not for the first time with them, she felt nervous. "I am known as Echo of the Frost."

"Frost fits," Xan mumbled.

"It was *just* a sleeping draught," Beth said with exasperation. "You're all fine!"

"You administered a sleeping draught to a group of men who had protected you for days, weeks even, who were tired and exhausted from fighting the zyvarg that followed *you*," Bastian told her coldly. "And who had just fought atchen in the woods beside the place where they were still protecting *you*, and *you* drugged them, leaving them defenceless. So no, *Echo*, it was not *just* a sleeping draught."

Wetting her lips nervously, Beth looked at Kase, who was avoiding eye contact. "I"—she swallowed hard—"I didn't think of it like that, my lord." A little shaken with the truth, Beth apologised. "I'm sorry, truly I am. I never thought of the consequences of leaving you unguarded." Trying for some even ground, she offered a smile. "And some of my friends would still call me Beth."

Bastian turned his attention to his Lord Commander. "What is it that *Echo* of the Frost has asked of the Order?"

Wincing as he spoke her name with such indifference, Beth exchanged a look with Tyria, who was gnawing at her lower lip. It was clear that Tyria hadn't thought of the atchen either in their haste to leave undetected. It was also clear that Kase *had* and left them unprotected anyway. She wasn't sure what to make of that.

"Are the introductions over?" she asked tiredly. They may have acted carelessly, but maybe if the men hadn't also been hiding secrets, then they wouldn't have needed to. "You ask us to share all, but as usual, you give nothing in return?"

The queen watched on as they all bounced off each other. There was obvious tension between the knights and the handmaiden and her companions, and it was obvious to Aeryn that there was caution being demonstrated by the knights to their Lord Commander. That fascinated her more than the issues between the woman and Bastian, but still she thought Echo had a point.

"Bastian," Aeryn directed. "It seems you are remiss, as ever, in your manners."

"The presence of my Lord Commander prohibits me from telling you what I think of your opinion," Bastian told her flippantly, ignoring the queen's eye roll. "Or theirs," he added as he jerked a thumb at the others. Taking a seat, Bastian decided he needed a drink after all and took a goblet of wine, drinking from it deeply.

Ax laughed in the heavy silence. "Let me rectify matters," he said with flair and a deep bow to Aeryn. She watched as the more carefree of the three presented himself to the three strangers. Although not as unknown to each other as she thought, they were still far from friends. She wasn't sure she would even describe them as acquaintances.

Ax pointed at Xan. "Knight of the Order of the Ravens, Sir Xan deVanya."

"DeVanya?" Tyria asked Xan. "Of the Pavolyn deVanyas?"

"Aye," Xan answered gruffly.

"What's the issue?" Kase asked, looking between the two of them.

"Sir Xan's father is the Marquess Cerxan deVanya." Tyria's voice wavered only slightly.

Kase considered the man in front of him. "Oh, is that all?"

Ax laughed heartily as he looked at Kase, smiling widely. "That is all," he told him. "Whatever title we may have held from the fortunes of our birth is removed when we enter the Order." Ax gave Tyria a broad wink. "There are only three ranks in the Order: squire, sergeant, and knight. And within that, the only titles that matter are general, Lord Commander and Grand Master."

"Simpler," Tyria said, rubbing her hands over her skirts. "Your name, Sir Knight?"

Ax was positively brimming with glee as he bowed low, and as he rose, his grey eyes holding her own as he kept his back bent slightly. "Axanyial…Barsgaard, at your service."

Tyria's hands flew to her mouth to stifle her groan. "Barsgaard?" she bemoaned.

"Afraid so." Ax straightened. "And I'm truly sorry to never have met your acquaintance…cousin, would it be?" he mocked her.

"You know as well as I do I'm not related to you, sir," Tyria snapped, her face red with embarrassment. "What were the chances that you were *actually* a Barsgaard?"

"You should always be sure who you mean to imitate before committing yourself," Ax chided gently. "Especially when my family is quite small."

"And *quite* powerful," Tyria grouched. "I took a gamble," she confessed.

"This is why you would not share your name when we first met," Kase directed at Bastian. "You are all of the nobility."

"*We*," Bastian answered as he scowled at his empty goblet, "are knights of the Order; titles mean nothing."

"Then why conceal your identities?" Kase challenged him.

"Why indeed?" Bastian snorted, returning Kase's challenge, which the man ignored as he looked away. Bastian shook his head in disgust. "Titles mean nothing to *us*. That doesn't mean that they don't mean a lot to others."

"So, you're who? Earl? Baron? Viscount?" Kase, who had turned back to look at Bastian as he spoke, asked with a sneer, which let them know titles meant little to him either.

"He is Bastian *dal'Leif*," Queen Aeryn said with a sharpness that caused Kase to lose his attitude. "And *he* is my brother."

"You're a prince?" Tyria gaped at him.

For the first time since she had met him, Bastian looked uncomfortable. "No, I am a Knight of the Order of the Ravens," he stated firmly.

"He bleeds the same colour as the rest of us," Ax said light-heartedly. "His shi—"

"Axanyial!" Draxon cut him off.

"Well, you get the idea," Ax said with a careless shrug, sharing a quick grin with Xan.

"So now that we all know each other," Bastian said as he stood. "Can we get to the part where a handmaiden of the Temple is seeking assistance from the Order of the Conclave?"

"Does your Temple Maiden know you are here?" Lord

Commander Draxon asked Echo. "*Not* the Temple in Pavolyn that is a sanctuary for any of the handmaidens, I mean the Temple Maiden of the Temple of the Frost."

"No."

"Beth, what mischief have you got yourself into?" Xan asked with a sly chuckle. "Or do we call you Echo?"

"You do not address the handmaiden by her name," Kase snapped angrily.

"Her name? Which one? Beth? Or Echo?" Ax asked with a frown. "I'm not saying Echo of the Frost every time —it's pretentious."

"Your father is right hand to the king of Bordyre," Tyria told him with wide eyes. "*He's* a duke." She pointed at Xan. "And he's a…" She hesitated as her finger shook slightly as she pointed at Bastian. "I don't know exactly, but the point is, I think you can handle saying Echo of the Frost!"

"I don't walk around saying Sir Axanyial Barsgaard, Knight of the Order of the Ravens, do I?" Ax countered hotly as he threw his hands in the air with exasperation. "No, I say *hello, I'm Ax*. See? Simple. Plain. No pretension. Bastian, does he mention his sister is the queen of Kestornia? Or that his father is the king of Kalzynia? No, he says *nice to meet you, I'm Bastian*."

"But he didn't," Echo cut in. "It wasn't until Bez was in danger that we learned his name." Slipping her hands into the inner pockets of her heavy blue cloak, she looked around. "And now we know why. He told us then there was a lot of power in a name, and in Bastian's case, that is true. As it is in my own, but you are right." Turning to face Ax fully, Echo dipped her head slightly in a quick bow. "Hello,

I'm Echo of the Frost, handmaiden to the Gods, and I serve in the Temple of the Frost."

Ax studied her for a long moment, and then slowly, a smile creased his face. "Can I call you Echo? Echo of the Frost is a lot to say in a hurry."

Echo smiled, her green eyes alight with mirth. It was impossible to remain grouchy at Ax. He had an appealing innocence about him that softened him, unlike the others. "You may call me Echo."

Aeryn watched their interaction, gauging the reactions of the others in the room. Her brother had reclaimed his seat and was focused on the table in front of him, seemingly removed from the conversation around him. But Aeryn knew her brother well; he was not as distant as he appeared to be. Xan was watching the tall plainsman, who was scowling at Ax. The serving lady, Tyria, was watching the entertaining exchange between her lady and the knight. Draxon, who sat next to her, was staring pointedly at Bastian, who was ignoring his Lord Commander and everyone else.

"Echo—" Aeryn paused. "I can also call you Echo?"

"Of course, your grace," Echo replied warmly.

"When you were here earlier, you had some outlandish claims to be shared. Can I ask that you share them again?"

Echo flicked her eyes to Bastian, whose attention was still elsewhere. "I would ask I speak of it to you and the Lord Commander alone," Echo requested again.

"Why?" Xan asked. "What is it that you have to say that is so dire that you think our Lord Commander will not share with us?" Xan looked over at Aeryn. "Or that our queen won't confide to her brother?"

Echo sighed heavily. "Because I know he will say no."

Startled at the sense of resignation that was heavy in the words from the handmaiden, Draxon asked, "Who? Me?"

"No, my lord," Echo answered, looking down.

"We have wasted enough time, handmaiden," Draxon said gruffly. "Why do you request aid from me and the Order of the Conclave?"

Echo raised her head and met his inquisitive stare fully. "Because a war is coming, and I need your Order's help to stop it." Ignoring the snort coming from the man on the couch, she continued. "I saw my first vision when I was three. I was but a child and thought it no more than a dream. I had the same dream every night. When I was five, my mother took me to the temple near our town." Echo stared out towards the balcony. The breeze blew at the thin sheer curtains, allowing glimpses out to the night sky beyond. "I told the Maiden of the Temple what I saw, and I was tested for my affinity to the Temple when I was six. I trained in the temple near my home until I was nine, and I entered the Temple of the Frost shortly thereafter."

"Nine is young," Ax murmured in sympathy.

"I made a fast friend." Echo looked at Tyria with fondness. "I have served in the Temple of the Frost in the Blue City since I was nine." Echo looked at them all as she spoke. "And I have had the same vision of the Gods every night until…"

"Until?" Draxon prompted.

"Within the last year, the vision has changed. It has always been the Gods reaching for me, taking me to the water's edge, and protecting me from the wrath of Mankla, the God of the sea. But now on the sand, there is a man beside me. Chanting. He's trying to stop me from hearing the Gods. He is dangerous, evil I am sure, and he is the voice of the old Gods."

"Or it is the old Gods who protect you from the new?" Xan countered.

"It is the five *new* Gods who come from the water to take my hands."

"Who is the man who stands beside you?" Draxon asked.

"I do not know."

"How is this connected with the Order of the Conclave?" Ax asked. "We are soldiers of the Gods," he reminded her, "and they are *not* the Gods that you serve."

"I know." Echo gave a small laugh as she once again marvelled at the irony. "I know. But I am to find an artefact, and I see the cloaks of the red. I see the breastplates of armour with the wings of a bird on them, and I know it is Knights of the Order. One stands beside me cast in shadow, but...I *know* in the very core of my being that he stands *beside* me, *not* against me."

"And who do they fight against as they stand beside you?" Draxon asked. "A dream?"

Echo had expected the mockery, and she was unfazed by it. "He calls himself the Mystic."

Bastian's head snapped up for the first time since she had begun to tell them why she was here. Light blue eyes the colour of the summer sky stared at her, clouded with suspicion.

"The Mystic is no longer a problem for the Five King-doms," Draxon scoffed. Picking up a goblet of wine, his finger caressed the curve of the goblet as he thought back to a darker time. "He died many years ago," he told her curtly, putting the wine to the side, not taking a drink.

"Then the Gods have imbued someone else with the power you fear so much," Echo spoke boldly.

Draxon had a plate with some food beside him, and his hand paused as he reached for the sweet pastries. "I do not fear the power of a dead man." Sitting back in his chair, he regarded Echo coldly. "Lexyck ManValen died a cowardly death, like the fraud he was."

"He was also a prophet of the new Gods, not the old," Bastian spoke for the first time since Echo had finally revealed why she and the others were there. "Your Mystic may not be the adversary that you think he is." His firm words were said in a reasonable tone, yet Echo still felt chastised.

"You are Temple of the Frost," Xan added. "Your affinity is water, correct?"

"Obviously," Echo muttered.

"Why would a handmaiden fear the sea?" Xan asked her shrewdly. "You command the water; it is your gift, correct?"

"It's why the rain fell from a clear sky over Wrazyth," Ax said in sudden understanding.

"You made it rain?" Aeryn asked with surprise as she looked at the handmaiden with a level of new respect. "You must truly be powerful."

"I have a gift the same as many of the others in the Temple."

"How many can make rain fall without clouds?" Xan asked sneeringly.

"We lose the reason I am here," Echo reminded them,

not wanting the power of her gift to be the centre of their attention, but when Bastian spoke, she knew it didn't matter.

"You took to the water when we left the Sand Seas," Bastian said quietly. "We knew you immersed yourself in the spring—you were dripping wet," he went on. "I thought it was to feel cleansed from the desert plains, but it was to replenish your gift." Bastian looked down at his hands clenched tightly into fists. "Your *gift* could have saved the very ground from crumbling under us as we travelled through the Sand Seas."

"Bastian, if I had used it, you—"

"If you had used your gift, he would not have fallen." Bastian rose to his feet and stood straight as he looked her up and down. His breastplate shone as it caught the light in the room, his red cloak draped over broad shoulders, and his left hand rested on the pommel of his sword. The sight was so familiar to Echo that her breath caught.

"It's you," Echo whispered. "In my vision, you are the red-cloaked knight beside me." Looking excitedly to Kase and Tyria, she missed Kase's sour glare at the knight, and Tyria jabbing him in the side because Tyria *did* notice.

"Ask why you are here, handmaiden." Bastian watched Echo, watched as the excitement leached from her expression as she anticipated what was coming.

"Bastian." Echo's plea was low, but it could be heard by all as she took a step forward, her hand half raised from her side in supplication.

"*Ask.*"

Echo dropped her hand as she turned her head away from the angry knight, knowing the answer already. "Bastian dal'Leif, Knight of the Order of the Ravens, will you join me on my quest to find the artefact so I can stop this war before it truly begins?"

"No."

Echo closed her eyes at the pain he caused with one word. With her head turned, she heard others get to their feet, no doubt Ax and Xan, and she knew they left the room with Bastian. Hanging her head, she fought the tears that threatened. She needed them, and without them, she was already failing in her mission to stop this war.

"Well," Aeryn said as she cleared her throat. "You were right, he said no."

Echo's thoughts were racing, her mind overwhelmed with everything they had learned this evening, and then realising that the man she needed to fulfil her duty had been beside her these last few weeks, it had shaken her. Dimly she heard the queen's comment and the grunt of agreement from someone in the room. Remembering she was not alone, Echo also remembered that Draxon was still here. Raising her head, she spoke to the Lord Commander, fuelled with renewed determination. "He *can't* say no. You command him…you command *all* of them. You can make him join me as I seek to fulfil what has been asked of me."

Lord Commander Draxon gave an empty smile. "Now, why would I do that?" he asked her with contempt. "Your *story* is nonsense. Your attempt at raising panic amongst us with tales of a man long dead is laughable at best." Draxon stood and, giving a formal bow to the queen that she acknowledged with merely a slight dip of her head, he turned back to Echo with a look of scorn. "I've heard more than enough from *you*." He walked past her and out of the room.

Echo felt the sense of hopelessness once more and knew that her only prospect was the queen. "Your grace?" she asked hopefully.

"Could you have saved him? Bez? Could you have stopped it?"

Echo shook her head slightly as she blinked back tears. "I don't know," she answered honestly. "My affinity is water; the affinity of clay is not mine."

"But the land crumbled because it was too dry. *You* could have changed that." The queen's challenge was in her words. "So, I ask you, handmaiden who can make a cloudless sky spill rain, could you have helped him?"

Echo shook her head, unwilling to admit that she had asked herself the same question many times and unwilling to admit what she *had* done. "I don't know if I could have saved Bez."

"Until you do, you will find no aid from the Order of the Conclave or my kingdom." The queen gestured to her guards. "Leave. Your audience is over."

CHAPTER 23

BASTIAN LAY ON HIS BED, STARING UPWARD BUT NOT TRULY seeing the ceiling overhead. He, Ax and Xan had not lingered at the palace. He had heard enough, and he was irrationally irked at his sister for hosting an audience with a handmaiden of the Temple with no knights accompanying her. It wasn't because *she* was the handmaiden, it was that Aeryn knew better. She knew they were dangerous. He had taught his sister to be more careful, to take precautions to guard her safety.

Bastian didn't care that the handmaidens represented the new Gods, but most of the handmaidens he had met were fanatical, and they encouraged their followers to be as zealous as them. He and his men had been called into service more times than he liked in order to quell a disturbance of the peace caused by citizens who had been whipped into a religious frenzy from handmaidens enticing riots. Whether the handmaiden intended that or not didn't matter; the fact that it happened more and more frequently was the problem.

Bastian thought about what Beth—no, not Beth, *Echo*—had told them. Vyka had asked him not to share the symbol being shown in Wrazyth, and he had kept it to himself, but he hadn't expected to see Echo again. She had seen it, and now he knew exactly why she had been so keen to see it preserved.

It had been almost ten years since the Mystic had walked this earth. Lexyck ManValen had been a farmer living in a small croft northeast of the Grey City of Kalzynia, where the land was hard to work and the crops fought to grow. All accounts of the man had him as quiet, unassuming, and plain. He had no wife and no children, and his neighbours had said he was always willing to help with their farms and asked for nothing in return. A typical decent man.

Until he claimed he was visited in his fields by the God Hal. As Lexyck toiled at the earth, Hal descended from the heavens to tell him that he, Lexyck, was a chosen messenger of the new Gods. The accounts of the retelling of the visitation stated that Lexyck, being a man of sense and surety, had rejected the God. Lexyck was a believer of the Gods he knew. At every harvest and spring, he had given his tithe to the Goddess Zynia in order for the Goddess of the land to grace him with a good crop.

The retellings said that Lexyck rejected Hal, but the mighty God Hal was not to be deterred. Adamant that his messenger listen to him, Hal sent a rain to wash away the seed Lexyck had planted, and then Hal called forth his sister the Goddess Syr to bless Lexyck's lands. From the sodden, flooded fields sprung a bountiful crop from land where no seed had been buried in the soil.

On seeing the miracle of growth, Lexyck was said to have fallen to his knees and begged Hal's forgiveness. Infused with his belief, Lexyck demanded that Hal tell him the message he was to spread on his belief. On seeing how devout Lexyck had become, Syr called forth her sister Mayv'd, the Goddess of divination, who gifted Lexyck with the gift of inner sight. Hal granted him magic in order that Lexyck could go forth and spread the message of the goodness of the new Gods and heal the people and the land.

Bastian thought about the wars that one man with one message had caused. The Temples, which had been small and had only a small following, sprang up and seemed to spread like wildfire in a dry forest. Soon there were four distinct temples, affiliated with the four elements of earth, air, water, and fire. The Maidens focused on the knowledge that every visible thing in the world was made up of a mix of the four elements. As the Orders of the Conclave were, the Temples divided into smaller elements, each focused on one of the elements. The Temple of the Frost represented water, the Temple of the Flame for fire, the Temple of the Wind for air, and the Temple of the Clay for earth, clay because people, like the earth, could still be moulded.

Sitting up, Bastian rubbed his forehead wearily. Personally, he had no real aversion to the Temples. Much like the new Gods, they were something that were of little concern to him or his spiritual wellbeing. He served the old Gods and believed in them. That others believed something else, did not change Bastian's belief or life.

Khaldan enjoyed eggs that had been stored in vinegar, but Bastian did not care for them. It did not mean Khaldan was any less of a man for eating them, and Bastian did not judge him for it. Although Bastian *did* judge him for the stench Khaldan left in the washrooms after eating them.

Getting off the bed, he began to pace. Zyvarg and atchen in the southern kingdoms bothered him. Were they here because of unrest between old and new Gods? It was unlikely. If they were all creations of the Gods, then either old or new were responsible for the monsters just as much as they were for the newborn babe.

For months he had felt it, the sense of unease. The land was stirring, something else brewed within, and he would be very surprised if it was a heavenly tussle between celestial beings.

Which brought him back to Echo and her claim that she was tasked with a mission to retrieve an artefact for the new Gods, with the soldiers of the old Gods by her side. Shaking his head, he crossed to his window, and pulling back the curtains, he stared out at the night sky. Pavolyn lay quietly in the dark. Covered in the blanket of night, the city slept. But Bastian knew not all of its citizens would be safely ensconced in the land of dreams. There would be many, like him, that would find little rest, either from their own heavy thoughts or for other matters that happened within the covering of darkness.

Echo and her companions had also heard the rumours of the Mystic. It seemed they had actively sought him out, which Bastian questioned Kase's judgement on. He was supposed to be her protector, was he not? Bastian wondered if this new Mystic knew the fate of the last one. Lexyck had been held in the dungeon within this very building. He had been interrogated by the then Lord Commander Fernyn, and in the end of a very long, and Bastian supposed painful, capture for Lexyck, the rulers of the Five Kingdoms had voted unanimously to put him to the death.

Bastian had been in training at the academy in Bordyre having already completed his training in Kalzynia. His father had wanted to ensure that if his son was sure to waste his future on serving Gods, he would be trained to be the best soldier he could be. But for the public death of the Mystic, all knights of the Order were called to Pavolyn to witness the event.

Fresh from the academy, ready to serve, Bastian and Khaldan had sat as Vyka took a knife to the throat of a beaten and broken man. He remembered well the rumble of thunder that sounded in the sky that afternoon, their Lord Commander saying it was a sign that the God Hoxka was pleased with their action. The Temples said it was a sign from the God Rym that he was displeased with the action.

Not long after punishment was delivered to the Mystic, as the knights of the Order of the Conclave restored order throughout the kingdoms by halting any further unrest and stopping further infractions, the leaders of the kingdoms whispered amongst themselves about uglier truths. New rumours began to spread, rumours that were revealed from conversations of monarchs about the Order of the Conclave.

Lord Commander Fernyn had been playing politics. Several of his generals had aided him in the manoeuvring of monarchies and battles their kingdoms had endured. Aid had always been sent when the rulers called for it, but as the ruling families discussed their affairs long after the death of the Mystic, they realised that the aid they had been granted sometimes was at too great a cost.

As doubt rose amongst them at the actions of the leader of the soldiers of the Gods, and as some royal coffers could not quite stretch to the debt still owed, it was too easy for the rulers to take up the mantle of new Gods and declare the Order of the Conclave corrupt and untrustworthy. As kings and queens called out the political agenda of the Order of the Conclave, some were undoubtedly guilty of the charge, Bastian knew, but some were not.

He was not.

But Bastian was born of royalty, and he knew the inner workings and scheming of the type of men who gave counsel to kings. With a snort of contempt, Bastian turned from the window.

His reminiscing of the past did not solve the problem of the present. Towards the end of Lexyck ManValen's campaign, fearing that his faithful were floundering under the hardship of war, Lexyck claimed he had yet again been visited by his Gods, and on his skin was inked four symbols, each representing the four elements.

One of the symbols was the design in the blooms at the festival. Very few people knew of their existence, and the fact that this new mystic was citing the same symbols for the old Gods worried Bastian.

How were they the same yet now on opposing sides? And where did *she* fit in? She claimed the Mystic was evil, but she was eager to embrace the symbol. Were they not the same thing? Were there two threats? And if there were two, which one was Echo of the Frost?

A soft rap on his door pulled him out of his contemplation. Striding over to the door, he opened it, surprised to see the squire. "Clem? What is it?"

"A visitor, my lord. They would not be deterred," he added apologetically.

"Who?" Bastian scowled when Clem told him, and closed the door to get dressed.

The nave was empty at this time of night, as it should be. Bastian's boots echoed loudly on the stone floor as he approached the altar and the person who stood in front of it. "It's an ungodly hour for a house visit," he said quietly as he came to stand beside her.

Her deep blue hood was pulled up over her dark hair, shielding her face from him, her head tilted slightly back to look at the marble sigils of the Gods. "Ungodly hour," Echo murmured, turning to look at him as her gloved hands rose and pushed her hood back slightly. "A strange turn of phrase, is it not?"

Bastian ignored her question as he looked over his shoulder to the empty room. "You seem to be alone," he commented.

"I am alone."

"Your protector will not be pleased, handmaiden."

"No, he would not understand why I need to speak to you privately." Echo looked back up at the sigils. "It's beautiful work," she noted. "The marble is flawless."

"If you came to talk to me about the talents of a stone master in the middle of the night, handmaiden, I'm afraid I will have to retire to my bedchamber."

Echo smiled at his dry sarcasm. "I want to explain," she said, sobering as she turned from the altar. "Is there somewhere we could talk in private?"

Bastian barked out a laugh that rattled around the silence of the nave. "You're in the nave of the Order of the Conclave. If you want quieter, my only other offer is my chambers, and I do not think either of us wish for that rumour to begin."

"If it is private, who would know?" Echo challenged.

"Because the shadows are always watching," he said gruffly.

"Even here?"

"Especially here," Bastian said with a sigh. "You're in a building of men, and I should not have to tell you, handmaiden, there are no bigger gossips than men."

Echo smiled widely. "I'm a woman from a fishing town," she agreed. "I am aware of the loose tongues of those who cannot hold their ale, never mind their secrets."

Bastian cocked his head to the side as he considered her. "Follow me," he instructed, making his decision.

"To your bedchamber?" Echo asked, feeling slightly alarmed at the prospect, even though it was her suggestion, and earning her an equally scandalised look from Bastian.

"No," he said in exasperation. "I am aware that your opinion of me is low, handmaiden, but I do have a sense of propriety, as should you," he added primly.

Echo pressed her lips tightly together to stop the burst of laughter from escaping. That this hardened warrior and stern man would be affronted at the mere suggestion she be taken to his bedchamber, even just to talk, contrasted with everything that she thought she knew about him.

Bastian led her through a narrow corridor with twists and turns, and when he eventually stopped at a wooden door, Echo no longer knew how she would know how to get back to where they came from. Bastian rapped his knuckles on the door, and after waiting a moment with his ear close to the door, he tried the handle and pushed the door open. Bastian motioned for her to follow, and as he turned the lanterns up higher, Echo looked around the small compact office space.

"This is my general's office," Bastian explained as he motioned for her to sit on a chair that looked old and unreliable. Seeing her dubious look, he smiled. "It'll hold your weight; it holds me," he assured her. When Echo was seated, he turned back to the door. "Give me a moment."

Surprised that she was being left alone in his commander's room, Echo took the opportunity to look around. The walls were bare stone, they hadn't even been painted, and the window was high and uncovered, but even were it daylight, little natural light would seep into this room. The desk was large and dominated the room, but unlike her Temple Maiden's desk, this one was bare, with no papers or parchments waiting for attention. The room held the chair behind the desk, the chair she sat on, and one other. That was it. The office of the general of the Order of the Ravens had bare walls, a large desk and three chairs. She felt strangely let down.

Echo knew that some of the knights in the Order of the Conclave took the vow of chastity, but she knew not all of them did, nor were they required to. However, looking around the room, she wondered if the general had chosen the life of a monk.

The door opening made her jump slightly, but it was only Bastian returning with a tray. On it was a pitcher and two simple wooden cups. Placing it on the desk, Bastian looked at her as he picked up the pitcher. "Water?"

"Yes, thank you."

With both cups poured, he crossed to the other side of the room, turning to face her, with his left hand resting on the back of the other chair. "The purpose of your visit?"

Repressing her sigh that he seemed to have reverted to his familiar self, Echo sipped her water. "I wanted the chance to talk to you regarding my duty and…" His hard unwavering stare was making her nervous. "Other things," she finished lamely.

"Things?" Bastian asked, his tone severe. "Bez is a thing now?"

"I spoke to the queen after you left." Echo decided to carry on regardless. "She told me that you would not help me with my task until I can answer your question that you ask of me."

"I have asked nothing from you, handmaiden," Bastian answered coldly.

"You do. You may not have voiced it as such, but you want to know if I could have used my gift to stop his fall. Don't you?"

Bastian's expression didn't change as he waited. "And could it?"

"The queen asked me the same thing, and I told her that I didn't know."

Bastian huffed as he turned his head away from her, taking a drink of his water. "You need not have roused me from my bed for this," he said to her, moving to the desk and placing his cup on the tray.

"You misunderstand me," Echo spoke quietly. "I don't know if I could have saved Bez."

"Yes," Bastian snapped. "You told me. I heard you and I just don't believe yo—"

"I don't know if I could have saved you *both!*" She cut him off sharply.

Bastian's mouth snapped shut as he frowned. "Both?"

Glaring at him in anger, Echo shook her head as she fought to say the words she hadn't told anyone. "I *did* use my gift. I pushed the water into the earth, I scrambled to strengthen the ground on which you lay, and it was *not enough*," she stressed. "Not for both of you. You were falling, you were *both* falling. I sent all that I had into the ground to try and save…one."

Bastian watched her. He knew he wasn't hiding his surprise, but looking at her, seeing her internal struggle, he knew there was more. "Why did you not say that?"

"Would you have heard me earlier? Would you have listened?" Echo finished her water and placed her cup on the tray. "Well?"

Bastian looked to the high window, noticing that the sky was turning to grey. "What else are you not saying?"

"Nothing," Echo told him hurriedly.

Running his tongue over the top of his teeth, he seemed to chew on her answer as he avoided looking at her directly. "Is that all you came for?" he asked her finally with a practiced indifference.

Echo bit her lip in frustration as she rose to her feet. "You know it is not," she said, her temper flaring despite her best efforts. "Will you come with me? Will you help me? You're the knight in the shadow that stands beside me, Bastian. I know it."

The dark-haired knight stood in front of her, in dark trousers and a loose shirt that was open at the neck. He was free of any of his clothing that marked him as a Knight of the Order, but still the invisible shield he wrapped around himself was impenetrable, and he appeared as unapproachable as he ever had when wrapped in his armour.

"Bastian? I've spoken the truth," Echo spoke softly.

Bastian nodded but she felt it was more to let her know he heard her, not agreeing with her. Glancing at the door, he crossed the small room, opening it and revealing the man who had escorted her to the nave earlier. "Clem will see you out," he told her.

"Bastian!" Echo called, trying to stop him from leaving. "Please?"

With his back to her, his head turned as if to look back over his shoulder, but his eyes were downcast, and his answer was loud in the quiet of the room before he even spoke it. "No."

CHAPTER 24

BASTIAN WAS IN THE TRAINING YARD TWO DAYS LATER, practicing his swordsmanship with the Master at Arms and enjoying the simplicity of the task. He had returned to the palace the day before after spending the morning grooming Ghost, and then spent a few hours with his sister, the queen. He was right, she loved the silk purse he had bought for his nephew's first tooth.

Kestornia was the only kingdom of the Five Kingdoms that was ruled by the king *and* queen, meaning that both monarchs had the same authority and neither deferred to the other. Aeryn's husband, King Dlayvon, believed that the partnership of marriage extended to the partnership of the throne, and much to his delight, Aeryn took to the throne with a confidence that shook the rulers of the other kingdoms. They had thought to overwhelm her with their politics and their underhanded offers of trade deals, thinking she was simply a woman, but she had been ready for them all.

Bastian smiled to himself as he recalled the swift severity with which Aeryn had shown her peers exactly who she was as queen of Kestornia. Now they gave her the respect she was due, but it didn't stop Bastian from worrying that she was very much a target for others' ambition. Dlayvon was a good king, but Bastian knew it was his sister who was the more capable ruler.

However, it wasn't her position on the throne that had been a thorn in Bastian's side for the last year when it came to dealing with her. Much to his abject horror, his sister was determined to find him a wife. Bastian wasn't sure why Aeryn seemed to hate her species so much to inflict a poor woman to embrace the life of a wife of a knight. Or perhaps knowing how often they were far from home, Aeryn thought she would be thanked for it. Nevertheless, it had made his visits to the palace shorter and less frequent as he avoided Aeryn and her court of willing sacrifices, ready to throw themselves into the shackles of marriage to a man they did not know and who had no interest in knowing *them*.

As Bastian moved across the training room, parrying his opponent's blows, he felt the familiar sense of frustration as he recalled the lady that Aeryn made join them for refreshment yesterday. He'd already forgotten her name, but he had not forgotten that the woman's hands had shaken so badly with nerves. Bastian had glared at his sister until she showed mercy and released the lady from their company. The speed with which the lady had departed had been his first, and only, source of amusement that day.

Then Aeryn ruined their lunch further by talking about the handmaiden, Echo. Which is when he had gotten up and left the palace.

"Easy, my lord," the Master at Arms wheezed, "I'm not your enemy."

Caught off guard with the warning, Bastian stopped his advance abruptly. "Apologies, I seem to have gotten caught up in the moment." Bastian was ready to resume their training when his attention was caught by Xan, who was striding towards him, his face set in a hard mask. Excusing himself, Bastian met Xan in the middle of the training yard. "What is it?"

"You need to come with me," Xan told him curtly. "I need you to see it for yourself."

Bastian looked at his companion curiously, but having known the man for half of his life, he followed silently. Biting his tongue from his questions was hard, especially when Xan opened Vyka's office door without knocking.

Bastian stopped suddenly as he looked at the crowded room. Khaldan was standing to the side of the front of the desk. Bastian hadn't known he had returned. Ax was leaning casually against the wall under the window, Vyka sat rigidly in his seat, and all three of them turned their attention to the door when Xan and Bastian walked in, but it was the woman in the chair who held Bastian's attention.

"Why?" he demanded as he closed the door behind him, his eyes flicking to Kase, who sat in the other chair. "Why are you here again?"

Kase's disgruntlement at the revelation this was not his lady's first visit did not go unnoticed, but Echo gave Bastian a serene smile. "Sir Bastian," she greeted him politely.

"Cut the bulsyn dung," he snapped. "Why are you here? I told you no. Twice."

"And I heard you, my lord," Echo answered him, her eyes tightening in anger. "But you are not why I am here."

With barely restrained patience, Bastian looked at Vyka for an explanation. "You called her here?"

"No," Khaldan spoke up. "I accompanied the hand-maiden here."

If Ax had suddenly stripped naked and done a cart-wheel, Bastian wouldn't have been more surprised. Actually, Ax had done that to him once before, so maybe Ax was a bad example for rating shock factors. Realising his brain was flailing in his shock, Bastian shook his head to clear his thoughts. "What did you say?"

"I heard and *listened* to handmaiden Echo of the Frost, and I brought her here to tell the general that I will be accompanying her on her journey," Khaldan spoke clearly, a challenge in his brown eyes as he regarded his closest friend.

"Why?" Bastian was stupefied. "Was Rhexynia truly intolerable this visit?"

"Careful, brother," Khaldan murmured quietly. "That's my lady wife you insult."

"I know." Bastian nodded in acceptance of his rudeness and lost some of his aggression as he regarded his best friend. "Khaldan? Can you help me understand why you would agree to this…madness?"

"I'm going as well," Ax piped up.

Bastian's eyes widened fractionally, and then he remembered Xan's furious expression as he crossed the training ground. "Xan? Don't tell me you as well?"

The contemptuous snort was enough of an answer. Bastian reached out and clasped the other man's shoulder. "You were right to get me," he said gravely. Turning to Vyka, Bastian inhaled deeply. "General?"

"I could order you to go," Vyka said with a sigh.

"I am aware," Bastian told him dryly. "You can also order these knights, my men, *not* to go."

Vyka gave a rueful laugh. "I could, but we both know that I *can't*." Pointing tiredly at Khaldan, he spoke. "*He's* already committed, and *that* fool"—he jerked his thumb at Ax, who was smiling widely—"would only go anyway, no matter what I ordered."

Bastian glanced at Echo and Kase. "Give us the room,"

he said curtly. Swiftly Kase stood and Echo followed. Xan held the door open, closing it firmly behind them when they left. Bastian turned to his comrades. "Ax? You heard the same story as we did at the palace. What's happened since then?"

"Nothing," Ax said easily. "I would have said yes then, but you got all forbidding and obstinate." He shrugged casually. "I knew I just needed to wait."

"For?"

"Khaldan," Ax answered.

"Khaldan?" Bastian searched his friend's face, looking for a sign that this was a weirdly elaborate ruse.

"Other than your rage at the loss of Bez, at the *guilt* you feel at the loss of Bez," Khaldan said to him, "you know you would have heard what I did, heard what your grief deafens you to. It's *war*, Bastian. The Mystic? The Gods warring? She can *stop* it; why would we *not* aid in that? It's our duty."

"A war of Gods is not for man to mix in," Bastian snapped angrily. "And Bez? Really? You think my judgement is skewed because of the loss of my sergeant? You think that I, of anyone here, do not know what duty means?"

"You're angry," Khaldan said with a heavy sigh. "I know, I understand."

"Do you?" Bastian snarled. "Do you understand that she *told* me she sent her gift into the ground, and she *told* me she had the power to do it."

"She saved you?" Ax asked, straightening in excitement. "Then why would you not help when she asks for it?"

"Because she *lied*!" Bastian roared angrily. "Because the very ground that crumbled beneath us? It crumbled because she *took* the moisture from it! Think of it. They had never been in the Sand Seas before, but did they suffer? Did they falter? No. *She* was aiding them; she wasn't aiding *you*. Why are you not *thinking*?" Rubbing his hands over his hair in frustration, he looked at them both. "I'm not listening because of my *grief*?" Bastian said with derision, shaking his head in astonishment at Khaldan's words. He looked up at the ceiling. "I *am* listening, and I hear the lies and deception in *every* word that she speaks."

"As do I," Xan said quietly. "To go is folly. They are shrouded in duplicity and deceit."

"I think she has been very open," Ax disagreed in the quiet of the room.

"You would," Xan said in exasperation.

Ax continued as if Xan hadn't spoken. "And I remember that she was carried out of the Sand Seas, and now I know it's because she spent herself using her gift on saving *you*."

Xan was not to be dissuaded by Ax's positivity. "Why is no one asking who the plainsman is? He refuses to answer queries on his Clan, why?"

Bastian grunted in agreement. "There is too much, brothers, that we still do not know. To follow blindly… Khaldan, listen to me. This is *not* our fight," Bastian appealed to Khaldan, hoping to get through to him. "If you knew—"

"Bastian!" Vyka interrupted him, and with a clenched jaw, he bit back his words.

Khaldan looked between his general and Bastian, knowing there was more that wasn't being said. "Seems there is more than one person being deceitful," he sneered.

"Khaldan," Bastian appealed to the other man.

"I'm going," Khaldan told him gruffly. "And you can't stop me." With a heavy sigh, he gestured to Ax. "We need to be ready to leave tomorrow," he told him as he headed to the door, leaving the office and the door open. Ax hesitated, and with an unhappy sigh, he followed Khaldan.

Bastian stood in the centre of the room with his arms at his side, his head bent forward.

"Bastian, this is not good," Xan warned him quietly.

"I know," Bastian replied. "I need to speak to the general. Go make sure that they both don't leave without us knowing." He waited until the door closed once more before he looked up at Vyka. "What in the name of the Gods was that?" he demanded angrily.

Vyka sat back in his chair and shook his head. "He came in like a *beobayr* from the Shingles," Vyka scoffed, and Bastian could imagine the scene. The beobayr was a mutation from the Before. Mountain bears with black shaggy coats. The poisoned rains that fell centuries ago had warped and twisted the animals into the monsters they were now. Bears with venomous fangs and warped bear claws that caused them pain as they aged, causing temperaments that were always angry.

"What did Ax hear that I didn't?" Bastian asked in wonder. "Xan heard what I did, why didn't Ax? Why didn't Khaldan?"

"Xan is suspicious of everything," Vyka reasoned. "I did not know all of what she said to you and the Lord Commander at the palace," Vyka softly rebuked him for his earlier omissions. "Do you think they are right? Is your anger at the loss of Bez clouding your judgement?"

"No." Bastian sat on the chair, looking at the floor.

"Am I angry that he died in front of me? Yes, I'm furious. Do I feel responsible? Of course I do. He was my sergeant, in my company of men. Am I the reason he died? No, I am not." Bastian raised his head to look at his general. "It took a few days to accept it, but I have. I did not let go, Bez did. He knew we would both fall if he did not; *he* saved me."

"You blame the handmaiden for his death."

"I blame her in part," Bastian confirmed. "But it's a small part," he acknowledged reluctantly.

"It's still blame."

"Yes. It is."

They sat, both looking at the other. When Vyka went to speak, Bastian groaned. "Do not say it."

"You need to go with them."

"I told you not to say it," Bastian muttered with a sigh. "We don't need to be involved."

"Khaldan and Ax accompanying the handmaiden means the Order of the Ravens is already involved," Vyka reminded him sourly.

"I need to tell them why she's dangerous," Bastian stated firmly. "They need to know, and I cannot lie to them."

"It's not a lie," Vyka said gravely.

"Is it the truth?" Bastian snapped as he stood. "Why? Tell me why I need to keep this secret."

Vyka opened the top drawer of his desk and took out a flask. He ignored Bastian as he took a healthy swig of rum. "Do you know the only time I need a drink of this is after you or one of your men are in my office?" he said after taking another swig.

"The fact that I make you turn to alcohol is not news to

me," Bastian said lightly. "You've been telling me since the first week of my training," he reminded him.

"Sit, Bastian," Vyka said tiredly. "You know I hate it when you hover over me." Bastian went to argue, but reluctantly he resumed his seat. "You've been in my command since the first day your father walked into the Keep and handed you over to my care."

"I'm aware of how long you've known me, general. I was there after all."

Vyka ignored the sarcasm. "Ten years old you were, and you wore the same look of impatience then as you do now." Vyka studied the man in front of him. "Your defiance is just as strong, but your sense of duty, your fight for what you believe in, is stronger. You entered the Order of the Ravens on your sixteenth birthday. You completed your final trials one year later, automatically a knight due to rank, but you earned your right to your title within *these* walls."

"Is there a reason for the history lesson?" Bastian asked acerbically.

"When the corruption of the Order of the Conclave was exposed, it made no sense to me that Fernyn was guilty," Vyka confessed. "He was such a self-righteous arse…he was too blinded by his loyalty to the Gods to have the wit to play kingdoms against one another." Vyka took another swig from his flask. "You did not serve under him for long, but did you see the mastermind they accused him of being?" Vyka asked.

"You've never spoken of this before," Bastian said instead of answering and admitting to his general he thought that the former Lord Commander was a pompous twit.

"I've kept my own counsel for some time," Vyka admitted. Putting the flask away, he rested his elbows on the desk, and leaning forward, he met Bastian's guarded expression with a determined gleam in his eye. "You *need* to go with them," he told him. "I have for some time doubted Fernyn's guilt, but I do not doubt that strings were being pulled by knights inside the Orders, and this? A handmaiden of the new Gods seeking and…demanding that red cloaks aid her in her quest? I know when someone's pulling at strings to make us dance, Bastian."

"You think she purposefully deceives us?" Bastian speculated.

"No," Vyka contradicted his own words. "I think she genuinely believes it, and that's so much worse."

"What are you saying to me, Vyka? You've reminded me how long you have known me, yet you talk in circles when you know I do not like riddles."

"The corruption of the Order of the Conclave did not dispel with Fernyn's imprisonment. It just became less noticeable."

"Vyka?" When the general said nothing, Bastian spoke for him. "The corrupt and the immoral have long been removed from these halls, Vyka." Bastian's tone was sharp. "I saw to a number of the removals myself, under your command."

"And do you think we are washed clean? Absolved of our brethren's error and greed? You may set many traps to catch a rat, but you will never catch them all."

Bastian felt frustrated as he sat in front of his general. "Twenty years," Bastian told him. "I have known you twenty years, and I am lost to what you are trying to say to me."

"A rot lies within our core, Bastian. It exists still. I tasted it when the accusations came ten years ago, and I taste it still. There is something at work here. It is not solely the work of rival Gods." Vyka frowned at Bastian. "You need to accompany them if only to prove her fraudulent for your own means."

"You don't think she is," Bastian said carefully.

"I believe she doesn't know she is being used," Vyka admitted. "But it worries me that our Lord Commander's audience with her was in the presence of you and your sister."

Bastian blinked in confusion. "What's the significance?"

"The handmaiden had requested an audience with him long before she sought out the ear of the queen."

"She planned to come directly to the Order?" Bastian asked.

"Yes."

"How do you know?"

"Because I received the letter three months ago."

Bastian gaped. "Three months?"

"Echo and her companions have travelled a long way to get here," Vyka told him. "I received the letter, and I gave it to Draxon, and he burned it. I know he received another three."

"He didn't react like he wasn't hearing her story for the first time," Bastian mused. "And she didn't mention that she had reached out to him, why would she keep that to herself? Although he would have denied it and she would have had no proof that she reached out to him." Bastian closed his eyes in realisation. "She was why you sent me north."

"I had hoped you would intercept them," Vyka admitted. "I was not expecting the whole of the events you told upon your return, and I had thought she would have been more open."

"But the handmaiden, the tale of warring Gods, those you expected? Because she had already communicated it to our Order?"

"Yes. It would have helped had she been honest with you in why she was coming to Pavolyn."

"Deceit and deception indeed," Bastian scoffed in disgust as he rose to his feet. "Is there anything else I need to know before I leave?"

"Yes." Vyka cleared his throat. "I know where the artefact is that she seeks."

Bastian gaped at his general in astonishment. "How?"

"*How* is not important, *where* is."

"How is *very* important," Bastian countered. "Tell me where it is."

"The last watchtower before the Barrens."

Bastian barked out a laugh. "Of course it is," he said in disgust. "Why wouldn't it be at the very end of the Five Kingdoms at the most dangerous point?" he asked, his words sarcastic. "What is it?"

"A staff."

"Whose?"

"That, I don't know."

"Why is it important?" Bastian asked as he fixed his glare on the wall above his general.

"Echo will know that better than I."

Bastian's gaze dropped to meet the tired eyes of his general. "You gave us five days—this is why? You knew she would seek out the Conclave."

"I suspected." Vyka scratched his cheek as he watched the man in front of him, who was failing to hide his anger. "Now do you see why you can't mention the symbols?"

"Because if the Order is corrupt and it goes as high as you suspect, all the way to the Lord Commander, then they will know that we know they have planted a false lead and we can expose them."

"You were ever a fast learner."

"I wish I wasn't," Bastian grumbled.

"I don't trust anyone else with this, Bastian." Vyka hesitated. "Neither should you."

Bastian said nothing. "Do you know what I hate more than anything?" he asked suddenly.

"The lies?" Vyka guessed.

"The manipulation." Bastian turned and strode to the door. "Make sure my sister is guarded while I'm on this fool's journey," he said as he left the room, the door slamming behind him.

Vyka winced at the loud slam of the door. Opening his top drawer, he retrieved his flask again. "Well, that could have been worse," he muttered as he unscrewed the lid and took a deep pull, ignoring the voice in his head that said it could have also gone a lot better.

CHAPTER 25

BASTIAN WALKED ANGRILY DOWN THE HALLS, IGNORING THE calls of greeting from his fellow knights as he made his way to Khaldan's suites. As Khaldan was married, he was granted a larger room in the Order's compound for him and his lady wife, should she choose to visit.

Jogging up the stairs to the upper levels, Bastian strode quickly to his comrade's room, knocking lightly before he pushed the door open.

Khaldan glared at him from the centre of the room. "You lost all of your manners?" he asked him, surprised at his friend's boldness to walk into his rooms.

Bastian shrugged. Crossing the room, he picked up Rhexynia's hand and kissed the back of it. The woman looked at him shrewdly, her eyes flicking between Khaldan and Bastian. "Scoundrel," she greeted him. "Why have you upset my husband?"

"Because your husband believes in the good of everyone," Bastian told her as he straightened. "I mean, he married you after all."

Rhexynia scowled at him and then stuck her tongue out at him, causing them both to laugh. Warmly she embraced Bastian. "I've missed you," she said with fondness. "You're avoiding me again."

"You do have a very piercing, shrill voice when you're angry," Bastian told her as he stepped back. "And you're usually angry."

"It's called passion," Rhexynia corrected him. "And you would do well to find yourself a woman who has some."

Bastian's grimace made her chuckle again. "My sister has taken that task upon herself, it seems," he told her sadly.

"Ugh, no wonder you're grouchy. Aeryn is a wonderful queen, but I can only imagine the simpering fools she's putting in front of you. Leave it with me, I'll have you a wife in no time."

Bastian felt true fear as Khaldan's wife nodded with determination. "I really don't think you need to trouble yourself, Rhex." He tried to be diplomatic, but he was sure his horror at the prospect of Rhexynia matchmaking on his behalf was not being concealed.

"Hush now, you know I'm right," she scolded. "Now, why aren't you going with Khaldan? What's this rift between the two of you?" she demanded.

Bastian turned to look at Khaldan. "I was hoping to talk to him about that," he said as he watched Khaldan observing them both.

"So, walking into my room unannounced was your best way to start this?" Khaldan jeered.

"I wasn't sure you would let me in," Bastian admitted quietly.

Khaldan grunted as he looked away. "Well, you did insult my wife," he said with a sly look to Bastian, and had they been alone, Bastian would have punched him for throwing him to the wolf like that.

"You insulted me?" Rhexynia said, her voice rising several octaves.

"I merely pointed out your strong vocal range," Bastian

hastily answered, hoping that was enough, but he saw the calculating look in Khaldan's eye, and he hurried on, "and that Khaldan may have taken this task to avoid spending more time with you, because…" He hesitated. The glare in the woman's eye was more intimidating than any Lord Commanders he had served under. "Because, you know… the volume."

Rhexynia stood, smoothing her soft pink satin dress over her hips. "For that Bastian, I am going to ensure your future wife is part ogre. *Then* you'll know volume." Rhexynia walked over to her husband, and Khaldan dipped his head, giving her less stretch to rise up and kiss his cheek. "Don't kill him," Rhexynia told him as she stroked her husband's cheek. She glanced at Bastian. "But you can make him suffer for the insults."

Khaldan chuckled as she kissed his cheek again. Pointing at Bastian, Rhexynia scowled. "You! Apologise to my husband, and if you so much as dare leave things troubled between you when you leave this room, I shall move myself and my four children into this sanctuary that you are so fond of hiding in." She left the room with more grace than Bastian had entered it, leaving both Khaldan and Bastian staring after her, one in admiration, the other in worry, knowing she was more than capable of carrying out her threat.

"I believe her." Bastian broke the silence after she left.

"I would if I were you," Khaldan agreed cheerfully as he took a seat beside the small table in the room. "Well? Get it off your chest."

"I spoke to Vyka." Bastian watched as Khaldan said

nothing and merely waited. "He has some reservations about this mission."

"I don't care what Vyka thinks."

Bastian frowned. "He is your general, you should care."

"I don't care about what Vyka thinks," Khaldan repeated. "I care what *you* think."

"I think it's a mistake."

"You already told me that. I don't need you to tell me again." Khaldan drummed his fingers off the top of the table.

"You didn't listen to me the first time," Bastian countered as he took a seat in the upholstered chair that Rhexynia had recently vacated. "And…I didn't listen to *you*. So, I'm here."

"I can see that," Khaldan said dryly.

"Tell me what you heard; tell me why *you* believed it."

"And you'll listen?" Khaldan cast him a sideways glance.

Bastian loosened his stiff shoulders and laughed as he tried to relax. "Look at us. Four days apart, and a rift has been caused because of a handmaiden. This isn't us. Talk to me, Khaldan."

Khaldan's attention was on his fingers as they drummed silently on the table. "Ax visited me at home. He told me of the visit to the palace and the revelations. Ax is many things, carefree and easy-going, yes, but unlike what Vyka said, he is no fool." Khaldan looked up at Bastian with a hard glare. "And *you* know that. He is also, out of all of us, the most pious. He told me what he heard, and I heard *his* belief that this was the right thing to do."

"You're going for Ax?"

"No, Bastian," Khaldan huffed in frustration. "I'm going because I spoke to Beth, I mean Echo." He smiled ruefully. "That will take a while before I get used to it," he admitted. "I spoke to her, and I listened to what she said, with an open mind. She is a handmaiden of the new Gods, yes, but she is not the enemy."

"I'm sure the old Gods would argue with that," Bastian muttered.

"And they may," Khaldan answered truthfully. "But *you* wouldn't. Not normally. How many times have you told us that what happens between the Gods is between the Gods and that what happens on the ground is our concern?"

Bastian frowned as he sent a sour look Khaldan's way. "I would appreciate not having my own words thrown back at me," he grumbled.

"Too bad," Khaldan told him bluntly, and Bastian fought the smile at his friend's backtalk. "She has had visions since she was three? She has enough power to cause the rain? She has enough power to strengthen desert land? Bastian, think about it." Khaldan leaned forward in earnest. "She is strong in her gift *and* in her belief, but yet she still needs us?" He looked at Bastian expectantly.

Bastian knew he was missing the point. "And…"

"The *Gods* are telling us! We are their soldiers on earth, and they are telling us that we need to fight this fight."

Bastian had grave doubts that the Gods old or new were saying any such thing, but he did not doubt that Khaldan believed it. "Okay."

Khaldan sat back in surprise. "Okay?"

"You believe her, and you're committed." Bastian stood

and rolled his shoulder as he stretched his sword arm. "I think I'm going to take Ghost for a ride. I saw him two days ago. He bit me twice," he added with a fond smile at the memory.

Khaldan looked at him with wide eyes. "That's it? *Okay* and you're going for a ride?"

"Yep." Bastian strolled to the door.

"You don't want to know who I plan on taking with me?" Khaldan asked with suspicion.

"Nope." Bastian smiled at him over his shoulder. "I have little faith in Echo of the Frost, my friend, but I have faith in you, please never doubt that." Opening the door, he called out to him, "I'll see you at supper. Convince your wife to leave my marital status alone!"

Khaldan watched the door close and sat for a long moment before he stood and followed Bastian out of the room. He had no idea what Bastian was up to, but it wasn't going to deter him from this. As Bastian said, he was committed to this mission, and he needed to get the men ready to leave.

BASTIAN WENT VIA XAN'S ROOMS ON HIS WAY TO THE stables. Rapping his knuckles on the door, he waited. He knew better than to walk into this room unannounced. Last time he had done it, he had narrowly missed the dagger that had been thrown at the door.

"Come," Xan barked from inside.

Bastian entered the room, and his words died on his

tongue when he saw Xan's pack open on his bed. "What's going on?"

Xan turned, giving him a flat look. "Mission."

"With Khaldan?" Bastian asked, wondering if his job of convincing Xan to accompany them was going to be easier than he thought.

"No," Xan snorted in contempt. "They're both being idiots," he added with disgust, his eyes flicking up to meet Bastian's. He groaned at the sheepish look on his fellow knight's face. "Which one got to you?"

"Vyka," Bastian admitted. "And then I spoke to Khaldan."

Xan resumed packing his pack. "Of course." He rolled some clothing into tight balls and shoved them to the bottom of his pack. "You know it's more than she says?"

"I do."

Xan nodded. "Well, that's something, I guess."

"Where are you heading?" Bastian asked him as he watched Xan unroll his weapons belt and check the contents.

"East," Xan grunted.

"The Prairie?" Bastian guessed. Xan's suspicion of Kase was obvious. "You could just ask him," he suggested lightly.

"I would, but orders are orders."

Bastian blinked in surprise. "You've been ordered to go?" he asked, and Xan nodded. "By whom?"

Xan gave him another flat stare. "Draxon."

Bastian's eyebrows rose in surprise, thinking on what Vyka had said to him. "I see."

"Do you?" Xan asked him as he fastened his pack. "Because you're going to need to," he added grimly.

Bastian nodded slowly. "I do and I know. It's a far bigger picture than the one that was painted to us at the palace."

Xan shouldered his pack and checked the room for anything he may have left behind. "Walk me out?"

"Yes." Bastian was still thinking. "I was going to take Ghost for a ride," he told him.

"Good," Xan said as they left his room. "You can accompany me out of the city."

Together they headed to the stables. Bastian had already sent the request to have Ghost saddled, and a horse was also waiting for Xan. The black stallion bared his teeth as Bastian approached.

"You can be as angry as you like," he told the horse. "You're just another one to add to the list."

"There's a list?" Xan asked in amusement as he mounted his horse.

"There's always a list," Bastian grouched as he got on Ghost, who immediately bucked in protest. "Two words, Ghost," Bastian warned him, holding the reins tight. "*Glue factory.*"

Xan watched as the horse's ears pricked up, and then with a toss of his head, Ghost settled. "It's uncanny watching you and that horse. I swear he understands you."

"Of course he does," Bastian said as he patted Ghost's neck. "And unlike some of my friends, he listens."

Xan laughed as Ghost gnashed his teeth. "Yeah, you tell yourself that, friend." Chuckling still at Bastian, Xan rode out of the stables with Bastian, heading to the southern gate.

Outside of the city's walls, they both let their horses stretch their legs, and they enjoyed a brisk canter as they rode to the coast. When they were far enough from the city and in open countryside, they slowed to a walk where they could talk comfortably.

"Vyka suspects there is still corruption in the Orders," Bastian told Xan.

"Of course there is," Xan said gruffly. "As it's written in the *History of the Falling*, where there is men, there is greed."

"You've been reading the old scriptures," Bastian said with amusement. "I thought Ax was the scholar."

"Ax is many things," Xan said with a grin. "A studious man he is not."

Bastian laughed freely in the summer afternoon. "Very true," he acknowledged. "What prompted you to visit the archives?"

"A handmaiden's tale about visions, mystics and soldiers of Gods fighting beside her."

"You really mistrust her?" Bastian observed thoughtfully.

"Not really," Xan grudgingly admitted. "The plainsman? Yes. Echo's task that she is the one to stop a war of the Gods before it starts? Yes."

"She believes it," Bastian said softly. "She really does."

"And it makes her dangerous. Those that believe they are chosen for something mighty are the most reckless of all."

"Agreed," Bastian told him. "Or we could be cynical bastards?"

"Or we could be realistic," Xan countered sarcastically. He pulled slightly on the reins of his horse, slowing it to a stop. "This is where we part."

Bastian looked towards the cliffs overlooking the sea and to the trail leading east. "Do you know where to go?"

"To get to the Prairie?" Xan asked him, grinning widely. "Yes, I keep riding east until I hit the long grass."

"Don't be facetious. I meant once you are there."

"I plan to head to the Green City and simply ask if anyone's missing a large grumpy Clansman with a penchant for the sword and not the axe."

Bastian gave Xan a long look. "I would suggest more subtlety."

"Really?" Xan appeared to consider it. "I prefer the more direct approach."

Bastian knew that he did and held in a sigh. "Try not to die."

"Try to remain alert," Xan said with a grim scowl back at the Golden City. "There's too much happening, and too many want to keep us in the shadows."

"According to the handmaiden's vision, we're already in shadow," Bastian reminded him.

"According to the handmaiden's vision, she can commune with the Gods," Xan scoffed. "I wouldn't rely too much on what she says to keep you steady, my friend."

Bastian chuckled as he reached out and clasped Xan's forearm in goodbye. "Stay safe. If you sense danger, ride *away* from it, Xan. Not *towards* it."

Xan's grin was wicked. "Now, Bastian, where would the fun be in that?" Nudging his heels into his horse's side, he rode away, the wind carrying his laughter back to Bastian.

Bastian watched Xan go, the feeling of unease settling back in his gut. Twisting in his saddle, he looked back towards the Golden City as Ghost grazed underneath him. Turning back around, he looked the way Xan had gone, his figure getting smaller the further he rode. Facing the sea,

Bastian thought about everything that had happened in the last few months. With a sigh, he looked west. The far west of Kestornia was pretty remote, with lots of isolation and few townships. Even though it was a hard land to live in, it was beautiful and rugged country.

Turning Ghost, Bastian headed back to the Golden City and his duty, his heart wishing he was riding west.

CHAPTER 26

WHEN BASTIAN RETURNED TO THE ORDER OF THE Conclave, Ax was waiting for him in the stables. "What is it?" Bastian asked as he dismounted, patting Ghost's neck.

"We've hit an obstacle," Ax told him. "The Lord Commander has prohibited us from aiding the handmaiden." Ax looked at the stable hands, who moved quietly about their duties, and tilted his head subtly to the doors.

Bastian knew he sought privacy, and quickly they left the stables so they could talk more freely. "Did he say why?"

"He is calling the handmaiden Echo of the Frost a heretic and has issued a warrant for her immediate apprehension."

Bastian almost stumbled as he stared at Ax in disbelief. Schooling his features for anyone watching, he nodded. "As is his right," Bastian said plainly. "How did Khaldan take it?" he asked under his breath.

"He is currently demanding an audience with the Lord Commander," Ax told him quietly.

"By the Gods, Ax, why are you here waiting on me?" Bastian snapped angrily. "Clem could have told me this! You should be with Khaldan, talking him down from his madness." Bastian picked up his pace as he hurried to the offices of the Lord Commander.

"I was, but they were sending Kedda to fetch you! I thought there may be less bloodshed if I did it," Ax growled. "Do not make me justify my actions, Bastian. I am not best tested at the moment."

"Sorry," Bastian apologised. "Where is Rhexynia?"

"At the palace. She is visiting with your sister."

"Good, she needs to be kept from here," Bastian spoke quietly.

"Agreed. I sent Fylip to delay her return," Ax told him. "You know, just in case."

Bastian *did* know and appreciated the fact that Ax had the wit about him to act fast. As they approached the offices, Bastian saw the many knights gathered in the waiting rooms. Knights of the Order of the Hawks and Order of the Cardinals were already looking towards him, many of them straightening as he approached. Too many of them reaching for their pommels.

"You need to trust me," Bastian whispered to Ax. "Can you do that?"

"Always," Ax answered readily.

"Where is Khaldan?" Bastian demanded loudly as he looked around the room, not seeing his fellow soldier.

"Inside." Kedda stepped forward. "You can't go in," he added with a smirk.

"Said who?" Bastian challenged.

"Said the Lord Commander," General Crux said from behind him. Bastian turned and looked at the older knight, feeling some of his anger deflate.

"General," Bastian greeted. "Is there a reason why I am being prohibited from entering?"

"I would think it has a lot to do with the fact Khaldan has made an ass of himself, and you have not," Crux answered. With a sigh, he gestured impatiently to Bastian. "Come, help me sit."

Bastian hesitated, but duty and respect for the older man had him stepping forward and offering his arm.

"Be steadfast, lad," Crux whispered in caution as he put on a show of being lowered to the seat.

Bastian's eyes flicked to Crux's, and he saw the warning in them. "My lord," Bastian murmured as he stepped back.

"Do you need anything, Uncle?" Ax asked as he came to stand beside them.

"A glorious death," Crux said with a grunt. "But no," he said as he patted his nephew's hand. "Just your patience."

Vyka arrived not long after, and Bastian left the side of Crux and stood beside his general, very aware of the gleeful grin of malice on Kedda's face.

"What's happening?" Bastian asked his general quietly.

"The rot spreads," Vyka said, his lips barely moving. "You need to be ready…and sensible."

Bastian wanted to remind his general that Khaldan was the sensible one, when the Lord Commander's office doors opened and Khaldan was led out with two knights of the Order of the Cardinals on either side of him, holding Khaldan's arms behind his back. Bastian stepped forward, but Vyka's hand gripped him from behind.

"*Sensible*, Bastian," Vyka whispered urgently as he quickly dropped his hand.

Khaldan was looking straight ahead as he was escorted from the rooms, and in a fog, Bastian heard Ax's raised voice protesting against what was happening. Lord Commander Draxon stepped out of his office. "Sir Axanyial, is there a problem?"

"Where is Khaldan being taken?" Ax asked angrily as he pushed his blond hair off his face.

"To the holding cells," Draxon told the room pompously. "He needs a night, or two," he added with an insincere smile, "to remember his place."

"His place?" Ax asked incredulously, his attention flicking to Bastian briefly. "His place is not in a holding cell in the building of the Order of the Conclave that he serves faithfully."

Draxon inhaled loudly and let out a loud sigh. "Are you questioning me, your Lord Commander?"

Bastian willed Ax not to speak, but unfortunately, the Gods were not listening to him.

"Of course I'm questioning you!" Ax answered hotly. "This is horse dung, and you know it!"

"Sir Kedda," Draxon called. "Sir Axanyial yearns to keep his fellow Raven company. Escort him there to see that it's so."

Bastian focused all of his attention on the way that Kedda strode forward and roughly grabbed at Ax. Ax went to resist, but Crux spoke up. "Ax, you forgot yourself," Crux berated him. "Your duty is to your Order and your Lord Commander."

Ax opened his mouth to protest as Kedda gripped him tighter.

"Kedda," Bastian spoke quietly, his eyes hard as stone as he looked at the other man. "The Lord Commander said *escort* him, not bruise him."

Draxon turned to Bastian. "You have no words of protest, Sir Bastian?"

"You are the Lord Commander," Bastian told him as he dipped his head in a bow. "If my fellow knights have offended, then I apologise on behalf of the Order of the

Ravens."

Draxon's reaction was more composed than Kedda's, whose mouth was hanging open. "As you should, and you should, Vyka," Draxon said imperiously.

"I will see to them as soon as you release them, Lord Commander," Vyka said grimly as he shook his head at Ax. "Your actions are unwelcome here," Vyka admonished him.

Ax looked between his fellow knights and hung his head. Draxon, seeing his compliance, signalled Kedda to take him away.

Looking around the gathered knights of various Orders, Draxon lifted his hand as if to speak, and then with a loud sigh, he dropped it to his side as he shook his head in despair. "A handmaiden," he started, his head bent in sorrow. "A handmaiden of the Temple of the Frost has whispered poison in their ears." Draxon raised his head as he looked at each of the knights gathered, with his eyes finally meeting Bastian's. "She has spoken lies, and although I have discredited her, they still planned to aid her in a wild chase that only serves as a distraction. Leading them into danger on a trail of a false prophet." Draxon kept his gaze steady on Bastian. "Do you doubt me?"

"I heard the same words as you, my lord," Bastian answered. "It is a tall tale indeed."

Draxon smiled beatifically at Bastian. "Indeed, it is." Turning, he spoke to the room. "She *is* the false prophet!" His voice was wild in the quiet of the room. "She seeks to ruin our Order of the Conclave with her deceit and corruption." Draxon raised his arms in supplication. "Join me! Join me in praying for your brethren's freedom from her wicked web of deceit."

Draxon bowed his head as did all the knights in the room, including Bastian and Vyka. Bastian glared at the stone slabs beneath his feet, fury burning in his veins.

"My Gods, hear my words. I ask you to look after your faithful flock and help those that have wandered, help them see the path of righteousness, and aid their way back to right." Draxon's words sounded loudly in the room. "May we fly high in your glory."

"May we fly high in your glory," the knights murmured as they lifted their heads.

"You may go," Draxon dismissed them all. "Vyka, Bastian, a word," he called as Bastian made to leave the room.

Bastian shared a look with Crux, who was still sitting, but he turned and followed his Lord Commander into the office, Vyka beside him.

Draxon walked around his desk, a large, heavily ornate, garish thing that Bastian despised. "It is a sad day," Draxon began. "I am glad I was not alone when Khaldan attacked me."

"Attacked you?" Bastian asked, knowing he hadn't hidden his disbelief.

"Yes," Draxon regarded Bastian coldly. "It was a shock to me too."

"I bet it was," Bastian murmured too low for the Lord Commander to hear, but Vyka did.

"Forgive my knights, Lord Commander," Vyka spoke smoothly. "They have been out on missions for so long now they sometimes forget their way within the walls of the Order of the Conclave."

"It is unfortunate," Draxon agreed. "I know it is not like Khaldan to act like this. The handmaiden told a convincing lie." He hesitated. "But a lie it was. Don't you agree?" Draxon asked Bastian again.

"I heard many falsehoods," Bastian agreed.

"And you had the sense to ignore them," Draxon praised him, happy with the knight's agreement. The door opened as his personal guard returned. Turning, Bastian looked at them and back at his Lord Commander. "They need to remain in the cells until they have been liberated of her influence."

Bastian's tongue swept over his front teeth before he clenched his jaw from replying.

"Agreed," Vyka said. "And when they are released?"

Draxon appeared to think about it, and Bastian forced himself to stay still. "I think you are right, Vyka, too long have we relied on the Order of the Ravens to go out into the kingdoms and undertake missions. We need to make changes, keep them closer to the Order of the Conclave, here in Pavolyn."

"Khaldan and Ax?" Bastian asked.

"All of you, I think." Draxon cocked his head to the right as he considered both men. "Yes, I think the flight of the Raven should remain closer to home for the foreseeable future."

"I think that would be agreeable to some," Vyka said thoughtfully.

"Are there any questions?" Draxon asked, looking between them both.

"No, Lord Commander," Vyka answered quickly.

Draxon looked pleased. "Sir Bastian?"

"No, Lord Commander," Bastian said evenly.

"You're dismissed."

Vyka and Bastian left the Lord Commander's office, and Bastian was unsurprised to see Crux still in the chair. "My lord, can I assist?" Bastian asked him.

"That would be most welcome," Crux told him and reached out as Vyka offered his arm. "A sad day," Crux said loudly as he steadied himself on his feet.

"Indeed," Vyka agreed, and the three of them made their way out of the Lord Commander's offices.

Slowly they walked in silence as they made their way back to their Orders' wings. As they reached the corridor that led to the Order of the Hawks, Crux turned to them both.

"Fly high," he said, holding Bastian's eye.

"Fly high," Vyka and Bastian's answer was automatic.

"Keep him safe," Crux said lowly as he started down the corridor to his Order's rooms. Bastian had no doubt who he referred to.

When they were back in Vyka's office, with the door closed firmly behind them, Bastian dropped wearily into the chair, and Vyka was in his drawer, his flask gripped firmly in his grasp.

"What a dung heap," Bastian swore. Vyka grunted but said nothing. "What possessed him to openly challenge Draxon?"

"A handmaiden allegedly," Vyka answered dryly. "That one usually so stoic could fall under the spell of a temptress is sorrowful." Bastian looked at his general sharply and saw Vyka's eye roll. "Horse shit." Vyka put the flask back and began to pace.

"You seem agitated," Bastian said, remarking on the reversal of the behaviour.

"I *am* agitated," Vyka snapped. "I thank the Gods Xan wasn't here for that performance," he said as he rubbed his forehead and then stopped as he looked at Bastian. "Where is he? Do I want to know?"

Bastian sat up straighter. "I thought you would know? He's gone to Tzenyth."

Vyka gaped at him, then tilted his head back and groaned. "The plainsman?"

Vyka cursed savagely, causing Bastian to startle. His general never lost his composure. "Yes." Bastian gripped the chair. "General, I thought you knew."

"Why would I *know*?" Vyka scoffed. "The day any of you four tell me anything…" Seeing Bastian's expression, Vyka stopped. "Bastian?"

"He told me he had been ordered to go," he answered slowly.

"Draxon," they both said at the same time.

"Gods dammit, Bastian!" Vyka berated him. "Why didn't you stop him?"

"Because he didn't tell me you didn't know!" Bastian argued. "And I agree with him! Kase is hiding more than what Clan he comes from." Vyka was gritting his teeth so hard Bastian could hear them grinding. "General, what am I missing?" Bastian asked him cautiously.

Vyka's palms were flat on the desk as he leaned on it, looking down. "The artefact is in the northmost watchtower," Vyka told him. "Khaldan and Ax are in the holding cells."

"And?"

"And the *fool's errand* hasn't changed," Vyka bit out,

pushing himself away from the desk. "Only now it needs to be done with stealth."

"Is that all? I can be stealthy," Bastian told him easily. "I'm not new to this," he reminded the general.

"You need to be stealthy and avoid being seen or caught." Vyka focused on the knight in front of him. "You need to avoid towns, villages… They will search for you."

Bastian was nodding in agreement. "I know, a small party, that's all we need. That's all it should have ever been," he added, giving it some thought.

"Bastian!" Vyka barked at him, breaking him from his deliberations. "You need *Xan* to get through!"

And Bastian realised what his general was telling him. "Ah, shit."

"Exactly. They won't let anyone but their own through," Vyka told him tightly.

"Well…that just made it more difficult, not impossible," Bastian said with determination.

"You'll fail."

Bastian thought about it and who he was travelling with. "All due respect, general, you don't know her," Bastian commented wryly. "She'll make sure she gets north."

Vyka regarded him seriously. "I'm more worried about her making sure my men don't give their lives for her goal."

"We won't." Standing, he smiled at the general. "I've got this under control."

"Bastian, this is so far from your control it's not even funny," Vyka mumbled. "Where are you going?"

Bastian inhaled deeply, clasping his hands behind his back. "I think I shall spend this evening dining with my sister at the palace and spending some time with my nephew."

Vyka gave him a long-suffering look. "Really? Aeryn?"

"Yes, she has been telling me how well attended her dinners are. The court is quite busy," Bastian said as he opened the door, looking at his general. "Aeryn is keen for me to witness the popularity of it."

"Well, enjoy your evening." Vyka gave him a conspiratorial smile as he realised Bastian was creating an alibi. "Fly high, Bastian," he added softly.

Bastian dipped his head and then went to his rooms, very conscious of those who watched from the shadows. As Vyka had taught him many years ago, the best way to lose a shadow was to stand in the light, and the light he intended to stand in this evening was none other than the brightest light in Pavolyn. That of his sister's court.

CHAPTER 27

CHANGING SWIFTLY BEHIND HIS SISTER'S SCREEN, BASTIAN pulled his shirt over his head, tucking it quickly into his dark trousers. Emerging from behind the screen in her suite, he tossed his fancier clothes on the chaise lounge beside her.

"I need those to disappear," he said as he pulled his leather cuirass from his pack.

"I'll burn them myself," Aeryn told him as she stood to help him tie the leather breastplate. "If I have nothing to worry about, why are you entering the very Order you serve wearing armour?"

"Because I'm being cautious," Bastian answered. "I told you this."

"I can't believe he arrested Khaldan," Aeryn said quietly as she went to pick up Bastian's boots.

"And Ax," Bastian growled. "Aeryn, I can put on my own boots," he said to her as he took them off her.

"If you get caught and he arrests you, Bastian," Aeryn warned.

"For the hundredth time, they haven't been formally arrested. They are being held as a warning only. They'll be free in two days max."

"So why not wait?" Aeryn challenged.

"Because we need to leave." Bastian paused as he looked at his sister. "Will you please stop worrying?" He resumed lacing his boots. "This is not the first time I've left on a mission," he reminded her.

"This is the first time you're breaking your fellow Ravens out of jail!" Aeryn snapped.

Bastian grinned at her. "It's not the first time. Actually it's not even the tenth time," he said with a wink. "Do you know how much trouble Ax is when he's in his cups? Or how easily Xan's fists fly when he's cheated at cards?"

Aeryn rolled her eyes as she flopped very un-queenlike onto her couch. "And you call yourselves gentlemen," she snorted.

"No, we call ourselves knights. No one ever mentioned being a gentleman," Bastian joked as he straightened. "My cloak." He held his hand out, and Aeryn grunted as she pulled it out from under her.

"I'm not happy about this," she reminded him.

"I know."

"And you're leaving me to deal with Rhex," she added.

Bastian grimaced. "For that, I am *truly* sorry," he told her. "But if you want to invite handmaidens to the palace for an audience, you only have yourself to blame," he chastised her.

"I told you why I did it!" Aeryn countered hotly.

"I know, it was either you or Dlayvon, and I agree, you are the more sensible option. But you should have waited for me."

"Because you were so willing to hear her," Aeryn scoffed. "And if I had to wait for you every time I held an audience, brother, the kingdom would never see me."

Bastian thought about it. "I don't have an issue with that," he admitted.

"You're ridiculous," Aeryn grumbled.

"I'm your brother; it's my job to protect you."

"You can't be it all, Bastian," Aeryn said quietly. "You can't be a soldier of the Gods, brothers to the Ravens, and protector to me." She sighed loudly. "Or heir to a throne."

"Aeryn," Bastian warned. "Not now."

"Of course," she snapped as she stood. "Never the right time, is it?"

"I'm away to commit a great offence, little sister; can we please leave the petty squabble until after I have returned?"

"You said it was a little thing," Aeryn told him with wide eyes.

"You're not stupid. You know as well as I do the severity of what I'm about to do." Bastian checked his weapons. "Okay, I have everything." Looking at her, he saw her eyes fill with tears. "Aeryn…"

"If you get killed, I will not be happy," she sniffled.

"Well, I don't expect you to be. I want you to be suitably miserable," he jested gently. When his sister didn't seem appeased by his attempt at humour, he caught her hand and squeezed gently. "Trust me, I do this all the time."

Aeryn rubbed her nose as she cast him a doubtful look. "You say things like this, and it worries me the kind of men who supposedly serve our Gods."

Bastian chuckled as he pulled her in for a quick hug, kissing the top of her head briefly. "Be careful, watch everyone, trust no one, tell Dlayvon the same." He took a deep breath. "And if it gets too much…call for father."

Aeryn's eyes were wide as saucers. "Bastian?"

"He'll come if he knows I'm not here," he added gruffly, not meeting his sister's troubled stare. "Now, go fix yourself. You're supposed to be…queenly."

Aeryn looked down at her dress, the crystals shining

back at her from the small stones sewn into it. "I don't look the part?"

"You look like you've been crying," he told her. "You need to be untouchable for when they come to question you, and he *will* come."

"I'll fix myself before I go back out."

Together they walked to the wall in the corner of the room, and both stared at each other. Quickly Bastian kissed her cheek. "I'll see you soon," he promised her.

Aeryn pressed into the wall the small stone that caused the door to swing open. "Fly high, brother," she whispered as Bastian ducked through the opening. "I love you," she murmured as she watched him disappear down the dark tunnel. With a final look, Aeryn closed the panel and ensured nothing was out of place. Bastian was right, she couldn't afford to slip up. Wiping her eyes and straightening her dress, the queen rolled her shoulders as she tried to loosen the tension she carried. With her head held high, she used a different secret passage, taking her brother's clothes with her and leaving them in the passage for now. She pushed the panel at the end of the tunnel, coming out of the wall that led to her husband's bedchamber. Dlayvon waited patiently, and when she closed the panel behind her, he took her hand, pulling her into his embrace.

"He'll be fine," he assured his wife. "The man is blessed by the Gods even if he is their most disobedient servant," he joked.

Aeryn embraced her husband tightly. She knew how lucky she was to have a husband who loved her as he did. Not all arranged marriages could boast that. With a nod and a smile plastered on her face, the two of them exited his room and made their way back to court, ignoring the hushed whispers of the courtiers that the king and queen had snuck off to enjoy some time together. Aeryn smiled through it all and dropped a few not-so-subtle winks to her ladies in waiting as she flamed the fire of the rumours of her court, all the while trying not to let her thoughts linger on the dangerous path her brother was on.

***

KHALDAN SAT WITH HIS BACK TO THE WALL, HIS EYES ON THE torch on the outside of his cell. He could see Ax, who lay on the cot in the cell opposite him. Neither of them had spoken since Ax had followed him down not long after Khaldan had been detained.

Two of the knights from the Order of the Starlings sat in the middle of the narrow walkway between the cells. They were playing cards and talking quietly about the upcoming harvest festival. Khaldan had been listening as the men talked about nonsense.

His wife was going to skin him alive, he mused, which actually made him smile. He hoped she was at the palace, but he also entertained the thought of Rhexynia giving Draxon a tongue lashing in her fury at him being detained. And she would be furious… Khaldan really hoped she was at the palace with the queen, although he pitied the man who tried to detain Rhex.

Ax was napping—he wasn't even pretending to be asleep. His light snores had been a steady constant for the last hour.

Khaldan thought about Echo. The name suited her.

She was always cool and reserved, well, apart from that one time she lost her temper in the Sand Seas. And that other time Bastian manipulated her into securing herself in the inn, and then there was the time that she was angry after the town set on fire. Khaldan rubbed his lips, maybe *cool* wasn't the best adjective to describe Echo's temperament.

He wondered if Bastian would at least have gone to the inn where Echo and the others were and told her that knights of the Order would not be accompanying her on her journey. Her journey. He banged his head lightly off the wall behind him. He didn't even know where they were going; he just knew he was willing to take her.

That Bastian had not heard it, not felt it, the sense of *rightness* in his core when she spoke… Her words had roused something in Khaldan, Ax too, he knew. How had Xan and Bastian not heard it? Felt it?

When Ax and he had left them at the inn, he had asked Ax several times if Echo had added anything in her retelling, but Ax had assured him it was exactly as she had told them at the palace. Khaldan was not prepared to not fulfil his role in his part, in his duty, as a knight of the Order, so it puzzled him that Bastian was so unswerving in his refusal.

Several hours later, the two knights on duty finished their game of cards and, shortly after, served Khaldan and Ax both a cup of water. Khaldan took his, but he noted Ax was still asleep, and the knight guard simply laid it on the ground.

"Rest well," one of the knights said with a commiserating smile before he took the torch and left them in the darkness in the cells. Khaldan closed his eyes and decided maybe Ax had the right idea and he should have slept.

"Are they gone?" Ax said quietly from the other cell, startling Khaldan. "By the Gods, it's dark in here."

"You slept most of the evening," Khaldan said as he closed his eyes again. "Of course you would wake when I want to sleep."

"You wish to sleep?" Ax asked in surprise. Khaldan heard Ax moving. "No time for sleep. He'll be here soon."

Khaldan was tempted to ask *who* but instead closed his eyes. If Ax thought they were to be rescued, he needed his head checked by the healers. Bastian probably agreed with the judgement of the Lord Commander, though he hoped that he did not.

Trying to tune out Ax moving around his cell, Khaldan willed for sleep.

He was jostled awake with a start.

"If you're trying to make me feel guilty for not being here sooner," Bastian whispered beside him, "I get it, but it's not my fault it's so late."

"Bastian?" Khaldan whispered tersely in the darkness as Bastian hauled him to his feet. "What in the name of Hoxka are you doing?"

"Knitting," Bastian hissed. "What do you think I'm doing?" He tugged his arm. "Move, we haven't much time."

Bastian pulled him out of the cell and towards the door. "Wait! Ax!" Khaldan hissed.

"He's already out," Bastian assured him. "Watch the table," he warned.

"Watch?" Khaldan deadpanned in the complete darkness where he could see nothing. "Ironic."

"Quit yammering," Bastian scolded.

Khaldan snapped his mouth closed from his reply and then tried not to feel too aggrieved that Bastian got Ax out first.

As they moved up the steps from the cells, Khaldan's familiarity with the building overtook his senses. Confidently, he and Bastian made their way to the ground level, and slowly, with measured care, Bastian led them to the seldom used back entrance.

With his finger to his lips, Bastian slowed as he looked around the corner. "Fast and low, brother," he instructed. "We need to be swift."

Khaldan nodded and on Bastian's signal, they moved quickly across the floor, hugging the wall, hidden by the shadows as they approached the door. The door opened a fraction, and Khaldan almost slowed, but Bastian anticipating his move, grabbed him and pulled him alongside him, almost pushing him through the door.

Khaldan met Fylip's grin with one of his own, as the three of them ran across the old training ground under the cover of darkness.

Khaldan had so many questions, but he knew now was not the time, but the appreciation he had for the man who led him rose unchecked in his chest, choking him. Clamping down his emotions, he kept his head down as the three of them turned out of the main building of the Order of the Conclave. Although Khaldan wanted to know why they were running to the western gate, he trusted the men in front.

At the gate, Fylip stopped. "Not too hard," he cautioned

just before Bastian punched him, hard, effectively knocking him out.

Khaldan's eyes widened as Bastian lay Fylip on the stone slabs. "What?" Bastian asked him evenly. "It needs to be believable."

Khaldan saw the crumpled form of another knight and looked accusingly at Bastian, who pulled a face at him and then was gently easing the gate open.

The western gate squeaked. The whole compound knew it, but few knew that if you lifted as you pushed, the squeak lessened. Xan knew and, as a good knight should, told his closest friends, and it was a secret they kept to themselves.

Picking something up from the ground, Bastian thrust it into Khaldan's arms, and realising it was his own heavy dark brown travelling cloak, Khaldan put it on, pulling the hood low.

"Let's go," Bastian instructed, similarly attired. They began to walk quickly, but not too quickly to attract attention, into the streets of Pavolyn, rounding a corner, free from the shadow of the Order of the Conclave. Khaldan went to speak, but the figure that detached from the shadows made both men draw up short.

"I knew you would do this," Kedda sneered as he looked at them both in triumph. His red cloak would bring attention to them, and as he stood in front of them, with his hands on his hips, Khaldan felt Bastian make his decision. "You both think you're so smart," he jeered. "But I found you."

"How many times have I told you to be aware of your surroundings?" Bastian said dryly as he relaxed beside Khaldan, noticing the man much broader than Kedda stepping out of the shadows. With the hilt of his sword, he struck Kedda across the head, knocking him out.

"What in the name of the Goddess is taking so long?" Kase demanded of them both.

"Kase?" Khaldan gaped.

"What? You expecting someone else?" Kase snorted before turning on his heel and leading them to the furthest gate where Ax waited.

"He took Ax," Khaldan realised, looking at Bastian with a smile.

"Of course he took Ax," Bastian said carelessly. "I couldn't risk getting caught and leaving Ax behind." Khaldan lowered his head to stop Bastian seeing his guilt. "You think I wouldn't choose you first?" Bastian murmured so no one else could hear.

Khaldan's smile was bitter. He *had*, and he should have known better. "We have a lot to talk about," he said instead.

Ax gave him a wide smile as they joined him. "We good?" he whispered.

"Let's move," Bastian said with a sharp nod.

Stealthily the four of them exited the city through the western gate, and breaking into a run, they headed for the cover of the treeline. Two figures waited, hidden in a copse of trees, and as they slowed, Khaldan saw the horses. Echo pushed her hood back as she looked them over, searching them all to make sure they were alright.

"We're good," Kase told her gruffly, recognising her look.

Tyria looked at Bastian with a scowl. "Your horse is possessed by a spirit of the underworld," she hissed. "He bit me."

"He bites everyone, don't take it personally," Bastian said as he took Ghost's reins. "Don't you, boy?" he greeted the mean-tempered horse and fed him a sugar cube before mounting him smoothly.

Tyria mumbled but got on her own horse, and Khaldan said nothing about the ease with which she did so or that she wore tight-fitting breeches and rode like a man. Kase lifted Echo up, and Khaldan looked away as the handmaiden's legs were bared as she too sat astride the horse.

"I wear breeches, my lord," Echo's soft voice carried in the night.

Kase was on his horse in one smooth motion. In the dark of the moonlight, in the copse of the trees, the plainsman had never looked more ferocious. His topknot was gathered tight, his leather tunic had two leather straps that crossed over his chest, and on his back was a huge broadsword.

Kase caught Khaldan looking and grinned wickedly. Nudging his horse's sides, he started forward, his two companions close behind him.

Ax looked at Bastian and Khaldan both. "He's Dy'lit-shi," Ax hissed.

Bastian said nothing as he nudged Ghost forward, seething internally at not seeing the obvious. It made sense that Kase would be one of the elite fighters of the Plains of Tzenyth.

"Wait!" Ax called. "Where's Xan?"

"Not here," Bastian growled. "Move," he ordered sharply. "We have much to discuss."

CHAPTER 28

THEY RODE IN SILENCE THROUGH THE NIGHT AND MOST OF the following morning. Bastian noted that Kase needed no urging to avoid the farming towns and the larger townships. The Tzenythian kept them off the beaten path, and Bastian would like very much to know how well versed the plainsman was in the kingdom of Kestornia. Mid-afternoon, Kase slowed his horse, and turning to look at them, he checked his lady first. "We have enough distance from your flock?" Kase asked the three men with a twist of his lips.

"It's possible Draxon knows where we are heading," Bastian conceded.

"Do *we* know where we're heading?" Khaldan asked them.

"Aye." Bastian turned in his saddle, looking back the way they had come. He felt the gnawing in his gut. "We need a few more hours," he told Kase.

Kase looked over Bastian's shoulder. "Agreed," he said gruffly. Looking around where he had stopped them, he pointed to a gathering of some rocks, overgrown with moss and vegetation. It was difficult to tell if it used to be a building or was just a natural formation. "Back in a moment," Kase said as he smoothly dismounted and tossed his reins to Tyria, who caught them deftly, as the tall man headed behind the rocks.

"Bordyre has few female horse trainers," Ax said conversationally.

"And they suffer for it," Tyria retorted as she pulled her long red braid over her shoulder.

"Strange that you would not know to not use my family's name," Ax said as he cocked his head in question.

Tyria sighed. "I wasn't thinking," she admitted. "Barsgaard was the first name I thought of." Getting off her horse, she looked up at Echo. "We won't be stopping for a while," she told her.

"I'd say ladies first," Bastian cut in. "But since Kase is already there," he added with a shrug. He dismounted and handed Ghost's reins to Khaldan. Kase was walking back as Bastian approached and he slowed. "You know where we're going?" Bastian asked quietly.

"Not truly," Kase admitted. "She says it's north."

Bastian huffed out a laugh. "It's north alright." He carried on walking, and as he relieved himself behind the rocks, Ax joined him.

"Bastian," Ax greeted. "Where's Xan?"

"On a wild turkey chase," Bastian told him, finishing up. Grabbing some grass, he rubbed it quickly between his hands, tossing it on the ground when he was done.

"He was never going to join us," Ax said with a disappointed sigh.

"No," Bastian agreed. "He needed to know more about who you travelled with."

"They were concealing more than some black ink on her wrists," Ax said as they both walked back, Ax stopping and plucking a dock leaf from the grass. He rubbed it between his hands and handed the remainder to Bastian. "Better than grass," he said. Bastian took the large dark green leaf and used it vigorously.

When Tyria and Echo had used the rocks for their own comfort break, they all took the opportunity to walk off the long night.

"What made you change your mind?" Echo asked Bastian.

"What made you send a letter to the Lord Commander three months ago and then omit that you had already approached him in the palace?"

Echo glanced at Kase, who was frowning. "I had my reasons."

Bastian nodded and then smiled beatifically. "As do I." He hesitated and then asked anyway. "You can create a safety barrier? In the Teeth, Xan said the zyvarg couldn't get too close to you. Nor could he?" Bastian watched her closely, her face giving nothing away. "Why do you need us if you can use your gift to keep you safe?"

"It drains my energy," Echo admitted. "Plus, I don't always know how to use it or control it." She looked away from his steady gaze. "I don't know how to do a lot," she admitted softly. She could see that the man in front of her was still sceptical. "We need to learn to trust each other if we're going to do this," Echo told him in frustration.

"Okay," Bastian agreed. "You first." Echo opened her mouth and then closed it again. She had told him enough. "That's what I thought," Bastian said with a smirk. Looking at Kase, he got back on Ghost. "A good few more leagues before we stop properly."

"Agreed," Kase said. "You ready?" he asked Echo, who hadn't gotten back on her horse yet. The big man was off his horse and lifting Echo onto hers in one smooth motion. "You good?" he asked her as she sorted her skirts.

"Yes." She smiled down at him.

Bastian watched the interaction, and Echo caught him staring. "Is there a problem?" she asked as she pushed at her skirts again.

"Queen Aeryn has riding skirts," Bastian said. "I admit I don't know the mechanics of it all, but it allows her to ride with ease."

"The queen does not ride sidesaddle?" Echo asked him in surprise.

"The queen does many things that are unconventional," Bastian answered. Nudging Ghost, he encouraged him to a trot. "We should make haste."

They rode for hours, their pace fast, stopping briefly to water the horses, but the breaks were so short no words were exchanged. In a small farming town, far from the well beaten path to the kingdom of Bordyre, they stopped.

"Still object to a hay loft?" Bastian asked Kase as they rode along a track where Bastian saw a farmhouse lying up ahead.

Glancing at the sky, seeing the heavy clouds, he didn't need a handmaiden with an affinity for water to tell him rain wasn't far. "I wouldn't mind a roof tonight," he said to Bastian.

"Agreed." They led the others towards the farmhouse, but as they got closer, Bastian slowed Ghost, and reaching out, he snatched Kase's reins. "Careful," he cautioned.

"Bastian?" Khaldan was already off his horse, Tyria taking the reins. "Something isn't right here," Khaldan warned as he drew his sword.

Wordlessly Bastian dismounted. Ghost came to a halt

and Bastian rubbed his nose as he passed him. "Stay," he commanded.

Ax followed them, as Kase stayed with Echo, his duty to the handmaiden and only her.

"Good Gods," Khaldan whispered. "Do you smell it?"

"Atchen," Bastian said grimly. "Be ready."

The farmhouse lay quiet, and as Bastian pushed the door to the house open, the door creaked loudly.

"Well, there goes the element of surprise," Khaldan muttered.

Bastian walked into the house, his sword drawn, but on inspection of the home, they found it empty. The stench of dead atchen was strong though.

"Why is it so strong when there are none here?" Ax asked, keeping his voice low.

Bastian was already looking at the floors. "No trap doors," he said. Looking up, he considered the rafters. "Too dense to go upwards and there's nowhere to hide," he commented. "The barn?"

"Ugh," Khaldan muttered as they made their way to the outbuildings. "It's always the barn."

The smell was overpowering before the barn doors were even opened. Grimly, Bastian kicked the door open, all three of them stepping back as the smell rolled over them in a putrid wave.

Carcasses of animals lay rotting within. Slowly the three men entered, their cloaks covering their mouths and noses, but still they choked. Nothing lived, and nothing had lived for many days. In a far corner, Ax found either the farmer's wife or a daughter. It was hard to tell, given the state of the damage to the body and the decomposition. Pushing open the other barn door, he found the farmer and another body that looked to be a small child.

"Ax?" Bastian called.

"All dead," Ax confirmed. "I have bodies," he added. He heard someone walk up behind him, and turning he looked at Bastian. "They need to be given proper burials."

"Aye," Bastian grunted. Turning back, he looked at the barn. "Come on."

Khaldan fell into step with them as they made their way back to the others. Kase and Tyria had dismounted, but Echo was still mounted.

"Anyone?" Kase asked gruffly.

"No," Khaldan confirmed.

"We move on?" Tyria asked them, taking in their expressions.

"Aye," Bastian said as he searched his pack.

"Is it very bad?" Echo asked, looking towards the farmhouse.

"It is." Ax looked away.

"I can help perform the rites," she said, getting ready to dismount.

"No need," Bastian said as he pulled his pouch from his pack. "Your affinity isn't needed."

"Fire?" Kase said with understanding. "I'll help move them free."

"No need," Bastian repeated as he started to walk back to the farmhouse.

"What?" Kase asked Khaldan in frustration. "He thinks we'll sit and let him carry this out alone?"

"No," Khaldan answered. "It's a one-man job."

"He's going to burn it all?" Tyria said in sudden understanding, seeing Ax nod. "It will bring attention," she cautioned.

"It should," Ax snapped. "They've been dead for days. Someone else had to have noticed."

Echo looked towards the scattering of houses they had seen from the hills as they approached. "Or there's no one left to see."

Bastian set about starting fires in the house. Finding some rubbing alcohol to use as an accelerant and a discarded torch, he cut linen into strips, carefully dipping the ends in the alcohol. As the flames caught, he stepped outside and headed to the barn, taking the torch and the linens with him. Steadily he moved through the barn, lighting the cloths and tossing them on the dead, ensuring the fire caught, and gradually he worked his way through the barn until he was outside. At the bodies of the farmer and his child, Bastian whispered a quick rite of passage, as he had done for the woman inside the barn. The anger at the atrocity burned within him as he dropped the final strip along with the torch onto the bodies. He watched the flames for a moment longer, ensuring they had caught and would spread throughout the barn.

Far from satisfied that he had righted this wrong, he turned away from the barn. Pulling his hood over low, he made his way back to the others.

Echo watched him approach and her memory caught on the familiar sight, a slice of a vision from before. "I've seen this," she said to no one, trying to remember what the vision had entailed. Why had she seen Bastian walking away from burning buildings? Snatches of her vision taunted her as she tried to grab onto the memory. The sense of *wrong* she was feeling was not from the hooded figure in front of her. Twisting in her saddle, Echo looked behind her and gave a startled yelp when she saw the man standing not that far a distance behind them. He was close enough that they should have heard his approach but far enough away that he still maintained a distance. He was also hooded, the cloak lighter in colour than the ones the knights wore but fashioned much the same. The man stood in the open, watching them, making no move to harm them, but Echo could feel the *wrongness* radiating from him.

"Kase," Echo called quietly as she kept her eyes on the stranger. "Tell me you can see him."

She felt their response as they all turned, and she dared not blink as Kase moved his horse in front of her. "I see him."

"Do we know him?" Bastian asked sharply, and she hadn't realised he had been so close. "Is he an ally?"

"He's a dream," Echo answered quietly.

"He looks quite real," Ax said from beside her. "But see how his cloak remains steady," he added. "I…" He sounded unsure. "I don't think he's here. He casts no shadow."

"How?" Kase asked, looking the figure over and seeing the blond knight was right, the cloak the figure was wearing was still, and he stood in front of them with the moon to the side, but there was no shadowy imprint of him on the ground. A knife flew past them and right through the figure, causing it to waver and vanish.

Everyone turned to look at Khaldan. "What?" he said gruffly. "Now we know for sure that it wasn't real. And now it's gone."

"That was quite the throw," Kase said as he looked

between the spot where Khaldan sat on his horse and where the knife had fallen.

"Aye. Remember that, plainsman," Khaldan said lightly, "next time you think to offer me anything *extra* in my tea."

Bastian was glad the hood covered his reaction to Khaldan's words; it didn't seem right to wear such a wide grin so soon after what he had just left behind him—and the ominous thought of what lay in front of them. "Let's move," he instructed them all. "We have a lot to discuss, and I don't need to tell you that we're being watched." He got on Ghost, and the six of them left the farm burning wildly behind them, already thinking of the next danger they would encounter.

"It's quite the trick," Ax mused as they rode. "To do that."

"What?" Tyria asked when no one else answered.

"Projection," Ax explained. "It's one of the old tricks of magic, to appear but not appear."

"Magic of the old Gods, you mean?" Tyria asked him in challenge.

Ax didn't rise to the bait. "Old or new Gods, it's not natural to be able to do, so it's magic. I have never seen it myself," he told her, "until today." Looking around them, he smiled. "Two days into our journey only. I wonder what we'll encounter next?"

"Let's hope we have some time to rest before we find out," Bastian told him dryly. As they rode, they passed a few more homes, but all were empty, none like the first farmhouse they had encountered. Mounting Ghost after checking the last structure, Bastian looked at Echo. He wondered if she knew her hood had fallen. Her dark hair shone in the moonlight, and her white pale skin looked translucent. "Handmaiden," Bastian said quietly. "Cover your hair. If there are any people left here, we don't want them to notice and remember you."

Echo did as she was told, but he saw her puzzled frown before her hood concealed her features. "Won't they remember the six of us anyway?" she asked, and he knew by her tone it was a genuine question, not a sarcastic comment.

"Probably, but in this part of Kestornia, it is very rare for the woman to wear their hair as long as yours and Tyria's," Bastian explained.

"Why is that?" Tyria asked curiously.

"This is hard land to work. These people are more concerned with surviving winter than their appearance." Bastian knew his words could be considered inflammatory, so he hastened to add, "Long hair, on either women or men, is seen by some to be a sign of wealth." Looking around the countryside and the few buildings they had passed, Bastian nudged Ghost forward. "This is not a land of wealth," he added quietly as they entered the small village.

"This is a place of death," Kase said gruffly, pointing to the smoking pyre where bodies had recently been burned.

"And someone's been here, to do that," Khaldan said as he drew his sword. "Let's see if they still are."

CHAPTER 20

THE VILLAGE, IF YOU COULD CALL IT THAT, WAS DESERTED.
They checked every structure and found no one, not even a
dog. Echo hadn't thought about it, but when Ax mentioned
there were no animals, Bastian had turned to look at him
and then made a motion with his hand, which she didn't
understand, but Khaldan and Ax did, and the three of them
formed a small group. Kase seemed to know what it meant
too as he joined them, leaving Tyria and her on the outskirts
of the quick huddle.

"There's no sound," Tyria said beside her. "I didn't
notice it either, but listen. All I hear is our horses."

"Everyone is dead or left," Echo told her.

"Listen," Tyria said more firmly. "There's no birdsong.
No buzzing of flies, no sign of life at all."

Echo heard it. The silence. Now that she was aware of
it, her skin prickled with unease. "What does that mean?"
she asked Tyria, her voice hardly a whisper.

"Nothing good," Tyria told her grimly.

The small meeting broke apart, and Kase strode over
to them both. "There's nothing left," he told them. "But
this is not like the first place we saw." Looking around, his
eyes sweeping over the buildings as if they housed his
answer, he shook his head. "They either fled or were
removed."

"We move on?" Echo asked.

"No." Kase turned back to look at her. "This place is…
empty." Again, he eyed the town with suspicion as if he was

issuing a challenge to it, to prove him wrong. "But it's not evil."

"Evil?" Echo asked him, surprised at his terminology.

"The last place." He shuddered. "Evil things were done there. Here…" Kase glanced at her. "Here is just…empty."

"You want us to sleep here?" Tyria asked in surprise.

"We need to rest. We have a long way to go," Kase said as he met Echo's frown. "You still think north?"

"Yes," she told him as she looked to the other three. Bastian had moved closer and was listening. "North, my lord?"

"Yes," Bastian answered gruffly. "All the way north."

Kase turned to him in surprise. "You know where we need to go?"

"Don't you?" Bastian cocked his head slightly to the right, and Echo wondered if he knew he did it as often as he did. Or that it was as infuriating as it was. When she thought about it, he probably *did* know. The man could infuriate a sack of grain.

Not surprisingly, Kase ignored the question and turned back to her. "*He* knows?" She saw the accusation in his eyes and suppressed her snappy reply that she was sorry she didn't, but the Gods hadn't shown her yet, and until they did, that's *why* they needed the knights of the Order.

"Where do you suppose we rest?" she asked Bastian instead. "I am not sure I can find comfort in this place."

"Don't need you to be comfortable," Bastian told her with a grunt. "Just need you to sleep. We have a long journey ahead, time is not on our side, and I need you alert enough to stay in the saddle."

Echo almost snapped at him too, but she saw Tyria

nodding in agreement, and she recognised she was irritable because she was exhausted. "Very well, if you all agree," she told them. Kase helped her dismount, and together the six of them looked for a place to sleep.

Khaldan picked the house. It had three beds and a long kitchen table, which Ax declared was good enough for him.

"If you don't mind sharing?" he asked Tyria and Echo.

"It's fine," Tyria said with a low chuckle. "You can have your plank of wood," she added.

"I'll take first watch," Bastian told Kase, who didn't object, and Echo realised they were all tired.

"We should eat," she said as she moved to the kitchen, but Bastian's hand on her arm stopped her, and he shook his head.

"Doesn't feel right to take the food," Khaldan said behind her, and looking, she saw the others agree.

"I only wanted to draw water from the well," she said as she pointed to the well in the corner. "Boil some water."

"Use ours," Bastian said as he removed his hand. "We don't have time to test the water."

Realising he meant for poisons, Echo moved to the small worktable beside the well. "Very well, Tyria, bring me the flasks." Opening a cupboard, she took out some simple wooden cups. "This is okay?" she asked them all. When she received several nods, she busied herself with a large mixing bowl and some tea leaves. Khaldan watched her as she mixed and stirred.

"More tea?"

"I think we need something to warm us," Echo told him as she brewed the tea.

"A fire is not a good idea," Khaldan said dubiously.

Echo smiled as she heard Kase chuckle. "My affinity is water, Sir Knight," she said as she kept her head down. "And now that I do not have to conceal who I am"—she looked up at him as the steam began to rise from the bowl—"we can enjoy a hot cup of tea." Dipping a ladle into the bowl, she poured him a cup and held it out to him. "Please drink."

The fact that Khaldan hesitated caused a brief flash of hurt that she wasn't expecting even though she had given them no reason to trust her. When Bastian leaned over and took the proffered cup instead, she looked back down at the bowl, grateful for his silent support.

"Huh." Bastian took another drink.

Irritation flaring, Echo looked back up at him, ready for whatever barbed comment he was ready to throw. "What is it?"

Bastian took another drink. "Could be warmer," he said, and picking up his pack, he left the house and took up first watch.

Busying herself with the mixing bowl, Echo was smiling as she poured the other cups, her smile wider when Khaldan reached forward and took his.

Tyria took two cups and picked the bed furthest in the room. Her cup was already drained, and she was lying down on top of the blankets when Echo joined her. Moving over, she made room for Echo.

"You okay?" Tyria asked her softly.

"I think so," she answered just as quietly. "We're getting closer, I can feel it," she said almost inaudibly as she sipped her own tea. Tyria said nothing in response, her eyes already closed. "Ty?" Echo poked her gently in the ribs, using an old nickname for her friend. "You won't sleep if you don't say it," she told her knowingly.

"It's good you feel that we are getting closer," Tyria said. "I just don't think closer means closer to the end."

Echo went to argue, but she accepted the truth of her friend's words. Getting the artefact was the first step. The first of many. Closing her eyes to get the rest they told her she would need, she wondered how many steps she still had to take.

Bastian watched the dead town, and he could feel it watching him back. He knew they were alone; there wasn't a sound to be heard other than the movements from within the house and the sound of Ghost and the other horses at the rear. Nothing stirred. Yet he was on high alert. His hand gripped his pommel tightly, and his other hand had a throwing knife as he waited in the growing darkness. Never quite able to relax, he spent his watch with a tense knot growing and spreading between his shoulders.

Ax relieved him a while later, and Bastian ignored the wooden table his friend had been so eager to sleep on, instead taking a spot on the floor against the wall. Leaning his head back, he closed his eyes.

The wind whipped at him as the rain slashed at his face like a thousand needles scratching against his skin. The storm was wild, and the waves crashed behind him as he looked up at the dark rock. He heard the scream over the wind and turned, stumbling on the black sand. The hooded figure was cowering on the sand a few feet from him. He couldn't see what assaulted them, but the scream they gave was one of pain, not one of fear.

Thunder boomed in the air, and Bastian jumped as lightning lit the sky, illuminating the dark shape that crouched in the sand. Arms flew up to protect their head as another invisible blow struck against it.

Bastian moved forward but a roaring sound, too close to be thunder, made him turn, and he yelled out as the wave engulfed him.

Jerking awake, Bastian looked around. The house was quiet, the sounds of the others sleeping the only noise. Rubbing his eyes clear of sleep, he froze as he felt the moisture on his hands. Cautiously, he felt his cloak as he struggled to understand what was happening. His clothes were wet, and getting to his feet, he almost yelled out loud when cold hands took his.

Echo led him out of the house, stepping over Kase, who slept outside, the horses nearby.

Silently, Echo led him away from the others. "Is everything wet?" she asked, her voice low and husky.

"I think so," he answered. "What was that?"

"It's my fault. My sleep was unguarded."

"Unguarded?" Bastian struggled to understand as Echo ran her hands over his shoulders. "What are you doing, handmaiden?"

"Drying you," Echo told him. "Shh, I need to concentrate."

He felt his clothes dry as he stood, as she worked her hands smoothly over his outer clothing, drawing the moisture into her body. Finally, she dropped her hands and looked up at Bastian in the clouded moonlight, her eyes heavy with exhaustion.

"Better?"

Patting his clothing cautiously, Bastian nodded, his gaze never leaving hers. "Explain."

"I sometimes pull others into my dreams. It's not

happened for a long time," she admitted quietly. "I usually have better control." Tiredly she rubbed her forehead. "I thought it better to try and dry you rather than create more distrust with the others."

"You think I'm not going to mention that you pulled me into whatever you dreamed, and I woke up wet?" Bastian knew he sounded dubious.

Echo sighed heavily. "I know it's a lot to ask, but I don't have the answers to the questions they'll ask." Turning her head away from him, she looked back at the house. "It won't happen again." When he said nothing, she took it for agreement and hurried back to the others and her bed.

Bastian stood and watched her go as he self-consciously patted at his clothes. She said it wouldn't happen again? Should he tell her it had already happened before, or was it one more thing to add to the list of why he didn't trust her?

Following her back to the house, he wasn't at all surprised to see Kase's eyes were open, and he had no doubt been watching them in the dark.

Khaldan slept soundly in the bed he had taken, and not wanting to disturb him, Bastian relieved Ax of his watch, brushing off the other man's protests with a firm order to sleep. Sleep was the last thing Bastian wanted; his thoughts were too crowded for sleep.

<hr>

They rode for another two days before they stopped on the outskirts of another village, this one a little larger than the small farming community they had slept in two nights ago.

They hovered on the edge, watching the glow from the lanterns and the sound of people that carried through the night.

"At least this one has the living," Tyria mumbled as she tugged on her braid tiredly. "A bed and some hot food would be welcome, my lady."

"Agreed." Echo looked at Kase and then Bastian. "Sir knight?"

"Cautiously," Bastian warned them all. "Also, we split up."

"Why?" Kase asked him suspiciously.

"A few people are less noticeable than a group," Khaldan told him. "Ax. You're with me." Khaldan turned to Bastian. "You and one of the women go first," he instructed. "Make sure there's a bed to be had."

Nodding, Bastian nudged Ghost. "Tyria, let's go find that hot food."

Tyria's startled look met that of her lady's. She hadn't expected to be paired with Bastian, but the promise of food had her following the knight on the dark road.

"There'll be a tavern," Ax told Khaldan. "We'll seek that out."

"You go to drink?" Kase asked him contemptuously.

"Men in their cups are looser with their secrets," Echo said, remembering her conversation with Bastian. "Be careful, both of you."

Ax winked at her, and he and Khaldan followed Bastian into the village.

"And where do we go?" Kase asked her quietly. "Inn or tavern?"

"Inn," Echo told him with a fond smile.

"Alright." Kase nodded as he looked up at the sky as it darkened. "We'll give them some time. Too many questions to be asked if we arrive too close behind them. We need to appear to be apart." Kase slipped to the ground, already readying his pack and removing most of his stuff from it.

"What are you doing?" Echo asked him curiously.

"Well, he's not going to take that big ugly warhorse into that village," Kase told her. "They may pay no mind to us, but they'll remember the horse." Pulling a blanket free from the saddle, he rolled it. "So, if it was my horse, I'd keep it close but not too close to be noticed. The animal's smart enough to stay close, loyal enough to wait for him," he added with grudging respect.

"And you're doing the same?" Echo asked him. "But your horse isn't memorable."

"No." Kase smiled at her as he patted his horse's nose. "She doesn't mean it. You're a fine horse," he mock whispered to it. "But two horses for two people means wealth these people don't have. He's right about that too." Kase cast a look over his shoulder, almost as if he was worried Bastian would hear him.

Echo's lips twitched but she schooled her features. "And a husband would let his lady ride while he walked beside the horse," she said in understanding.

"Aye." Kase sniffed as he avoided looking at her.

"Well, this is new," Echo said with a smile. "We've not been husband and wife before."

Kase bit his tongue and slapped his horse's hindquarters, sure it would seek out the other horse in the night.

As they walked the path into town, Echo looked down at him. It wasn't far—he was level with her hip. Kase was so tall he would stand out anywhere. "Cover your head, husband, your hair will draw far more attention than the length of mine."

"Aye." Kase did as he was bid, and they walked in silence for a while longer.

Echo heard the distant whinnying, and seeing Kase turn in the same direction, she guessed that Ghost had rounded up the other man's mare.

"You know," Echo said with a smile, "you're lucky Ghost never heard you call him ugly," she teased. "I think he would bite you had he heard."

"He's a mean-spirited brute," Kase grouched as he looked up at her. "As is his master."

As they entered the village, Echo was glad the hood hid her from Kase's unspoken challenge. Bastian *was* suited to his horse, but the more they journeyed with him, the less she thought of Bastian as the brute that she once did.

CHAPTER 30

AFTER ALL THEIR CAREFUL PRECAUTIONS, THE VILLAGERS didn't care that they entered their compact village in pairs. The small inn that there was had three rooms in total, and Kase had reluctantly accepted the offer of the hayloft with a dangerous gleam in his eye that Echo was sure Ax would pay for later.

As Kase brushed down the horse and made sure it had oats, Echo looked around the hayloft. There were blankets and some pillows piled to the side, and she set about making them both a bed each. Kase said nothing about the sleeping arrangements, merely headed back into the inn and came back with two bowls of stew, which they ate in silence.

"It's quite cosy," Echo commented as she looked around. "I thought it would smell more," she admitted.

"Give it time," Kase grunted, moving his makeshift bed further from her.

Echo said nothing, as she was used to the plainsman and his ways. Although, in fairness, she knew he was doing this in the act of chivalry—or something equally eye roll worthy. Looking at her cup of water, Echo dipped her finger into it, channelling some of her gift into the shallow depth of the cup. Lost in her own thoughts, she played with the water, causing patterns and waves, heating it and then cooling it rapidly after. Concentrating, she cooled the water more. First, a slight frost on the sides of the cup appeared, which deepened as she watched the fractals bloom across the surface. When she held a cup of solid water, she realised she was no longer touching the surface of the water at all. A throat being cleared made her look up, and she met Kase's frown with one of her own.

"Ice?" he questioned.

"Yes." Echo hastily put the cup down, hiding it with her skirts. "We should sleep." For once, she was grateful for the plainsman's silent ways as he took to his bed and asked no more questions.

A body landing heavily on her woke her from her sleep, and her yelp of surprise was drowned out by Kase's angry roar and raised voices shouting over each other to be heard.

"Echo?" Ax sounded in surprise. "You're in the hayloft?"

Pushing against him, Echo struggled out from under the playful knight. "I am."

"What are you doing here?"

"I was sleeping!" she scolded him. A lantern was lit, and she looked at the three men in consternation. "What in the name of the Gods is going on?" she asked as she pushed her hair off her face and tried to sit up straighter.

"Inn's full," Ax told her as he bit into a chunk of bread, waving it around in front of him. "Hayloft." He chewed his bread as if those three words explained everything.

Echo looked at him in exasperation and tried Khaldan. "Is he drunk?"

Khaldan nodded as he scratched his beard. "Could be."

"He *could* be?" Echo asked incredulously. "Is that really appropriate?"

"Yes?" Khaldan said tentatively as if he wasn't sure of the answer she wanted to hear.

"Khaldan? Are you in your cups too?" she asked suspiciously, and when he grinned happily at her, she guessed why they said his wife was angry a lot. With wide eyes, she stared at Kase who, to her shock, was hiding his laughter behind his hand. "It's funny?" she demanded of him.

"It's a little bit funny," he mumbled.

"I thought we were all being careful?" Echo snapped. "How are these two being in their cups helpful?"

"No one suspects of them, I would guess," Bastian said from under them on the barn floor.

Ax peered over the edge of the hayloft, and Echo grabbed him when he teetered. "Sir, your companion's wayward," she scolded him too. And when she looked over the ledge, he was also grinning, while Echo was sure it wasn't funny.

"Ax, lay down and sleep," Bastian commanded. "Khaldan, how many?"

Khaldan inhaled deeply and then belched loudly, much to Echo's distress. Kase's snort of laughter at his lady's pained expression slipped free, and he clamped his hand tighter over his mouth.

"Khaldan?" Bastian asked again, firmer this time.

"Seven. Mean-looking brutes," Khaldan told him as he dropped onto a hay bale and lifted his foot to take his boot off. "Had very unkind things to say about the birds. Suspicious they were too."

Kase, Echo noticed, had lost his laughter and was watching closely.

"And where are they?" Bastian asked from the ground, and Echo looked down at him. Standing looking up, his hands on his hips, he wore a smile, which grew when he saw her agitation.

"Oh, they're much drunker than us," Khaldan told him happily. "No wagging tongues there."

"They can still talk," Kase said as he too looked down at Bastian, his humour gone.

"But we'll have left by the time they're coherent enough to string a sentence together," Bastian assured him. "Seven men who got drunk with passing strangers is talked about less than seven men who fought two knights."

"I'll check it out anyway," Kase said as he quickly climbed down the ladder. "Echo?"

"Go, I'll be fine." She looked back at the two knights. Ax was already sound asleep, and Khaldan was dozing with one boot still dangling off of his foot.

Looking back to the ladder, she was startled when Bastian looked back at her from the top of it, his grin once again wide.

"It's not funny," she admonished him.

"You have straw in your hair," he said as he leaned his elbows on the mezzanine floor. "You look like someone who's had some fun in the hayloft with a suitor." He looked at his companions. "Maybe two?" he added with a wink.

Echo picked the straw from her hair. "Well, that one," she said as she nudged Ax in the side none too gently, "fell on me."

Bastian chuckled and extended his hand. "Come on, there's a bed in with Tyria."

"They'll be okay?" Echo asked as she took his hand and he helped her down the ladder.

"Ax can sleep anywhere," Bastian told her as he stepped back. "He's like a cat. Khaldan's not slept properly since the holding cell. He needs the rest."

"Oh." Echo looked back up to the hayloft. "I feel a little guilty for scolding him now."

Bastian laughed again. "Don't be. They deserve it for waking you." Walking back to the side door that led to the back entrance to the inn, he checked over his shoulder to see if she was following. But Echo wasn't behind him. She was facing the main barn doors, her body still. "Handmaiden?" Bastian lost all sense of humour as he stepped towards her.

Echo walked forward, and cautiously he followed. "*Echo*," he cautioned as she pushed the door open, letting the moonlight stream in.

Either she never heard him or she chose to ignore him, but the handmaiden walked out into the night as if in a trance.

Bastian followed and when she stopped several steps from the barn, he drew alongside her, his eyes darting around the shadows, looking for threats.

The man stepped out of the shadow, taller than he had been when they had seen him earlier. Bastian cursed the hidden moonlight, as he had no way to tell if this was the man or the projection until the air stirred his cloak.

"Who are you?" Echo asked him, proud that her voice was steady even with her fists balled tightly at her sides.

"Who do you want me to be, Echo of the Frost?" His voice was rich and deep. Some would say it was pleasant.

"Show yourself," Echo demanded and stiffened when she heard the low, soft laughter.

"You think looking upon me will make a difference?" he mocked. Pushing his hood back, he uncovered straight darkish hair that framed a square face. The darkness of the night didn't allow them to see him clearly, but Echo guessed he would appear as any other man. "Happier?" he sneered at her.

"What do you want?" Bastian asked him.

"I want what she wants," the man answered. "And I'm going to let you in on a secret." He leaned forward as if he was indeed sharing a secret amongst friends. "I'm going to get there first."

Bastian's knife threw true through the darkness, much like Khaldan's had done, but to both his and Echo's shock, the blade stopped in front of the man's face. Raising his hand, he made a circling motion with his finger, and the dagger turned in the air, pointing back at them.

"Tsk tsk, Bastian, didn't your mother teach you not to play with knives?" He dropped his hand, and the dagger came flying back towards Bastian and Echo.

Grabbing the handmaiden, Bastian pulled her out of the way, wrapping an arm protectively around her. He heard the dagger drop on the path behind them.

"See you soon," the man mocked, and Echo shivered as he vanished in front of them.

Bastian stepped away from her and looked around. "We're not safe here," he spoke to himself.

"He can vanish into thin air." Echo wrapped her arms around her middle. "Are we safe anywhere?"

"Do you know what it is that you seek?" Bastian asked her suddenly. When Echo nodded, he leaned forward and spoke into her ear. "Do you know where it is?" When she shook her head, he whispered the location.

"How do you know?" Echo asked him.

"My general," Bastian confessed. "We took a risk here, but we can't stop again."

Echo nodded in agreement, but she pulled on Bastian's arm when he went to walk away. "He could already have it."

"No. If he did, he wouldn't be here boasting to us."

"Bastian…" She hesitated. "He's…"

"Not of the old Gods," Bastian said with a grim look. "Nor your new ones, I think. Unless the Temple of the Maiden started letting men in?"

Echo shook her head in denial. "He feels—"

"Wrong," Bastian finished. "It's felt wrong for months now," he said half to himself. "Which means we need to be faster."

Together they rushed back into the barn to wake their companions, to hurry their journey north. Ax and Khaldan needed strong coffee before they started, and they crowded into the small room Bastian had secured for Tyria and himself.

"I don't know of any magic that can make someone vanish." Ax rubbed his forehead repeatedly. "Maybe he shot up into the air?"

"He didn't fly," Bastian snapped impatiently. "He vanished."

"Are you sure it's the watchtower?" Khaldan asked Bastian, who nodded. Shaking his head in frustration, he looked upwards. "Of course it bloody would be. Furthest thing there is north."

Bastian didn't comment that had been his reaction too.

"The Barrens are further," Ax supplied unhelpfully.

"We could try the forest," Tyria suggested uncertainly. "It may not be as bad as they say."

"It's worse," Khaldan grunted.

"You've been through it?" Tyria asked him with surprise.

"Aye."

"It's just a forest," Echo added. "No?" she asked when she saw their expressions. "I'm from Eloysth; I don't know about your creepy forest," she snapped in exasperation.

"Finakyn Forest is ruled by the De'xynaith," Bastian explained. "They are not really of this world, and they are not ruled by the Gods, old or new."

"And to enter their forest is death," Ax added with a snarl.

"We could go by sea. It's a detour to go back the way we have come," Khaldan grumbled as he drank his coffee. "But still, we could sail right past it."

Echo and Bastian exchanged a quick look. "I'd rather not be on the water right now," Echo said in a low voice.

"You're a *water* affinity," Ax challenged her. "I'm surprised you're not already racing us over the waves strapped to the back of one of the *dalphyne*."

Echo blinked in surprise at the strange image he painted. The dalphyne were sea mammals that had been changed when the world from before twisted all of its creatures as man poisoned the land and seas. Grey sleek creatures that used to dance on the waves were now transformations of what they had been. Blistered skin from where the rain had burned them as they came up for air had burned beneath their skin. Sores that would never close seeped poison into their blood, and the once graceful creatures of the sea were distorted mutations.

Unused to Ax's bitterness, Echo was saved from defending herself when Bastian spoke instead. "I agree, the sea is a foe right now. We've all heard the handmaiden's visions." Bastian finished his coffee and poured more for Ax. "Drink this—your mind's in a dark place."

"Come," Bastian spoke to the others, "we should get ready."

"Why can't we go through the forest?" Echo asked again. "Is it so bad? If we explained—"

Ax's cup crashed off the opposing wall, causing Echo and Tyria to jump. "We can't go through the forest," he yelled furiously. "We can't get *past*, and he *knew* that."

"Who?" Kase asked quietly as Khaldan spoke inaudibly to his comrade, calming his temper.

"My—" Bastian corrected himself. "*The* Lord Commander knew where we needed to go. We could have passed through, but he made sure that was not a possibility for us."

"How?" Echo asked as she looked at them all, still not understanding.

"Xan," Tyria said in sudden realisation. "He's—"

"Yes," Bastian cut her off.

"There are still too many secrets." Kase looked between them with fresh suspicion.

Tyria surprised them all when she spoke. "There are some secrets that are not ours to share." Reaching for Echo, she pulled her forward. "Come, we need to prepare to leave. We have weeks of travel ahead."

Even with the women out of the room, it was still crowded with the four men in it.

"Nothing's changed," Bastian told his fellow knights. "We skirt the forest," Bastian said with a sigh. "We head to the town of Flakyn and pass around it. We need to believe they're still behind us."

"Pass Flakyn and into Bordyre," Khaldan agreed with a nod. "Keep to the treeline. Only fools travel close to it. We'll know if we're being followed."

"Aye." Bastian studied them and saw the resignation in their faces. "We haven't lost the fight yet," he reminded them.

Ax smoothed his hair back, regaining his composure. "I need more coffee," he told no one in particular. "Then we'll ride."

Bastian caught Khaldan's eye, and with a slight nod, he left them in the room, Kase following him. They found Echo was in the barn, checking packs.

"Where's Tyria?" Kase asked sharply.

"The innkeeper told her that there was a meat merchant who opened his stall early for the hunters." Echo looked up at them. "She went to get food."

Kase closed his eyes briefly. "Alone?" With an angry look at Bastian and the unspoken question, Bastian made the motion for him to go.

Echo heard him go but kept on with her task. "Tyria is more than capable to haggle with a meat merchant," she tsked.

"I have no doubts," Bastian said as he began to get Ghost ready to leave. "About Tyria," he added.

Echo's hands stilled for a moment. "But you have doubts?"

"Don't you?"

"I am clear in my task," she told him as she avoided eye contact with him.

"I do not doubt that either," Bastian said under his breath, but she heard him.

"You doubt me then," she said as she stood and faced him.

Bastian had several answers he could give her; instead, he surprised them both when he spoke next. "Kase is right, there are still too many secrets." Turning, he glanced at her. "Tell me, Echo of the Frost, are you the figure being struck on the beach?"

Echo paled. "Wh-what?"

"You pulled me into the dream. Tell me, are you the one being struck? Or are you the one striking them?"

Echo looked down at her hands. "I'm the one being struck. The old Gods beat me."

Bastian resumed his task. "And when I called to you all those weeks ago, and you ran up the rocks, where did you go?"

"That was you?" she asked as she took a step forward.

"And when the quicksand took me, was it the old Gods that pushed me under? Or you?"

"What? No!" Echo hurried to him, her hand covering his, stopping him from his actions of getting Ghost saddled. "Bastian, *no*. I did not push you down."

Her wide green eyes stared up at him in earnest, and he gave a jerk of his head, pulling his hand from under hers and resuming his task. "So, who is it?"

"I thought the enemy in my visions were the old Gods," Echo said as she moved back to the packs. "But the old Gods wouldn't hurt their soldier," she said. "Even if it is you," she added as she thought about it, ignoring his low chuckle. Echo looked at him in surprise as she realised. "*Especially* if it was you." Excitement rushed through her.

"Bastian, do you know what this means?" she asked him. "You've been in the vision *without* me."

"Lucky me," he mocked as he started readying Ax's horse.

"Bastian!" Echo snapped irritably. "Don't you see what this *means*? It means we're on the *same* side."

"I thought that was obvious when I broke my friends out of jail in the middle of the night."

"It's impossible to talk to you," she grouched at him. "I'm on this journey as a messenger of the Gods, don't you *see*? You're having visions too. You're the same as me."

Bastian looked the handmaiden over. "Echo, I am the furthest thing from you. I am a soldier. You're a handmaiden. We're on the same path because you told my men a convincing tale that may have some truth in it." He shrugged. "I don't know, but trust me on this, we are *not* the same."

"And the Mystic? You saw him. Is he part of my convincing story?" she challenged him.

"I don't know what he is," Bastian admitted. "I do know he is man, and I know one more thing."

"Which is?"

"Men bleed." Bastian finished with the horse. "I'll fetch the others," he told her as he looked over her shoulder.

Surprised he would leave her alone, Echo turned to see Tyria and Kase behind her, and realised he hadn't left her alone after all. "I thought we were making progress," she told them sadly. Looking back at the door to the inn, she rubbed her hands over her upper arms, creating some warmth from the chill she suddenly felt.

"Progress or not, they cannot be trusted," Kase

reminded her as he started leading the horses from the stables, careful of Ghost's bite.

"We're on the right path," Tyria said, attempting to cheer her up. "We've come a long way. Stay true to that."

Echo smiled, letting her know she was, even though she felt heavy with disappointment. The three knights of the Order of the Ravens walked through the door to the barn, and quickly they had their horses and were ready to depart.

As Kase helped her mount, Echo couldn't help looking over at the three men who had taken up her task with her. Two believed her, but one still did not, even though he was clearly far more involved than he wanted to admit.

"Echo." Kase brought her attention back to him. "We need to ride hard. They'll be on our heels. There are still so many obstacles in our way." The tall plainsman caught her hand gently. "They may be our allies, but they are not our friends." His harsh words caused her to wince inside, but she didn't let him see it. "Are you ready for this?" he asked as he looked up at her.

Wetting her lips, she gave a shallow nod. "Of course," she assured him. "This is our task."

The knights were ready and talking amongst themselves and then Tyria as she joined them. They were eager to start their journey north, waiting only for her and Kase. Ax and Khaldan looked back once or twice, but Kase stood by her horse, waiting to make sure she was with him, that she was focused on her goal.

"Echo," he started.

"I'm fine, Kase," she said with perhaps more sharpness than she intended. Bastian looked back and met her stare, his eyebrow rising in question at the delay. Kase saw it too and mounted his horse, and the two of them started to walk their horses to join the others.

"This will work out," she told him confidently as she watched Ax laugh at something Tyria said with a smile, glad the surliness from earlier had gone from the light-hearted knight. "It takes time," she reminded him.

"Time is something we don't have," Kase reminded her grimly.

"He's in the visions," she said softly. "It has to mean something."

"Or it means nothing," Kase argued. "Don't forget who they are and what they represent."

"I don't," Echo said with a long-suffering sigh at his overprotectiveness. "But we got this far with them; let's give them the benefit of the doubt. We get to the watchtower, we claim the artefact, and we take it from there. Okay?"

Kase's hard stare continued to watch the three knights. "Do you know what they call a flock of ravens?" he asked under his breath.

Echo shook her head no, and Kase's next words made her question everything she had just said as her skin broke out in goose bumps.

"A conspiracy."

EPILOGUE

From the shadows, he watched the six of them ride from the town, the three wingless ones in front, the horse trainer laughing along with them like they were *friends*.

Snarling, he looked at the handmaiden and the Clanless one beside her, always beside her. Only in her dreams could he get her alone, and now the dark-haired *crow* fluttered at the edges.

He had come too far and sacrificed too much to lose to a fool who didn't even believe in what he fought for.

He believed.

He was worthy of the call.

He was chosen…and he would not be stopped.

Ava Speirs is the alter ego of USA Today bestselling author Eve L. Mitchell.

Ava is a huge fantasy fan and grew up reading stories that captured her imagination and took her on journeys of action and adventure. Her favourite stories to write are ones where the possibilities are endless and reality is what she creates. Ava favours the grumpy, sometimes reluctant hero and the fearless, usually sarcastic heroine.

Ava lives in the North East of Scotland with her significant other, Mr M. When not writing, Ava adores all things Dean Winchester, quaffs coffee like a champion, and still has no idea what a dangling modifier is. She is quite fond of a cliffhanger though...

Want to know more?
Follow Ava Speirs

ACKNOWLEDGEMENTS

My first thanks has to be to my readers. You are the reason I get to keep doing this, you keep asking for stories and I keep (trying) to deliver.

For those of you who jumped onto Ava's book as easily as you jump onto Eve L. Mitchell's, THANK YOU. Thank you for reading and coming back for more. For those of you who are new to Ava, thank you for taking the chance. I hope it was worth it.

To all my readers, whether old or new, please know that every word that I write comes from the many conversations with the voices in my head, in addition to lots of time daydreaming about how scenes should flow and then taking the time to craft them in a way that does flow.

Speaking of flow…to Helayna Trask, my editor who battles in my corner tirelessly and I promise you, I've been sent multiple examples and explanations of the dreaded dangling modifier, but I just can't stop them happening. I write them. She cries. I make a joke about it. She smiles through her tears with a clenched jaw. She is patient, she is kind, she laughs at all (most of) my jokes, and I am so very lucky that she sticks with me.

To my two alpha readers for this book, Julie, and Renee, thank you for gobbling down the chapters that I fed you in drips, thank you for your patience and for reading, and your positivity about this book.

To the bloggers and bookstagrammers who helped share this release. Thank you for loving books, your work is deeply appreciated, and I am so grateful for your time.

To every person who leaves a review, thank you. Reviews

are the life blood for an author and taking that time to leave one or two sentences means more than you know.

To my mum and dad, who shared their love of books with me. We were strong believers of the phrase "just one more chapter" in my house growing up. I still mutter it at one a.m. when I have work the next morning but know I won't sleep until I get that next all-important chapter read. I blame my parents for being the influences that they were in encouraging me to read, and thank them for giving me my love of books.

To my dear patient Mr M. I know I got worse than normal with this book, and you patiently waited while I wandered off into my head chasing down scenes, listening to conversations only I can hear, created spreadsheets of stuff you know I wouldn't use and then there was that week where I didn't write a word as I decided to be a mapmaker (shudders)… I know how much you put up with, and I am grateful you still make me coffee while I pursue the story. Your support is endless, and I can't do any of this without you.

And finally, to the readers whose imagination knows no limit, welcome into mine, and thank you for the chance to take you on this adventure.

Ava x